The Last Celt

The Phantom of Annwn

D. Osborne Hughes

Copyright © 2023 by D. Osborne Hughes

All Rights Reserved.

No part of this book may be used or reproduced by any means, graphic, electronic, or mechanical, including photocopying, recording, taping, or by any information storage retrieval system without the written permission of the publisher except in the case of brief quotations embodied in critical articles and reviews.

Publisher D. Osborne Hughes

dosbornehughes.com

thelastcelt@btinternet.com

Cover illustration by D Osborne Hughes

Models: Mark Weir, Ameliamary and David Eaton

Note

'The Phantom of Annwn', is the second book in 'The Last Celt' series. It is the sequel to, and follows the storyline from 'The Last Celt, Waking Dreams' and as such, I would always recommend you read 'Waking Dreams' first, although I have tried to write in such a way that it stands alone, with some semblance of the full story.

Annwn: 'Hades' to the Greeks and Romans; the closest Christian translation would be 'Hell', but from my limited knowledge – gleaned from the modern-day commentaries of the Celt's obscure beliefs – I have come to understand 'Annwn' as a Spirit World, the place from which we have wandered and, following our deaths, that place to which we will return; – if only for a short time – a world of spirits, encompassing both good and evil.

'The Phantom of Annwn' portrays violence; it is a natural part of its narrative, but I have not sought to glory or degrade in its telling. The stories behind its brutality, however, have not been gleaned from our history books, (Although we are undoubtedly the legacy of a brutal and violent past), but to our shame, they have been gathered from incidents hidden within the news reports of our, so-called, more enlightened times.

No matter how hard I seek the answer; the question posed in the Folk Song, 'Where Have all the Flowers Gone?' still haunts me;

"When will they ever learn?"

NB. There are some more comprehensive notes at the rear of the book: including, the meaning and pronunciation of certain words and names I use; also some explanations of the different languages I portray.

As planning a battle, Alexander the Great, in negotiation with the Celtic Chieftains, demanded they be in a certain position on the battlefield, at a precise moment of the battle. The Celts swore with an oath, affirming they would accomplish everything demanded of them; vowing,

"Unless the Sky Falls Down!"

To Martin and Rachael

Prologue

My Grandfather was christened, John Hugh Hughes, but was known to his work-mates as 'Jack-the-lamp'; a reference to his job in the local lead mine. John, after his father, John Hughes: Hugh, after his grandfather, Hugh Hughes, the son of Benjamin Hughes, the son of Benjamin Siôn Hughes, the son of Siôn Hughes and so on, back through all my generations, back through history; back to the people who first settled the lands of Moel-y-Crio (The Mountain of Tears) many lifetimes ago; back to the people who dwelt in these lands before the meridian of time; back to those we have a want to call the Celts.

It seems incredible to me that I should associate such a kind, gentle, man, as my grandfather, with an ancient race of people such as the Celts. A people whose power came from strength in arms and courage on the battlefield. I could never, as a child, imagined my grandfather painted in woad, all arrayed in his battle garb, ready for war, and yet, the quiet power he possessed, which shone from somewhere deep inside, was perhaps more formidable than any Celtic army.

The Romans described the Celts as living 'Beyond the Pillars of Hercules', but if we look behind the popular veil of contemporary history, we find the Celts were a valued ally of the Greeks, in both culture and war. Great lovers of poetry, language and art, they were a refined people, but despite the Celt's culture, they were a fierce warrior nation.

A Celtic Warrior never lacked valour on the battlefield. They were constant and steadfast, fighting to their last breath in defence of their sacred religion, freedom and the protection of their homes and families. Their unwavering devotion to their sacred religion gave them a firm conviction of the eternal nature of life and they fought as immortals, which made them formidable adversaries. To a Celt, death was an integral part of their eternal progression: a voyage leading beyond the gates of celestial realms, to where the Gods of the sun dwell.

Early Rome suffered great defeats at their hands, but in the twilight of the Celt's existence, a once beautiful and courageous people appear to have been decimated and the last of the Celts were left to resist Rome's oppression, in the lands we know as Bretton, Cornwall, Scotland and Wales. No amount of courage on the battlefield could ever match the Romans' sophisticated and barbarous fighting machine, but among the mountains of Scotland and Wales, the Celts once more worried and tested their weary opponents.

It is of these people my story tells and their blood runs deep in my veins, handed down through the generations. They are my people if that can be said with any surety, following the Celt's tumultuous history and after the pure blood of time has been mixed with the life's-blood of people the Celts have conquered and the clouded blood of people who have conquered the Celts. But my blood, tainted and diluted as it may be, doesn't just flow inside me; in some way – I don't know how or why these things work – I can feel their influence swelling deep in my heart and what little remains of their blood, ebbs and flows, streaming relentlessly through me, stirring my mind. Despite the cauldrons of time and maybe even because of them,

I am still intensely proud of who I am, where I have come from, and the people who have gone before me.

My people have written a poem deep inside me; its rhymes echo forever in my heart, sealed up there by words my grandfather whispered to me as a child. They are words that have constantly conjured images, pictures that relentlessly track my imagination, following a story that has eventually floated free from the tenuous strands of my mind. Nevertheless, these faint whispers of distant generations have been watched over by the unseen presence of my Taid (Grandfather), who, whilst long since departed from this life: is yet a giant of a man, whom I still know and love.

My story chronicles dark and disturbing tales of the past. It speaks of the precious people who, I believe, were responsible for holding my life in trust, and in the darkest most terrifying times of my life, it is this people's influence I have felt deep inside me. They have instilled in me a power, passed down from generation to generation, and I stand here with the might of my grandfather and all his people, flowing through me. Stumbling through the menacing shadows in the forests of life, I feel their familiar presence walking at my side, indicating the way I should go. And so, I walk through the maze of pathways set in life's woods, without any fear.

In quiet times the drift of my dreams seeps into silent moments, where the familiar spirit of my grandfather waits patiently for me to rise above my fears. Maybe he begged the sentinels who guard the way, unable to make his voyage without those lives he loves, more than his own. In the silence of life's shadows, his words continue to guide me and in the blindness of the mists that surround me, I know I am not alone.

If the sun refused its light to shine upon me; if all the stars drained from their celestial courts on high; if earthquakes prevented my path; if tempestuous winds became my enemy raining down the combined elements to hedge up my way; if the wild horses of the sea galloped after me, trampling my soul under their thunderous hooves; if the Dragons jaws gaped open after me, with his fiery breath pursuing me into the molten furnaces of Annwn itself; I know this: Unless the sky fell down, crushing his body into the dirt of this earth, he would stand at my side with his love to support me.

No matter where I go, no matter who stands at my side or how much love surrounds me and no matter how many lifetimes fall between us, his love is the light that gently leads me on, and I know he waits at that gate, beyond my voyage of tears.

So, until that day, like a seer, I peep back through time and search for all my generation's sacred names, but one name shines brighter than them all and in the dark spaces forged in the hearts of a forgotten people, I hear that name whispered, 'Hyw bach'.

Introduction

"Be quick and tarry not…gird ye…for the time is far spent and we must be hence. I am thy guide. For those of ye who hath not drawn nigh to me before, I must instruct thee as to mine duties. Nothing shalt be shielded from thee other than to save the dignity and shame of those we view.

Ye may seeth me as a spirit, an apparition, even, but some wouldst say 'I am an angel' – in the understanding of thy tongue – although I am, but a witness. I am not a guardian of the gate, nor am I a sentinel, who walks the path or guards the way; I hath no power or influence and am forbidden to touch or change and so, at times, mine own task is grievous. The guardians and sentinels art set in their duties, we may see them, but thou shalt not follow after them. I am what I am and ye may follow after me, but pay heed to mine own words, I hath been called upon to witness and only to witness. I am condemned to record the deeds of the boy's life and am nothing more than a lowly scribe.

Mine own true name cannot be uttered save only in one place. A place I keep sacred, but mine own given name is Siôn. Yes…I wast once born of this place; I am the boy's great grandfather and we shalt witness at the boy's side by and by. I wast once part of this story, but anon I passed beyond mine life before I knew much of his force. Having been called, as I am, to witness his life; I hast seen much. Mine own people were once fearsome warriors, having lived by the feud, 'Blood for Blood'. I too hast stepped into the fray, mine own blade bright with the blood of mine enemies, but never before hath I seen one so valiant and steadfast as he, and never hath I witnessed such unwavering courage.

So if thou art willing, I will guide thee, and if thou art true, ye may see all I see, and many other things pertaining to his life. Ye may even hear his thoughts, but whether ye possess the understanding to view his dreams, I canst not say.

He hath the 'Seeing Eye'; visions, if ye prefer. The veil is thin around him. So treadeth ye lightly, keep thy tongue and do not disturb his thoughts' for only the Sentinels' art clothed with the power and authority that he seeketh. His 'Waking Dreams' hath haunted his childhood; their apparitions break into his waking mind. Mine own son, his all-seeing, but blind, grandfather, hath told him they are a blessing in his life, but as a child, he doubted those words and as a man, they continue to plague his life.

For those of ye who were witnesses to his childhood, ye may have greater understanding, but it sufficeth me to say, all that wast precious to him, hath been ripped from him. All those he did love, hath been mutilated and murdered; Bryn and Isobel, mine own grandson and his betrothed, Hyw's loving parents; Ywel, mine own son and the boy's beloved grandfather; Bayr his beautiful and precious sister. All art gone; murdered. All hath been put to the slaughter, and he rides out for revenge, 'Blood for Blood' and their blood boils within him, souring his anger.

Come, followeth me, for the veil is drawn nigh and we must be hence. The leaves art falling and soon the bitter cold of winter shall beset him, for he hath wandered afar from the warmth of his home. Here...step beneath these darkling trees. I canst see what path his steed hath taken, nor do I *know the taiga. Tis sore in the darkling shadows where he abides: canst thou see him sat astride that grey palfrey? The horse's head bows down as it engluts itself on the grass by the side of the path. How long the gentle mare hath carried him thus, I cannot say*

Hush and be still...let us see what time hath made. Canst thou see him? No longer a boy; but a man sits high on the ghostly grey mare. His torso is bare to the waist and daubed in the woad of battle, but it canst hide the dirt on his face. Look at his body; his constant hammering of the metal hath sculpted a power in him that waxes strong. Wo, Wo, unto those who hath murdered those he loves, for he is no longer a suckling babe. The heart of a warrior beats in his breast, and he rides out to bring a swift death to Māthōg and his Blood Red Crows.

But mine charge is lost in some melancholy and his mind is broken. Asleep in some stupor his enemies may find him unawares. His eyes art as sharp and precise as the blade of his arrows, but tortured by his nightmares his eyes wilt not wake. Behold, his bow is almost falling from his lap where it hangs loosely down. His eyes art brimmed with sorrow: a sorrow he may never overcome. Guilt and shame stalk him, and his inability to save those he loves haunts his 'Waking Dreams'.

Abide ye and watch, there is danger in these woods. See there, along the path? A figure presses ever towards him. Is that a blade in his hand? Lost, mine charges mind will not wake and I fear lest he follows after those he loves, to the world beyond.

Hush ye anon, his name is Hyw and his mind is broken; when it wakes, I do not know, nor can I say, what will remain of his life.

Chapter One

Sat high on his ghostly grey mare, Hyw is lost to the world, haunted by the nightmares of his Waking Dreams.

The grey mare saunters forward, along a strange path. It stops and stands still for a moment and then she drops her head to graze on the sparse woodland grass at the side of the way.

A numbing silence pervades as Hyw's sapping melancholy slowly suffocates him. Madness has arrested all sense of lucidity within him as his life drifts into the pervading gloom. Lost in unfathomable darkness, his tortured mind seems never to stir again, but slowly the faintest glow of light stirs his crippled consciousness.

"Look to the light Hyw bach." His grandfather's words echo inside his memories, but before they can wake his mind, he hears another voice.

"Save thy sister Hyw Bach!" His mother's words chase his sanity down through the haunted corridors of time and Hyw's heart aches within his breast.

Whether in this world or the next, the groping tendrils of some darkness seem to grip his mind and he gradually breathes in the stifling air of some lifeless wilderness. Mist surrounds him and he is transfixed amid a sea of creeping ghostly smog. There is no shape or silhouette, no trees or rocks, no mountain or river, track or way, no clearing and no home set above the valley; only the stifling gloom of some lost realm, which seems to relentlessly suffocate him.

"Save thy sister Hyw Bach!" His heart breaks, again and again, hearing his mother's plea, but still, he cannot move. Panic sets in as the mist's incantations begin to throng around him. The floor is hard beneath his feet and a spark of dread swells inside him as he searches his memories, for any sight or sound, scent or smell; anything he can recognise and fix his thoughts to.

"Save thy sister Hyw bach!" His mother's desperate words chase after him as he looks back through time.

Instantly, he wakes to his prison and although still sitting on the mare; in his nightmares, he is surrounded by dark mists and he realises he is chained to the great rock, set above the cliff in front of his precious home.

Suddenly, the dread of his memories pounces on him: Māthōg! The pulse and heave, sight and sound and guarded fears of all his lurid nightmares suddenly appear before him, with his father's huge sword thrashing through the air. The machinations of all his childhood fears conspire against him and the grotesque Scotti giant rages towards him, his cold eyes flashing like lightning from the storm of his thickly bearded face.

Cowering in shock, Hyw is defenceless as the cruel Scotti Chieftain rises up, towering above him. But he is no longer a child; the constant hammering of the metal has sculpted him into a powerful warrior.

Readying himself for the sudden fray, Hyw tries to roll to one side but is held fast in his chains. Unable to move, he is helpless. Erect as a great standing stone, Hyw clenches his fists, but looking down he realises he is an eight-year-old child once more.

"Save thy sister Hyw bach!" In an instant, he turns towards the dread of his enemy, but Māthōg is no longer towering above him.

With a crushing squeeze pressing him into the dirt, he remembers in dred and realises he is trapped beneath The Scotti Grot(Grotesque) he killed as a child. Fighting with all his might, time seems to slow. Eventually, he gains his feet only to feel, Bayr, his helpless baby sister, clinging to him as if she would never let go.

All his memories seem to flood through him as he finds himself surrounded by the terrifying turmoil of Māthōg's first attack on his home. The Scotti marauders, 'The Blood Red Crows', have despatched his father and the pain again seizes Hyw's heart. The splinters of his first faulty and knotted bow lay shattered around him. In his memories, he searches back through the years and finds his broken arrow. Grasping its tip in his hand, holding it like a dagger, he knows it is the only weapon available to him.

"Save thy sister Hyw bach!" Dread fills him, as his mother's demands call him back through time.

"The Roman whore is mine!" Māthōg's thunderous roar fills the air as he pins Hyw's mother, Isobel, into the dirt. In utter terror, the desolation of his mother's struggle again plays out before him. Māthōg is ripping at her body. With her clothes in tatters, he sits astride her; writhing on her; pounding her into the teaming mould.

Bayr continues to cling to his side. Above the building clamour, Hyw hears her tears. She pulls at his arm and he knows he is her last hope, but he cannot think of saving his sister until he has saved his mother and Isobel's screams, wake him to that purpose.

Time slows and in her desperate struggle, Isobel slowly turns her head toward her son. Her stare catches his, and her very being seems to reach inside him. With his heart bursting she whispers in his ear.

"Save thy sister Hyw bach!" Freeing himself and with the broken arrow gripped firmly in his hand, the wild cat claws at the ground and taking five swift paces, he leaps onto Māthōg, as if no power on earth could stem the flow of his anger. Snatching a large swathe of the giant's hair, he pulls vigorously, and as Māthōg's head tilts back, he hammers his other fist into his face. Still gripping his broken arrow tightly in his hand, he drags it down over Māthōg's eye and cheek, drawing a great roar of agony. All of Māthōg's torturous intentions are instantly bent towards Hyw; with the blood of his attack spewing from Māthōg's face. With a thunderous blow, Hyw is slammed into the dirt.

Gasping for air he manages to gain his feet and with the arrowhead still clenched firmly in his hand, he grabs his sister and drags her across the clearing. The torturous sight of his mother being trampled beneath the hooves of the charging stallion infests his mind as its rider, Scar Face, screams a warning, but Māthōg's mind does not stir as he watches Hyw and Bayr run to where they have no escape.

Bundling his sister through the door of the shack set above their deep midden pit, Hyw looks back to see the light in his mother's eyes burning low, but a faint glow still stirs. Their eyes meet and Hyw remembers her last words.

"Save thy sister, Hyw bach!"

Isobel's words chase him through their toilet door as her head sinks slowly to the ground and his mother is gone.

Heaving his sister through the hole in their toilet seat, he drops her into the stench of the deep and in his memories, he again rolls forward into the darkness. Keeping his grip on the seat long enough to snatch the broken arrow back, he too drops into the deep. Looking back through the torturous memories of his Waking Dreams, he remembers Māthōg's huge body blocking out the daylight as extending his father's sword toward him. Standing above his sister with the broken arrowhead gripped between his trembling fingers, he remembers Māthōg's threats.

"I'll be back fo'thee an' tha sister…to be sure…Dost thou hear moi? Runt! Dead on…come back for thee oi will!"

The huge glob of congealed spittle Māthōg gobbed at him, again trickles down his face and its putrid mass eventually drips from his chin, but still, he stands guard over his sister; holding the broken arrow up towards the light. With nothing left inside him, he remembers the gush of dread as his own urine washes down the inside of his leg. Weeping and crying, kneeling in chains on the back of 'The Rock of his Family's Throne' he remembers; he remembers everything.

Leaves begin to fall around him, they become thicker and turn to rain with the rain turning to snow. The snow gathers deep around him and he feels its clutching frozen fingers. The snow melts and gives way to flowers that begin to grow amongst the green grasses of the spring meadows. The summer grasses lighten and dry as they wilt and leaves begin to fall again as the years roll ever by with the nightmares of his memories quenching themselves into his tortured soul.

Watching his sister, Bayr, growing into a beautiful young woman, Hyw rises to his feet, straining with all his might against the chains that bind him, but still, he dares to dream and in his nightmares, he dreams he can save her.

Māthōg keeps his promise.

'Hyw!' The piercing scream is inside his head and it wakes a panicked fear that rises through him. His crippled hallucinations roll incessantly on as Bayr calls his name.

"Hyw…!"

Ywel, Hyw's beloved grandfather, lies crippled in the dirt of the clearing, moaning in his agonies and spitting blood from his mortally wounded body following the Scotti's brutal attack and Hyw realises 'The Blood Red Crows' have his sister. He remembers his chase through the woods with his sister calling to him through the trees

"Hyw," His mother's words whispering in his ears,

"Save thy sister Hyw bach, save thy sister."

And his grandfather's words pursuing him,

"Go…Go, Hyw bach…Go…bring her back to us!"

Turning to the chase, with all the hosts of Annwn following, Hyw remembers the rush in his veins thumping inside his head as he mounts the powerful steed of his rage. Bayr's cries scream out over and over again,

"Hyw…Hyw… Hyw…!"

His swift pursuit gains the marauders before they can escape his feathered warriors.

"No…No…please no!" Bayr's cries call his heart to battle as she struggles with her captor. Remembering the awful sound of her dress ripping he is there once more, his feet clawing at the path behind the last rider. Rage sears through him on seeing his sister for the first time, her dress, ripped open at the front, with the filthy Slag torturing her and Hyw fights to quell his fury. Bayr's eyes meet his and her confidence waxes, sensing the victory of her brother's impending battle.

Bending his powerful hunting bow, he had despatched the closest Grot and racing forward, he gains on the slag that holds his sister bound. Advancing into Annwn, he pleads and begs for Bayr's life. Pausing, only for a moment, he swiftly bends his bow and releases his hungry Hawk. With its eyes uncovered, it can see the neck of its vile prey.

Straining at the leash of the chains that bind him, he watches the horse stubble and no matter how he wills or prays it not to be; the horse stumbles over and over in his nightmares, and he knows his arrow will not make its mark.

In an explosion of red flesh, a gaudy phosphorescence of blood spews out, as the feathered warrior rips into the bulging muscle of the Slag's shoulder. A roar of agony echoes out between the trees and the assassin pulls back on his reins while struggling to stay astride his horse. Looking back at Hyw, the slag is defenceless against the full might of Hyw's arrows, but Hyw has loosed his last feathered warrior.

In his nightmares, Hyw knows the order of things. Begging to the Gods, he pleads that his bow should never bend again, but he watches in a pained agony as he bends his bow toward the grot, as if drawing an arrow across his bow. The avalanche of his memories powers forward. The effect is instant and the wounded Slag frantically spurs his poor nag forward, expecting to be despatched at any moment. Gripping his hand he grabs a fist full of Bayr's hair, ripping her from his horse in a desperate effort to gain greater speed.

Bayr screams as she is catapulted to the floor and, rolling from the path, she disappears down the steep bank towards the stream and her screams fall silent.

Before the last horse disappears from his view, Hyw scrambles from the path, half slipping, half stumbling down to where Bayr has fallen, his grief building inside. Gaining his sister's side, dragging her from the water, cradling her head in his hand: in his nightmares, Hyw's fingers once again feel the bones of her broken skull. With her life's blood seeping into the palm of his hand he screams up to the heavens. Hyw's waking dreams continue to roll over and over again, but the conflict in his mind gives way to a strange awakening that slowly permeates through him and whispering in his grief, he mutters,

"I could not save them!"

Chapter Two

"Whose there then?"

A voice calls out, shattering the darkness and Hyw's sanity wakes in an explosive clamour. Fumbling at his side, he panics, not knowing where he is. With his eyes scanning the shifting shadows around him, his crippled mind still is not fully lucid. Expecting Māthōg to swing the great blade and cut him down; in the confusion, he drops his bow. Frantically turning and hopelessly raging against the darkness of his waking dreams; finally, he manages to draw his new blade and brings it to bear.

"Hold on Hyw bach, it is I!" The old man steps out in front of him and Hyw can just make out his tattooed face. It is Sián's grandfather, Mordda; the old warrior stumbles slightly as he bends to pick up Hyw's bow.

Hyw's memories drift back to the day he first saw the old warrior; the day he walked out into the valley with his Grandfather. The day they had met his young friends, Sián and Enydd.

Returning piece by piece, Hyw's gathering sanity ebbs and flows as he slowly lowers the blade. Gradually becoming lucid, his memories stray back through his hallucinations. His last lucid memory was of his watching the love of his life, Sián, from beneath the trees in the Black Woods. She was swaying from side to side as she beat a rug into submission. He remembers watching her body from beneath her dress and a feeling of wanting coming over him, but then he hears her cries as he rode away.

'What is this? Where am I…? What incantations have brought me here?

As Hyw struggles to make sense of his sudden awakening, the old man stares up into his woad-painted, dirty face. Not quite believing what he sees, suddenly the sight of Hyw arrayed for battle seems to grip Mordda's imagination as he hands the bow back to Hyw.

"Going after Māthōg are we?" Smiling, Mordda turns and looks up at the mountain.

"Rumour is they passed by the Shade of the Mountain only this morning. They've been out in the borders, plying their awful trade!" Mordda's eyes are bloodshot and even from where Hyw sits, high on his grey mare, he can smell the grog on the old man's breath.

"Wait for me, Hyw bach…We have scores to settle…Blood for Blood…Blood for…!" Mordda chokes and his words falter, remembering Māthōg's slaughter of his precious granddaughter.

"Wait for…!" Before he can finish, he turns.

"Don't leave without me…Hyw bach!" Scurrying off into the darkness of the trees, the old man disappears. Hyw hears a low thud and a muted cry as something crashes through the undergrowth. Stumbling in his drunken haze; Mordda has fallen into a ditch by the river. On hearing his moans, Hyw pulls at the reins, coaxing his gentle companion back to the trail as he places the sword back in its scabbard.

Cursing to himself, Mordda is in a daze, tangled in the uprooted and spinning darkness.

"I'll be all right, I'll be there now!" He shouts out to the waiting night. The old man stumbles again and Hyw pauses on the path, listening to the low moans coming from the base of the hedge, but they subside and give way to drunken breathing as Mordda begins to snore.

Tapping his heels at his horse's side, the grey mare walks on.

Staring at the sword in its scabbard, some sense of reason enters his mind. In all his life, he has never swung a blade in anger. He had played with sticks as a boy and watched his father's precise practice with the great blade, but Hyw's skill rests in his use of the bow. Ywel had long told him of his father's expertise with the blade, but for some reason, Hyw has never been shown its skills.

Riding over the hill, he sees the beacon fires lining the mountains as he ponders his path; and also, his wisdom. Thoughts of Mordda come flooding into his mind.

"I let a drunken old man find me off guard!" Hyw begins to talk to himself.

'Thou wast dozing. What if he were Māthōg and his men? Ye wouldst be dead, that's what!'

Māthōg; the mere thought starts his blood boiling inside him and all his pain, his rage and anger burn in the flames of his madness.

Tapping his heels again on the sides of his gentle beast of burden, he calls in no more than a forced whisper.

"Garl up!" And the grey mare breaks into a trot as Hyw continues to question and reason with himself.

"Well, there's no turning back now."

"Of course ye can…just turn around and follow the path…go call on Sián…beg her to forgive thee…tell her how wrong ye have been…tell her how beautiful she is…tell her…how ye long to run thy fingers through her hair…to feel it against thy skin…tell her, how ye long for the feel of her soft warm body next to thee…beg her to bear thee thy children…"

"Oh that'll do it, I'm sure…?"

"No, I must continue."

"Why? Dust thou want to end up a drunken old fool, stripped of thy dignity by the pains thy life has brought to thee…go back…build a home for Sián and thee; have a family…build thyself a life."

"What's the point? Māthōg has ripped everything I have ever loved, from me…while he lives, I will never rest!"

The argument in his mind ceases and he begins to plan his journey.

"Go and visit my brother…he will know what to do!" His Grandfather's words come flooding into his mind. Pondering on a brother he had only ever glimpsed in the uncertain light of a dying fire, he thinks on.

"Maybe I will…Maybe I will?" Hyw thinks about his Grandfather's brother, a man that has Waking Dreams; just as he does. A man that had followed his dreams had led their family to sacred islands, a man that had found a Holy Man, who had blessed them and given them a purpose and direction. However, in his racing thoughts, his mind stumbles and he rides on.

"Thou wilt ne'r survive, not even the first night…ye must pay more attention to thy surroundings…thou canst not just ride blindly on!" It is his grandfather, Ywel, who begins to reason inside his head. Clearing his mind and purging his guilt over the way he has treated his childhood sweetheart, Sián, he continues to walk forward, convinced the path he treads will one day lead him home.

Skirting around the tavern and the few crofts that form the Shade of the Mountain, he presses forward. The faint sounds of people shouting and crying in drunken laughter echo out into the night.

Beginning to shiver without his smock, he jumps down and rummages in the bundle on the back of his perplexed companion and to his relief he sees he has packed all he will need. Finding his hunting smock, wrapped in the middle of the roll, he takes it out. Slipping the smock over his head, he climbs back into the saddle. Laying the bow over the front of his saddle with an arrow across its centre, he drags his father's wolf-skin blanket over his shoulders and ties it at the front of his neck; eventually, he is ready. Dressed in his woad, set for the fray, he would at least be warm when he eventually gets there; wherever there becomes.

Following the path, he climbs up past the gold mines. Soon he is close to the top of The Dragon's Back and the summit of the Mother Mountain, where he pauses, sitting astride his silent companion. Staring out over the mountains, he can just make out the silhouette of the Druid's Eerie Mountains. The stars are just beginning to peep through the clouds and with a lull in proceedings, the mare drops her head and quietly munches on the short mountain fodder.

Turning in his saddle, Hyw looks back to the east and can see the faint glow of the Great Warrior of the night. Feeling, somehow, safe and secure he imagines those he loves watching over him and looking down from the stars.

Leaving the trail, he looks out to the distant mountains and wonders if his journey will take him to their lofty heights, but before he drops further down the mountain, he looks back to his own mountain home and wonders if he will ever see it again.

Looking across to King's Mount and then down into the valley spreading out between them; he pats the horse on its neck and strokes its mane. The grey mare neighs softly at the unexpected attention and Hyw points them both towards the flickering light of a campfire burning amongst the foothills of the mountains.

'There is no dwelling there.' He thinks to himself. The fire's small luminous glow wanes, but occasionally, someone stirs its light, sending a billowing glow of bright sparks scurrying up into the night. As the fire's distant light gets closer and closer, the blood of the warrior scalds through him and he fights to prevent it from boiling over. Gripping his bow firmly in his hand, he holds it out to one side with one finger looped around his feathered warrior.

The horse silently treads a path towards the fire and, somewhere in his distant memories, he remembers the promise he made to the beast. A promise of never again having to ride into battle.

"How many compromises and promises wilt I break before my journey's done?" The words go unspoken and the pain of promises made and broken is burnt up in his rage for Māthōg and his Blood Red Crows.

Drawing closer and closer to the fire's small glow, his senses seem to heighten. A short distance from the fire the horse stops, turning slightly to one side as if he knows his master's thoughts in advance. Its head drops to give Hyw room to manoeuvre, and the silent animal doesn't munch on the grass; its discipline is immaculate.

Hyw can see four men in the fire's dying glow. There are several bundles of blankets on the ground to the rear of the fire, but they are close enough to feel its warmth. Heads are sticking out of two of the bundles; one with blankets pulled almost over its hair. A third man is lying with the blankets up to his waist, leaning on one elbow, talking to a fourth man who is squatting to the left of the fire.

The man at the fire is older, with his long grey hair tied at the back of his head. Poking at the dying embers, sparks dance high into the night. Throwing another log onto the simmering blaze, he half squats, half leans on his crook, with its stick resting on his shoulder. In an instant, Hyw can see they are shepherds and he hears the unmistakable bleating of Old Soay sheep coming from somewhere beyond where the men are gathered around the fire's warm light.

The dark silhouette of a hedge and trees against the night, forms the far side of the sheep's open pen, but in the darkness, Hyw cannot make out any other fencing, or if the sheep are tended by another, but he guessed there would be others on watch.

The man squatting by the fire coughs and then, clearing his throat, he spits into the fire as if to ward off evil. Hyw can't quite make out what the two men are saying and he wonders why so many men are out in the fields guarding the flock.

Gently nudging at the mare, they move slowly forward with Hyw holding his bow loosely at his side. Entering the circle of light, the men stop talking, hearing the horse for the first time. The great beast stops before they are too close and turns again, giving Hyw room to bring his bow to bear. All the time Hyw's eyes constantly scan the surrounding darkness and his ears strain to listen to every spark of noise. Again, he recognises his horse's great discipline and he is forced, to remember his promise to the beast. Catching sight of his dark silhouette in the shadows; the old boy calls out.

"Who's there then?" The man's voice is low but loud. Immediately the second man, lying on the ground grabs his crook and gets to his feet, with one of the sleeping men rousing and slowly sitting up, not understanding the danger he is in.

Hyw is a fearsome sight as the old shepherd looks up into his face, with the flickering light of the fire's renewed flames. Obviously shaken, he slowly gets to his feet and seems, somehow, to calm his feelings.

Continuing to scan the darkness beyond where the shepherds are gathered; they are all made acutely aware of Hyw's presence. Suddenly a fifth man steps into the circle with a sword in his hand and a sixth man is skirting around to his right, under the cover of darkness. Quickly raising his arm, Hyw bends his bow; its deadly shaft aimed straight at the heart of the man with the sword and the old shepherd calls out.

"Wait…Stop…wait a moment!" The man in the shadows stops and, feeling the acute nearness of Hyw's watchful blade, the man with the sword holds it out to his side, his other arm held up; its hand open. Slowly opening his empty hand, he looks straight into Hyw. Seeing and sensing little danger, Hyw lowers his aim, letting the tension between his powerful arms ease, much to the relief of the shepherds who have been caught off guard.

"I look for the one they call Māthōg!" Hyw says in a voice that seems, somehow, alien to him. With a surge of hate rushing through him at the name of his foe, he wonders about that other entity that is taking over his senses.

The sixth shepherd moves towards the light and Hyw stares across at him as he edges into view. The old man relaxes and slowly crouches back down by the fire.

"And what would a young man like thee want with the Scotti…have ye a want for Annwn?" Hyw remains silent and the old shepherd stares up at his pitiful sight. Bowing his head again, the old shepherd goes to speak.

"Thou art too late…they've been and gone!" There is venom in his voice as the old man stares into the furnace of the fire.

"Thou hast seen them then?" The man remains cautious of Hyw.

"Yes, we've seen them!" The man with the sword says, placing his sword in its scabbard.

"They killed his brother!" His words are full of hate as he points to a young man who steps into the light from where he stood in the shadows, an arrow notched into the string of his own bow.

"They killed his brother and stole our sheep!" One of the others joins in the conversation and their anger at the Scotti is obvious.

"Why dust thou think it takes six of us to tend our flocks?" Hyw's head bows at the news, but he raises it again as the old shepherd continues to speak.

"What business dust thou have with men such as these?" But as soon as he poses the question he realises he will not gain an answer. Looking up at Hyw, the shepherd can only imagine the horrors he has suffered and he doesn't push the matter further. His pity for the boy sat astride the ghostly grey mare in front of him waxes.

"Come, sit awhile. We have food and the fire is warm…we will talk!"

Hyw stares down at the fire's inviting glow, but he silently shakes his head as he continues to ask questions.

"How many…?" The old man gets to his feet and points out across the valley.

"There are nine or ten…all of them drunk with ale from the Shade of the Mountain. We're not sure, but we think they took the path up between the Lost Woods and the High Moors!" Turning back towards Hyw, he hesitates before he looks back, again pointing his finger along the trail.

"The light of a strange fire glows on the far side of the valley…See it…there?" The shepherd points out a tiny pinprick of light. Hyw looks out and can barely make out its faint glow, but its position is set firmly in his mind.

"I doubt it's their fire though…In too much of a hurry to stay in one place long, they were."

Hyw breathes in the chilled night air as he reaches out with all his senses and he knows it is their fire. Crouching back down the old shepherd looks up at where Hyw still sits astride his horse.

"They carry one who is wounded…Looked like death itself, he did!" He pauses slightly before continuing.

"Thy work…maybe?" Hyw looks straight into him and nods his head as the shepherd smiles.

"May the Gods and all their power go with thee my friend…give 'em nothing. Don't turn thy back on those wolves for a moment." Hyw pulls on the reins while kicking at the sides of his gentle companion and the horse turns towards the dim light of a distant fire as the old shepherd looks back down. He doesn't look up again as Hyw rides away but speaks quietly to his companions.

"That young man's looking for a kingdom of trouble…but it's nothing to the dark realms he has seen!" The man's words fall silent as Hyw's image fades from his mind.

Placing his arrows and bow away so he can ride hard, Hyw pushes the grey mare into the darkness of an uncertain night.

Chapter Three

Hyw slows his tired companion as they approach the borders of the Lost Woods. The chilled morning air cools them as the dawn's slow light edges into the sky behind where they ride. Having lost sight of the fire, he steers the horse forward to a lull in the trees, knowing their camp is near.

The Lost Woods are a foreboding tangle of bent and twisted trees with thick firs at their heart. Hyw's people call them the Lost Woods, but those who live within their borders call them Coed-y-Teg; The Woods of the Fair Ones. The woods stretch out as far as the eye can see and disappear over the distant horizon. The thick mires and murky desolation of the high moors are almost as foreboding, but of the two, Hyw would prefer to follow a path towards the moors. The woods line the southern borders of the meandering trail westward, with the high moors rising to the north.

Steam rises from the grey mare and large swaths of sweat run down its neck and legs, frothing at its mouth. It had been a long haul; pressing hard into the night. They had stopped at the river and had rested at every stream and spring, but only long enough for her to drink. In front of them, the path meanders up to the distant hills and onto the moors.

The fire's small heart has long since faded, but Hyw has marked its location well. Searching through the thin veils of mist draped between the trees and over the moors, he can smell the faintest scent of wood smoke. Its meagre fare is too scant for him to follow, but his bridled companion seems to catch its odour and follows its invitations. Eventually, Hyw spies a thin ribbon of smoke drifting out between the trees.

Jumping down, he throws his father's wolf skin coat over the horse and lets the reins drop, trusting the mare's loyalty. Scrambling up a small bank, he peers into the darkness and can just make out the dying embers where the fire once burnt. Scanning for any sign of life, he sees a fallen tree and strewn beneath it, fixes his eyes on a bundle of dirty rags that were once blankets. Smoke obscures his view slightly, but he is sure there is someone wrapped up in the paltry coverings. With the smoke clearing slightly, he can make out a ghostly face bereft of any discernable life.

Waiting patiently, constantly checking for any sign of the Scotti, Hyw hears a low moan and the rags heave and turn with a further muffled cry, then nothing. Silently, Hyw moves back to where his horse waits patiently, nibbling at the hedgerow. Reaching up; Hyw draws the sword from its scabbard and turns back to the trees making no sound, he crawls back to his original position. Constantly checking that all is clear, he continues crawling on his belly as the wild cat inside him, stalks its prey. Drawing closer, he clearly sees where the ghostly figure lies. When he reaches the fire, he inches to his feet, crouching then standing, all the while carefully keeping watch on the tattered rags.

'If the others appear I can run off through the trees and nothing will be lost!' he thinks to himself.

'Yes…but why the sword…why oh why did ye pick the sword?' Hyw grips the blade tighter in his hand as he purges the voice from his head. Thoughts of disappearing comfort and settle his mind, but he is certain there is no one lying in wait.

Staring down at the pathetic sight, Hyw's ears begin to ring with Bayr's woeful cries and a vision of the Slag teasing at her infests his mind. Only the last light of the fire stands between this dirty slag and the point of his blade.

The mess his stray arrow has caused is partially open to his view and he stares down at the ashen face of the wretch as large beads of sweat trickle from his forehead. The fiend groans in a stupor of agony as he rolls onto his side. His shattered shoulder turns towards Hyw who marvels how this Grot could have continued in the weeks that have passed.

Catching the stench of the wound in his nostrils, Hyw almost heaves at the sight and smell of the open, maggoty wound that invades his nostrils. The dark red flesh at its centre is swollen out of all proportion and is surrounded by yellow and white blisters of puss. Beads of sweat dribble inside it and Hyw can see his pathetic victim is burning up in a deep fever. The Slag's deathly white skin seems to boil as he rambles in delirium, but he is about to be woken to the reality of all his nightmares.

The painful image of Bayr lying motionless in the crimson water, tears at Hyw's heart as her blood cries up from the palm of his hand cupped under the broken bones of her skull. Being so close rankles inside Hyw, and he grips the handle of the blade as he slowly extends it out. Making no sound, he steps over the fire and points the blade down towards the wound. With its honed tip, he pokes callously at the slags festering shoulder and a volcano of puss spurts out. The Grot instantly wakes, tortured and reeling in his agonies.

Stepping back, Hyw gives him chance to focus as the old shepherds' words haunt his mind.

"Give them nothing!"

Fear and fever strip all dignity from the quivering Grot. Crawling to his knees, he doubles over holding his gut, while rambling incoherently. Begging for his life, he tries to grip the end of Hyw's blade, but Hyw keeps a good distance with his impatient blade waiting for its baptism.

Staring down at the pitiful sight before him; his anger and rage are tempered slightly.

'He is not long for this life, no matter what I do!' The thought is silenced.

'Thy heart is not in this, Hyw bach!' The voice in his head is that of his grandfather, but the presence he feels deep in his heart is the familiar spirit of his mother, and pity flows through him as the Slag begs for his life.

'Run him through!' Again, the voice in his head.

'No, no… I can't do it!' The voice in his head laughs as it goads him on.

'Don't be a fool…Remember thy sister; do what ye came here to do!'

'No…I, can't…I, just can't…He'll be dead soon, my first attack was enough…I'll go call on Sián and beg her to forgive me!' And Hyw turns to go.

'Give 'em nothing…' The shepherd's words echo in his mind once more.

Suddenly the Slag moves and Hyw realises his mistake. The Slag's movement is heavy on the ground and a rush of uncertain power surges in Hyw as the blood of the warrior burns inside him. Quickly turning his head, Hyw sees the dagger in the Grot's hand. Spinning around; the Grot lunges forward. With the sword held firmly in both hands, Hyw swings the blade, trying to aim its power, but in his inexperience, he misses his aim and only the flat of his blade strikes the upper arm of the resurrected Slag.

His arm is thrown wide with the force of the sword smashing into him, but although deflected from his deadly course, he still manages to keep his blade and his feet. Spinning out of control with the weight of the sword, Hyw finds himself with his back to the swift blade of an accomplished killer. The Slag renews his attack as cries fill Hyw's head, stifling any clear thought.

Throwing the sword quickly into the air and reversing his grip, Hyw thrusts the sword quickly behind him with its sharp edges narrowly missing his leg. Holding it rigid, he cowers from the Slag's impending attack. In his delirium, the Grot pounces on Hyw, with all the might his crippled body can muster, but his attack is short-lived as he impales himself on Hyw's waiting blade.

Hyw feels the hungry point of his sword puncturing the Grot's belly, its blade jolting as it slams into the Grot's spine. Pushing sharply back, its keenly honed edges grate through the bones, vibrating down its handle into Hyw's hands and arms. Warmblood spills out onto the back of Hyw's legs and in the fray of battle, he hopes it is not his own. Standing, he steps quickly forward tugging at the blade as its steel grates once more against the Slag's bones. It exits his foe's crippled body, and he manages to stand for only a moment before he collapses onto the fire. Coughing and spluttering, Hyw turns to watch as the Grot's life spills into the ashes.

Exhausted, Hyw drops to his knees; the fray had lasted only a moment, but all his energy is drained. Taking in deep gulps of air, he fights to gain control of his senses. Images of Bayr's struggle fill his head; boiling in the cauldron of his rage then suddenly, without reason and with no conscious thought inside him, he falls on the wretched Grot, pounding him with his fists.

All pity leaves him as dark shadows infest his mind. Blood splashes up from his face, where Hyw's fists continue to rain down. Continuing his senseless attack, Hyw vents the vials of his wrath and his fists beat like the pounding of his hammer on the slag's lifeless remains.

Time passes and Hyw finally comes to, lying on his back staring up at the branches of the trees above him. His face and clothes are splattered with blood and dirt. Slowly staggering to his feet, he picks up his bloodstained blade and wipes it on a tuft of ferns.

There is little feeling left inside him as he looks down at the Slag's mutilated body. Only one end befits such a criminal and grabbing handfuls of dry leaves, he kindles a spark that breathes life back into the fire. Moving beyond the fallen tree, he picks up the end of two fallen branches, one of which still has its dried leaves hanging from its bough. Throwing them on the fire he goes searching for more. Building up the fire around the Grot's burning carcass, it roars into a towering blaze. Thick smoke climbs high into the morning sky and the shepherds stare across the valley in muted wonder.

'There's no turning back!'

'I know!' Hyw admits to himself.

'Ye did it; thou hast killed him!' He hangs his head.

'Yes I killed him,' Somewhere, deep inside, he is ashamed and struggles to come to terms with what he has done. He had faced death before, but somehow this was different. Ywel had always encouraged him to 'face life' and he ponders on his grandfather's wisdom.

The grey mare is munching on fern nuts as Hyw walks over to her. Cradling the gentle animal's head in his arms, there is nothing left inside him as he whispers into the horse's ears. They are quiet words of comfort, but he dares not make the beast any further promises.

'No more swordplay!' Hyw thinks as he places the blade in its scabbard.

"No swordplay!" He repeats the words out loud. The grey mare looks back at him with sad eyes.

"Stick with what ye know Hyw bach!" He hears his grandfather's voice inside his head. Patting the great horse on her hindquarters.

"I have broken my promise to thee!" The horse neighs softly.

"Go if thou wilt, but I must stay!" Whispering to the beast, as scratching around the mare's ears, Hyw rests his head against hers. They both stand, each looking into the other's eyes. Silent words pass between them until both their minds are set with unspoken vows hanging in the air.

Turning towards the high moors, Hyw gazes at the dark clouds gathering over The Druids Mountains. Mounting his ghostly companion, he gently taps at the horse's sides and they ride towards a billowing storm.

Chapter Four

Sitting on the ghostly grey mare, wandering like some phantom through the shadows of the woods, Hyw wraps himself up against the coming winter's chill that is blowing down off the moors. Māthōg and his men have cut a swath through the landscape a child could follow. Scanning the moors to the north and then to the west where the trail eventually turns, his path leads up to the high moors, rising over distant horizons.

Looking out, hunger drags at him as his eyes grow heavy and he cannot remember the last time he slept. Waking with a start, the horse has stopped to graze on short grass. Rousing himself and the horse, he chivvies them on, but his eyes are soon closing again.

Echoes of those he has loved and lost, feed his want for revenge; revenge tempered only by thoughts of justice. Drawing his father's wolfskin coat over his shoulders, he looks behind him, to the mountains of his home.

Turning again, he lifts his eyes to the Druid's Mountains, to the land of the Eagles Eerie where dark clouds shroud their rocky crags.

The day burns steadily on as he rides through the edge of the forest, climbing to distant heights with the storm drawing ever closer. Hyw stops where the trail leads out of the woods and onto the moors. Soon they will be engulfed in the billow clouds and the fury of the storm. Watching and waiting, his want for food and sleep drags at him as the mare drops her head once more to the sparse fodder at her feet and Hyw's eyes fade.

A thicket of bushes and brush erupts in a scurry of movement with the cackling laugh of the Roman's Fowl. Jumping to attention, Hyw bends his bow towards the bush and its dry autumn thicket. The Roman's Fowl flies out, hugging the tops of the heather. Waiting, he searches for his aim. Checking the wind and the bird's flight, he releases his hungry hawk. Swooping towards its prey with its talons outstretched, his arrow kills the unfortunate fowl in an instant.

Jumping down, Hyw bounds and leaps over the heather to retrieve the pheasant, slitting its throat as he does so. Marching back into the trees, he hangs the bird from a suitable bough. Its blood drips to the ground as he leads the mare beneath the shelter of the trees.

"It is time to rest and take stock, my friend," Hyw says quietly and the horse neighs softly to him, as though she understands and agrees with his words.

Nearby is a giant fir whose thick branches hang down, in places, almost touching the ground, and Hyw makes his camp beneath its cover. Gathering as much wood as he can from the forest floor, he stacks enough for a fire, against the impending storm and the cold of the night. Stripping his quiet companion of her load, Hyw tethers her beneath the tree. They will both need shelter.

If Hyw had looked all day he could not have found a better place to hole up. The tree's thick branches afford them good cover but are open enough to have a commanding view of the moors and any approach.

Unrolling the bundle wrapped in two large thick woollen blankets, he immediately throws one of the blankets over the mare, tying it at the front. The horse whinnies and briskly nods its head in appreciation. Taking the net of hay, he drapes it from a broken branch where she can reach it. Then opening the sack of crushed horse oats he spreads some on the ground.

"What more dust thou need?" Hyw asks and the horse neighs softly again, stopping chomping on the food for only a moment.

"Tis time to name thee, my friend!" Hyw steps around to the front of the gentle beast that raises her head to meet his eyes. Scratching at the tuft of hair between her ears, Hyw runs his hand down her face. Cupping his fingers, he places his hand over her mouth. The horse gently nibbles at Hyw's fingers with her soft hairy lips.

"Sarn…yes Sarn. Thou art my path, a highway on which I wouldst travel!" Hyw hugs the horse's head to his.

"What dust thou think my friend…hey Sarn bach?" The horse neighs and lifts its head out of Hyw's arms.

"Sarn it is then!" Patting the horse's neck, it goes back to its oats and nuts.

Returning to his preparations, spreading out the second blanket as a groundsheet, he rolls out his bed of finer woollen blankets and his father's wolf skin cloak, placing all his worldly goods around him. Loosening the saddle, Hyw puts it next to the trunk of the tree and lays out the horse's blanket as a pillow for his head.

Sián has done him proud, there is a stock of salted and smoked meats with some bread and nuts, but he too has also packed well: two tinderboxes; a stock of charcoal for kindling and a host of bowstrings. There is also a spare smock and shirt with an arsenal of arrows enough to supply a small army.

Picking up one of the tinderboxes, he sparks a fire. Carefully tending the flame, blowing occasionally. Soon he has a roaring blaze and he turns his attention to the fowl. It is soon stripped and cleaned and the smell of its roasting flesh over the fire becomes almost unbearable. He would usually hang the fowl for at least a week, but there is no time for refined living. Work brings new vigour to His mind.

Keeping his bow close at hand, he keeps his belt around his waist with its quiver and knives. Soon everything is set and he sits below the eves of the great fir, ripping the hot meat of the Roman's Fowl apart. It is succulent and its swelling warmth fills his belly.

The cold wind edges into the woods, but there is a strange silence at its heart. Drawing the blankets and furs higher, he begins to drift. In his dreams, he is safe and snugly wrapped up at his mother's side but with crashing concern, he turns to her as she calls to him.

"Save thy sister, Hyw bach…save thy sister!" Her words are gently spoken, but their urgency haunts his sanity.

Sarn's frightened squeal and whinnies slowly stir him awake, but dull to her fears, his mind has a want to continue his dreams. Another low growl murmurs through the woods and wakes him in an instant. Gripping the handle of his bow, he quickly notches an arrow into place. Turning, he stands, bringing his bow to bear. The wolves scurry off through the woods at his sudden movement, but they will soon be back. Sarn's eyes are wide with her fear as she looks anxiously back at her master.

"Come Sarn bach!" Hyw digs into the bag containing her food and raises his hand towards her.

"Come…come by here then!" Hyw sucks through his teeth and then trots his tongue against the roof of his mouth as the huge beast bows her head and walks over to his side. Nibbling cautiously at his hand, Sarn is still full of fear. The sound of wolves moves through the darkness of the forest, but Hyw ignores their presence, petting and comforting Sarn. Eventually, he turns into the darkness, his eyes scanning every shadow and shape. The ravenous flickering shadows of the night are creeping closer still. Returning to the fire, Hyw stokes its smouldering embers and he throws several large armfuls of wood into its flames.

To one side lies the carcass of the Roman's Fowl. Picking up its cold remains, he tosses it towards the shadows of the wolves. Growls and the gnashing of teeth echo in the darkness and the squeals of a young cub can be heard, howling off between the trees. Its howls fade and Hyw turns back to the light of his fire.

"If they dare to come back, Sarn Bach, they'll have some of this!" Hyw smiles at the mare as he points to the blade of his feathered warrior. Looking out to the moors, Hyw can see the storm has passed and the night skies are clear and he realises he has slept through its howling torrent. The moon is glistening on the first snows of winter, thick on the high moors, but only a scattering on the lower ground by the woods.

Moving out into the open; the chill of the clear night bites into his face. His breath blows great clouds in front of him and he looks up into the eternity of stars above.

Looking at the high moors, Māthōg's trail has been obliterated by the snow. Turning to the east, he fixes his eyes on the stars beyond which the God of his grandfather dwells. Their light shines down on the mountains of his home. Pondering the course of his life he falls over his thoughts.

'There is no divine plan…No path set for me, to follow!' His thoughts betray his anger and his memories taunt his visions as they flash inside him.

'Life is surely left to its misfortune…No God of love could have ordered these things I have suffered…and what of those things I have yet to face?'

Looking, he can see only dark shadows in his waking dreams and he rages at the night.

"If ye want me...?" Hyw's baying words reach up to the heavens, crying at the stars and quickly bending his bow his feathered warrior pursues them up into the night. Its talons are set against that place, beyond the stars, where the God of his grandfather dwells, but the moment he releases his shaft, Hyw regrets his anger. The arrow is woefully short of its mark and falls to the earth, but his eyes remain fixed on the stars. The glistening pathway of the night stretches out above him and the four corners of the earth, ruled over by the three gods, with the 'One True God' at their centre. They all shine down serenely to where he drops to his knees in tears.

The ravenous wolves have dared to trouble his camp again; he can hear their snarls and they're snapping at each other. Running quickly forward, he roars into the shadows of the woods scattering their hunger once more. All patience has left him and notching an arrow into place, Hyw loses his anger at one of the creeping shadows. With a sudden squeal and cry, the wolves run for the safety of the night and do not venture back.

Tethering Sarn closer to the fire, Hyw stokes its flames again and lies back on his bed, but sleep eludes him for what remains of the night. Lying back staring up into the sad eyes of his faithful companion, he looks past her to the stars.

Riding out of the trees, the sun is already above the mountains of his home. Beginning along the path, Hyw can no longer see the trail Mathog and his men had made. It is lost beneath the sparse coverings of the snow. Approaching the brow of the first rise, his eyes scan back to his own mountains and he catches the faintest sight of something blowing in the breeze just above the heather. It is the arrow he launched into the night. Jumping down, bounding over the brush, he walks back, wiping the dirt from the blade of his arrow.

"I wish my words were as easy to retrieve… hey, Sarn bach!" The horse neighs softly and shakes its head at his voice.

The snow is only thin and the rising sun is already melting its cold heart. The skies are clear and blue, with only a slight breeze in the air, but its slow breath lifts the cold from the ground and Hyw pulls the wolf skins in closely around him. The trail is well worn, but whether Mathog and his Blood Red Crows had passed this way, Hyw has no way of telling.

The day saunters slowly on as clouds gather above the mountains to the west. The high moors have their own desolate beauty; thick bogs and quagmires are set on either side of the path as it meanders through the undulating landscape. Occasionally the trail circumscribes small ponds and larger lakes and there is a constant sound of seeping water at Sarn's feet and the smell of peat. The moors seem awash with water as it bleeds through a mess of heather and peat, oozing, dripping, trickling, and eventually flowing into small streams. In its hollows, it would be easy for someone to lose their way, but while the light lasts the path is sufficient for Hyw to follow.

In the mid-afternoon sun, a traveller comes along the trail towards him, walking over the high moor, an old man with a shepherd's crook and long wisps of willow for wattle, bundled over his shoulders. His head is bowed in front of him, but at the sight of Hyw, he scurries off onto the moors and hides behind an outcrop of rock, the only feature on the face of the barren landscape. Hyw isn't surprised. His horse and armour alone would fill even the stoutest heart with trepidation, but Hyw is still covered with the stench and dirt of death and looks every bit a phantom of some dark realm.

In the late afternoon, the moors break into patches of high grassland, strewn with rocks and boulders. The grassy slopes steadily drop towards distant woodlands. He passes a few sheepfolds and a tumbledown shepherd's croft. Low windswept hedges and badly maintained dry stone walls start to appear on either side of the track and he can see stacks of smoke rising from the valley below.

Suddenly a group of small birds are startled from the hedge and Hyw catches sight of the hawk as it darts, swooping from one side of the hedge to the other, taking one of the birds in flight.

The evening is fast falling around the two lonely wanderers, but the valley is still a good ride below as Sarn picks her way through lengthening shadows. She slows at a patch of long grass and grazes for a while then, stepping forward, she stops to graze again. A dog barks in a distant yard and Hyw suddenly wakes. Rousing the sleep from him, he gently kicks at Sarn's sides.

"Not yet Sarn bach!" The horse neighs as she reluctantly moves on into the gathering dusk. A stream flows somewhere to the side of the path, but soon its babbling brook cuts across the path and Hyw and Sarn refresh themselves in its pure waters. It tumbles over a small waterfall somewhere not too far from where they drink. Waiting while his gentle companion grazes, foraging in the bundle on her back, he brings out a piece of dried meat for himself.

Thinking of Sián, he wonders how he could ever reconcile his feelings toward her. His heart burns inside him as he contemplates his lost love.

The path leads slowly on; following the stream into the dark shadows of the coming night. Tumbling over rocks and falls, the familiar sound of the water comforts him as he thinks of the stream that tumbles past his own small mountain home and again he fights the rage building inside him.

One step blurs into the next as time drifts slowly by. Shadows lengthen and then disappear into the night. The strains of a reed chanter moan in the distant darkness. A light flickers from a window as it gazes out at the passing lonely strangers. The croft is half-hidden in a thicket of trees, but there is laughter beyond its door and Hyw longs for company and conversation around a dying fire, he longs for the quiet laughter of friends; of people he loves and cares for; he longs for a life free from anger and fear, but most of all, Hyw longs for love as he sits quietly, wrapped up in the ghostly, but comforting arms of his mother.

A dog barks having picked up their scent on the air. The laughter from beyond the windows dies and the door opens.

"Who's there then?" A tired voice calls out. The dog stops calling and the door closes, dousing its light.

In the valley, the stream joins a river. Calmly meandering through meadows and grassland. Hyw looks for a place to rest for the night. It is too exposed for a fire and Hyw huddles at the base of a huge oak as he sinks slowly into a restless sleep. Trapped somewhere between death and dawn, he listens to the river's gentle flow. Sarn chomps on the dying grasses of the meadow and Hyw struggles in his haunted dreams. In his nightmares, he constantly follows Māthōg's trail as they circle back to set a trap, having heard his following footsteps. A feathered warrior from a Scotti bow thrashes out of the shadows and Hyw wakes suddenly from his troubled sleep. Sarn has wandered off from her stake and is grazing a short distance from where Hyw is shaking off the night.

"Come Sarn bach!" His quiet call goes unheeded as Hyw gets to his feet. Sarn has wandered over to the other side of the meadow where the grass is slightly sweeter. She is feeding in the shadow of a small wood that runs between the river and an unknown track. Hyw calls again.

"Here, Sarn bach!" Sarn raises her head and turns towards Hyw and then ignoring his call, she continues to chomp on the long grass again. Trotting his tongue against the roof of his mouth, Sarn ignores him. His calls become louder.

"Sarn!" Sarn grazes on.

Hyw bends to pick up his bow, holding an arrow loosely at its grip as he walks out into the dim light of the field towards where Sarn is still intent on grazing.

Halfway across the pasture, a shadow disturbs the slumber of Hyw's waking thoughts, bringing his full senses immediately to attention. A feathered shaft breaks loose from the shadows and instantly notching an arrow into place, Hyw flings himself aside. The arrow thrashes past his head and Hyw bends his bow towards a dark silhouette in the bushes by the track. His arrow is swift and deadly, but before his blade makes its mark, the cries of Māthōg and his men fill the air. They break from the shadow of the woods and charge at Hyw, who is alone and exposed in the centre of the long field.

The thunderous hooves of Māthōg's warhorse vibrate through the ground as the Red Raiders gallop towards him, past where Sarn is grazing. In the excitement of the moment Sarn turns and gallops toward her master, but Māthōg is well ahead of her eager heart. Hyw curses to himself, staring at his empty hands.

There is no way he can beat the deadly charge back to his nest of arrows, laying abandoned beneath the tree with his belt and knives. His only chance is to dodge the flashing steal of Māthōg's blade.

Another arrow whistles past his head and in the madness of the moment he scoffs at the inadequate aim of his foe. Seeing his hopeless situation, Māthōg's men slow their charge and leave Māthōg, alone with his helpless quarry.

The great warhorse thunders forward aimed directly at Hyw, but just before its snorting charge tramples over him, Hyw dives to the side. Looking up at Sarn, Hyw can see she has been caught by one of Māthōg's men and he looks on helplessly as the Grot draws Hyw's sword from its scabbard.

Māthōg turns and slows his charge slashing at the air with the blade. Ducking and weaving, Hyw makes for the front of the warhorse narrowly escaping the hungry edge of his father's deadly captured blade. Gripping the bit in the horse's mouth he ducks from Māthōg's repeated attacks. Māthōg lunges forward with his blade and his horse whinnies as lifting its head, breaking Hyw's grip. Hyw screams as the tip of Māthōg's blade rips through his clothes and he wakes from his nightmares to the touch of

Sarn's soft lips gently nibbling and dribbling on his face. Hyw jumps back with a start but then hugs Sarn to him.

"My dear Sarn bach!" Hyw says out loud as Sarn neighs softly. The dream had seemed so real.

The first grey light of the morning is seeping into the sky, but the meadow is quiet and Sarn is safely tethered where Hyw had staked her the night before. Checking his belt, all is as it should be, with his feathered warriors nesting safely in their quiver, but Hyw remains cautious as he moves warily towards the river's edge.

Trout flit and dart beneath its glimmering surface as they dance to and fro at the presence of his looming shadow. Flitting to the underbelly of their rocks; they disappear from Hyw's keen sight. Stepping out onto a large rock where he has seen two fish, run and hide, he stoops and kneels on its slippery surface. Rolling up his sleeve, he gradually immerses his hand in the freezing waters. Feeling under the rock, his hand is soon rubbing the underbelly of a large brook trout and within a short time, he has caught two for his morning's meal.

Chapter Five

The grey blank giant silhouettes of trees seep solemnly by like lonely giants; barely visible in the bubbling mire of damp fog that hangs in the air. Only the sound of trickling water breaks through the silence as Sarn slowly saunters through the gathering gloom. The darkness deepens as misty rain begins to fall. Lost and alone to all, but her new master, Sarn trudges on.

High above the trees, a buzzard soars unseen, crying for the pity of the world below. Stalking from the chill of one shadow into the next, they pass people who point and stare. Only one name is uttered, falling from the lips of suspicious mothers as they whisper in dread;

'The Phantom of Annwn'.

Days slip endlessly by as Hyw's melancholy seems to sink in the bubbling misty mires and all intent of his search for Māthōg and his blood-red crows is lost. The two lonely companions wander through forests strewn with brambles and briars as pasture and field give way to sheer banks and the unforgiving rocks of perilous and swollen rivers. Time and again, Sarn is forced back by the thick undergrowth, and in the darkness beneath the trees, gradually all sense of sanity ebbs from Hyw's mind.

The river tumbles ever on, down the steep sides of the valley with its sheer banks dwarfed by mountains on every side. Sickened by the shadows, Sarn climbs the steep sides of a wood-strewn mountain. Finding a rocky outcrop, she stands like a statue, staring down into the heart of an unknown valley, where a small gathering of crofts is nestled by the fork of the relentless river. Above the treetops, a huddle of smokestacks drift up into the drizzle of the day. The smell of wood smoke sparks a light in Hyw's mind and he can feel the warmth of their fires dragging him home.

The ghostly silhouette of Hyw sitting high on Sarn's back has caught the gaze of one young child and gathering around her, the people stare up at where she points. With no conscious thought inside him, he returns their stare as a whisper ripples through those gathered;

'The Phantom of Annwn'.

Sarn bows her head with the rain pouring relentlessly through her ghostly passenger. Time seems to slow as if one-moment struggles to find the next. Guided, as if by some other hand, Sarn turns and slowly saunters down the mountainside, picking her way through the Sacred Birch Woods, towards the light and warmth of uncertain fires. Stepping from the trees onto the path, the roar of the river eludes Hyw's senses.

Walking slowly on, people disappear, scurrying for the safety and warmth of forgotten hearths. The frightened cry of a child wakes Hyw, but he still struggles in his madness. The people scatter to and fro, children clinging to the safety of their mother's arms, but unaware of their fears, Sarn plods on.

Ambling through the borders of the village, they round the corner of the first croft with only one man left standing on the track. Almost as young as Hyw, he has a tangle of long hair that hangs down, wet with rain. Eyes peer out from his scantly bearded face. With a sodden blanket thrown over his shoulders, his bright blue eyes scrutinise Hyw and an uncertain light is cast into his worried gaze. His face begins to contort and twitch in his growing fears, but he continues to stand his ground.

Carrying a bow, a young woman rushes forward, her long bright hair blowing in the breeze. Running towards the young man, her dress flows free, hugging her soft warm body. Even at such a distance, her familiar beauty is open to Hyw's imagination.

'Sián!' The thought lights a fire in his mind and Sián's image brushes his memories, like autumn leaves blown through the end-of-summer grasses. Ever since he met Sián and her sister Enydd, his childhood fantasies had been caught in the brambles of their long flowing hair. Nothing complicated, just playing and dreaming, dreaming and playing, and that thought of wanting trickles through him once again.

Through his awful Waking Dreams, he had witnessed the nightmare of Enydd's slaughter at the hands of Māthōg and his Blood Red Crows as if he had been standing and watching her awful mutilation. Hiding beneath the big old tree, he had heard Sián's cries in his head and the nightmares of his visions had shown him Sián's hiding place. Telling his Grandfather, men from the village had eventually rescued Sián from her nightmare.

But unbeknown to Hyw, Sián had felt his presence there. Somehow, she believed he had been there; watching over her and ever since that dreadful day, there had always been a connection between them as children.

Memories of Sián suddenly wake his mind to the day he rode off and he remembers; he remembers everything.

"Go call on Sián!" The words of his grandfather echo in his visions.

The doubt that filled his addled mind grips him again and as he watches himself riding away, it is his own voice that begins to infest his mind; pleading and begging at himself.

"Stay…Stay…I love thee Sián Bach!" And he begins to mumble the words and they splash down his cheeks with his tears. His waking dream surges forward. Although his memories are clouded he can hear Sián's tears crying in his head, dragging him back to the day he rode from his home and those he loves, to seek Blood for Blood.

Like an apparition Sián's face appears before him, with tears in her eyes. Begging him to stay, her words drag at his heart. In an instant his waking dreams grip him and he sees himself sitting astride Sarn, with the dirt of his work still caked on his skin with the dried rivers of tears down his cheeks. Unable to recognise himself for a moment, he peers beyond the thick fingers of woad daubed on his cheeks and across his bare torso. Gaining full recognition, the whites of Hyw's eyes seem to glow as he stares vacantly out at himself, but there is no discernible sign of life within him.

Hyw witnesses the pains and care of all those who loved him and their efforts to prevent his path and stop him from riding off to seek blood for blood.

"Hyw bach…it's me cariad." The voice is raised and its great love and concern warm through him, tempting him from his madness.

"Hyw bach…it is Olwyn, cariad." Although looking back through time, Olwyn's voice breaks into his continuing madness and he witnesses her care for him. Her eyes, barely able to take in the sight of his wretched figure blindly passing her gate.

After the murder of his parents, Olwyn had taken Bayr and Hyw into the bosom of her heart; raising Bayr as her own. Olwyn's voice is the only thing on the face of the whole earth strong enough to reach him and she calls through time as stepping out in front of Sarn. Coming to a halt, Sarn breathes a sigh of relief, begging the sentinels to release her from her torturous charge.

The dirt of his work, reforging the Scotti blade, is still caked on his skin, with his dried tears forging rivers down his face and through the thick fingers of woad painted on his cheeks and torso. Naked from the waist up, the whites of Hyw's eyes seem to glow, but there is no discernible sign of life within them.

Unable to reach him, Hyw watches as Olwyn and all those he loves fuss around him. She prevents Hefyn, her son, Hyw's greatest friend, from riding off with him, to seek blood for blood. Sián's tears drag at his heart, with hands pulling at him. Into the melee rides Megan, her bow in hand and Hyw watches as Pwyll drags her from their gelding. She screams and fights and they both fall to the ground. Continuing her struggle, a shudder of tears quakes through her and she screams out through her tears.

Her brutal torture at the hands of Māthōg and his Blood Red Crows still boils inside her.

"I need to go with him!" And into Hyw's nightmare, Megan's kidnap and desolation play before him, over and over again.

"Hyw bach." Olwyn's gentle voice fades with his nightmares and he wakes to face the people of the Sacred Birch Woods.

Looking again, the young woman slows a few paces from the man standing some way in front of him, but it is Megan's awful desolation that echoes through Hyw's broken mind.

"Thy bow, Gwion" The young woman sounds out of breath as she hands her man the bow with several arrows and she quickly retreats, running for the security of their croft. Notching an arrow into place, Gwion bends his bow. Fingers strain as they cup around the string and he begins to tremble under the pressure building on his fingers. His aim is dubious at best and exactly how much danger Hyw is in, even Gwion cannot be sure, but he tracks Sarn's every move and unconcerned, Sarn saunters forward.

Remaining still and quiet with his bow held loosely at his side, Hyw is still fighting to shake off the shadows of the dark realm that held him captive and thoughts of Sián, and those he loves, have warmed his senses.

Sarn steps closer, the steady fall of her hooves making no sound. Looking hard into Hyw, Gwion momentarily lowers his aim, not quite believing his eyes, but then, as if confirming it to himself; he raises the bow again.

"Annwn preserve us." Whispering, half under his breath, Gwion lowers his aim once more, and a cold chill runs through him. The dirt and stench of death is still thick on Hyw's face and hands. Wrapped up against the rain under the stained colours of a thick woollen blanket, which Hyw has draped over his head and shoulders, reaches down over Sarn's hindquarters. Dirt has washed down over Sarn and her wet, grey almost white coat, is filthy with the same stench of death. Hyw's eyes are empty and dark as he looks blankly back at the young man, but Gwion's fears turn to pity. Hyw finds the presence of mind to speak, but only just in time.

"Māthōg…I seek Māthōg and his wolves?" Hyw's voice is quiet, but it conveys all his fears and rage with pity turning to pain as Gwion is left to wonder about the tragedies that have befallen his life.

"Ye won't find Māthōg here!" Gwion stumbles over his tongue as he quickly averts his gaze, staring towards the ground, unable to keep his eyes on the awful sight before him.

"He dwells beyond the seas and rides secret paths only he knows; he hides from our new masters the Warriors of Gododdyn. They too hunt him, but he does no harm to us and we leave him be…leave now, ye must leave, go in peace!" Gwion hesitates at his thoughtless words, but his eyes are fixed and resolute.

Starring beyond the man, to the doorway of his croft, Hyw looks up to where the young woman stands. Peering over the stile of its gate is a child, a young girl with fine red hair hanging in wavy wafts as it flows down over her rosy cheeks, but it is her eyes that catch Hyw's gaze. They are shaped like two half-moons and he has seen them before. They are the eyes of one of the children in his waking dreams and Hyw knows he has stepped back onto the path he is destined to tread.

The child smiles across at him, a smile that warms his very soul. Somehow she is not afraid of his terrifying figure and Hyw begins to smile back, but as he smiles, his fears grow for the young girl knowing the omens his visions convey.

The woman pulls at the child, trying to keep the gate shut, but her efforts fail as the strength of the girl pushes past her. Gwion looks back to where they struggle at the gate and he shouts back at them.

"Get thee inside woman and take the child with thee!" The young man snaps. Hyw's mind is slow, but his concerns grow for the child and the hidden meanings of his haunted visions.

"Māthōg's heart is set against the beauty of our people; guard thy family well, my friend, guard them well!" The man nods almost in disbelief at Hyw's concern for him and his family.

The battle of wills is lost and the gate flies open. The child runs down the few rocky steps to where her father stands. She is quickly followed by her mother. The child runs with a strange lolloping gait, and bandy legs and her arms seem slightly gangly as if they are too long for her body.

The young man looks down at the child who is standing at his side holding up her hands towards him. Shaking his head from side to side in frustration he takes his daughter in his arms. Hyw smiles again, as the child looks up at him. The man sits her on his hip and Hyw's heart melts as he becomes fully lucid.

53

"Go now Da…no noise… 'Annon' no like noise Da!" The girl speaks quickly and quietly, looking cautiously up at Hyw. Unable to form her words fully, Hyw has to listen hard to understand her meaning. The man kisses his daughter's soft hair as it falls in damp waves over her glowing smile.

"Come Da…no noise now… Annon go now!" The strangely beautiful girl, tugs at her father's neck.

"Shush…Rhyannon," He says sharply and she pauses for a moment as another warm smile spreads out on her face looking up at Hyw. Tears start to well in his eyes as the child conjures thoughts of Bayr. Trotting his tongue against the roof of his mouth, Sarn brushes past where the man and his family stand.

"Wait up!" The young man calls after him, and Sarn comes to an eager halt.

"Ye cannot leave like this…We are in grave danger if we help thee, but I cannot let thee leave this way…I dare not give thee food or shelter, but what I know is maybe of more worth. The Warriors of Gododdyn seek after thee…They have heard whispers of thee and their Sires quake at thy name,

'The Phantom Annwn'!" Hyw turns towards the young man whose hair hangs over his face with rain dripping from its straggly ends. They each look deep into the other's eyes, but Hyw says nothing.

"Well, thou art a fearsome sight!" He smiles up at Hyw, but Hyw's senses are numb and he just stares blindly back. Feeling awkward, the man talks quickly.

"They have placed a price on thy head and wouldst hunt thee as the boar. They will pass this way by and by and many will bend their ears with news of thy presence!" Hyw thinks back on his memories, of meeting Geddyn and his men, on The Mother Mountain. He thinks of his grandfather's token and remembers the trust it bought. They had visited his home and shared in the hospitality of their food.

'They are warriors of honour,' he thinks to himself, 'How have I become their prey?'

Hyw looks at the man and nods in recognition of what he has said and then turns to go.

"I'm sorry it could not be more!"   In turning, Hyw's eyes meet those of the young woman. He senses a certain frustration in her, whether it is that of struggling with the child or a lifetime of unfulfilled dreams, he cannot tell, but the woman smiles and then quickly turns away. There is something there, something between them and Hyw struggles to hold on to his feelings. Looking again, there is a familiar light in her eyes and he finds himself looking at Sián once more, with her radiant smile warming through him.

When he breathes again he is by the river with Sarn stepping down into its flow. The villagers watch through the towering rain. Sarn carefully fords the swollen river, climbing out onto the far bank and disappearing into the tree hedge of the woods.

Slowly sinking back inside himself, Hyw is haunted once more by his madness, as tears track familiar paths down his cheeks and he cries in his grief for his lost love.

"Oh, Sián…Sián, why did I ever leave thee?"

The woods give way to thin strips of sparse pasture between the trees, but they are meagre breaks and are quickly swallowed up by the never-ending forest. Secret ways crisscross his path through the shadowy haunts and leafy labyrinths of the 'Fair Ones'. Ywel had always scoffed at talk of the fair folk, but Hyw sees them on every side as the night steals through the woods with him.

Plodding slowly on, Sarn picks her way through the darkness between the trees. Coming to a small clearing she stops, but Hyw's waking dreams devour him and he is lost to his gentle companion's uncertainty. How long he struggles in their grasp he cannot tell, he only knows he is tired of running from their awful images. A faint light sparks in his mind but searching, he can no longer see the elusive glow.

The ebb and sway of some unseen water washes onto the shores of his mind as he slumbers beneath thin veils of early morning mists. Turning in his sleep, he finds himself looking out over a large lake. A shimmer of light ripples across the surface of the water as the morning sun sparkles in the breeze. In his dreams, there is someone caught in the reflections of the shimmering light.

"Sián!" Hyw calls out in his sleep.

"Sián…Sián…" He mumbles again and again, and Sarn whinnies uncertain if her master will ever wake.

Chapter Six

Hyw's visions quicken as his eyes open to a bright new day. Lying amid the knotted and tangled roots of a great Beech Tree, he struggles to wake his senses. Looking out from his knobbly bed, his eyes gaze over a small lake where the sun has indeed caught the ripple of its shimmering surface and he shivers in the chill and ripple of a soft breeze that drifts off the lake. There is no blanket or fur wrapped around him and he is lying where he fell in the stupor and madness of his dark night.

A Dipper, twitters then flies from a nearby rock, but the host of the morning birds have long since finished their dawn's waking chant. Sarn is quietly grazing on some sweet grass a short distance from where he has fallen, but she pauses, looking across at her master who is finally rousing.

The world seems to tumble by. Taking in a deep breath, Hyw stirs his life and feels the bruising ache to his arm and hip that broke his fall. The cares that have so long troubled his mind fade as he tries to wake his memories, but he cannot remember ordering his sleep.

Raising himself onto his elbows, Hyw surveys the scene before him. The huge beech stands at the edge of the Sacred Birch Woods and less than a stone's throw in front of him is the shore of a crystal-clear lake. Its waters are still and calm with the breeze occasionally blurring its mirrored halls. Edged with thick beds of reeds, its far shore is less than half an arrow's flight. The hills surrounding the lake are crowded with dense firs which tumble down to the margins of the lake. A feeling of peace comes over him as he forgets his torment for a while.

Sitting up, he calls to Sarn, sucking between his teeth. Holding out his hand, Sarn is tempted and walks towards her master, but seeing no food she drops her head and continues to graze. Dragging himself from the harshness of his bed, Hyw moves over to where Sarn munches on grass and he scratches around her neck and ears. Raising her head, she bathes in the attention he pours on her.

"Well Sarn bach, whence should we tread?" Hyw asks, almost in a whisper. Sarn nods and whinnies as looking dolefully up at him. Somehow he had managed to take his belt kit off and a few of his feathered warriors have escaped the quiver. His bow is lying on the ground a few paces from where he slept. Picking up the arrows, he leans his bow against the tree and stands the quiver next to it.

There is something new and fresh about the morning and he stretches himself as he takes in another deep breath, once again feeling the ache of his fall. The flickering shadows of his visions seem to have dimmed and even distant memories and the dark visions, of his restless night, have vanished from his mind.

Walking towards the lake's cool waters; its pure clean stream will soon cleanse all hurt from him. The sun is high above the far hills and it warms into his tired limbs. The day is cloudy bright and quite warm for the time of year, but it is not warm enough to bathe and Hyw only strips to the waist. Kneeling by the lake he bends slowly forward towards its mirror, but he jumps back in terror. Mustering all his courage he creeps forward and looks hesitantly toward his reflection. The horror of his image is more than he can bear and he shudders at his neglect. Sunken black eyes peer out from behind the daubed mess of blood, dirt and faded woad that seemed to be daubed all over his body. Gaunt and grey, the stench of death is almost suffocating as he stares down at the horrific sight of 'The Phantom of Annwn'.

Plunging his face into the lake, he scrubs until he is forced to come up for air. His body is splattered with the same stench and dirt and he splashes and scrubs at every mark and blemish. Cut and bruised, his torso and arms are covered with a myriad of scratches and tares from the briars and thorns that have lined his path. It is as though he is seeing and feeling for the very first time and the realisation of his squalid life cuts into him. More worrying are the wounds he has received without any knowledge or memory.

Calming himself, he again peers down at the surface of the lake, looking for his reflection, but as the surface of the lake clears, a shrill laugh and the squeals of playful excitement dance across the pool towards him. Looking slowly up, his eyes follow the ripples his bathing has made and his stare looks out towards the far bank.

Behind the reeds running along the lake's far shore, Hyw can see the thick trunks of stunted willows, their heads shorn close. The bundles of their thin whips are stacked in their shadows. The reeds that line the far bank have not yet been harvested and are reflected in the surface of the water. A stack of smoke rises from a chimney hidden behind part of the reed beds.

Two girls are playing in an opening at the water's edge, splashing each other as they bathe. Having thrown their dresses over the reeds, to one side, and dressed only in thin petticoats, they are also washing away the cobwebs of the night. One of the girls splashes again and then the other, as the cold chase of water squeals through them. Their white petticoats gape at the neck and Hyw glimpses their bare breasts that tease and groan inside him.

Continuing their games, the girls are oblivious to Hyw as he watches every splash they make, but something seems to spark inside one of the young women; as if someone whispers in her ear. Stopping her games, she listens. Continuing to splash at the edge of the water, her sister seems to catch the moment. One of the girls looks slowly up, followed by the other and they both gawp, in silence, at Hyw.

Feeling caught out in some way, the thought of running crosses Hyw's mind; like a child. Trapped in the flash of distant memories he cannot take his eyes off the girls. There is a moment between them, but then, one of them shrieks as she turns and runs out of his sight.

Slowly kneeling back down, the remaining girl looks quizzically at him, as she gently cups her hand under the neck of her petticoat barring any further intrusion. Time passes, as an uncertain smile seeps out onto her face.

Her beauty is plain and unadorned, but she has an alluring presence that grips Hyw's imagination. Pensive deep green eyes cover her thoughts and Hyw cannot turn his gaze from her. Her long dark hair has fallen onto the surface of the lake, hiding her soft warm body from his hungry gaze. Her sister's beauty was perhaps a little more obvious, but Hyw's eyes feast on something more than beauty. There is a certain way about her; something in her eyes, in the way she moves, in the way she holds her hand and arm across her chest, in her smile; something he cannot place, but the feeling warms and excites him.

Both the girl's similarities are striking and there can't be many years between them, if any, and instantly, Hyw surmises they are twins. He had heard of children being born together but never had he seen any with his own eyes.

Hyw smiles back as the girl slowly rises to her feet. Picking one of the dresses off the reeds, she holds it across the front of her body. Unable to look away, Hyw continues to stare, his eyes wide like an owl. Stepping cautiously inside the neck of her dress, the girl's full beauty momentarily opens to him. The damp petticoat is scant covering and every line and curve of her body momentarily shows through. He smiles and an uncertain smile eases out onto the girl's face.

The first girl returns, dragging her father behind her as her mother steps from the doorway of the croft and they all look out towards where Hyw is still crouched at the far shore of the lake. A brother or maybe even a husband to one of the girls is standing in the doorway of a tent and the girl's father beckons for his son to stay.

There is a newly finished croft and another under construction. Hyw can see a covered wagon and a thin plume of smoke from a second fire situated somewhere beyond the first. Beyond their camp, animals graze on a small spread of pasture. They appear to be new to the land and like Hyw they are strangers. There are others, but he cannot pick out all their detail.

"Mynddy!" The older man calls out and the first girl stands at his side repeating her father's stern warning to her sister.

"Mynddy!"

Returning his attention to the water's edge, the girl does not move. Combing her fingers through her hair, she drags it back over her head as she holds his gaze. All her beauty is caught in the mirror of the lake's shimmering surface as the sun catches and dances on the water and she is momentarily lost in the brilliance of its sparkling ripples. Instantly her father is at her side and he looks long and hard at Hyw, who still isn't fully clean.

"Back to the croft girls…come now!" He calls to his daughters, but they wait, each looking and smiling. Turning to go the girl who had dared to stay turns again and smiles as her sister collects her dress from the reed bed.

Hyw waits for Sián's image to interrupt the vision, but his thoughts and memories are lost in the dancing miasma of his racing thoughts. Both girls step behind their father but they do not leave.

Hyw stoops and dips his hands in the lake to wash again, watched carefully by the man. Cupping his hands, he splashes his face with water then dips his head into its cold, scrubbing relentlessly.

Standing, he looks back at the man. A broad and powerfully built middle-aged man with a barrel chest looks quizzically back, and his stature stirs memories of his father, Bryn. The man's hair is cropped at the back of his neck and his beard has been shorn from his face. What little remains of his hair is thick and wavy with barely a touch of grey painted within it. Nodding his approval, he turns to go as Hyw nods back.

Walking past his daughters the man passes out of Hyw's sight as Hyw's attention returns to the girls, but their father returns and shepherds them back towards their mother and mutters something as he does so. When all is safely gathered in, the man turns again, checking Hyw is still there and then he disappears into the croft.

The girls both turn and look at Hyw, poking fun; each at the other, giggling as they do so, but the girl they call Mynddy, takes time to smile at him. Wild feelings run through him and he cannot move, his heart pounding inside his breast as his longings for Sián grow.

Bitter regret floods through him as haunted memories of his last words to Sián and his turning from her, grate inside him. Pondering on all his misjudgement, he turns to go with a heavy heart. Again thinking of Sián; he sees the child she once was, hiding behind her mother's dress. The image moves on and Hyw can see her, standing barefoot in the rear yard of their croft as she beats a sheepskin rug into submission. Watching his memories fade, he yearns for her soft touch and the familiar warmth of love, but not just any love. Hyw yearns for the love of someone who knows and understands, someone who can dry away his tears, someone who, no matter how dark the night, would always understand and be at his side.

"Maybe I should go home and beg her to forgive me..." The thought reasons inside him, but is spoken out loud.

"Or maybe I should try and find Taid's brother...he will understand those things I seek!" Hyw whispers all his thoughts to Sarn and she snorts and whinnies, nodding her head as if she understands every word spoken, but unseen in the shadows, a girl stares out to where Hyw is trying to reorder his life.

It had been a complete shock to him when his grandfather had told him that he had a brother; a Holy Man, who lived on a sacred island, but the greatest shock was the revelation that his grandfather's brother had Waking Dreams, much the same as Hyw and he thinks back, trying to remember all his grandfather's words.

It is time to take stock and Hyw collects all around him. Unloading Sarn, he realises his father's wolf skin coat is missing. Collecting his bow and putting on his belt kit, Hyw retraces Sarn's tracks and finds the coat a short distance from where he had fallen in the darkness.

Returning, Sarn is waiting. In just a few short weeks she has grown to trust her new master. Hyw recognises her loyalty and rewards her with a few handfuls of crushed oats.

Sitting awhile, with no discernable thoughts to brighten his mind he waits as if someone will come to reorder his life for him. The trickle of a stream is somewhere just beyond the great beech tree, where he had slept. Collecting his bow, he walks beyond the trees to find its falling waters.

The brook flows between two large rocks, tumbling into the waters of the lake. Stooping then kneeling, he drinks. Draining his hand several times, he hears approaching footsteps from behind him. Quickly turning, his bow held firmly in his hand, Hyw's eyes rest on Sarn, who is eager to drink herself.

"Come my friend, take thy fill!" Hyw trots his tongue against the roof of his mouth and Sarn walks forward to the stream. They both drink, side by side until their thirst is quenched.

"Enough is enough!" Hyw says and Sarn whinnies and nods her head at his words. Turning his thoughts to food, he looks at the stream's tumbling water, imagining the trout its rocks must hide. Stepping out onto the first rock he crouches and rubs his hand along its hidden ledges. With no sign of trout, he steps onto another rock, then another. On the fourth attempt, he touches the head of a large trout, which is hidden from his view. A sudden rush jumps through his hungry hand and he is left watching the fleeting shadow of the fish, scurrying off downstream as it disappears into the lake.

"Well my friend, it looks as though I must be content with dry meat again!" Sarn nods politely.

"Funny friend ye turned out to be; nodding at my misfortune. No more oats for thee, Sarn bach!" He smiles as he talks.

The crack of a twig wakes his cautious senses and he grips the handle of his bow with an arrow instantly notched into place.

"Art thou there?" A man's voice breaks through the trees and the father of the girl's steps out where Hyw can see him. In his hand is a plate with steam rising from hot food piled up at its centre. The man offers the plate forward, but Hyw remains cautious.

"It's good…my wife is a good cook and ye look hungry my friend!" The man has an easy way about him. His voice is low and thick, but softly spoken and Hyw is instantly put at ease. Reaching up for the plate, he smiles and nods.

"I thank thee!" Hyw says, picking up the fork and stabbing it into a large piece of meat in the stew.

"Ye must be cold. Come and warm thyself at our fire. We have more to spare and thou art welcome!" The man speaks the language of Hyw's forefathers, but his speech is not local, and it is not the speech of the painted men of the north; nor does he wear a skirt as they wore. Hyw takes time to think about the man's invitation.

"Thou art a stranger to these parts?" The man states as he stares deep into Hyw's eyes as if he is looking and searching through his hidden thoughts.

"I perceive thou art a stranger thyself!" A smile hides Hyw's thoughts. The man reminds him so much of his own father, but although he fills Hyw with confidence, for some reason, he declines his invitation.

"I must be away."

"What troubles thee? Come, my friend. Come join us; at least for a while." The man pauses.

"Ye could at least rest for a while."

"I thank thee," Hyw says quietly.

"I thank thee for thy kind offer, but my path lies to the west and my presence here would only bring thee and thy family danger." The man is slow to speak, sensing much pain in Hyw.

"I know not what ghosts follow thee, but when they are purged, thou art welcome back this way and we will give thee rest!" Hyw is drawn in by the man's words, but something stops him from attending their camp. There is an urgency to his thoughts, his journey and his want for revenge and all his mixed emotions seem to plague his senses.

"My path leads only to…!" Hyw's words fall silent as he thinks about all his grandfather had told him. The man drops his head, looking down and thinking.

"Whom doth thy vengeance seek?" Raising their heads, they both look deep, each in the other's eyes.

"Māthōg!" Hyw says calmly.

"Māthōg and his Crows. Have ye seen them?" The man's head drops again.

"I have heard murmur of him, but as for seeing the Scotti, I hope never to lay my eyes on them" The man speaks quietly, only imagining the suffering Hyw has seen in his short life and Hyw senses his quiet understanding.

"Guard thy family well. Māthōg's sword is set against our people and he bathes in the blood of many we hold dear!" Hyw's words fall silent and the man knows not to push his feelings, so he extends his hand forward and taking Hyw's hand in his, he shakes it.

When Hyw has emptied the plate the man collects it and turns to go, but standing in the trees behind him is his daughter. Both Hyw and her father see her at the same time.

"Mynddy, I told thee to stay. Get thee gone girl." The man walks off past his daughter who stares for long moments at Hyw. There is a quiet beauty about her, something that shines in the bright fire that burns in the catch-light of her eyes. Her skin is pale and glows like the silver winter moon; her dark hair falls in tresses past her bright eyes; eyes which reflect the colour of summers long since past and they smile out at Hyw. Caught in the web of his confused feelings, all he can do is smile as she turns to go.

Gathering his things together he grips Sarn's reins and climbs up onto her back, and turning her towards the dark woods and the west, he has a new determination.

"I must follow Māthōg's trail…to foreign shores if necessary…I must rid myself of this pain."

As Sarn makes her way through the trees following the shore of the lake, Hyw looks across for the last time at the small camp. He sees Mynddy loitering, looking back at him. Their eyes meet briefly, which causes a flutter of feelings in him as he disappears through the trees, with any thought of the girl drifting slowly from his mind.

Chapter Seven

A large cloud covers the sun and the chilled fingers of the coming winter bite into Hyw. Pulling his father's wolf skin cloak around him, he keeps his bow in hand. The day is long as Sarn picks her way back through the woods towards the river they forded the previous evening. Avoiding the small riverside community, they skirt along and up a second stream; stepping from the dank darkness of one shadow into the next.

Pausing for a moment, Hyw looks up, his eyes searching the huddle of crofts for the curious bright-faced little girl from his Waking Dreams and he wonders if she will play any further part in his life. She had sparked a light in the shadows of his madness, melting the gloom that had gathered around him. Drifting in his thoughts, he is swallowed up by the moment and the image of the girl intrudes into his thoughts; she smiles up at him warming his mind once more, but the image quickly fades as Sarn continues to pick her way through the dense forest.

The trees thin out as the rugged mountains of the Eagles Eerie rise before them. Some sheep and cattle are grazing on sparse pasture with a shepherd sitting on a small outcrop of rocks on the far side of the cruel, almost indistinguishable fields of the mountains. Climbing out of the valley, he avoids the shepherd's attention as the woods and sparse fields give way to rough, rocky terrain. A few crofts litter the unforgiving landscape with their smoke rising high on the back of the cold breeze off the mountains.

Pausing in the shadows beneath a diminishing treeline, he sees two warriors sitting astride warhorses in front of a small windswept croft. They appear to be guarding the head of the valley, blocking the way ahead. Each is facing the other; talking, occasionally pointing and constantly looking around them. Their conversation doesn't appear urgent, but their eyes are keen and Hyw instantly recognises their dress and knows he must avoid the Son's of Gododdyn.

Standing at the gate of the croft is an old man and one of the warriors calls to him, riding over to where he is standing. A short conversation takes place before the warrior returns to his comrade.

Hyw scans the landscape, carefully accessing his next move. A large hillock rises above the croft, crowned with a circle of tall Beech trees, with rocks at their centre and strewn down the side of the hill. The hillock would make an easily defendable shelter for the night, but the night is a long way off and the journey west is pressing him to move forward.

To the north, the forest follows the high ground, which backs onto yet more hills and mountains, but following the line of the trees, they circle back to the west. Turning Sarn north, Hyw makes his way deeper into the woods as they climb the steep sides of the valley. Progress is slow as Hyw constantly scans for danger.

The trees thin out again and looking back to where the warriors had sat, he can see no sign of them; there is only the old man standing at his gate, looking out. Too far away to be certain, the old man seems to be scanning the tree line where Hyw rides.

The woods peter out forming a thin line of trees, ferns and scrub, which offers little cover and Hyw is in danger of being sky-lined on the high ground. Silhouetted against the light, he would not be difficult to spot, with Sarn struggling through the heavy undergrowth.

Sarn is jittery and Hyw has learnt to pay heed to her keen senses, but scanning again he can see nothing. A thick wood lies ahead of them; an arrow's flight away, maybe a little further. Sarn would have to sprint across open ground to make the safety of its cover. Choices are limited; back to the woods or a short ride, to wider woods leading west. The distant tree line is strewn with evergreens which make an inviting cover. A quick sprint and they would be walking at their ease.

"Art thou ready my old friend?" Hyw whispers in Sarn's ear and then he nudges her out into the open. Goaded into life, Sarn covers the ground quickly and her swift pace would soon find the haven of darker shadows, but as they break the first rise a shout empties into the two fugitives.

"Thee Phantom!" Unseen, above where he has broken cover, the main body of Warriors lies in wait, with a smaller band of horsemen making their way up from the valley below. Glancing momentarily behind him, Hyw recognises his pursuers;

'The Sons of Gododdyn'; the 'Painted Men of the North'.

Their cries fill the air and the hunt is on with Hyw leaning into the wind as he pats Sarn on the neck, whispering into the breeze.

"Not far my brave friend and we shall hide from their poisoned blades!" Sarn's eyes are wide and her mouth contorted with the bit, but she pricks up her ears and her master's words seem to raise her spirits.

"Garl up!" Hyw calls as Sarn's stride eats the ground beneath her hooves.

An arrow shoots past them and dives into a tuft of grass as another arrow whistles past Hyw's head. Glancing back, the band of warriors is in hot pursuit, but they are some way behind him. Sarn approaches the tree line where a small Juniper is spread at the side of the path and from beneath its moss-green branches, a large rabbit flinches and then scurries across the startled ground; zigzagging furiously until it remembers where it has misplaced its burrow.

Again patting Sarn on her neck, he whispers.

"Well done my friend!" His words are calm as they reach the edge of the wood. The pursuit is still some way off, but as they break through the trees, Hyw sees the barren heart of the woods and the sparse bare trees at its centre offer them little, if any, cover. There is nowhere to hide as the ground drops away from them.

Quickly turning Sarn aside, they swiftly edge through the coverings of yew bushes and firs. Secreting themselves at their heart, they wait for the worst. Sarn quietly backs further into the thicket of the tree line, as horses seem to crash through the hedge on either side of them.

Sitting in silence, the chase spills through every opening and charges downhill into the bare winter woods in front of them. Almost twenty warriors swoop past their position, yelling, hollering and crying, as they search for any sign of The Phantom, but the Phantom has vanished. Their cries echo as they disappear into the distance, but Hyw and Sarn remain perfectly still. Sarn's ears prick up and Hyw gently pats her neck knowing the message she conveys, and he prepares his bow for the fray.

A twig cracks and Hyw is aware of more horses behind where he sits. They are close, too close for comfort. Surely his hiding place will be discovered if it hasn't been already, but he dare not move; knowing, if he remains still, there is a chance he won't be seen. Opening his mouth slightly, he tries to control his breathing, as every beat of his heart pounds inside his breast. Sarn is remarkably composed after her sudden burst across the ground, but she too can feel the anxieties of her young master as steam rises from her head and neck.

Branches sway as further twigs crack underfoot and the leader of the men appears just to one side of Hyw. The warrior's horse walks forward; away from Hyw's position, but Hyw instantly recognises him,

'Geddyn'.

Memories of his mountaintop walk with his blind grandfather, guiding them over the Dragon's Back of mountains as a child, come flooding back through the years. Geddyn's thicket of bright red hair is streaked with some grey, but it is, most definitely, the same warrior. Geddyn's horse comes to a halt as he is joined by two others. Hyw cannot be sure of the older one, but the larger of the two is most certainly the one they called Maddrōg. Suddenly a fourth warrior joins them, a young lad; perhaps a little younger than Hyw, but dressed in the same wrapped skirts as the others.

If they turn he would surely be seen.

"This canna be nae Phantom…unless his horse can fly… an' no Phantom I ken, wid run and hide from such petulant men!" Geddyn exclaims as Maddrōg joins him.

"An' have ye seen a Phantom afore then?" Maddrōg says.

Geddyn laughs out loud.

"Aye, but only in the stupor of Ale!" They all laugh.

"Should wae follow after them, Sire?"

"Nay they will tire from chasing shadows soon enough!"

Suddenly a shriek pierces the dank air and a squealing wild hog charges toward them; its hide being disturbed by the charge of warriors.

"Seems we have nae found a Phantom, but a great boar!" Maddrōg says with a worried tone to his voice, and Geddyn laughs again.

"Aye, maybe the Phantom has changed himself into a wee beastie!" The worried look on Maddrōg's face deepens. The crashing stampede of the hog is tearing through the woods towards them and if they stay still the panicking hog will not see them until the last moment. The older Warrior stands up in his stirrups and turns slightly to check the hog's advance. It is Dynōg and he looks out, but cannot see the pig.

"Have we nae got a bow to fell the wee beastie!" Maddrōg moves forward with a lance gripped firmly in his hand.

"Dinna worry, I'll take the wee beastie doon!"

The great savage boar is charging uphill and does not deviate, squealing as it charges through a small thicket of fern in the sparse winter woods. The shouts and cries of some of the other warriors can be heard in the distance, but they are lost in the shadows of the trees.

'The enemy of my enemy is my friend!' Hyw remembers Ywel's words and wonders about their wisdom. They had indeed become good friends, or so it seemed to Hyw as a child, but many years have passed since they visited his home. Straining to see, Hyw grips his legs around Sarn.

Maddrōg spurs his horse forward and launches his lance towards the charging boar, but the warrior heaves and sighs as his lance falls short. All eyes are fixed on the wild pig as it rushes over the brow of the hill into Hyw's eager gaze. Bending his bow and taking aim in one continuous movement, his first shaft is loosed towards the charging beast. There is a crash as the arrow unerringly finds its mark and the hog's legs crumble.

The great boar squeals and tumbles to the ground. Before anyone realises their danger, another deadly shaft is notched into place. Taking great, but swift care, Hyw releases his hungry hawk and its talons find their mark, just behind the joint in the boar's front leg, instantly silencing its squeals. In a blur of movement, another blade is notched into place and he bends his bow again, aiming its shaft towards his old friend as their eyes meet.

"The enemy of my enemy is my friend!" Hyw's words are spoken with authority and the sound of his voice surprises even him.

"Why dust thou hunt thy friends like the beast of the forest?" Hyw continues.

From deep in the woods, an arrow whistles through the dim light and flashes in front of Hyw. Geddyn raises quickly up into his stirrups and stretching out both his arms he calls for his men to stem their enthusiasm, but there is still a lonely blade hanging in the air. Hyw sees its honed edges as it arches towards him. Instantly relaxing his grip on his bow, he lies back onto Sarn's rump. The arrow narrowly passes over his taught stomach muscles and buries itself into the trunk of a fir tree behind him.

"Did ah no say, lower thy weapons!" Geddyn's voice booms out. Some of the warriors have realised their mistake and arc charging back up the hill to protect their master, but reluctantly they cease their charge. Sitting back down, Geddyn looks back at Hyw who has his bow bent once more towards his heart.

Chapter Eight

Hyw's fingers strain as his bow arm straightens and his fingers pull back against all the might of his hunting bow; placing his forefinger into the corner of his mouth, he takes great care aim.

"Who art thou, who calls tha-selv ma frien?" Geddyn strains his eyes and gradually he sees some strange familiarity through the years that pass between them.

"Once ye dined at my home and thy horses were shod at my father's hand. I was, but a boy…" Hyw pauses.

"The breath of the Dragon yet breathes in the Cymri!" Hyw's words seem to puzzle Geddyn, but then the fog lifts and a smile appears on his face. Hyw lowers his aim and Dynōg grabs at the handle of his sword.

"Dinna be rash. Can ye no see oor error. An his blade wid cut ye doon afore ye drew it!" Dynōg relaxes his grip and stands down at his master's bidding.

"Forgive ma frien; I could nae see the wee laddie I once knew in the warrior who sits afore me. The breath o' the dragon doth yet breathe in the Cymri. That was a keen blade, which fell yon beastie. Come we shall feast t'nicht on tha gift thou hast brought tee us. Ye ken, it is no by chance our paths cross again my young frien." Geddyn turns to his men and shouts his orders.

"String tha wee beastie up, an cut its thro't afore its meat is ruined; we dine t'nicht wit auld friens!" Turning towards Hyw.

"If ma memory serves me well, yer name is Hyw!"

Hyw nods.

"Tell ma of yer family Hyw. What has become of ye?" The warrior looks Hyw up and down with the faint sign of an awkward smile on his face, but Hyw's broken heart will not let him speak.

"Aye, an' what has become of thy grandfaither? He was a fine auld fellow. Aye, an I remember he seemed t'hav a strange power hidden behind his blind eyes!"

Hyw's head drops in his grief and the warrior's questions fall silent as unspoken words pass between them. Geddyn can see Hyw's pain and does not pursue his questions further, knowing the unseen pains of battle.

The men string up the boar between two horses and one of them cuts at the hog's throat. Its blood pours out onto the ground as all the warriors of Gododdyn gather around. They stare at Hyw, who, compared to them, is little more than a boy. They are rough brutes of men. Many of them bear the scars of battle, but they are a strange sight, to Hyw, so many warriors gathered for one cause.

"Come my young frein, let us ride tee-gether and talk of better times. We must thank ye for our feast; aye and for my life!"

Hyw is torn apart by an avalanche of feelings that tear through him and he is unable to speak. Geddyn again senses his unease but says nothing as he rides quietly at Hyw's side. Eventually, Geddyn speaks again.

"I do nae ken what troubles ye, but it wid honour our company if ye rested in our care t'nicht. Aye…we ha done ye a disservice. What say ye?" Geddyn leans over to Hyw, extending his open hand towards him.

"I am Geddyn, trusted sire to the king's guard and true warrior of Gododdyn and if ma memory serves me well, I seem to remember, thou art the trusted grandson of a wise auld man whose name was…Ywel…an if he were here, he wid be prud of the warrior who rides at my side!" Hyw nods his head in appreciation, still trying to rein in his feelings.

"I ken ye art troubled, but we shall nae spik o' these things until tha nicht comes and auld friends can sit doon among the ghosts of their past!"

Managing to control his feelings, the slow procession of warriors wends its way out of the woods into the bright light of a lazy afternoon. There is much irony in the way he feels, but riding at the rear of the Warriors of Gododdyn next to Geddyn he relaxes and his thoughts drift away to his youth and his family, but there is always pain in his memories. Feeling cradled somehow he rides in silence. A cosseted feeling begins to warm through him almost as though his mother is sitting astride Sarn with him, wrapping him up in the comfort of her arms.

They call back at the croft where the old man is waiting to greet them. The warriors have stored many of their provisions there. The hillock is steep and its sides are unforgiving. Sarn struggles, but only gives out long after all the other warriors are forced to dismount from their steeds.

Hyw looks out from the safety of the trees that crown the hill like tall ramparts. There is a commanding view across to where three tracks meet;

three ways, each leading into different valleys. The Roman's Way, which he and Sarn had followed from the east, rises out of the thickly wooded valley of The Sacred Birch Woods. A short distance beyond the hillock, its track turns to the north and disappears over the brow of a hill into a higher valley, but there is a third way; a track leading to the west and its path meanders along the shores of a winding stream, which leads between the Druid's Mountains. Staring out and along its path, Hyw imagines where it would lead him.

Every warrior busies himself with preparations. Two of them have a small fire sparked at the centre of the crown of trees and another is gathering wood. Geddyn lays out his bed and encourages Hyw to lay his roll next to his. Hyw works in silence. After stripping Sarn of her load, the youngest warrior, who had accompanied Geddyn, is eager to take Sarn away. With a mop of red hair and a few freckles strewn over the bridge of his nose, his looks are similar to those of Geddyn; he has the same stance and gait and his face seems to wrinkle with the same half-smile before he speaks. The lad tethers Sarn with the other horses and begins to feed and groom her with Hyw watching intently.

"He will take guid care o' her!" Geddyn says quietly and Hyw begins to relax.

No matter where Hyw moves through the camp, he is watched constantly. Geddyn's men are still suspicious of him and treat him with caution. The young lad smiles up at Hyw, with that same half-smile. Hyw smiles back as the boy turns his attention to Geddyn's horse. Sitting on his bed, Hyw studies his new friends as they busy themselves with the hog.

Time slips by as the afternoon drifts into the evening. Two further warriors arrive at their camp. Geddyn takes them to one side where a short conversation takes place and then they reluctantly turn to go constantly looking back at the hog slowly roasting. Two of the older warriors take turns to slowly turn the boar over the dying flames of the fire. Occasionally one of them takes his knife and stabs at the hog's sizzling flesh. Large droplets of fat spark and sizzle as they fall into the crack and spit of the glowing embers. Hyw is almost transfixed by the turning, spitting, sparking and hissing of the meat dripping into the furnace of the fire.

His mind drifts off to the rock of his family's throne. He remembers the last night he spent with Bayr and Ywel as they huddled together, talking until the dawn's slow light. In the drift of his dreams, Hyw doesn't notice Geddyn approaching.

"An where d' ye wander in thy dreams, Laddie?" His mother's words burn inside him.

"Over the hills and far away!" Her ghostly words whisper in his ear.

"D' ye wander tae thy home amid yon hills?" Hyw wakes from his dreams and looks up at Geddyn, half smiling at him. To Hyw, Geddyn's eyes seem, somehow, tired, but his smile is the smile of someone he trusts. Hyw nods. Geddyn slowly squats, sitting on his bedroll. A moment of silence passes between them.

"It will be cold t'nicht, but a fine feast an' fire will warm our hearts!" Geddyn doesn't push at Hyw's drifting thoughts.

Finally, the feast is ready. Geddyn leads him forward through his men. They are all standing, waiting to commence the feast, but before they are allowed to cut at the sizzling flesh of the hog, Geddyn speaks to them. Putting his arm around Hyw and placing his other hand on his shoulder, he calls out.

"This is Hyw...an auld frein t'oor people...ye ken...an t'nicht we extend him the respect he is due!" Geddyn indicates towards the roasting hog, for Hyw to cut his meat.

The hog's strong, but tender flesh warms through him as he sits on his bed. Geddyn sits quietly next to him with the young lad sitting on a roll of blankets on the other side. Geddyn watches as Hyw stabs at the meat on his board. He seems to be studying the knife in Hyw's hand as he raises it to his mouth.

"Tha faither's work?" Geddyn asks as he points to the finely honed blade.

Hyw nods.

"May I?" Geddyn holds out his hand. Hyw hands him the knife and he examines its fine workmanship, rolling it between his fingers, and then scraping his thumb over its blade. After careful examination, Geddyn hands it back. Looking down at Hyw's belt, he sees the smaller of the two blades and again he asks

"Thy faither's work?" Geddyn is desperate to hear Hyw's voice, but still, he does not speak and only nods his reply. Geddyn turns his attention toward the sword hanging from the side of Hyw's saddle, which has been placed as his pillow.

"Thy faither's work laddie?" Geddyn asks again, but this time, Hyw shakes his head. Geddyn breathes a sigh of relief as he finally finds the answer he has been looking for, but he asks the question nonetheless.

"Thy work?" Hyw nods.

"May I?"

Hyw points to the sword whose handle is facing Geddyn and he stands as his friend draws the blade from its sheath. Admiring the finely honed and precious metal, Geddyn sees the magnificent change Hyw has wrought on the Scotti Slag's evil blade, and he smiles.

"Well, ma frein, thou art a master of thy father's science and craft!" Geddyn exclaims while handling the blade.

The young lad stands, watching, seeing the sword in his father's certain grip. Geddyn points to the blade and the lad's young eyes are wide with wonder as they trace the swords continuing path as it slices through the air.

"Aye Laddie 'tis a wondrous weapon indeed!" Geddyn stops his swordplay for a moment and beckons the young lad forward. Placing his arm around the young man he turns to Hyw.

"Hyw, this is ma son, Cilydd. I have bin trying to educate him in the finer arts of the blade, but he has nae a sword of his own!" Geddyn has one arm around his son and the other brandishes the blade.

"What say ye to making such a blade for ma Laddie? Aye, an I'd reward ye weel for yer troubles!" Geddyn is teasing at Hyw's mind, but not with any cruel intentions. Hyw's head drops a little and so does Geddyn's heart, but he is surprised at Hyw's response.

"He may take the blade; I have no further use for it!" Hyw says almost to himself.

"What laddie? I could nae… I had no wish to take it from ye. Why wid ye give such a princely prize?"

Some of Geddyn's men gather around them on hearing the exchange of words.

A long silence passes as Hyw gathers his thoughts and the young lad's eyes grow large in anticipation. Hyw remembers the awful visions that gripped him when he first took hold of the blade and its continuing nightmares as he reforged its polluted metal. Remembering his pitiful efforts to wield the sword and the pain it brought to his life as killing the wounded Grot, he struggles to find the words he needs.

"I have no skill with the blade and it has brought me only misfortune. If thy son requires a blade, it is his, and I wish him greater fortunes than I!"

"Why…why wid ye do such a thing… why wid ye give up such a noble prize?" Geddyn bends himself low towards where Hyw is still sitting on his bedroll.

"My grandfather once placed his trust in thee. In his blindness, he could see what was barred to me. The sword will right a wrong wrought in me…Do with it as ye please!"

Geddyn cannot speak as his men gather around and gaze down at Hyw.

One of the older warriors steps forward through the crowd, pushing at some of the others. There is a strange light in his eyes; a light of some familiar recognition. His want to be where he can hear Geddyn's words shows keenly on his face, but his eyes are upon Hyw. Long braids of hair are tied at the back of his head and he is slightly built, in comparison to most of his companions. Stepping out in front of the other warriors he catches Hyw's attention and Hyw stares back into the most piercing slate-grey eyes he has ever seen, but he turns back to Geddyn as he begins to speak.

"We were once warriors o' this land, afore mae teem. Oor forefaithers left when the Romans came, but we have returned ta tha land we once forsook. Ye have full right ta mistrust us laddie, but because of tha cares of yer heart, I accept this thing ye give and must give ye a gift in return!" Geddyn pauses again, thinking.

"What can I give ye?" Hyw mulls the question over in his mind.

"Take whatever ye need…if it is mine ta give it is thine for tha keeping!" Geddyn reaches out. Hyw slowly raises his hand to Geddyn's and Geddyn takes hold of it pulling Hyw to his feet.

"Ye shall hae free passage o' this land and none shall molest ye. I shall make it known that tha Phantom of Annwn is ma frein and ye shall live under this pledge as long as ma bairn an I live. This blade will ne'er be set against thee…Will ye no ride with us? I should make thee a noble and ye wid hae fine clothes and riches in my faither's house!" Geddyn takes hold of Hyw's head and bending it forward, kisses his hair, but Hyw backs away slightly.

"I thank thee for this honour, but my path leads to the west, beyond the mountains!"

"Far wid ye go and why? Tell me what ails ye, Laddie?"

Hyw remains silent.

Geddyn hands the sword to his son and Cilydd is instantly led away by a crowd of jostling warriors. They are eager to see his new prize. Only the warrior with the braided hair remains. Geddyn watches his son in all his excitement.

The old warrior with braided hair steps forward until he is almost at the side of Hyw and Geddyn. Suddenly he reaches out, taking hold of the leather thong around Hyw's neck. Pulling at it, Bayr's arrowhead emerges from under Hyw's smock. Hyw goes to grab it, but something holds him back. The warrior pulls at a thong hidden around his own neck and a similar arrowhead, decorated with a feather and a small faceted stone, comes away from his breast. The warrior holds Hyw's arrowhead in the palm of his hand and then he closes his hand tightly around it.

"Ah tha' Cymri…ah will nae understand tha ways if I live to be a hundred, but nae bother!" Geddyn steps forward.

"He wid nae give me his pledge until I showed him this!" And then Geddyn takes Ywel's token, from around his own neck and shows it to Hyw.

"I doo nae know what power this holds, but I wish it was mine to wield… yer people are stubborn in giving their pledge, but this seems to buy some favour wit some!"

They all smile at each other, but the older warrior has many questions on his tongue and Hyw's mind is racing. Seeing a thirst in his friend's eyes, Geddyn turns from them and walks over to his son, who is still in the centre of a maul of warriors.

The warrior with the braided hair looks straight into Hyw, taking hold of his shoulders.

"Who art thou Hyw bach? Who art thy kin and whence have ye come?"

Hyw stumbles in his thoughts for a moment but looks straight into the warrior's deep grey eyes. They seem to pierce his very being and hold his gaze. The warrior speaks again.

"They call me Blaidd, but it is not my given name, nor is it my promised name!" Hyw is slightly confused, but he gathers his thoughts enough to speak.

"I am Hyw the son of Bryn Alwyn, the son of Ywel and the people of the Mountain of Tears!" At this, Blaidd throws his arms around him and hugs him to his breast. Hyw feels awkward as the warrior wraps him in his arms, but Blaidd does not let go and tightens his grip. Just when Hyw thinks Blaidd is about to let go, the warrior squeezes again. His embrace is firm, not constrictive, but Hyw is slightly embarrassed at the actions of this stranger, even though he carries the same token as his grandfather.

Blaidd eventually pulls away from him and Hyw can see tears in the old warrior's eyes. Taking hold of his shoulders, Hyw can see tears on his cheeks. Finding it difficult to talk he speaks, almost in a whisper.

"I rode with thy Da and Tad. I knew them well and I keep the oaths we made! An I hath waited these many years for thee," Hyw is taken aback by what he is saying and he cannot fathom their meaning. Blaidd places the arrowhead back beneath his smock and breastplate. Hyw's eyes quickly glaze over at the mention of his family, but he controls his feelings well. There is a myriad of questions storming through his mind, but Blaidd places a finger over his lips and quickly says.

"We will talk again. I have pledged my oath to Geddyn, but I keep ma sacred oaths tha family and I made!"

Geddyn coughs as he approaches and Blaidd gives Hyw a knowing look as they part.

"Come let us sit ageen and talk o' men and majesty!" Geddyn takes Hyw under his arm and leads him down to the fire, which is set in a slight hollow. The remains of the hog have been stripped and its carcass burns in the flames. Blaidd throws more wood onto its dying embers. The stumps of some felled trees surround the fire and there are great logs of wood set between them as seats. The hillock is well used by Geddyn and his men and he calls out.

"Set a guard, we wid nae want Māthōg and his men t'steal upon us noo, would we laddie?" Geddyn turns his words to Hyw, who becomes uneasy at the mention of Māthōg. Geddyn pulls him in close under his arm and he can see Hyw's disquiet.

As they sit around the fire, Cilydd comes to thank Hyw for his great gift and then sits next to his father.

"Aye Hyw tis a magnificent gift and I have nae paid thee any part of what it is worth laddie!"

Blaidd moves closer and then drawers up a stump of wood, so he can catch Hyw's gaze.

The sun quenches itself into the thick clouds bubbling above the mountains as the rise and fall of the warrior's settling conversations drone melodiously on. Younger warriors talk of their skirmishes and glory in battle, while older heads smile and listen to their tales. Tales turn to boasting and bragging as the fire burns brightly between them and the guard is changed before they retire.

Geddyn half sits and half lies on his bedroll at Hyw's side with Blaidd constantly watching and listening. Cilydd is seduced away by the fanciful tales of one group of rowdy older warriors, but Geddyn is biding his time.

"D'ye ken this young laddie, Blaidd?" His question is friendly, but Blaidd hesitates, which Geddyn mistakes for silence. Geddyn reaches inside his shirt feeling for the arrowhead, watched eagerly by both Hyw and Blaidd. He holds it out and asks, without any hope of a reply.

"An' what secrets are bound in this wee token!" Blaidd deflects the prying eyes of the second question by answering the first.

"I rode with Hyw's father... and his grandfather and I have told thee something of our journeys, sire!"

Geddyn muses over Blaidd's words.

"Ye hav telt may 'something' of tha journeys, but I wish to ken all my frien...I wish to learn!" Geddyn looks down at the arrowhead.

"Aye, an' I wish t'ken more of the man who gave me this token!"

"I hiv told ye all I can sire and I canna say more!" His words are for Geddyn, but his eyes look straight into Hyw, who is becoming uneasy about where the conversation is leading.

"Ye canna or ye will nae?" Geddyn asks.

"I am bound by an oath greater than the pledge I have made to thee and would die before I broke it!" Blaidd says.

"Then I will nae ask again!" Geddyn replies, knowing his comrade's resolve.

"Then tell me of the old man who gave me his trust and tell me of Māthōg again!"

Hyw is confused and uneasy. The question cannot have been for him, he had made no mention of Māthōg. Blaidd is a warrior and having fought in many battles, his mind has been dulled somewhat by the fight. His words are simple although there is much power in his blade but, in turn, Geddyn turns to Hyw.

"I perceive Māthōg has deen ye wrong. Is this fa whom ye seek?"

Hyw remains silent, but the pains of his memories are written on his face.

"Who has din ye wrong t'bring ye from tha bosom of yer kin an' what horrors have befallen ye Hyw?" Geddyn knows his questions are too much, but he still pursues them.

"We will hunt him together as a rogue wolf. Tell me an' it's thine. Just gi' me tha leave an' it is thine; blood fee blood!"

Hyw stares up into Blaidd's piercing grey eyes. Blaidd is anxious to hear more, but he dares not disturb Hyw's thoughts and can only wonder about the tragedy that has befallen his friends. But he knows that while there is breath in Bryn or Ywel they would not allow Hyw to venture out alone.

Geddyn has almost given up hope of Hyw's words when Hyw begins to speak. His words are quiet and low, to begin with, and some of Geddyn's men have ceased their idle prattle in the hope of learning more.

"I am the last!" Hyw begins. Blaidd sighs as his worst fears are confirmed to him.

"I am the last!" Hyw repeats thinking back to his grandfather's dying words to him as he struggled to hold onto his life long enough to teach his grandson.

"Dead…Hyw bach?" Blaidd asks as rage burns inside Geddyn, but he holds his tongue and his feelings go unseen.

Tears start to gather in Blaidd's eyes as the drone of all the warriors' varying conversations subsides.

"Māthōg and his…he put them all to the sword and my life is bound up in his fate!" Hyw's words fall slowly at first, but he finds strength in them.

"I was, but eight when they attacked our home for the first time!" Hyw begins his sorrowful tale as he tells them of Māthōg's murderous destruction of his parents, but he is circumspect in what he says. He tells them of his father's great battle with Māthōg's men and his mother's sacrifice in trying to bring Bryn the blade his father wrought. Telling of his own small efforts and the breaking of his bow, he does not mention his killing of the two Grots, nor his attack on Māthōg with his broken arrow.

Hyw's words fall silent as he thinks of Ywel's love; love strong enough to shore him up in the years between the two attacks, but Geddyn suspects more.

"An' what of tha scar on Māthōg's face? Tha work, laddie?" Geddyn asks, clenching his fist in his lap.

Hyw barely nods as a murmur ripples out through Geddyn's men and one of the warriors is heard to say.

"Aye I ken it… did no I tell ye…he's tha one!"

Geddyn looks up at the warrior's indiscretion, but undeterred, Hyw continues to tell them of the two he had killed and his attack on Māthōg; drawing the blade of his broken arrow down Māthōg's face. He shows no pride in his tale and is almost ashamed of his feeble efforts, but he does not tell of how he had escaped Māthōg's rage by hiding with his sister in the stench of their toilet. Nor does he mention the fear that had gripped him as his own piss ran down his leg.

Talking of the years between the two attacks, Hyw tells them of his sister's beauty and her hopes of marriage; telling of Ywel's heartache and his years of sacrifice. Finally, Hyw tells all gathered, of Māthōg's second attack and his chase through the woods. Hyw is unusually calm as speaks, but Geddyn's men become unsettled, although they do not show their disquiet to Hyw.

Hyw does not mention his grandfather's fight with death, nor does he mention the old man's words to him on that one long night, but knowing the period of time which must have elapsed and knowing the determination of his old friend, Blaidd has an idea of what must have taken place that night. At the end of his words, all falls silent. Not a ripple murmurs through the gathering.

"We shall hunt him as a dog. Aye, we shall ride with ye and recover thy faither's blade for thee!"

Geddyn's words are full of venom, but Hyw does not share Geddyn's want. Instead, he just shakes his head.

"This battle is mine…I must face him alone…I have sworn it to…!" Hyw cannot finish his words.

"Māthōg has worried our lands fa too lang noo… his blade has spilt t'much blood for me to turn ma een from him. I canna tell ma men to turn from their quest, but if we triumph oor him, thy faither's blade will be kept for thee!"

Geddyn holds out his hand to Hyw and Hyw takes it as they shake on his word.

Wrestling in their want; slowly every warrior turns from his tale and Hyw is eventually able to find some peace as he sleeps under the protection of their watch.

Chapter Nine

The camp slumbers amid the constant snores and coughs of its sleeping warriors, but before the slow grey light of the morning appears, Hyw eases from his bed and gathers his blankets, together with his saddle. Picking his way quietly through their dreams, the guards watch his every move. Saddling Sarn, Hyw leads her out to the tree line.

A thick blanket of fog covers the valley below with only the mountains and tallest trees forming islands protruding from its veil and their silhouettes fade into the distance. Pausing, Hyw thinks about his life and the path set before him; his want for revenge no longer chokes his thoughts, although Māthōg still infests his nightmares. Thinking of Ywel's brother, Hyw wonders about an old man he only saw once as a child, and then only for a fleeting moment in the obscure light cast by a dying fire. Closing his eyes, drawing in a deep breath, Hyw searches for the old man's presence and smiling to himself, he is content with the message his visions bear. Searching back through the years, he rehearses

Ywel's directions to the sacred Isle, then leaning forward he pats Sarn's neck.

"Well my girl, ye have another journey ahead!" Sarn neighs softly at his words and Hyw climbs into the saddle as she begins the descent towards the misty ocean before them. But in the fleeting moment, Hyw is still not convinced of the path he should take.

Hearing footsteps from behind, he turns to see Blaidd stumbling towards him; his bare feet picking their way between the rocks. Stubbing his toe, he cries out in his pain.

"Wait Hyw bach…wait up!" Sarn comes to a halt and Blaidd catches his breath as he nurses his foot.

"Leaving so soon? I should like to ride with thee if I may…I have Geddyn's leave…It would not take me long to prepare myself!"

'Hyw Bach!' The words drag at his memories and he longs for home, but the nightmares that accompany any thought of his home weigh heavy on his mind. A moment of silence passes between them as he thinks on many things, but eventually, he shakes his head. Why he refuses Blaidd, he cannot tell, he only knows some unseen force rankles inside him; pushing forward and in his Waking Dreams, he can only see Sarn and himself, walking their lonely path.

Blaidd's head drops, but he soon raises his gaze back up to Hyw.

"Keep thy secrets safe Hyw bach, keep them…!" Blaidd pauses slightly. "We shall talk again by and by!"

At these words, Hyw calls softly to Sarn and the gentle mare begins her descent, picking her way between the rocks and boulders.

"Wait Hyw!" Cilydd's voice disturbs the quiet of the morning's slumber as a low sun creeps over the mountains, its light piercing the trees behind where he stands.

"Afore ye go I must thank thee for thy gift, an' one day I too shall repay thee!" Hyw smiles at them both as Blaidd places one of his hands on Cilydd's shoulder. Behind where they stand, loitering in the shadows of the tree line, Geddyn watches and waits. Hyw catches sight of his silhouette and half-smiles, but bowing his head he turns to go.

Slowly Sarn wades down into a sea of mist and they disappear from view, but as Hyw immerses himself in an ocean of smog, he begins to drown in his visions and restless dreams, where Māthōg relentlessly pursues him.

Sarn's footfall is certain as she tracks westward, following the path by the meandering stream with mountains rising on every side. Her master jumps and moans, suffering in his memories. The cry of a hawk breaks through the blanket of fog as it soars up towards the sun.

"BAYR!" Hyw cries out, but again he is too late. Shuddering, he shivers under the blanket of fog, but the warmth of the sun begins to burn the mist from the land and as the mist clears his nightmares fade.

"I will never be free while Māthōg lives!" Sarn shakes her head and snorts at Hyw's words.

"We must hold our journey awhile Sarn bach…we must find a place to make our stand and then we shall wait!"

There is only one certainty that his dreams bring to him.

'I will one day face Māthōg…I must be ready.' It flashes inside him, but he is unusually calm at that thought. Of the place and time he cannot say, but whether to track forward or back, it is no mind, Māthōg would somehow always find him. It is as though their lives are set; inextricably linked by some wretched and evil enchantment spell cast in Annwn, and until Hyw breaks its power he will never be free.

"Sorry Sarn bach!" Hyw looks up to the top of the mountains and then down into the valley in front of them. The track drops sharply to a low wooded plain, where, through the thinning mist, Hyw can just make out a great lake fed by a meandering river whose streams tumble from the mountains on every side. There are a few scattered crofts along its southern shore with mountains towering above it, to the north. Looking up to the mountains and remembering Ywel's words, he coaxes Sarn from the path and they begin to climb.

The day is long and slowly they climb out above the mists and clouds. In the saddle between two mountains, Hyw turns to the west, following a path towards the highest peak. Sarn slowly plods on as the sun burns the last of the mist from the mountains and their full majesty is unveiled. Pools and lakes wait silently between the steep sides of the mountains and the continuous trickle and fall of water, fills his ears.

They reach a large lake and have to skirt around its northern shore as they climb again. After a short time, they come to the shores of yet another lake, surrounded by mountains, except for the thin path that climbs to greater grandeur. This highest of all the lakes is dark and strangely coloured and Sarn refuses to drink or walk too close to its shoreline.

Climbing higher and higher, Sarn begins to struggle as the rocky terrain steepens, but Hyw is patient and looks for the surer path. Finally, they climb out onto the ridge between the highest peaks. Surrounded, the scenery is breathtaking, an eternity of mountains rising to meet his gaze in every direction, misty layers stretching on forever, silhouetted in the day's low sun.

An eagle soars below where they stand. It swoops down over the highest lake that is an eternity beneath them and moments later it is above their heads, climbing high into the wild blue yonder of the heavens. Awestruck, Hyw ponders on the great bird's grace and power. Sarn saunters towards the top. The Eagle soars at their side as if to check on the two strangers who have dared to intrude upon its mountain.

Looking continuously to the west, Hyw tries to make out the waters of the sea and the sacred isle, but his gaze is lost amid the continuous scene of misty mountains. He searches for the path he should tread, firstly scouring the landscape and then looking inside, to his visions, but he cannot divine a way forward.

Hyw pauses for only a moment at the top before following the ridge on the other side of the summit and they wend their way down the mountain's rocky sides. Two more eagles join the first. Having to dismount continuously, Hyw guides Sarn down large rocky steps in the mountain, but Sarn seems content with her load as he talks quietly to her.

They eventually reach softer terrain where boggy slopes squelch and ooze at their feet. Dropping her head to feed, Hyw nudges his gentle companion forward, but then he relents and they pause for a while as Sarn munches on the mountain's sparse fodder.

There are diggings on the steep slopes of the mountain, where men are breaking rocks and loading carts. It looks like slate workings, but Hyw cannot be sure at the distance. Coaxing Sarn forward, she walks steadily on, skirting unseen around the quarry. A shepherd is watching his flock on the opposite slope but immersed in his care for his flock he pays no attention to the two lonely strangers in his midst.

Water flows continuously from the mountain, seeping, oozing, trickling and dripping into small channels that flow down into streams that eventually form a cascading river that tumbles ever on. Both Sarn and Hyw stop to drink at one of the streams. The ice-cold water is crystal clear and sweet to the taste of the weary travellers.

Their path and the river lead down towards a gap between the steep sides of two further mountains where the river falls from view. Reaching the gap Hyw is mesmerised. The stream tumbles over huge drops in the mountain as it falls towards the valley below. He has never before seen such cascades in his life. The stream that flows past his own small home is, but a trickle in comparison and hasn't the same force, even in the floods of winter.

Climbing down, Hyw walks next to the river's cascades. Huge waterfalls crash and roar into crystal-clear pools and Hyw can feel the water's power and energy flowing through him. Sarn walks a little way behind her master, grazing occasionally, but keeping up with Hyw, not allowing him to stray too far from her side. At the bottom of the waterfalls, the path and the river part-company as the river falls, crashing over a sheer drop. Never in his wildest dreams could Hyw have ever imagined such a scene.

Standing, watching, as if transfixed by the wonder of it all, Hyw realises there is another cascade, hidden from his view, beneath some trees and bushes. Climbing from the path, Hyw walks towards the lowest pool, close to where it tumbles over the edge of the world and he gazes back up the mountain stream in awe. There beneath the trees is the most beautiful little scene; a waterfall dropping into a large round pool hidden away from the path above. An old tree, set with thick bushes surrounding it, spreads its branches out over the crystal clear waters. A grassy ledge protrudes out over the river and Hyw sits awhile in the shade of the tree. Sarn leaves her munching on the mountain's short grass and comes to drink from the stream's clear waters.

The sun has drifted over its low skies and the short day will soon be coming to a close. It is still warm for the time of year and the sun thaws into Hyw as he slips away in his dreams. Thinking of Sián, Hyw wishes she were lazing at his side. His dream continues and he can feel the cool waters of the pool as they swim together. He imagines a splash of water as Sián turns to him, her full beauty open to his eyes, but looking up he doesn't recognise her face. His feelings tumble, like the water of the stream over its falls and he wakes with a start. Trying to conjure the scene once more in his mind, to his horror, Hyw cannot picture Sián's face.

Suddenly the vision of Māthōg breaks into his mind and Hyw jumps grabbing at his bow. Looking all around him, he is cautious, but there is no one there. Sarn is slightly perplexed and looks out over the mountainside, but, not seeing any danger, she quickly returns her attention to the cool waters of the stream.

Standing, Hyw walks across to where his lonely companion is still drinking and he tentatively steps out onto a rock in the stream. Stepping from rock to rock, he traverses its fast flow with Sarn following him. They walk together out onto the mountain, leaving the path behind as the day slowly fades.

Māthōg has once more disturbed Hyw's dreams and he knows he will gain no peace until he has faced him. He cannot dream of love or Sián or his home until he has rid himself of the nightmares Māthōg has cast into his life.

"What shall we do then my friend?" Hyw asks Sarn.

"Shall we scour the land or shall we wait in ambush or shall we…?" Sarn nods her head and snorts.

"Well it could be a long wait old girl, but we shall make ourselves comfy!"

They descend the steep slopes until Hyw can see the whole valley from a point about halfway along the lake. A point he had seen that morning through a haze of mist.

It is a huge hillock of rock rising, out of the lake's waters, on its northern shore, just below where he stands. Climbing down, onto its back, Hyw finds an old shepherd's shelter lying in ruins and he immediately sets to work, making it habitable for the night. It is split into two small rooms although the roof has long since fallen in and the walls are in urgent need of repair.

Hyw looks out over the valley as he works. The track on the opposite shoreline is clearly in view and he has a commanding view of the crofts and woods. To the east, at the head of the valley, is the way he had taken that morning and looking to the west, where the sun is fast waning, he surveys the fields and scattered woods of the valley's watery plain.

Hyw gathers kindling for a fire and as the light of the day fades completely, he builds up the walls of the shelter. Labouring in the flickering shadows of the fire's meagre light. He spreads a blanket over the shelter's rotting beams for a roof. Tethering Sarn close to the entrance, she would be able to gain some shelter from the elements and feel at least a little warmth from the fire. Setting large flat stones on their edges on either side of his blaze, he hides the light of his fire from the valley below and soon the two travellers are snug and warm.

The hillock of rock on which he sits would be easy to defend. On every side, there are almost sheer drops except for a narrow path at the rear of the fold. He looks up at Sarn who is finishing the last of her oats.

"Our rear is thy responsibility Sarn bach!" Sarn neighs softly at Hyw's attention.

"Keep thine eyes open my old friend!"

Listening to the trickle of water off the mountain and the lapping of the lake beneath him, Hyw drifts off into the night. An owl cries and screeches as hunting. It swoops from a tree and snatches a mouse from the side of a large boulder. The mouse hangs helplessly from the owl's beak as it flies back to the tree to eat its feast. A wolf howls and Hyw instinctively pulls his father's fur blanket further over his shoulders. Wrestling in his nightmares, he wakes with a start and cries out. Sarn's ghost-like figure stares down at him.

"Don't wake me again Sarn bach… Dost thou hear me!" She whinnies quietly as sleep catches him once more and drags him off to his nightmares and the darkly wooded night of his Waking Dreams. Every moan and cry, each jump and start of his tortured dreams is watched over by his gentle companion.

The morning brings him some relief and he busies himself with his new work. Building walls and making a place to dwell; a lookout; a secure habitat where he would wait for Māthōg. Nothing, not even the power of Annwn would drag him from his path. Days pass into weeks. Mending all the walls, Hyw raises them so Sarn can shelter from the winter's cold in the second chamber he creates. Fishing in the streams and rivers that run off the mountains, and hunting through the woods, Hyw provides for his needs. Gathering fallen logs, he builds a store of fuel for the winter's cold, all carried on Sarn's sturdy back. Even slate for a roof is purchased from the men of the mountain, but through all his work, he is constant in his watch over the valley.

His days are full of fishing, hunting and gathering and when his nightmares become too much for him, he climbs to the mountains and their rocky grandeur seems to lift his spirits. Often he gazes out to the west, looking to the islands of the sea as he listens to his grandfather's words whispering inside his head, but he cannot step over his bitter thoughts of Māthōg. In the evening's dying light, Hyw ponders and plans his attack.

'I will have to keep my head…no reckless or impulsive assault…Māthōg would surely win the day that way…if I wait, holding back my attack, he will surely come to me.'

Occasionally he sees a sign of Geddyn's men at the head of the valley. They look over to where he keeps his watch, but they do not enter the valley. Hyw knows they keep watch for both Māthōg and him, but still, he keeps his silent vigil. It rains continually for what seems like weeks as he checks and re-checks the security of his little shelter.

In the harshness of winter, he is sometimes forced to compete with the wild animals scavenging for food. The bite of winter grinds slowly by and the New Year brings little relief from its creeping fingers. The snow begins to fall late one afternoon and doesn't stop for two full days. Both Sarn and Hyw stay close to the warmth of the shelter with Hyw keeping a roaring fire. The wind howls in through the gaps in the walls, which Hyw fills with mud and small rocks. The snow builds outside and drifts up against the curtained doorway.

On the third day, an eerie silence surrounds them as he sits by his fire wrapped in his father's wolfskin blanket. The silence is overwhelming and Sarn is uneasy. Her ears prick back and she raises her head, listening to something on the breeze. Grabbing his bow from by the door, he swiftly notches an arrow into its string. Someone is approaching around the top of the huge rock; even Hyw can hear their horse's footfall.

"Art thou there, Hyw bach?"

It's Blaidd. Rising from his crouched position, Blaidd sees Hyw's feathered warrior notched into his bow. The sound of his friend's voice raises his spirits and even Sarn seems pleased to see the visitor.

"May God pour his richest blessings on thy head Hyw bach!" As Blaidd asks God's blessings on him, Hyw thinks back to his grandfather and the blessings he would ask over all the people of their valley. Emerging fully into the light of day, he greets his guests. Rounding the corner of his little croft he sees Cilydd, riding a short distance behind Blaidd. Overwhelmed with joy; it is a feeling that has long eluded him.

"How art thou Hyw bach? We bring thee gifts…food and grain from Geddyn and he sends his best regards!" Cilydd smiles at Hyw. He is pleased to see him again but hadn't realised he had been living in such squalor. Blaidd is more understanding.

"Thou hast made thyself comfy Hyw bach…ye have all the comforts of home!"

The snow is still piled in high drifts and the horses are sweating and panting from their struggle. Steam from their sweat rises from their hindquarters as they rest awhile. Blaidd apologises and says they cannot stay long; there has been no word or sign of Māthōg and his men. The warriors of Gododdyn have been set with responsibility for all the main paths, but Blaidd doubts Māthōg uses the main pathways and says he is more likely to journey through the mountain passes. Cilydd is eager to speak.

"Ma faither has left this valley t'tha care Hyw; ye have it 'sewn in a bag'…he says; tha could nae have picked a better place t'ambush Māthōg, himself!" Cilydd thinks this is a good thing to say and is pleased with the message he bears, but Hyw pays the words little attention, other than for the word they bear of Māthōg. But he delights in the company of good friends.

Soon he is watching his friends struggling back through the deep drifts of snow. They slowly climb down to the far end of the lake where they skirt around the marshes at its head, crossing its river and they begin the climb up and out of the valley, but before they break the brow of the distant hills, they both turn and wave back to where Hyw is standing.

The thaw is slow and well over a week later there are still large swathes of snow, covering the mountains, hills and trees, but spring is already pushing its wildflowers up through the valley's winter coverings.

In the still of clearer nights, Hyw sits in the doorway of his shelter looking up at the galleries of the endless stars. The Morning Star shines brightly from just above the mountains and Hyw traces its guiding light, wondering about the secrets it holds. The words of his grandfather come echoing down the forgotten passages of time that have finally fallen between them and he drowns in the silent waters of his thoughts.

A Red Breast has adopted Hyw's shelter as its own. It flits in through a gap between the curtained doorway and the wall and perches itself just above the fire. Hyw feeds it crumbs from both his meat and Sarn's oats and nuts. It stays warm and grows fat on his titbits, but Sarn and Hyw both appreciate their newfound friend. The small bird sometimes flies over and sits on Sarn's back or explores the nether regions of Hyw's comfy shelter. Trying to feed it from his hand, the bird is brazen but does not find the courage to take food directly from Hyw.

Weeks go by and the rains eventually wash all signs of the snow into the river and lake; only the tops of the mountains remain white. Venturing out into the valley, he still keeps himself to himself, remaining quiet and unseen to the tenants and shepherds who work the land, but each knows of his resting place. Geddyn has kept his word and all the residents of the valley feel safe, as Hyw keeps his vigil over them.

The rains eventually give way to clear blue skies and the sundries down on the two friends and their shelter. A chorus of birds greets them every morning as busying themselves with courting and nest building. Even the redbreast finds a mate and they begin to build their own home in the eaves of Hyw's shelter. The first lambs are out on the mountainsides where their ewes shelter them from the prying eyes of eagles. The mountain streams are swollen with the thaw off their slopes and trout flit and jump over their rocks and waterfalls.

A young family of Redbreasts wakes him every morning; their singing brings untold joy to Hyw's heart, but it is a double-edged sword and thoughts of his own family or finding a wife and raising children, cut him to the quick.

Spring breathes life back into the valley all around him, as sits high above the lake, watching the two riders as they approach. Their horses struggle up the path towards him. Sarn pays them little mind, having heard their footfall before. There are two large sacks of provisions hung over the haunches of their stallions, which he surmises are for him. Blaidd is again riding with Cilydd, his old blade hung at Cilydd's side.

Continuing to sit in the curtained doorway of the sheepfold, Hyw waits for his two friends to dismount and walk around to where he is sitting. His eyes are tracking an eagle, soaring high on the back of a warm spring breeze. Its wings seem to collapse as it tumbles, swooping then gliding low over the meadows. It glides, hugging the nap of the mountainside. Hyw can see a hare someway in front of the great bird as lambs run for the shelter of their mother's underbellies. Silently slicing through the air, it seems to extend its fingers out and up; it bobs slightly and the hare is gone.

Blaidd again calls for the richest blessings to be poured out on his friend. Depositing the sacks of supplies just inside the doorway, he sits on a rock opposite Hyw, as Cilydd stands to one side hardly able to contain himself. Blaidd sits awhile looking, searching with his eyes before he speaks.

"There are rumours abroad…they whisper of Māthōg!" Hyw looks deep into Blaidd's piercing grey-blue eyes.

"The Men of Gododdyn ride to the north leaving only a few to guard thy rear, Hyw bach." Hyw looks up at Cilydd and then back to Blaidd.

"No Hyw bach, I begged to stay, but we must ride with Geddyn!" For some reason, Hyw is disappointed at the news that his friends will be leaving. He does not understand the secrets and power Ywel's token holds, but in the short time, he has known Blaidd it has forged a bond between them.

"Come wi' us Hyw. My faither has given his permission!" Cilydd's eager words tempt, but Hyw remains silent. There is silence for what seems like a lifetime. Cilydd cannot understand his new friends' hesitation, but Blaidd waits on Hyw's word.

"I will remain!" Hyw says quietly.

"I must face Māthōg alone…I have seen it!" Hyw has said too much, but Blaidd understands the secrets his words hold, having known the visions of Ywel's brother and Blaidd is instantly filled with some unseen power that seems to overcome his soul; building a peaceful feeling inside him.

Cilydd is disappointed and he can only smile at Hyw in his confusion.

"Ye must do as ye see, Hyw bach!" Blaidd stands and extends his hand forward. Hyw takes it as they both grip, each at the other's wrist. Then they fall into each other's arms as tears splash onto Blaidd's face. After a moment they separate and Hyw sees the tears as he wipes the tears from his face.

"Just an old man who has seen too much battle!" Hyw instantly understands.

"We shall talk again Hyw bach unless the sky falls down," Blaidd appears to want to say more but holds his words.

Hyw stands at the doorway of his rocky shack and watches his two friends ride up and out of the valley; with a final wave as they turn to go.

Chapter Ten

Sarn is restless, but Hyw sleeps on, struggling in some torrid nightmare. Wandering through the haunted woods of his dreams, he toils with some unseen adversary. Something tugs at his dream and a familiar voice whispers in his ear. Trying to wake himself, still haunted by his nightmares, Hyw cannot see who speaks, nor does he understand their words.

"Raise thyself and save thy sister, Hyw bach!" His mother's familiar words come flooding back through time, piercing his very soul. With his heartbreaking Isobel whispers again.

"Wake and arise Hyw bach, save thy sister… save thy sister Hyw bach!" Trying to rouse his senses, suddenly he wakes with a start and stares straight up into the fire that burns in his mother's eyes. Rubbing his own eyes, trying to shake off his visions, he cannot seem to rouse himself or free his thoughts from the grasp of the cruel apparition before him.

Fully awake, he is still staring deep into his mother's eyes. She stoops over him, pulling at his arm, repeating her words.

"Wake and arise Hyw bach, save thy sister… save thy sister Hyw bach!" Hyw jumps to his feet with his mother stepping back into the shadows of the shelter. Still not fully convinced he is in the real world; he stares hard into her careworn eyes as she loiters in the shadows, like some ghostly apparition. A smile begins to burn in her eyes and it warms his imagination, but he cannot speak. Behind the vision of his mother, standing silently in the shadows, Hyw can see a small throng of ghostly figures, but he cannot make out their faces or their form.

Sarn is waiting by the open curtain of the doorway; she has somehow been saddled and is ready for a swift journey. Nodding her head and neighing softly towards where he stands, struggling in a daze of confusion with the darkness of the night around him.

"Thy bow, Hyw bach!" Isobel whispers again. Hyw wakes his mind and instantly takes up his bow, strapping his father's belt around his waist.

"No time to pause Hyw bach; ye must fly!" Looking long and hard at his mother, his heart breaks over and over again, but the urgency of her words blazes through him.

"Sarn knows the way, we shall guide thy feet, but the fight is thine alone to bear!" Hyw is confused, but Isobel steps forward to take hold of her son by his head and bending it gently forward, she kisses his hair.

"Ye must be away…quick now…the wolves yet prowl around thy sister!" Hyw's heart is rent in two but without thought, he checks again on his belt for the knives and his quiver of arrows. Pausing for one short moment he searches his mother's eyes for some answers, but she quickly spurs him out of the door.

"Ride Hyw bach, ride…!" Hyw climbs into the saddle and tugging at the reins, he disappears into the night.

The darkness is thick around him and it will be some time before the morning's slow grey light rises above the mountains. Galloping ever on, as if possessed by the chasing demons of Annwn, Sarn seems to cut through the gloom of the night and forges ever on.

Hyw wonders on his journey home and he can only imagine what horrors his mother's familiar spirit has warned him of. At the crest of the valley, he looks for signs of Geddyn's men, but none stand guard. Charging ever on, Sarn enters the Sacred Grove of the Birch Woods.

Dawn is creeping slowly into the sky as they ford the river just below the huddle of small crofts. High above the opposite woods, Bare-Faced Crows are swirling and crying like the black shadows of giant bats; they are tumbling in some tormented dance in the dim light of the dawn.

There is no time for him to give thought to the black shadowy tormentors or their flight and he attempts to steer Sarn towards the path leading over the High Moors, but his trusted friend has greater hands pulling on the bit in her mouth and he has little control over the path she treads; all he can do is give her free rein as she turns towards the woods and the black tormentors.

They enter the woods as a guttural scream pierces his ears and Sarn jumps beneath him. With a renewed vigour, Hyw goads Sarn on dreading the secrets his mother's words convey. Questioning his sanity, Hyw trusts the faith he places in his dreams, and the love he bares for his sister drives him ever on.

Sarn gallops through the trees, whose every branch claws out at them as the roots of the fallen woods raise themselves up to slow their progress. In the shadows, every tree takes on the form of some ghoulish spectre or tormented demon and the twisted woods gather in around them, but Sarn presses on undaunted. The rooks cry and circle overhead as Sarn is spurred on by her celestial guides.

A plume of smoke rises above the trees as a dreadful thought shudders through Hyw and he remembers his friends by the lake. His journey takes on a new urgency as he hears the cries of men and Māthōg's unmistakable call to arms. The terrified screams of a young woman empty into Hyw and he spurs Sarn forward, notching an arrow into his bow.

Hyw breaks cover and sees the desperate struggle of his friends on the far side of the lake. Rage pulses through him as he trembles at the sight of Māthōg sitting high on his stead, shouting his sadistic orders to his bloodthirsty cohorts. In blind fury and forgetting all his winters' plans for a cold calculated attack, Hyw looses a reckless feathered warrior high into the air, but the moment his hawk takes to flight he regrets his impetuous actions.

The blade will not make its mark and will only serve as a warning to his old adversary. With the hungry talons of his lonely hawk about to give away his attack, only the surprise of a sustained onslaught will win the day. Letting out a cry that would wake the dead and, like an eagle on the breeze, Sarn swoops into Annwn.

His feathered hawk is not so amiss and it sinks into the hindquarters of Māthōg's warhorse, causing it to jump in pain and stagger in fright. It rears up with Māthōg struggling to stay in the saddle. His eyes find Hyw and fear seems to strike through him, like the lightning of the end of summer storms.

Hyw is a fearsome sight with the dirt of winter ground on his face. Streaked with sweat and set to the charge, his eyes are darkly menacing. Another deadly hawk is notched into place; its sharpened senses and talons are honed to one purpose as Sarn stampedes forward. Galloping around the top end of the lake, its waters erupt beneath her thunderous hooves.

An archer breaks cover, stepping onto the path in front of Sarn. Hyw's arrow is swift and furious, thrashing through the air. The feathered warrior shatters the Grot's neck, which instantly explodes, spraying its gaudy phosphorescent shower of blood into the air, but Hyw's attack continues forward unabated. With another arrow notched into place, he scans constantly back and forth as he screams towards his prey. Panicked, in the face of Hyw's furious attack, Māthōg frantically turns his horse while shouting a warning to his men. Battle, seems to rage everywhere and as he approaches the croft he can see the fury of the girl's brothers fending off a score of verminous Scotti Slags.

A cry calls out from the area of the croft then a low thud. Another of Māthōg's men steps from beyond the croft's outer wall. Surprise lights across the Grots face, but before he can raise his sword to protect himself, Hyw's shafted blade slams into his chest and he sinks slowly to his knees with his sword tumbling into the dirt.

Māthōg's horse tears at the ground in a hurried stampede for the tree line. Galloping towards the continuing battle, Sarn cautiously, but swiftly bears down on the awful scene playing before her.

The eldest son of Hyw's friends is in a frantic battle with several Red Raiders; without Hyw's help, it is a battle condemned to fail. Whether the Scotti have heard Māthōg's warning, Hyw isn't sure, but they are all fixed in the uncertain fray of their individual conflicts. One after the other his feathered warriors are despatched and they arch through the air towards Māthōg's Blood Red Crows. Sarn bears swiftly down on the battle. Two then three Grots quit their rage and slowly sink into the dirt.

Māthōg is out of sight and seeing the fury and aggression of Hyw's attack, some of his men are running for their steeds or the cover of the trees. Māthōg has brought a small army with him.

An arrow pierces one of the brother's sides and he struggles to stay on his feet. Hyw swiftly despatches the archer and is desperate to string another arrow into his bow, but his fumbling fingers are too late with one of the Scotti Slags thrusting a twisted blade into the young man's back. Hyw curses his clumsy fingers as his arrow cuts down the assassin. Scanning the tree line for the Scotti archer, yet more marauders flee the field. Every passing moment, Hyw expects to be despatched by Māthōg's concealed archers.

A lone swordsman wields his blade attacking the girl's only remaining brother. Hyw takes careful aim as an arrow whistles past his ear and the decision is made. Turning his aim to the edge of the woods where the Grot is fumbling at the string of his bow, Hyw's swift blade brings his frantic struggle to an end and the Grot falls from the cover of a large thicket of hazel.

Turning back to the girl's brother, another arrow finds the string of his bow. Another arrow breaks the cover of the trees, its feathers thrashing past Hyw. The girl's second brother has joined the first in Annwn and the last of his tormentors is running for the tree line. Despite the danger, Hyw knows his duty and the fleeing Grot does not make the safety of the woods.

Hyw's attack has stalled momentarily, but he has killed or driven almost all the Scotti marauders from the clearing. There are five of Māthōg's wolves frantically struggling to mount their frightened steeds close to the tree line. Another swift, but ill-aimed shaft breaks the cover of the tree line. Hyw's deadly hawk shrieks through the air and the low thud of it piercing the Grot's chest is followed by a muffled cry. Māthōg's flint-hearted marauders have gained control of their horses and Hyw braces himself for their impending attack.

A cry breaks the tree line. Unknown to Hyw, a third brother charges from the edge of the woods brandishing an axe. This brother cannot be as old as his sisters, but his attack is that of a man. Letting out a piercing cry he runs towards the four horsemen, but his charge is hopelessly in vain. Throwing his axe at the foremost Scotti Slag, it spins swiftly through the air as he grabs at the knife on his belt. The force of the axe hitting the Grot, square in the chest, instantly unseats him as the heavy blade rips through his chest and the young boy leaps onto the second Slag with his blade gripped tightly in his hand.

Sarn's heart is fit to burst, but she springs to the aid of their friend, another Slag is despatched by one of Hyw's hungry hawks, but despite her swift heart the last of the brothers is shrugged off and trampled underfoot. Quickly finding his feet, the last two Grots callously slash out with their swords and in a frenzy of flashing blades, the young boy is hewn down. Another feathered warrior finds one of the two remaining Slags, but he manages to stay astride his warhorse and they are quickly out of sight. There is still an archer hidden somewhere in the trees and Hyw is wary.

Slowing his attack and with all the Red Raiders out of view, Hyw searches the edges of the clearing. There is no time to mourn; Māthōg will be rallying his men for an attack. An arrow whistles past Hyw's ear; he has seen the archer's hiding place, but cannot see the archer. Straining his eyes he bends his bow. Seeing some movement in the bushes beyond the far corner of the croft, he waits momentarily, as another arrow is launched from behind a low bush. The shaft's intent is more accurate this time and Hyw quickly ducks as the Scotti blade whistles over his head.

Silence seems to open a space between Hyw and the hidden archer. There is a moment of indecision when the archer realises his impending doom. Breaking cover, he runs swiftly back through the woods, he trips on a root, and Sarn begins her charge. Following the frightened fleeing shadow, the Grot swiftly finds his feet, but Hyw releases another hungry hawk. The force of all Hyw's rage empties into the back of the startled archer and he falls to his knees. Slowly looking up at Hyw; the Slag trembles. Fingers helplessly fumble at the string of his bow as he half leans against its staff. A flash of panic dies as another feathered warrior smashes into his face. His head shudders with the force of the arrow and he crumbles into the dirt.

A girl's scream wakes Hyw to a desperate struggle taking place inside the croft. A Slag calls out from behind its curtained doorway.

"Hold her still!" Another voice calls out for more men to join them, but he cannot know the only person to hear his calls, is Hyw. Time seems to slow as Hyw jumps from Sarn's back running towards the croft.

The lifeless body of the girl's father is lying in the dirt just to one side of the doorway, with his sword still held securely in his hand. A large patch of blood, stains his smock and the side of his head has been cleaved open, cutting his ear in two. The gaping wound extends around to the back of his head. The blood-soaked bodies of two Red Raiders are lying on the ground just beyond where he lies. His valiant battle to protect his wife and daughters had finally been lost, but the time it has given Hyw, might be enough to save those lives a father loves, more than his own life.

Moans and cries sound out in unison, almost as though spirits from the unseen world cry out with those still struggling in this God-forsaken realm. Hyw is swift over the ground; if his heart were an arrow his flight would not have been any quicker. The haunting cries of the unseen young girl spurs him on. Before he makes the doorway a scream pierces Hyw's ears as a low thud is followed by yet another scream.

Time is passing quickly and Hyw seems transfixed unable to join the race to its end. The sobbing of a girl drags at his heart filling it to overflowing. It builds until he thinks it will burst under the immense agony it spills inside him.

Suddenly the curtained doorway explodes as a bloodstained Scotti fiend appears with his prize raised high into the air. Holding it out by the hair, he raises the severed head of the girl's mother.

In the stark bright daylight, the Slag is momentarily blinded. Expecting to show his trophy of a woman's severed head off to his kinsmen, he is met, only by Hyw and the anger of his bow. The force of Hyw's arrow striking into the Grot's unprotected body rips straight through his heart and only the feathers of his arrow can be seen protruding from the centre of his chest. Momentarily reeling in his agony the grot looks down at the white goose feathers as the severed head falls from his hand. Making no sound, he stands blocking Hyw's path, but Hyw has already wasted too much time.

'Māthōg must surely be returning,' The thought inside his head calls him to action.

With another shaft firmly notched in place, Hyw pulls at the Grot who staggers forward and then falls. With no discernable sound, Hyw steps beyond the curtained doorway. Standing in the pained darkness of the croft, his eyes strain as they search the shadows. Sweeping through the doorway he hears a low frightened gasp; it is more like a feeling than a sound, but someone has seen him slip into the enveloping shadows.

There is a moan, as a Grot groans and strains in the darkness. The girl winces as a sliver of pain cuts into her. Hyw stares down at a writhing shapeless heap in the centre of the room. The curtain in the doorway flaps in the morning's breeze, bringing an uncertain light and his eyes catch sight of the awful scene for the first time. An old Slag is lying on top of one of the girls, grinding her into the cold slate floor of the croft. This fiend of Annwn, suspecting more of his kinsmen have joined him for the fun, half calls out,

"Get her...!" He groans again not finishing what he was saying, grinding harder at the girl. Hyw's eyes can barely comprehend the awful scene as his attack falters and his crippling visions haunt his sanity.

For some reason, another awful scene takes the place of the first and he stands motionless in the shadows as his memories and waking visions torment him. Standing in another place; another time, he strains his tortured mind to understand the twisted vision playing before him. The realisation suddenly hits him. It is Sián's eyes through which his memories gaze and he watches all her torment as she witnesses the brutal torture and mutilation of her sister. All the horrors of Enydd's desecration and murder are open to his gaze.

Just as suddenly as the vision had infested his mind, it fades and Hyw is left staring down at the young woman's awful nightmare. A blade is being held across her throat, its honed edge has already drawn blood, which is dribbling down the side of her neck. Her once radiant face is wet with sweat and tears, tears of helpless submission. Fear is no longer part of what she feels as she submits herself to her fate. Looking behind where she lays, towards some large reed baskets that line the far wall, she cannot bring herself to look at her tormentor. Quietly sobbing, she moans at each course movement the Slag makes.

Hyw stands ready, his bow bent towards this evil marauder, but thinking carefully he relaxes his aim. Gripping at the handle of his father's knife, Hyw is ready, but before he can move the Red Raider draws his blade swiftly across the girl's throat, spilling her life's blood. Raising himself in the air by his arms, the Grot is engulfed in his sadistic pleasures.

Seizing the moment with the Grot's body pushed away from the girl, Hyw's shaft is swift and true, but to his horror, its honed edges have over penetrated and its deadly blade is protruding down towards the girl's heart. With her life slowly draining into the dirt, she sees Hyw standing above her. She can also see his blade as it protrudes from the Grot's body pointing towards her own. The Grot is still somehow managing to hold himself above her and he looks down between them. The girl smiles up through the dim light and with all her remaining strength she wraps her arms around the Slag's neck and pulls. The Grot instantly collapses and it is over.

Hyw scans the room for further signs of life, but there is nothing left in the silence and darkness. There is no time for remorse or regret. Māthōg and his Red Raiders will already be returning and he must retrieve arrows for the impending fray. Quickly turning for the door, Hyw senses something. Again the feeling of someone jumping in the shadows. He turns, scanning the darkness, but sees nothing.

'Maybe his young friends pull at life!' Hyw thinks to himself, but he lingers for valuable moments, to make sure there is no sign of life. The fight has stalled and will be lost if Hyw does not pursue Māthōg to the end.

Peering beyond the flapping curtain, Hyw looks towards the woods scanning the shadows beneath the trees, but there is no sign of Māthōg and his henchmen. Sarn is waiting patiently a short distance away and she looks up to where Hyw stands anticipating. She waits as her master loiters precious moments longer in the shadows behind the curtain.

She wonders about her master's hesitation. No danger lurks near and his indecision perplexes her. She raises her head and looks calmly into Hyw's hesitant eyes. Sensing Sarn's composure, he silently slips past the curtain into the stark light of day. Walking back through the devastation of his friend's lives, retrieving his feathered warriors, he tiptoes past death as though it would wake at any moment and seize him, dragging him down into that awful abyss.

"More haste, less speed," Remembering his grandfather's words, it is his mother's warning that breaks into his thoughts.

"Save thy sister Hyw Bach!" His urgency is circumspect and whilst the sister is not his own, that will not temper his fight.

Chapter Eleven

Striding up to his valiant dappled grey mare, Hyw climbs into the saddle. Sarn is ready; she is always ready; ready to carry her master anywhere he bids. Gentle and kind, he is unlike her previous owner who was a brutally, hard, cruel Slag; a heartless marauder who had killed the woman who had raised Sarn from a foal. Since her first owner's sad and brutal death, Sarn had been a witness to too much suffering and the awful pains the stench of death brings, troubles her gentle heart. She longs to be free just like Hyw, but their futures are inseparably connected.

Sarn has witnessed much, even with her new master, but somehow, her new master is different. Her master suffers; she knows and understands some of his pains and she will not live in peace and comfort for a long while yet, if ever but she had sworn with an oath to serve her new master until his or her life is over and only then would she rest; swearing it, to the head of those who follow.

Without a full understanding of those who follow, she sees them and at times, hears and understands those that look on; the Ancient Ones. They had been a constant presence, from the first time Hyw had rescued her in the woods. While still a young foal, Sarn had been instructed at the hands of her mother, about those things pertaining to this life and the next.

"Our kind may see them; other troubled beings, but humankind cannot and only occasionally can they feel their presence." Sarn's mother had told her. Sarn is sure, Hyw cannot see them, or at least she had been until that very morning.

"They are great and terrible spirits of the world beyond this one!" Sarn had been told.

"But do not fear them for they cannot touch thee. They whisper to persuade; their fiery blades cannot burn or cut thee my darling but when the ancient ones whisper, ye do well to listen!"

Throughout her life Sarn had, on occasions, seen those Ancient Ones; they would come and go but they had been a constant presence since her rescue. She sees them as Guardians and only the most beautiful of these had ever whispered to her.

"Let us covenant together my child!" Her words were sweet as the taste of the spring grass but had Sarn known of the terrible sights she would witness she might not have sworn her oath.

"Swear it; my son's life is in thy hands!" This Ancient One was somehow different to the others. A beautiful maiden of the celestial realms, with calm dark eyes that burned with a love and fire Sarn, had not seen before in any other creature. Looking deep into her dark eyes, Sarn could not refuse. Since that time she had witnessed many things to make her regret her oath, but still, she keeps her word.

Sarn had witnessed the Ancient Ones, in the woods, helping Hyw to lift his sister out of the deep crimson waters as he carried her home; they had stood as Sentinels, guarding him and the old man all through the night, with their flaming swords brightly blazing; they had walked silently among those who grieved at the graveside; with tears staining their cheeks they had watched Hyw's onslaught when he fell on the wounded Slag in the woods; they had chased the wolves off into the night, following after her master's feathered warrior and they had lined the woods and barred the way to Hyw's back when the Painted Men of the North had hunted him as the boar.

But it was that one beautiful guardian who had guided Sarn through the darkness of the trees when Hyw had slipped inside himself; she and she alone had held her bridle, watching her gentle footfall along the darkest trails of the night; it was she who had whispered to Sarn of the urgency of their cause and that morning her master had been woken by that one beautiful, but sad-eyed sentinel. She had spoken to him as humans speak, with Hyw recognising the Sentinel's voice.

Thoughts continue to trouble Sarn. The Ancient Ones of the night's long dark trail have all disappeared into the woods, following Māthōg and the Red Raiders. Only the most beautiful of all the Sentinels remain. She entered the croft just ahead of Hyw but Sarn has not seen her since, and without her to guide them, Sarn is concerned for their lives. What scene of devastation lies beyond the curtained doorway, Sarn cannot tell, but her heart is heavy and quietly troubled. Her master is ready and he gently coaxes her along the trail, following after Māthōg without the ever-present gaze of the Sentinels.

Again gently encouraging Sarn, she is hesitant. The fury of Hyw's attack has subsided and he is cautious, aware of everything around him. Sarn picks her way through the dead at her feet, but Hyw seems strangely unaware of their presence. Increasingly worried that Hyw is slipping back inside himself, she walks on, but then he leans forward, patting her on the neck.

"Well done Sarn bach!" Sarn whinnies and shakes her head in appreciation.

On entering the woods and beneath the trees, Sarn's troubles increase and Hyw senses her hesitation.

"Come, my friend," Hyw coaxes with a whisper and taps at her sides with his heels, but without the Ancient Ones, Sarn is uncertain. She looks anxiously around her for signs of their presence, but she can see nothing. They push on into the dim light beneath the trees. The green of spring is everywhere, with buds beginning to sprout on the trees, but Hyw keeps their footfall amid the evergreens, which offer them the greatest cover from the marauder's eyes and blades.

The woods thin slightly as a bright sun climbs higher in the sky. Both Sarn and Hyw look towards the borders of the woods, from beyond which they can hear shouts and the panicked cries of the Scotti. Things had not gone to plan. Māthōg's voice can be heard booming over the others and he shouts orders, cursing at his men. Somewhere in the pastures beyond the trees, the Red Raiders frantically rally themselves, continuously looking up into the shadows beneath the trees.

Sarn is tired from the night's ride, her legs are heavy, exhausted from the charge. Fearful of her master's plans they edge closer to the borders of the woods. They had taken their enemy by surprise, but they are not yet ready for another attack and the watching Sentinels have abandoned their cause. Sarn stops beneath a large group of firs, where juniper and yew cover the ground at the edge of the wood. Silence rains through the trees. Sarn wonders if the Red Raiders had given up thoughts of another attack, but Hyw knows better.

Looking out into the light, suddenly they see the silhouette of horsemen riding cautiously along the borders of the wood, but none dare to enter. They have the sun behind their attack and Hyw realises his disadvantage, so he remains motionless on Sarn's back as she stands bold, like a storm cloud. Deep in the shadows, Hyw knows Māthōg's men will not find his hiding place unless they ride right into it, but Sarn nonetheless slowly retreats deeper into the bushes.

The unmistakable silhouette of Māthōg breaks into their view causing a tremble to run through Sarn as Hyw's blood runs cold. Sat astride his wounded stead, he sits like some wretched demon of Annwn with the stench of death pervading all around him. Even his men keep their distance.

The powerful beast on which he sits is lame from the wound on its hindquarters and through the dim light, Hyw can see blood still flowing from where the broken shaft of his arrow protrudes from the top of the horse's back.

His stallion is grey like Sarn, if slightly darker, with what looks like a stain of brown over the top of its legs and a few small brown poker dots spread over the horse's rear getting larger the further back they spread. Even though the beast is lame, the animal holds itself well and somehow appears regal, stately even.

Looking closer, Hyw sees Māthōg's bearded face. It is as though he is looking straight into Hyw and he longs to bend his bow towards him, but the branches of the trees are too thick and at the distance, even Hyw could not be sure of his aim. Māthōg continues to stare into the shadows. Hyw can make out the scar running down his face and over his blind eye, which is blackened and dead. His eyes follow the line of the scar as it runs down Māthōg's face, disappearing into his beard.

Something jumps inside him as his eyes catch sight of his father's sword in Māthōg's hand. His anger builds and it is all he can do to prevent himself from kicking at Sarn's sides and being done with his life. Hyw looks closer to where he can see a second sword sheathed on the rump of Māthōg's beast.

Bringing his horse to a halt at the end of the path into the woods, Māthōg pauses for a few moments then kicks at his horse's sides. The animal jumps and whinnies, stumbling backwards and then with a succession of kicks from Māthōg, his sharp spurs puncturing the horse's flesh; the beast walks on, but it stops before it reaches the first tree.

"Useless Old Nag!" Māthōg shouts out kicking at the horse's sides again.

Regret at launching that first ill-tempered arrow into the air runs through him.

'Can he not see his horse's pain and fear? Is his mind that blind to all, but his own evil intents?' With fear dancing through the stricken animal, it stubbles forward again.

Sarn stands ready. Hyw sits astride his beast of burden, ready. The vision of his mother's dying smile burns deep in Hyw's mind and then the awful scene of his sister's broken body lying motionless in the crimson waters of the stream's endless flow runs through him. The time is right.

Māthōg's horse stumbles on the roots of the first tree, but from behind its thick trunk, the ghostly figure of a sentinel steps out in front of the stammering beast. Sarn looks quickly up and down the hedge of the woods and from every bush and tree along the edge of the wood, slowly and quietly the terrible forms of the guarding Sentinels step from the shadows with flaming swords held aloft in their clenched fists.

Unseen blades brightly blaze in the face of Māthōg and his men as they sit astride their steeds, but their horses are not blind and some rear up on seeing such an enemy with others squealing and bucking. One runs off into the depths of the meadow with its rider struggling to control his panicked beast.

Māthōg's horse rears and whinnies in unison with those of his men. He kicks and curses wildly at his stammering stallion, but the Ancient Ones have firmly barred the way. The horse spins wildly around, unable to bear the pain of its wounds with the weight of Māthōg's full grip churning the bit in its mouth and it snorts and bellows with fear flashing in its eyes.

Hyw can watch anymore and he bends his bow as he is tempted to try his aim and end the gentle beasts suffering, but Sarn is less certain. They can not charge down all his men and Hyw's quiver is dangerously low.

Māthōg manages to control his beast and from deep in the shadows Hyw calms his aim.

"Tha Gods are not with us!" Māthōg bellows to his men.

"But soon the whelp will boi moin!" Raising the great blade, high into the air, he calls out to the watching woods.

"Thoi family's blood hus warmed my bloide and soon, very soon… thoi blood will be upon its steel!" Hyw knows Māthōg is goading him to step out into the open, but Hyw remains safe in the shadows.

Turning his horse down the hill Māthōg rides out of Hyw's sight and with his tacit permission his men are only too willing to follow. Hidden beyond the brow in the pasture below, Hyw can still hear Māthōg's company. Curiosity gets the better of him and Hyw coaxes Sarn out to the furthermost shadows of the trees and he sits there watching Māthōg changing his wounded horse for another.

There is a coral of fresh horses, which two of Māthōg's men and a young boy have kept during the attack. Māthōg is cursing and swearing, with some of his men helping him while others, the most discerning of his group, slope off to avoid his wrath.

Nudging Sarn further and further out of the tree line, Hyw sits watching the spectacle, but he isn't wasting his time. He can count nine men including Māthōg; two are tending wounds, one, a young lad, is holding the stricken horse by its reins, and three more are keeping a careful watch of the tree line, and Hyw. Māthōg ignores their concerns and continues cursing at the poor animal as he scolds and brutalises it, slapping and punching out at the sad beast. The lad holding onto the horse struggles as it rears up wildly.

"Hold him still or thoi wilt suffer the same!" Māthōg barks while trying to get his saddle off the poor animal.

"Useless trash of a nag!" Māthōg growls. Hyw can barely stand to watch and rage builds inside him as he struggles with his desire to charge down the hill. Even Sarn's heart breaks for the poor animal as Māthōg mounts his new stead.

"Hold that useless cripple still!" Māthōg calls out to the lad. Leaning down he grabs at the broken shaft sticking out of the horse's hindquarters and without a thought for the beast, he pulls at the blade and it comes clean out.

The reaction is instant; Hyw shatters the air with a piercing cry, which echoes with the crippled horse's squeals as their attack begins. The wounded horse bucks and rears, with the youth unable to hold it any longer, but the thunder of Sarn's charge is heard in every frightened heart. Hyw continues to cry as Sarn swiftly careers downhill.

Māthōg's discarded stallion races off across the field as he swipes at the horse with his sword, but its sharp steel misses its mark. Hyw rampages downhill towards the Red Raiders with his bow bent to only one end: Māthōg. His cries wake Sarn's courage and she gallops full steam towards that one hopeless end. Riding to certain death, Hyw steels himself, but in his speed and fury, he would gain his revenge.

Māthōg has new legs beneath him and a good head start and is the first to leave the field, knowing the strength of Hyw's arm and the aim of his bow is set for him alone. His men quickly follow him, all, but the young lad who is desperately trying to control his own steed so he can gain his mount.

By the time he is on his horse, the lad is the only one left on the field and Hyw's aim turns to him. The boy is young, even for Māthōg's marauders. With Hyw's bow bent towards him, the lad is petrified, but Hyw seems to have lost all stomach for the kill, having spilt too much blood already. The death of this good-for-nothing wretch would gain him little.

Frozen in the panic of his fear he loses all control of himself. Trembling, all he can do is stare straight down the shaft of Hyw's blade.

Sarn tempers her charge as they draw closer, but Hyw's bow is still bent towards the lad's heart. Sarn comes to a halt and turns slightly so that her master can aim without hindrance. Staring deep into the young man's eyes, Hyw cannot release his hungry hawk. One day he may live to regret his inaction and the words of the old shepherd ring in his ears.

"Give 'em nothing." But still, Hyw cannot despatch the young Grot. On seeing Hyw's hesitation, the youth quickly scarpers and Hyw lowers his aim. Scanning the distant ridge for a sign of Māthōg's return, Hyw watches. But Māthōg's men will not be so easy to persuade back into battle; even against just one man.

Slowly making his way to the ridge, Hyw follows their track for only enough time to make sure he is safe. They have cut a swathe through the undergrowth that even a blind man could follow, but although they have left in a hurry Māthōg will soon rally his Blood Red Crows.

His blood boiling within him, Hyw wants to follow after Māthōg, but regaining his full senses, he knows Māthōg will set guards to wait in ambush. The time would come, but expedience drags him back and there is another life weighing heavy on his mind.

The wounded stallion is standing up at the top end of the field, close to where Hyw had begun his charge and Sarn slowly saunters back up the hill to where it stands. Hyw tries to steer Sarn past the stricken beast, but Sarn is stubborn and insists. Hyw is in no mood to argue and lets Sarn guide him. As they draw alongside the stallion, Hyw dismounts.

The horse is wary at first but, employing his natural ways with the animal, he is soon running his hands over its side and back. Talking calmly and quietly to the beast, he spends time stroking and patting its head. Working his hand down its neck and across its back, he examines the wound which is still flowing freely and in the chase, the animal has lost a lot of blood.

Sarn takes her turn and nuzzles up to the stallion until their heads meet, noses first and then rubbing their heads together they turn until they are almost side-by-side.

The wound is deep and Hyw looks up at Sarn, shaking his head.

"Sorry my old friend, but we can't waste time here, it's too deep…it is a shame to behold, for he was a fine animal!" Sarn looks at Hyw as though she has understood every word and she pulls away as Hyw reaches for her reins. Reaching up again, Hyw manages to catch hold, but he knows his quiet friend is still unhappy.

"Well, my friend…if he is strong enough to follow, I'll see what can be done, but we must return to the croft!" Sarn seems to relax and shakes her head as Hyw climbs on her back. She turns toward the stallion and somehow it knows. Climbing to the brow of the hill they pass under the first trees of the wood, followed by the crippled stallion.

Both Hyw and Sarn are cautious as their friend's camp comes into view. In the foray of their attack, Hyw knows he will have missed many things. Scanning the ground, he looks for the body of his young friend, the second daughter but cannot find her body. Despite his mother's warning, he had arrived too late and old feelings of guilt begin to trouble him.

Something leads Sarn towards the croft. She had seen the ghostly, but beautiful guardian, enter but had not seen her since. Nothing is moving; only a meandering thin wispy trail of smoke from a dying fire raises itself slowly up into the morning. The girl is nowhere to be seen. On reaching the curtained doorway, Hyw dismounts and steps cautiously towards the croft.

Raising his bow with an arrow firmly in place, he parts the curtain and steps into Annwn. The same feeling of someone jumping in the darkness touches his senses and he raises his aim, quickly bending his bow. Something jumps again, he can hear and see nothing, but someone's fear quickens inside him. Sián again jumps in the shadows of his memories and Hyw's heart is torn in two.

Checking the room thoroughly, he checks it again. The far wall is stacked high with rush-work baskets and furniture, which casts strange shapes and silhouettes in the shadows on the wall. Moving slowly through the room, he can almost feel something or someone breathing, but it is difficult to discern between his memories and reality.

'Maybe a Grot is hiding, wounded in the shadows and I have missed him.' Hyw keeps his bow bent as he checks each nook and alcove.

Eventually, he reaches the far wall where the baskets are stacked and he gently pulls at the first pile. They fall to the floor with a crash.

'There it is again!' He feels the same indiscernible tremor. Seeing all the room except for the small space beyond the last pile of baskets, Hyw steps carefully forward and hooks the baskets with the end of his bow. Standing back he swiftly brings his bow to bear and waits for the crash. Hidden in the shadows, someone is crouching behind the baskets and as they crash to the floor Hyw is ready for them. A tremor of fear almost leaps inside him and Hyw is about to despatch the last Grot when he catches the flash of fear in the young girl's eyes.

Memories of the bright young girl, full of life, who persuaded her father to feed him that first morning, splash onto his mind. Looking out and up to where Hyw stands with his bow bent towards her. It is as though the blade of his arrow were piercing his own heart as he thinks about what she must have witnessed.

'What must she think of me?' He had felt her jump in the darkness as her sister bled to death in front of her and she had eventually witnessed the blade of Hyw's swift arrow piercing her sister's heart.

Standing Hyw is unable to move for a long time; knowing the emptiness her grief will bring to her. Seeing all her terror, all her pain, his heart breaks for her loss and he is overwhelmed. Easing the grip on the string of his bow, Hyw lowers his aim while sinking to his knees. Tears are brimming in his eyes and he bows his head in shame. Unable to speak; he cannot find the words he needs. The girl is trembling in the corner, curled up like a baby with her arms hugging her knees into her chest. She is rocking back and forth, but not one tear falls out onto her pale cheeks.

Slowly Hyw raises himself and turns to go, but as he does so he feels the same jump inside him. Looking back at the pathetic sight huddled in the corner; Hyw tries to smile, but then turns again and lifts the curtain, he walks out of the door. There is nothing he can do and yet he feels he must.

Moving around to the far side of the croft Hyw piles all the family's stock of firewood onto the dying light of their morning's fire. Stepping over the bodies of his dead friends, he drags each Slag and Grot to the blaze; throwing their bodies onto its growing inferno. Retrieving as many of his feather warriors as he can, he cleans their shafts and places them one by one back into his quiver.

Finally, returning to the waiting darkness, he finds the young girl still huddled, trembling in the corner. Stepping over the headless body of her mother, Hyw leans over the two bodies in the centre of the room. The Slag is still lying on top of the girl's sister with his arrow pinning them both together.

Taking hold of the Slag he raises him off the girl; the arrow pulling through his torso. Throwing him to one side, Hyw kneels by the girl and takes out his father's blade. Working it around the base of the arrow it cuts clean through, just above where it has penetrated the girl's chest. Throwing the shaft of the blood-stained arrow to one side he realises the arrowhead may come free. Gently he tugs at its stub and the head eases out.

Hyw drags the Slag outside and tosses him into the flames. The bare flesh of the Scotti Slags is turning brown and black as the flames lick out at their hair and clothes. Its sickly sweet smell is turning Hyw's stomach as their hair singes in the fire, but still, he continues, throwing more wood on the flames in the hope the fire will consume them all the quicker.

One by one Hyw gathers his friend's bodies together and lays them out at the far end of the croft, on a small raised piece of ground at the head of the lake. All the men of the family lay at peace, side-by-side on the mound's gentle slope. Hesitating he looks back at the croft and then up at Sarn who has sauntered over to him.

"Sorry old girl, but I must take care of the dead before I can tend to thy newfound friend!" Trying to pluck up the courage to re-enter the croft; Hyw looks back up at Sarn.

"Oh, what's to be done Sarn bach?" Sarn nudges him with her snout pushing him to move and then she gives out a loud whinny while nodding her head.

Through the flapping curtained doorway, Sarn has witnessed some of the devastation but her watch is for that Ancient One. The other sentinels stand like guardians, lining the woods watching and waiting beneath the shadows of the trees. With tears staining their faces they keep their silent vigils.

Hyw returns to the doorway of the croft. Stooping, he picks up the severed head of the girl's mother. Walking back, he places the woman's head next to that of her husband. Returning once more, Hyw hesitates at the doorway and taking a deep breath he raises the curtain. Unable to look at the girl, not knowing what he can do or say, he stoops at her mother's side. Lifting her limp headless corps he carries her body outside.

When he returns he finds the girl kneeling by her sister, stroking her hair, oblivious to his presence. Not wanting to intrude he turns to leave. The girls had been hidden behind the baskets in the croft on Māthōg's attack. When the two Slags entered, the girls hiding place was secure. The two Slags had raged at the girl's mother, but still, their lives were secure. One of the two Slags suspected there were more females and he began a search.

Only when her sister was certain their hiding place would be found, did she break cover? It was all the interest the two Grots needed to prevent them from finding her sister.

'It is time,' Hyw thinks. Unsure if Māthōg and the Red Raiders will return, but he knows if they do, all their retribution would be piled onto this young girl. Stepping back into the gloom he kneels at the girl's side.

"It is time," He says quietly with no hope of recognition for his words. Bending forward he cradles the dead girl in his arms, her sister gives out a small sound; an ache or a moan; no decipherable word, almost a muffled cry, but Hyw continues, carefully scooping her sister from the straw and dirt. Standing, he carries her out into the light. Expecting her sister to follow, he looks back, but cannot see her. Laying her sister with her family Hyw returns to the croft and opens the curtain. The girl is still kneeling on the floor, her hands on her knees, turning something over and over, in her fingers. It is his broken arrowhead.

Bending down towards her, Hyw slowly pulls at one of the leather thongs around his neck and Bayr's arrowhead comes free and dangles between them, hanging in the dim light. The girl looks at the tip of the arrow in her hand and then up at the arrowhead around Hyw's neck. Trying to smile; it is a pinched and clouded smile and it fails to light a fire in the girl's eyes but there is a spark of silence between them. Slowly the girl reaches up to where Bayr's arrowhead hangs and she takes hold of it; examining it in her hand. Looking straight into Hyw's eyes only love and anger infests the space between them and their broken lives become one torturous moment in the dim light of the croft. Finally, Hyw tries to speak.

"I know…" Faltering, he cannot bring himself to finish his fruitless words. Breaking down, he can only wrap the girl in his arms. Pulling her to him. She wraps her arms around him as silent tears fall between them. but somehow, something changes and the girl shies away and in her uncertainty Hyw tries again.

"I hunt Māthōg and his Slags. Their blood will wash my pains away or I will die trying!" The girl's face softens slightly, but she remains silent.

Sarn is waiting. The curtain moves and Sarn looks up to where her master appears, walking with his arm around a young woman who, in turn, is cradled in the arms of that one most beautiful of all the Sentinels.

The day grinds slowly on. The girl kneels between her mother and sister, stroking and grooming their hair, but not one tear falls from her eyes. Hyw digs the pit for their graves and then harnesses Sarn and drags several large rocks from the edges of the lake and the clearing, to form the headstones for their funeral barque.

One by one they put her family to rest, but the girl struggles to let her sister go. She moans, lying prostrate next to her, hugging her limp body to her own. Finally, Hyw manages to separate them long enough to place the dead girl in the ground, but the girl only joins her sister in the pit. It is a pitiful sight and it breaks Hyw's heart over and over again, but he has given up asking, why? There are no answers; not in this dark realm.

Placing all her brother's and her father's weapons next to them in the grave, for some reason, the girl retrieves her father's sword and lays it across the headstone. She is caught up in her own painful world and even Hyw seems unable to reach out to her, but gradually she begins to put some order to what remains of her life.

A thought of taking her to the village lights inside him; surely they would take her in when they hear all she has suffered, but Hyw is quietly troubled by a growing determination he can see in the girl.

Before Hyw covers her family over, she goes to the croft and returns with jewellery to adorn her mother and her sister. Watching in silence, Hyw finally lays her loved ones to rest. Smiling awkwardly over to where she is kneeling at the graveside, he remembers his own suffering and he is helpless, feeling somehow responsible.

'I must end this…blood for blood as the law requires,' The thought is set in Hyw's mind and he cannot climb over it.

'I must face Māthōg or I will never be able to live!' The words are in his head and he thinks of his grandfather as his words swell inside him, but turning from his memories, Hyw walks over to his trusted companion.

"Alright, my friend we shall do what we can!" The stallion hobbles over towards Hyw and he examines the wound. It is deep and already closed over. Leading the horse to the water's edge, Hyw looks at the mirror of the lake's surface just as he had done the first time he had knelt at its shores. Watching the sway of the water, he sees his gruesome reflection with the dirt of winter ground on his face and neck. His eyes appear dark and sunken and his hair is greasy and unkempt.

Placing his bow to one side of the stallion, the horse starts to drink as Hyw washes the dirt from his face and body. He strips to the waist and splashes water over him, rubbing and scouring. The stallion nuzzles up to him and he begins the bathe its side close to the wound. Gently massaging his fingers into it, Hyw's fingers wash the injured area. Looking up momentarily the girl has vanished. Hyw's heart jumps and he reaches for his bow. Looking all around, he eventually catches sight of her foraging beneath the trees where he had slept.

Leading the stallion from the lake, the girl walks over with a mixture of various mosses and roots in her hand. Continuing past the two horses and Hyw, she disappears, rummaging in the cart at the far end of the croft. Returning moments later with a mortise and pestle, she places the roots and other herbs into the bowl and sets to work grinding them together.

Sitting quietly on the ground, Sarn walks over to her and sniffs at the mixture. Moving a little closer, the girl pushes the horse away, shooing the air with her fingers, indicating for the horse to leave her alone. Sarn is not put off so easily and she nuzzles at the girl's neck. The horse's warm breath moves slowly through her and she stops working for a moment. Sarn continues to nibble with her soft hairy lips and nudges gently at the girl. In the end, the girl continues mixing her potions, while accepting Sarn's attention.

When the mixture is the right consistency she gets to her feet and works it into the moss. Taking a handful of the potion, she walks over to the animal and begins to pack it into the wound. Even though she is gentle, the stallion jumps and Hyw has to hold its head. Speaking softly and quietly to the great beast. Watching Hyw comforting the beast, the girl recognises his quiet gentle ways.

With the wound packed, she moves down the horse's body stroking and caressing the stallion as she does so. Continuing, she moves to where Hyw has hold of the horse's head and she too scratches and strokes at the stallion's face and mane. Stepping to one side, Hyw gives her the space. Placing her forehead against the horse's face, they seem to find some connection and she cradles his head in her arms hugging the horse between her breasts.

She has a way with the animal and he is intrigued by her knowledge of the old ways, just as Olwyn had taught Bayr. He had often watched his sister as she made poultices for the horses he shod and watching the girl brings back those precious memories. The girl looks at him; there is a certain recognition between them, but Hyw purges it from his mind, knowing he must abandon her at the village.

Stepping back, Sarn moves into Hyw's place and the girl cradles both the horse's heads to her breast. Both seem at ease in her presence and as she caresses them, Sarn looks up at her master with sad eyes.

"It is time!" Hyw says quietly.

"We must leave now!" His words are met with silence, but it is followed by a slow realisation of the constraints her tragic life has brought to her. Walking over to the croft, she disappears inside. After some time she reappears, but only to walk immediately over to the wagon. Hyw watches. She roots and rummages in the back of the cart. Throwing a long old fur cape over her shoulders, she returns with unknown treasures wrapped up in a roll of blankets in one hand and a powerful bow in the other. Placing the bow on the ground, she ties the bundle to the back of Sarn's saddle.

Hyw can see there are no arrows to accompany the bow. His concerns grow, as he tries to fathom her intentions. Disappearing into the croft, she quickly emerges, this time with a handful of arrows. Fixed in her purpose, the expression on her face does not change. Her eyes scan the clearing and she finds what she is looking for; with no noticeable spark of recognition inside her; she picks up her eldest brother's belt with his knife still in its sheath. Unable to buckle the large belt around her waist, she ties it tightly around her and folds the end of the belt over itself and it hangs down the front of her smock.

Beginning to walk back to the horses, the girl collapses to the ground. Sitting amid the devastation of her life, tears still do not fall. Hyw remembers her smile and the feelings that had risen inside him watching her and her sister as they splashed and bathed in the lake. Kneeling, she is unable to gather her life to her and Hyw's heart softens as he reaches out.

Smiling, Hyw stands over her and he reaches down for the belt, which she unties and hands to him. The knife is intricately worked, but it is not to the same standard as his father's blades. Taking it from its sheath, he works the point of the blade through the leather, where he thinks it appropriate. Holding his hand out, he helps to lift her from the ground. Handing her the belt, she takes it and parting her mother's cape, places the belt around her waist.

Hyw notices her waist and he studies her. She is powerfully built in her arms and shoulders, but her waist is thin and she has a firm flat stomach. Not a child, she has the full figure of a woman. Hyw's eyes are intrusive and the girl hesitates slightly and pulls her cape around her. Smiling awkwardly, he knows he has been inappropriate. Trying to shepherd her towards the horses, raising one of his arms to place it across her shoulder, the girl shies away. On approaching the two animals the girl walks back to the grave and Hyw wonders if he will ever lead her away to the safety of the village.

"We must be away. We have tarried too long and…!" Hyw thinks before saying nothing. To mention Māthōg or his Slags would be too much. Kneeling at her family's grave for what could be the last time; the young woman picks up her father's blade from the headstone. Rising from her knees, she returns to where Hyw is waiting. Placing the blade in the empty scabbard on Sarn's saddle, she picks up her brother's bow with three arrows held at its handle and hands the others to Hyw who reluctantly places them in his quiver. Finally, she is ready.

Waiting for Hyw to mount she will follow where he leads, but Hyw indicates to Sarn and holds his hand out to help her up. Moving in to help her, in one smooth swift movement she steps up into the saddle and he again wonders about the qualities her sad continence conceals. Looking up at the girl, he says.

"I am Hyw, the son of Bryn Alwyn, the son of Ywel, the son of Bryn Ywel and the people of the Mountain of Tears!" There is silence between them as the girl looks at Hyw and says nothing.

"Mynddy!" Hyw doesn't know what else to say; if his memory is correct that is what her father had called her. There is a spark of recognition in her eyes. Maybe even a glad thought that he had remembered her name. Her father may have only uttered her name once, but Hyw had remembered it, for some reason.

"Well, I must call thee something and Mynddy is as nice a name as I can think, so until ye canst tell me otherwise," Hyw is toying with her, but it works and the hint of a clouded smile seeps onto her face.

"Mynddy it is then!" Struggling to fill the awkward silence between them, he takes hold of Sarn's bridle and guides her towards the woods with the stallion following behind. Mynddy notches an arrow into the string of her bow, but other than this one movement she rides as if in some stupor of thought as she slowly sinks back inside herself.

Chapter Eleven

The journey back to the village is slow. Mynddy still does not speak, but her silence is choked by the incessant cries of the circling rooks above the woods as the sluggish procession wends its way, down from the hills and into the valley below. Hyw walks, leading Sarn as the stallion saunters along behind them. They saunter through a patchwork of woods and fields, fallow pastures and forest glades, eventually reaching the river. They follow its banks by its swirling spring flow; looking for a place they can ford.

Sitting high on Sarn's back Mynddy's face is devoid of any discernable emotion; her eyes are blank and her face is stained with death. The light behind her eyes is slowly fading as shadows of her life gather around her.

"We must see if the people in the village will take thee!" Hyw says, without a flicker of recognition from Mynddy.

"I know the people there!" It is only half a lie, but he utters the words in the vain hope of calming any concerns the girl may have.

Sarn is quiet and ambles along the path with her only cares riding on her back and walking at her side. The stallion hobbles along watched over by both Hyw and Sarn. It sometimes lags, but the lonely procession stops to wait as Hyw wonders about the strange menagerie of broken souls following after him.

The afternoon becomes dull, as the bright skies give way to deep dark blankets of clouds that shroud the hills and valley. A steady breeze breaks out, ruffling at Mynddy's hair and the horse's manes. Dancing winds begin to ripple on the water and spray from its waterfalls is carried away on the breath of the day. A storm is brewing somewhere unseen beyond the mountains and it will soon be upon them.

Hyw looks out over the river to where he knows the villager's crofts are hidden in the tree line. The only sign of their presence is ribboning traces of smoke from their chimneys, buffeted by the wind. Looking upstream, he can see the Roman's Way and the bridge they built to span the river's wild waters, but Hyw will not tread above its arches and Sarn will not walk over its dry and solid track.

Reaching a suitable place in the river, he looks up at Mynddy, but nothing stirs inside her. Hesitating slightly, she jumps, as Hyw climbs up behind her. The warmth radiating from Mynddy's body seeps through him. It is a snug feeling; an old feeling, a feeling of somehow belonging and the sensation evokes something deep inside him and he wonders if Mynddy feels the same.

Whether Mynddy feels the same or not, she hasn't the mind to tell, but his presence seems to thaw into her. Quickly chasing the thought from his mind; he knows he cannot take her with him.

Gently kicking at Sarn's sides, she climbs down into the stream's fast flow. Hesitating again, he places his arms on either side of Mynddy's waist, taking hold of the reins. Sarn kicks and splashes as she wades through the river's cold, refreshing waters. She stumbles slightly on the rough rocks and as she does so, Hyw clasps his arms firmly around

Mynddy to steady her and he feels a tremble inside her body, but she is safe.

The Stallion follows in Sarn's wake and as they climb out onto the far side of the river the crofts of the village come into view. Looking to where he had first encountered the young man and his family, their croft is not yet in sight, but travelling a little further up the field, Hyw can see almost up to its door.

The people of the village have already seen the dishevelled company crossing the river. Sarn walks through the lower meadows as the crofters come out onto the track and stand at their gateways. Some scurry back and forth, but mostly they just watch and wait. The young man, who had confronted Hyw, on his first visit, is walking through the wicker gate of his croft. His bow is held in his hand, but he doesn't notch an arrow into place. Reaching the track, he leans against the staff of his bow with a perplexed look chiselled into his face.

The young man half-smiles as he wraps his arms around the top of his Yew staff. Hyw manages to smile back, but then his attention is drawn to the doorway of the croft, where the man's wife is struggling with their daughter who is frantic to join her father on the path. The battle is lost and the child runs to the wicker gate with her mother running after her. A warm smile radiates from the child's face from beneath her bonnet of bright red hair and a broad smile spreads across Hyw's face in return.

Stepping slowly out of the saddle, Hyw climbs down and stands in front of the young man, resting his own bow with its tip touching the ground between them.

The young man recognises the girl. Her family had moved from the east two seasons ago, but they had kept themselves to themselves. They were basket makers and Thatcher's, so far as he knew.

"The girl needs a place to stay. Her family…!" Hyw doesn't continue as he rearranges the thoughts and words in his head. The young man can see the devastation of her life, but although his heart is breaking for her, he does not speak. Hyw tries again.

"Her name is Mynddy; at least I think that is what she is called. Her tongue has been taken from her with the ..." Again Hyw thinks about what he is about to say and his words fall silent in the wake of greater feelings.

The young man can only guess at the pains Mynddy has suffered, but still, the fear he has for his family and friends will not free his mind. He looks out across the valley, over the river to the distant woods where Hyw and the girl have just ridden and Hyw follows the track of his eyes. There is a slow silence between them and Hyw watches the black specks of Bare-Faced-Crows circling above their distant nests. The young man interrupts the disquiet between them.

"They have been crying after the dead since the dawn!" His words are almost matter-of-fact and spoken to Hyw in a familiar way, almost as though they are neighbours who have both been kept awake by their incessant cries. His words slowly seep through him and their meanings return to haunt him. Looking up at Mynddy, who has shown no feeling or recognition or even understanding, his heart is torn again. Nodding at Hyw, he beckons with his head for him to move closer. They walk a little further up the path and find a space where they can speak quietly together.

Hyw looks up to the gateway of the man's croft, where his beautiful young wife struggles once again to contain their child inside the gate. Her struggle pauses and she half-smiles at him, but then goes back to her fight. The strange-looking child seems largely built and is strong for her age. She is twisting and wriggling, desperate to break out and stand with her father.

"Annon too, Annon too!" She calls out. Hyw looks across at her and the child momentarily stops her thrashing to smile and she points sideways up at him.

"Take her in woman. Keep her indoors!" The young man calls out, then, turning back to Hyw he says,

"We cannot take the girl in, I'm sorry," Hyw looks up at him in some surprise as the man continues.

"Māthōg and his men let us be…The Painted Men of the North give us little protection; they are interested only in our tribute. I dare not take her in if Māthōg has set his mind against her…his anger will be vent on us!" Hyw pauses, thinking quickly to himself.

A small crowd of villagers has gathered around where Sarn stands with Mynddy still sitting silently on her back. She seems to gaze back to where her broken home lies beyond the trees, but still, her countenance does not change.

The young man goes to speak, but Hyw has already turned back towards Mynddy and the man's words chase after him.

"Ye must understand; Māthōg…" His words fall silent as he realises the others are listening. Hyw marches straight up to Sarn's side. There is a certain purpose and determination in the way he strides back towards his faithful companion. All his intentions are fixed on Mynddy. Raising his arms, he beckons for her to dismount. Mynddy does not react. Hyw nudges at one of her legs, but still nothing. He nudges harder and slowly Mynddy seems to wake her senses looking down to where he stands with his arms raised towards her. Beckoning again, he shakes his arms, but nothing moves her. Suddenly he reaches up, grabs at Mynddy's waist and pulls her from the horse.

The moment Mynddy's feet touch the ground, Hyw turns, unties her belongings from Sarn's saddle and hands them quickly to her, but she fails to take hold of them and they fall to the ground. Climbing into the saddle, Hyw kicks at his horse's sides. Sarn seems to hesitate slightly but then begins to walk off up the trail, followed by the hobbling stallion. Mynddy stands in stunned silence with her bow in her hand and the bundle still rolling away from her. The young man's temper rises.

"I said she couldn't stay!" Hyw's eyes are fixed firmly on the trail as Sarn brushes past him. With his heartbreaking inside him, a confusion of thoughts quickly runs through Hyw's head. He remembers his mother's words.

"Save thy sister Hyw bach, save thy sister!"

'Why did she wake me…what is the girl to me…who is this broken soul I have rescued?' Hyw thinks of his sister's tormentors as a Waking Vision of his chase through the woods flickers in his mind. Her fall from the Grots steed flashes inside him, but his vision quickly changes as he peers into the frightened darkness through Sián's frightened eyes at Enydd's awful destruction. Sián's broken heart cries inside his own.

The vision flashes again and a different picture is etched on Hyw's mind as he witnesses Mynddy's pain that day. He sees and feels everything. How her mother had hidden the two girls behind the rush-work baskets and withstood the attack of Māthōg's evil assassins alone. Watching, his heart breaks as she gives her life to save her daughters. Remembering the sacrifice his mother made for her children and through the eyes of the child within him, he stares back across the clearing, all those years ago, to where the light in his mother's eyes fades before him, his heart breaking as his vision fades.

Sarn can feel the torment of her master rippling through her and she slows. A host of ghostly hands grip the bridle and bit in her mouth and she is forbidden to take another step.

Everything seems to happen at once. The battle of wills at the wicker gate has failed and the child runs towards her father. Sarn stops, and the young man turns, trying to grab at Sarn's reins, but his daughter has found her hero and she holds him fast. Life seems to spark inside Mynddy and taking two strides across the track she bends picking up the bundle. Then leaping forward, she pulls at the stallion's mane and somehow propels herself up onto its back. She lies over the horse at first, but then hooks one leg over its back and pulls herself up into place.

The stallion is badly lame, but as Mynddy kicks, at its sides, the great horse seems to find strength, and Mynddy is soon following Hyw up the trail. Behind where she rides there is another battle of wills taking place.

"Rhyannon!" The young man calls after his daughter, who has broken free from his grip. The child runs up the track followed closely by her father. "Annon too" She cries. Her father grabs her hand as her arms wrap around a young tree at the side of the path.

"Rhyannon…come now!" His words are sharp as he tugs at the child, scolding her, only with his tongue, but he pauses while looking up the trail to where Mynddy has made it to Hyw's side

"Annon come now!" The child's words are almost lost in a confusion of differing thoughts. Hyw's face is stained with tears as he turns to look at Mynddy.

"Ye cannot come where I ride!" Mynddy only looks to the trail that leads on and up through the trees. The stallion comes to a halt next to Sarn, who is still held fast by a ghostly throng, and Sarn cannot be coaxed to walk on. Looking at the crippled stallion and then up at Mynddy, without saying a word he holds his arm out. Mynddy slides across onto Sarn's back and settles herself there, tying her bundle back to the saddle as Sarn finally walks on. Something has woken Mynddy's senses and notching an arrow into the string of her brother's bow, she is ready.

They follow the small tributary of the river up through the valley, listening to the tune of wild waters. The horses stop to drink as the evening draws near. They emerge from the woods at the head of the three valleys and can see the storm clouds gathering above them; its winds howl through the trees and between the mountains.

Two of Geddyn's men are guarding the way and Hyw climbs down, walking over to talk to them. He tells them of all that has taken place and both look up at the blank expression on Mynddy's face.

"Māthōg rode east, but will circle back around before the day is done!" Hyw says. The two warriors appear to organise themselves, planning to ride north to inform their master. The older warrior looks away from Mynddy and talks quietly to Hyw.

"An' wit art ye to do then Hyw? Ye canna ride after Māthōg with the wee lassie an' a crippled horse?" There is some sense in what the warrior is saying.

"Let us take care o'her for thee and we can tak the horse tee," The warrior's words are not spoken with compassion and Mynddy becomes uneasy listening to the conversation. The older of the two warriors looks her up and down; his eyes burning into her.

"I thank thee, but I must take her west…to her family!" Another lie, but his mind is set and as he climbs back up behind where Mynddy sits the warrior side-smiles up at him.

"Ah, I can see now, that thine own eye is on the girl…it is a pity, she is a fine-looking Lassie!" Without speaking, Hyw nudges at Sarn's sides and she walks on. The warrior calls after him.

"What about tha Stallion?" But the stallion is close behind and the silent company continue to walk beneath the gathering clouds as the two warriors sidle away, watched closely by Hyw.

Thoughts of his grandfather's brother seep into his mind and echoing back through time, and Ywel's words sound in his ears.

"He too has dreams and visions…He has seen thee in his dreams, Hyw bach!"

'I have delayed my journey too long!' Hyw thinks to himself.

The storm breaks as they reach Hyw's winter quarters. Helping Mynddy down, she settles on his bed, sitting with her back against the cold stone wall, still wrapped up in her fur cape with the small bundle gathered to her.

Hyw busies himself with Sarn and the stallion, feeding and tending to their needs. The space he had built for Sarn is not ideal for both animals, but they seem at home together. Checking the stallion's wound, he redresses it the best he can. The poisons from his blade are starting to seep from the cut and he is unsure if it will heal, but Mynddy had tended it well. Before leaving Hyw pets and strokes at Sarn's back and head, all the time telling her how well she has done on the day's long and troublesome trail.

The rain pours down on the small shelter, but its roof is secure and all are safe inside. Mynddy continues to sit with her back against the stone wall. She hugs her knees up to her chest and rests her head on top of them, rocking gently back and forth. Placing his saddle at the head of the bed, Hyw does not sit down, seeing Mynddy's hesitation. Searching through the bags and bundles for extra bedding, he finds an old blanket. Gathering some food, he offers it to Mynddy, but again she shies away from him.

"Ye made a fine poultice for the animal's wound!" Hyw's words are intended to raise Mynddy's spirits as he searches for inspiration, but Mynddy remains silent. Reaching back, he gathers his father's wolfskin coat in his arms, then moving forward he holds it out towards Mynddy. With no discernable recognition of his offer, he steps in front of her and places it over her shoulders, closing it around her cape.

Raking at the dead ashes in the grate, Hyw crouches and gently blows until he coaxes life back into its cinders. It brings warmth and some light to the shelter and Mynddy seems to settle slightly.

The redbreast flits in through a gap and perches in front of Hyw above the fire. It is followed by its young family seeking shelter from the storm. Hyw stoops and rummages in one of the sacks and the redbreast flutters over onto Sarn's back, followed, one by one, by its family. Mynddy watches the family of birds but does not move. Standing back, Hyw holds out his hand with some crushed oats and nuts in it. Mynddy's eyes follow his movements. The redbreast is tempted for a moment but then holds back. He places the food on the ledge above the fire and the birds wait for him to move away before taking their feast.

Behind the wall where Mynddy sits, Sarn and the stallion munch on the last of their food. Sarn raises her head and peers over the wall, looking down at Mynddy. Turning her head up to where the grey mare is standing, Sarn's warm breath gently caresses Mynddy's cold face as she reaches to pet the horse. The stallion follows Sarn, lifting its head above the wall and both horses lean down towards Mynddy.

Hyw watches in silence as Sarn desperately tries to reach out to Mynddy's broken heart. There is a recognition between them, Hyw had seen it in the clearing after the attack and he wonders about Sarn's limited understanding, but Mynddy's hand lowers and she sinks back inside herself. The family of redbreasts flit about. One perches in a hole in the wall near where Mynddy sits. Her eyes follow where the bird flies. It cocks its head to one side and then to the other as it stares back at the stranger in their midst. Hyw continues to watch as the light in Mynddy's eyes glows brighter.

The rain still beats down outside and Hyw plugs every gap in the shelter's walls and doorway. He rests Mynddy's bow next to his and then leans her father's sword against the wall, next to her. First, he squats and then sits on a sack of crushed oats close to the fire. Staring across into Mynddy's expressionless face he smiles, but hopes of a smile in return are vain.

"We must go to see my uncle…he will know what to do!" Hyw says. His words are spoken out loud, but Mynddy shows no sign of recognition.

"Yes, he will know what to do!" Hyw looks up at Sarn and the stallion who appear to be the only ones paying his words any attention. The redbreast flits back to the ledge above the fire and Mynddy's eyes follow its fleeting movements as Hyw continues to talk.

"He lives on an island in the seas beyond the mountains!" Once Hyw starts he cannot stop his words. The fight of the day slowly drains from him as he begins to ache at every move, but talking seems to help somehow; ordering his thoughts and he puts some semblance of order back into his life. He talks of an old man whom he has never spoken to and whom he has only ever seen for a fleeting moment. He talks of a journey into the setting sun and of a holy man who has devoted his life to God. Hyw's thoughts stall as he thinks of the Gods, but he steps over his thoughts as he imagines the trail over the mountains.

Mynddy shivers under her fur wraps and Hyw places more wood on the fire. A flash of lightning suddenly lights up the shelter through the curtained doorway as the accompanying crack of thunder seems to shatter a tree somewhere just beyond the shelter's flimsy walls. Mynddy shivers uncontrollably. Hyw grabs the blanket as he moves to sit next to her. With the blanket over his shoulders, he sits, leaning with his back against the wall and holding his arm up, Mynddy tentatively leans into his side. Hyw pulls her in towards him and then pulls the covers over them. Mynddy continues to shake and shiver and he pulls her closer to his side. After what seems an age, the warmth of his body thaws into her and eventually, she falls asleep. Continuing to try and make her comfortable, she curls up awkwardly at his side. Leaning further over she is almost lying in his lap. Making sure the furs are around them, he cradles her head, wondering how he could ever have thought to leave her in the village.

Sometime in the early hours of the morning, Mynddy's nightmares begin. She jumps under Hyw's arm and moans in agony as she watches her mother and sister struggle, but in her tormented sleep Mynddy wraps an arm around Hyw, holding onto him. She jumps and moans again, they are the first sounds Hyw has heard her make, but in all her restless nightmares she does not utter a single word.

Chapter Twelve

Hyw stirs slightly then wakes with a start as his senses come to. The redbreast is singing its heart out, somewhere just beyond the shelter's walls. The horses snort and breathe in the comfort of their stable. A thin ribbon of smoke drifts up from the fire where what looks like Mynddy's dress is smouldering on the small mound of ashes, but Mynddy is gone.

Sunlight is struggling in through the door as Hyw rolls over onto his knees. Standing up, he looks across towards the two horses. Mynddy is standing quietly in front of them, cradling both their heads in her arms. She is feeding the stallion some oats and when she has finished, she scratches vigorously at its head, then their sad eyes stare up at her as she gently caresses them.

The sunlight is playing on the floor at the horse's feet where the bundle Mynddy had gathered together the day before is open on the ground. A dress is half unfolded at the centre of the bundle. Mynddy is wearing only a thin white lace petticoat and the morning's sun streams through its material as the two horses nuzzle up to her slim warm body. Hyw is transfixed. She leans slowly into the two animals and kisses the Stallion in the centre of its forehead and then turns her attention to Sarn who snorts and whinnies as Mynddy scratches between her ears.

Stooping slightly; Mynddy steps into the dress at her feet. Pulling it up and over the petticoat, she slips between the two animals. Hyw watches intently as she examines the stallion's wound. Her fingers nimbly work at the animal's side and he can see the wound is badly swollen. Engrossed in her care for the two horses, suddenly something startles her and, turning in an instant, she stares straight at Hyw. Feeling caught out in some way, he smiles up at her, awkwardly. Mynddy still appears to be in a stupor, but there is more colour in her cheeks. She turns back to the horses and Hyw turns towards the door.

Stoking the fire, he kneels to coax some heat from its ashes and the dress is soon consumed by its flames. Walking out, Mynddy is sitting on a rock looking out across the lake. The day is fine and the sun is drying away the night's storms. Small white lazy clouds drift slowly across a blue sky and their shadows ripple and fold, as they glide over the mountains. A hawk cries unseen in the blue forever above them. Mynddy remains silent as Hyw approaches.

"How art thou this morning?" Hyw asks. Mynddy shows no sign of recognition of his words, but he hadn't expected any reply and he changes direction in his thoughts.

"Would ye like some food?" Mynddy seems not to hear. The breeze ruffles at her long hair. It is dull from the dirt and degradation of the previous day's laments, but its rich dark hue still seems to radiate from its flowing gown as it falls over her shoulders and into the centre of her back. The sun warms into the rocks, but the morning's chill still shows on Mynddy's breath. Hyw tries to reach out to her again.

"Art thou cold Mynddy bach?" Knowing there will be no response, Hyw takes her the cape from where she has laid it over the wall of the stable.

He steps up behind her and drapes it loosely over her shoulders. She hesitates, looks up momentarily and then, gazes back out over the lake.

"I must bathe and tend to the horses," Hyw says and he turns to go. Opening the makeshift stable door, the horses saunter out into the day. They follow Hyw down the rocky pathway to the shores of the lake. As they walk, he peers back up to where Mynddy sits. A few days before, all he could think of was Māthōg and his revenge, but his thoughts have turned to the safety of Mynddy.

The stallion is still badly lame and struggles down to the edge of the water. Sarn waits patiently for her new companion and when the horse reaches the lake, Hyw feels to see if the animal has a fever. The horses are content for the moment, each in the other's company and they drink slowly knowing the protection they are under. A few paces from where Hyw is standing a large rock sticks out of the shoreline. Hyw has sat on its surface many times during the winter, but he is content to lean against it, watching Sarn and her new friend.

A sudden joy seems to leap inside him as he breathes in the day with all its sunlight and warmth struggling through the chill of the morning. Hyw cannot imagine where the feeling has come from. Looking back up toward his shelter; Mynddy is lost in a trance as she sits staring out over the valley. Turning back to the stallion, Hyw knows he will not be able to travel for a few days.

Propping his bow against the rock at his side, he watches the shimmering water of the lake as it ripples with its gentle swell lapping at his feet. The air is still and quiet after the night's storms and the reflection of Sarn and the stallion are cast into the mirror of the lake's clear waters.

'Somehow things will work out.' The words reason in his mind, but he is sure of it and a calm feeling comes over him.

A large flat rock lies just above the lake's surface and with a little effort he manages to jump out onto its smooth step. First, he stoops and then he kneels. Cupping his hands together, he drinks then, placing his hands on the rock he leans forward, looking at his reflection as the lake's surface settles like a mirror. His reflection is gaunt. Dipping his hands in the water, he splashes his face and hair. Fingers of cold water stab into him, refreshing every part of his tired and aching body.

Hearing something behind him he turns in an instant. It is Mynddy. Something has woken inside her and she is slowly making her way down to where Hyw bathes. In one hand she is carrying her brother's bow, but there is something small in the palm of her other hand and Hyw cannot quite make it out. Canting his head around, Hyw smiles up at her; even the horses turn their heads to watch as she picks her way down to the edge of the lake.

The dress she has put on is finely made and Hyw wonders again where her people are from. The dress is not the raiment of a basket weaver's daughter. It is gathered around in the front, hugging the shape and line of her breasts, but below its elaborate needlework, it flows freely down almost touching the ground. Under the dress, the petticoat is of intricate lace work and again indicates more than her apparent station in life, but the condition Hyw had seen her family in, did not indicate any stately blood or breeding.

The sun climbs higher in the sky, casting its gentle rays onto the rocks and surface of the lake, but its warmth will not find the depths of its waters for some weeks yet and even then it would be cold.

Mynddy walks over to the rock placing her bow next to Hyw's and then she stands looking vaguely in his direction. The sudden spark of life inside her is fading again and Mynddy stands with no discernable thought inside her. Hyw turns his attention to her.

'What can I do?' He thinks to himself as a procession of thoughts march over him.

'She means little to me…but I cannot abandon her…she is not my responsibility…so why did my mother warn me of her desperate plight? Oh, why did she not wake me sooner? I wish I could see the meaning of my dreams with more clarity?'

"Save thy sister Hyw bach, save thy sister!" Isobel's words break into his thoughts, tearing at his very being.

Turning on the surface of the rock, Hyw smiles up at Mynddy, but she continues to stare past him, showing no sign of recognition. Scooping water up in his hands, he splashes his face; gasping under the water's refreshing bite. Splashing again, Hyw runs his hand quickly through the water; Mynddy seems to jump at the sudden noise and the thrashing of the lake's surface. Splashing again, Mynddy stares down at his hand, with water dripping from his fingertips. Hyw smiles. There is still no recognition on Mynddy's face, but her eyes focus on him. Continuing to smile, something eventually lights up inside her.

Slowly she raises her arm toward him. Holding out her hand, she indicates to the small object in her palm and then throws it out to him. He jumps in surprise as he struggles to catch the block of oily soap. Mynddy nods slightly and then nods again, indicating with her hands for him to dip the block into the water and then rub his face, as though Hyw hasn't seen soap before and she is having to teach him like a child. Playing along, copying her actions, he soaps his face and hair.

Way back in his memories, Hyw can see his mother soaping her face and hair, but the people of Hyw's home had always used oils to wash with. Only occasionally had Bayr used blocks of soap.

Rinsing himself off, Hyw stands and turns towards her. She is sullen and the light in her eyes is fading again. She only seems to show sparks of life, glimpses of who she had been before Māthōg and his men, but after any lucid period, Mynddy quickly sinks back inside herself.

Hyw jumps from the rock, back to the shore. Kneeling next to Mynddy he points to the soap. Pretending to wash his face and he reaches out to her, but she shies away.

"Come now Mynddy!" Hyw's words seem to touch her as she looks into him.

"Mynddy!" Hyw speaks her name and she looks again.

"Mynddy…that is thy name, isn't it?" Mynddy slowly nods her head as a tear drops onto her cheek.

"Ye must wash and look after thy needs!" Hyw has little idea of what exactly he is saying, but he had heard Olwyn saying those same words to his sister. The words are enough and from somewhere deep inside her confused memories, she hears her mother softly talking to her.

Mynddy holds out her hand for Hyw to place the soap in it. She slowly gathers herself together and taking her feet from her sandals, she drops the shoulders of her dress and it slides down her arms. Letting the dress fall to the floor, she steps over it and wades out to the flat rock in the lake.

Hyw can see the cold of the water shivering through her, but Mynddy continues to walk, stepping up onto the rock. The sun blazes once more through the thin petticoat. Hyw tries not to look, to save her modesty, but his eyes are hungry and he looks for the briefest moments and then averts his gaze.

Turning to the horses, closing his eyes, Hyw listens. He can hear the water trickling back into the lake from Mynddy's long hair and he can hear horses slurping at the surface of the lake; he can hear a hound barking in a faraway wood, and as he listens, his life passes slowly by.

Mynddy steps down from the rock into the lake, but instead of walking back to the shore, she makes her way over to the stallion.

"He has a fever!" Hyw says, almost expecting Mynddy to reply, but she just continues towards the animal, cupping her hands under its mouth. "The wound is bad and needs more attention!" Hyw's words seem to fade into the day.

Mynddy steps back into slightly deeper water and she gathers the hem of her petticoat in one hand to prevent it from getting wet. Scooping the water with her other hand, she splashes it up, onto the Stallion's back. The horse stamps with its hoof on the surface of the lake and Mynddy steps forward washing the area of the wound. The great beast jumps, but Mynddy is gentle as she pours more of the freezing water onto the wound. Again and again, she dips her hands back into the water and eventually, a plug of congealed puss and matter works free from the animal's rump. The great beast whinnies and shakes its head, but Mynddy carries on bathing the wound. Doing all she can, Sarn comes over to thank the sad-eyed girl they had rescued.

Watching her every move, Hyw takes the whole scene in as she stands with her petticoat gathered up around her knees with the sun soaking through its dainty materials, and water dripping from its hem. In the numb ache of the water, Mynddy stumbles slightly on the pebbles at her feet. She steps back into deeper water and for a moment Hyw thinks she will fall in, but she manages to regain her balance. The sunlight blazes around her, catching every drop of water that drips from her hair and hands and the hem of her petticoat. The ripples, her movement, reflections, and the splashing of the water, were like a balm spilling across the surface of his mind. Mynddy stands momentarily in a halo of light and Hyw cannot avert his gaze. The reflection of the sun is almost blinding and it strips her naked. Mynddy steps out of the lake and as she does so, the vision fades. It takes Hyw a moment to recover his senses and his words are slow and uncertain.

"I had an idea to find my grandfather's brother... he is someone I can trust and he will know what to do!" Mynddy looks up towards him as she steps inside her dress and pulls it up over the damp petticoat.

"I will take thee wherever ye wish to go... before or after we have found the old man...I do not mind...If it is mine to give, it is thine, unless the sky falls down!" Mynddy gazes across towards him but shows no recognition of his words.

"Dust thou wish me to take thee home Mynddy?" Mynddy breathes in as her sad eyes stare into him and she slowly shakes her head.

"Where dust thou wish to go...with me?" There is no change to the expression on her face.

"We cannot stay here...I fear Māthōg and his men will be looking for us...he will not rest!" Hyw's words stir inside Mynddy, but the thought plays on his mind. Mynddy has dropped her gaze again and he knows he cannot abandon her.

"We shall travel west then...to the sacred isles of the sea, but it will not be easy...Māthōg and his men will hunt us as the boar for what I have done...there is much play between us. We must gather ourselves and prepare for whatever dangers may befall us, but I will watch over thee as my own, until the day we part or unless the sky falls down!" Mynddy's eyes seem to brighten slightly, but Hyw wonders about the wisdom of his words and the oath he makes.

Just as he finishes speaking a voice is carried on the morning's gentle breeze and as it touches his ear a waking dream clutches at his thoughts. Someone takes refuge in the shadows that infest his mind. The voice calls again; whether from this world or the next, he cannot tell, but a frightened child hides in some lost and dark realm.

"Rhyannon!" A long mournful cry breaks into his vision and he is free. The voice calls again.

"Rhyannon!" And he knows his young friend is in danger. Mynddy looks straight into Hyw knowing something troubles him.

"Something is wrong…I must go…thou wilt be safe here and I will return as soon as I can!"

Calling over to Sarn, Hyw turns and picking up his bow he races to his shelter, followed by his faithful companion, but Mynddy is not far behind him and as he emerges from his shelter she is sat astride the stallion with an arrow notched into her brother's bow. Hyw smiles up at her and relents without further thought.

"We cannot take the stallion…Sarn will have to carry us both…Make him as comfortable as ye can!" He says and Mynddy quietly tends to the steed.

"We must avoid Geddyn's men if we can…They will not aid us in our task!" Half talking to himself, he wonders at the task he is taking on, but Rhyannon jumps in the shadows of his waking dreams and he knows he must go.

Riding up and out of the valley, they escape the attention of Geddyn's men and cross over the small stream climbing down towards the Sacred Birch Woods. Sitting high on Sarn's back, Hyw talks quietly to Mynddy as he cradles her in his arms and she is happy to lean back into him, to feel his arms at her side and to rest her head on his shoulder. In the one long and treacherous day, he has spent with her, Hyw has grown accustomed to her presence and he is already protective of her. Pointing his trusted friend in the general direction, Sarn seems to know the path they must tread.

"Rhyannon!" A voice calls out, hidden somewhere in the trees. On hearing the name, Hyw trembles slightly, but then gains his senses. "Rhyannon. A man's voice is coming from somewhere up ahead in a thicket of trees. Suddenly he appears on the path in front of them. He is old and walks with the aid of a staff. A cloak is thrown over his shoulders and he is wrapped up against the chill of the day or probably the previous night. Hyw recognises him as one of the villagers. The crofter stops instantly on seeing Hyw and Mynddy and he is defenceless in front of the Phantom of Annwn.

Riding up to him, the old man seems to forget his fears.

"We have lost Rhyannon!" The old man is out of breath with his fear and his words are quickly spoken. Hyw does not care for the people of the village, but the young girl with the bonnet of fine red hair and bright half-moon eyes warmed Hyw's frozen heart and he could not turn his back on her, despite the suspicions of her people.

"The Druids came; they are desperate people. The Romans have taken their powers… they hide in the cracks of rocks until the danger passes and then they come out by secret ways and prey on the innocence of our people!"

"Enough old man…Rhyannon?" Shouting, he brings the old man swiftly to the point.

"One minute she was there…the next she was gone!" The old man frets on.

"She is so trusting of strangers, but she was not born as thee or me…the Gods have touched her. Gwion, her father, is out searching with some men, but we are precious few!" The man cannot contain his words.

"I fear the worst…Angharydd is beside herself!"

"Enough old man!" Hyw says, looking around him, trying to orientate exactly where he is; they are not far from the village.

"Lead on and we shall follow!" The old man begins to walk but stops and looks back to where Hyw and Mynddy are sitting.

"It will be quicker if I point the way!" The old man points ahead. "Through yonder, trees is the river and thou wilt see the village as ye reach the meadow!"

Hyw knows the way and is impatient to continue with Sarn pushing past the old boy. Continuing along the trail, Hyw and Mynddy can hear the

155

calls of the women and children throughout the surrounding woods; only one name falls from their lips.

"Rhyannon!"

Sarn moves quickly through the meadows and they ride towards the few scattered crofts of the village. An old lady stands comforting Rhyannon's mother. When Angharydd catches sight of Hyw she breaks free from her comforter and rushes to his side. Her beautiful face is raw and contorted from her crying. Hyw can barely make out a word as she sobs at him.

"They have taken my child, they have taken my Rhyannon!" The old lady tells a similar story to the old man's but adds that there were two strangers in the village that day.

"An old Druid and his young apprentice!" Angharydd is inconsolable and prostrates herself on the ground in front of Sarn, begging Hyw to find her child. She lifts herself and rushes to Hyw's side, pulling at his leg, crying and screaming.

"Please, Rhyannon, find Rhyannon!"

Hyw's heart is breaking as he nods his head towards Angharydd, accepting her pleas. Turning to go, the old lady follows Hyw a little way along the path and calls to him

"Wait. They have not told thee all… Māthōg has been seen, his rage is against all who stand in his path. Those who know these things say that he asks after The Phantom!" The old lady's words are whispered circumspectly, but Mynddy trembles at the mention of Māthōg's name.

"Whether it is the Druids or Māthōg and his wolves, I do not know, but I fear exceedingly for the little one!" The old lady turns as if to go but then turns again.

"Mind thy footfall well!" She bows her head as Hyw nods his appreciation for her warnings.

Sarn walks on. The news of Māthōg made little difference in Hyw's mind; greater powers force him forward and the child's destiny and his own are somehow one. Hyw speaks quickly and quietly to Mynddy.

"We must avoid the path, with Māthōg and his men hunting for us!" Hyw reaches his arm around Mynddy and gripping it around her waist he pulls her around him.

Leading Sarn higher up the sides of the valley into the foothills of the mountains, they search the thick woods for what remains of the morning and long into the afternoon. The cries and calls of the crofters can be heard fading in the distance. Progress is slow amid the darkness of the trees, but Hyw is certain they are on the right path and eventually Sarn steps out high above the valley.

They find themselves on the side of a mountain to the south of the hillock where Hyw had camped with Geddyn and his men. Sarn waits. Hyw watches as Mynddy wraps her arms tightly around him. A fire is burning at the heart of the trees on top of the hill and beyond its trees, Hyw can see two guards on horseback talking to the old man at the gate of the croft, but Hyw can see nothing else moving.

There is a distant cry of someone's name and although the words are indiscernible, Hyw knows the voice calls for Rhyannon. A fox barks in the woods and all the creatures of the night wake in the growing darkness. An owl screeches and hoots as it swoops on an unsuspecting vole.

Looking down to where the Sons of Gododdyn prepare for the night, Mynddy tightens her grip on Hyw's waist and takes cover behind his back. She had heard the old warrior at the head of the valley and had felt his eyes upon her. They are a danger to her. Hyw knows and understands Mynddy's concerns, but says nothing. Gently coaxing at Sarn's sides, Hyw senses hesitation in his old friend and Sarn seems reluctant to move.

"What dust thou see then Sarn bach?" He asks, knowing her keen ears and eyes so well. Stepping out of the saddle, Hyw climbs down from her back and scans all around. Walking a little higher up the mountainside, Hyw scans again, but he can see nothing. Looking back at Sarn, who is following him up the steep sides of the mountain; she stops momentarily, looks, listens, with her ears pricking up and then continues to follow her master.

Hyw climbs an outcrop of rocks. Jumping from one rock to another to gain a better view, and pausing to look. The sun has dropped behind the mountains, but it is casting its warm glow into distant clouds, which drip its glowing honey onto the mountaintops. Hyw struggles to take in every disappearing detail around him and he searches through his waking visions for a sign. There is nothing. The sky is clear and one by one the stars appear above them.

Again Hyw looks back at Sarn with Mynddy sitting silently on her back. The horse is looking across the mountainside to further peaks above a long lake. Hyw's eyes strain in the dimming light, but as the night grows something flickers in Hyw's mind. Turning his gaze toward Geddyn's campfire, a strange feeling surrounds him as his mind flickers with some hidden firelight, but it is not that of Geddyn's fire.

"Where art thou Rhyannon?" Hyw whispers to the night.

"Where art thou?"

Rhyannon's smile breaks across his mind as he closes his eyes. He can see her bright eyes smiling back at him and he calls again, no louder than a whisper.

"Where art thou Rhyannon?" Sarn has moved forward a little further and Hyw looks frantically in the direction she follows. His eyes strain in the night, but further up the mountain, the night sky flickers again. Staring through the darkness around him, Hyw can see a faint flickering glow further up the mountain. Certain of what he sees, he follows the strange glow.

Jumping from one rock to another; Hyw races towards Mynddy and Sarn. An arrow is notched into his bow and as he passes his companions he whispers.

"Well done Sarn bach!"

Mynddy spurs Sarn on as they chase Hyw further up the mountain, not knowing where he will lead them. Hyw stops suddenly and, turning back to Mynddy, holds his hand up with his palm held out towards her, indicating for her to stay.

Creeping slowly forward, he can make out the reflections of a campfire flickering on the rocks ahead of him. Its blaze is hidden from his view, but he gradually moves forward until he knows the fire is close. Still, its blaze is concealed, as if its fire burns within the rocks. Mynddy is walking behind him and he beckons for her to be silent, but when he turns she is at his side. They both creep towards the large outcrop of rocks. Slowly moving towards the flickering light, they approach a gigantic flat slab of granite held up at one end by two massive boulders.

Hyw checks and checks again. There is an opening under the rock, but no more than a couple of people could shelter comfortably beneath its roof. He is as certain as he can be; it is not Māthōg hiding amid the rocks. Suddenly a voice calls out.

"Is that thee, boy!"

Hyw rounds the corner of the first boulder and to his surprise, he sees what looks like a small cave hidden within the cluster of huge slabs of rock. Its entrance is just high enough for a squat man to walk under its roof without stooping. Behind a smaller boulder in the entrance to this cave is a fire and sitting behind the fire is an old man with a long flowing beard and fine grey hair tied at the back of his head in a ponytail. The old man is wearing sacred robes and an apron around his waist. The apron is decorated with a circle of oak leaves and contains a finely embroidered image of a spreading oak at its centre. He is sitting with his legs crossed and appears to be dragging the smoke from the fire towards him with his cupped hands.

Hyw bends his bow as he steps forward into the full view of the old man, but the old Druid doesn't jump or bother at Hyw's presence, he only cants his head to one side as he looks up at him. In doing so, Hyw notices his eye. The Druid is looking up through his one good eye and his other eye is white as chalk with a funny-shaped black scar at its centre. It is obvious that the Druid is struggling to focus his one good eye on Hyw and that he was expecting Hyw to be someone else. By the time the old Druid focuses his eye, Mynddy is standing at Hyw's side with her brother's bow bent towards the old man.

"Oh, good grief!" the old man exclaims on seeing both their bows bent towards him.

"Put away thy weapons of war. I am a holy man, a priest of the most high, a shaman…put away thy bows!" Both Mynddy and Hyw have arrows notched securely into place, but they relax their guard, seeing no danger.

"Step a little closer so I may see thee more clearly my children!" Hyw bends forward slightly as he steps into the entrance of the cave. As he does so he feels something jump in the shadows behind where the Druid sits. There is a muffled cry in Hyw's head and an uncertain tremor grips his senses. The same feelings he had felt in the darkness that had gathered in Mynddy's croft and he knows the Druid is not alone. Staring past Hyw the Old Druid casts his gaze over Mynddy.

"And what art thou doing here my child? Step closer so I may see thy beauty girl!"

Mynddy shrugs back from the old man's words and pulls her cape in around her. Suddenly the sound of Sarn rearing somewhere behind them breaks into the stillness of the night and Hyw turns away from the old man for only a moment. A cry empties into the cave and Hyw can see the charging silhouette of a young man with a sword held aloft in both his hands.

The Druid's apprentice had been given the task of protecting the old man. Secreting himself in the thick bracken on the mountainside, but in his inexperience, he had fallen asleep in the comfort of the evening's dimming light and it was only the old man's raised voice that had woken him. To his waking surprise, the apprentice had seen Hyw and Mynddy, with their weapons bent towards his master and commenced his charge toward them.

There is no time to think. Out of the corner of his eye, Hyw sees the old Druid reaching under a blanket for a blade he has concealed there. For his age, the Druid is surprisingly nimble and he moves quickly, standing and then advancing towards Hyw. Gaining full control of the sword in his hand the old man goes to step over the fire. Hyw struggles in his dilemma, with two blades swiftly approaching him.

The Druid bends his head forward under the low roof of the cave. In one swift movement, Hyw turns, bending his bow. The shaft of his arrow rages through the air. Its blade penetrates the top of the Druid's skull and does not stop until it is buried almost completely inside his body.

Mynddy has thrown the cloak off her shoulders and she turns with an arrow notched into the string of her brother's bow as Hyw struggles to notch another arrow into place. The young man screams towards them, his cries intensifying as he sees his master falling into the fire. Mynddy bends her bow towards the Druid's young apprentice, but for some reason, she freezes and cannot loose her deadly blade. The furious attack of Māthōg and his men flashes in her memory and Mynddy is caught, frozen in the frenzy of all her drowning fears.

Hyw can see her hesitation and fumbles at the string of his bow. The lad's furious charge is almost on them as Hyw advances, but his fumbling fingers have not yet found the nock of his arrow. In one desperately awkward moment, Hyw's bow bends and his feathered warrior finally thrashes toward its prey.

The momentum of the young boy's advance continues as Hyw pushes Mynddy to one side. She looses her own arrow, but its wild aim is launched high into the night. Hyw stands his ground as the sword falls towards him. The flickering light of the fire has found the young man's fear, with Hyw's feathered warrior protruding from his gut. The flashing blade still slices through the air towards them. There is a loud clash and sparks fly from the rock above Hyw's head where the blade strikes, but its honed edge still rains down on him. Hyw desperately tries to dodge the sword's stunted course, but the blade strikes him on the head finding a spring of blood, which gushes out, instantly running down his face and Hyw falls lifeless into the dirt.

Blood flows freely onto the ground as Mynddy rushes to Hyw's side. Dazed and confused, Mynddy is quick to paw over him. Quickly looking around she sees Sarn approaching. Running over to her she reaches up into the bundle on Sarn's back. Mynddy frantically tears at a piece of white cloth and rushes back to where Hyw lies moaning on the ground.

Slowly waking, Hyw comes to, with a start as Mynddy attempts to plug the wound to his forehead, but Hyw will not lay still. Getting to his feet he quickly makes his way to the rear of the cave where his eyes meet Rhyannon's frightened gaze. Jumping in her fears, Rhyannon struggles in a panic, bound and gagged in the cold and dark, having been forced into a large crack between two rocks.

Hyw bends down towards her and lifts her into his arms. She is shaking in terror as he cuts at the cords that bind her. Mynddy joins Hyw in a quickening of thoughts and removes the gag in Rhyannon's mouth, taking Rhyannon from Hyw and hugging her to her breast. Rhyannon throws her arms around Mynddy's neck as she looks nervously back towards Hyw, blood still pouring from the wound on his head.

"Annon safe!" Rhyannon calls out.

"Annon safe now!"

Hyw is confused at the child's reaction to him. He was sure he had gained her confidence but seems to be the enemy.

Picking up the already blooded cloth from the floor of the cave, Hyw dabs at his forehead. Feeling the wound through the cloth; its cut is only small, but it is some time before Hyw can bring the bleeding under control.

Dragging at the old Druid, Hyw pulls him out of the cave and onto the mountainside, and then he returns for the Druid's young apprentice. A stock of wood is piled to one side of the cave and thoughts of burning all the Druid's evil intents fire in Hyw's mind, but their presence on the mountain must not be conveyed to the valley below.

Hyw throws a little wood onto the small blaze at his feet and can see the remains of many other fires in the small hollow behind the boulder. As flames lick at the dry wood, Hyw can see its flickering light is cleverly concealed from the world below and he realises he had only seen the Druid's firelight through Sarn's keen senses and stumbling too close.

Hyw watches as Mynddy sits cuddling Rhyannon, who is playing a game, known only to her, with Mynddy's fingers. "We must wait here until the morning!" Mynddy looks up at Hyw as he speaks.

"It is too dangerous to travel back tonight… Māthōg is restless and the Warriors of Gododdyn may mistake us for their enemy!" Mynddy seems to relax at Hyw's words. She beckons for him to move closer and taking the cloth from him, she takes a turn dabbing the wound. Hyw looks around them.

"We must make ourselves comfortable. I think we will be safe here for the night, but I will keep watch!" Hyw goes out into the darkness after Sarn and leads her up to the entrance of the cave. There is food and water in the Druid's provisions, also a skin full of strong drink, which Hyw pours onto the flames of the fire causing it to rear up into the night.

Rhyannon is content playing for a while; Mynddy seems to have found a connection with the child, but she is soon calling for her mother and cries herself to sleep.

In turn, Mynddy suffers in restless dreams. Hyw tries to make her comfortable, wrapping her cape around both her and Rhyannon. Propped against the wall of one of the huge boulders, she is slumped awkwardly to one side and Hyw sits beside her, using her bundle as a pillow between them. Raising his arm above her, Hyw hesitates, not for the first time, before he places his arm down over her side and pulls her into his own. Dragging his father's wolf skin coat over both Rhyannon and Mynddy he stokes the fire with yet more logs. Staring out into the night, he rests his bow at his side with an arrow laid over its string.

"The darkness of the night is thine Sarn bach!" Hyw whispers as he sets his faithful friend to watch over them.

In the early hours of the morning, the first wolves appear on the mountainside. Sarn is nervous, but Hyw keeps his silent vigil over his faithful friend, and the wolves find enough to eat outside the walls of the cave.

The morning dew drips from the trees. Hyw walks in front, with Mynddy and Rhyannon riding in silence on Sarn's back. Rhyannon struggles to stay awake. They have crossed over the river onto the opposite side of the valley. Sarn has been uneasy for a while and Hyw had caught sight of some riders deeper in the woods, only shadows, but he didn't want to take any chances.

The morning is still and quiet and only a red breast dared to follow them along the path and even the red breast's stout heart eventually abandoned its cause. Moving higher up the sides of the valley, Hyw follows the course of the stream to where he knows it tumbles into the valley below, close to Rhyannon's home.

Mynddy seems to have found at least some joy, as she hugs Rhyannon to her. Rhyannon slowly wakes up and begins to play with Mynddy's fingers again. The girl appears to make signs with her hands as she tries to communicate with her silent new friend.

The path in front of them is obscure and several times Hyw pauses for long moments searching all around them, scanning every tree and bush that line their way. Twice he sees the shadows of riders between the trees, but through the woods, he can't make out their detail and just waits for them to disappear.

Eventually, the path leads down towards the village. The woods thin out and from their borders, Hyw looks out to where he can see riders on the other side of the river. He watches and waits in the shadows. It is Geddyn's men, but Geddyn himself is not with them and straining his eyes, Hyw cannot make out Blaidd or Cilydd among them.

Mynddy grips the reins not wanting Sarn to move or give away their position, but Sarn has greater discipline herself. Hyw nods up at her in recognition of her fears and he places his finger over his lips as smiling towards Rhyannon, but she has recognised her home and is becoming restless. Its secure walls are waiting for her, only an arrow's flight across the meadow.

Rhyannon goes to call out, pointing to where she can see her home. Mynddy is quick with her hand and covers Rhyannon's mouth. Hyw watches Mynddy with the child as she signs to Rhyannon, placing her finger over her mouth, indicating for Rhyannon to keep quiet. At first, Rhyannon struggles in Mynddy's arms, but Mynddy perseveres in her silence and finally, Rhyannon joins in the game.

Hyw turns as the warriors ride into the village, two riding up to Rhyannon's home. Gwion appears at the gate. The warrior is slow in his movements with his head bowed. Even at this distance, Hyw can see the devastation painted on Gwion's face. The apparent leader of the warriors turns in his saddle as he talks to Gwion. Rhyannon can now see her father and Mynddy struggles to keep control.

"Annon Da, Annon Da!" Rhyannon says excitedly, but placing a finger against her mouth she blows through her teeth.

"Shush. Annon shush!" Hyw smiles at Rhyannon who smiles back at him and then turns to Mynddy.

"No sad, Annon no sad!" Rhyannon reaches her hand up and gently strokes Mynddy's long dark hair and pats her on the head.

"Annon home now, Annon home…no sad now… no sad now!"

Hyw looks back to where Gwion is joined by Angharydd struggling in her grief. The old lady has a tight grip on Angharydd's shoulder and her other arm around her back. It is as though Angharydd has no strength left in her and the old woman drags at her listless body.

The warrior points over to the mountain on the other side of the valley and then back along the trail where they have ridden. He seems to talk quickly, but Hyw is out of earshot. The effect of his words is instant though, and Angharydd collapses to her knees, pawed over by Gwion who is also crying. Angharydd's cries fill Hyw's heart, but he dares not break his cover. Rhyannon watches in a perplexed silence.

The warriors turn to go and ride back up the track. Hyw watches and waits. After some time he smiles up at Mynddy and she nods back her approval as Hyw leads Sarn out into the open. They are still some way off from the village, but the old lady standing by Angharydd sees them break the cover of the tree line. First Gwion looks up and then Angharydd slowly raises her eyes. She looks out across the fields and suddenly breaks free from her friends.

"Rhyannon!" Angharydd shrieks out her daughter's name as she tears across the field towards her. Rhyannon struggles to get down as Hyw reaches up to her and taking both her arms he smiles as he places

Rhyannon at his feet. Angharydd is almost upon them as Rhyannon runs to her. Instantly bursting into tears, Angharydd sinks to her knees and wraps her precious daughter up in her arms. Her tears spill out onto her cheeks and all her feelings splash on her daughter's face and neck.

Hyw is stunned. Gwion races to hug his child and as he hugs his family to him, Angharydd looks up through her tears to where Hyw is standing.

"I thank thee." Angharydd mouths through her tears.

"I thank thee." She says out loud.

"How can we ever repay you?" Angharydd goes back to Rhyannon who is slightly confused by all the attention.

Hyw turns to Sarn and then smiles up at Mynddy. Mynddy takes her foot out of the stirrup as Hyw lifts his foot towards it. Stepping up he climbs onto Sarn's back behind where Mynddy is sitting and pulling at the reins, Sarn turns and begins to walk up through the meadow towards the track.

Mynddy looks back to where Gwion and Angharydd are still pawing over their daughter. The old lady follows Hyw up the field and calls out to him. Sarn stops. The old woman approaches and looks up to where Hyw is sitting. She reaches up and rests one of her hands on Hyw's leg, just above the knee.

Hyw looks down into the woman's tired eyes. Her hair was once coloured like ripened straw in the evening's sun, but now its grey almost white tresses are pulled back over her head and tied neatly with a dark comb. She is a thick-set woman, with robust shoulders and hips, which are covered by a dark skirt and smock.

Hyw makes no sound or gives no recognition of her presence, other than to stare back into her warm, but fading green eyes. But as he stares his heart warms to her. She had warned him of Māthōg and his intentions, but that isn't what warms Hyw's feelings. There is something about the woman that Hyw cannot see with his eyes; some familiar presence. Having never seen her before his travels, he feels comfortable, even secure in her presence. She reminds him of Olwyn and he thinks of his home and he longs to be there.

Mynddy takes hold of Hyw's arms around her and pulls them into her waist, and she feels Hyw's sadness trembling through her. Turning his thoughts to Sián, the old woman's words interrupt the image he has conjured in his head.

"It is a big thing thou hast done!" Her words are quietly spoken, but there is a lifetime of care wrapped up in them.

"I thank thee for the life of the child… there are not many in this world who would have done what ye did!" Her words pause slightly as she looks up at Mynddy.

"Stay. Stay with us, at least for a while. Ye can wash and bath, eat and make thyself ready for the trail. We have done thee wrong and have much to be forgiven of…please stay!"

"Yes stay!" The words are those of Gwion who has walked up the field to where the old woman has stopped them. Looking back at Gwion; Angharydd is standing just behind him with Rhyannon sitting on her hip. She struggles to hold her daughter's weight and hitches Rhyannon higher.

"Stay at least for a while, we will guard over thy sleep. We will keep the girl for thee!" Mynddy jumps at the words and squeezes Hyw's arms, hugging them tighter around her waist.

Rhyannon smiles up through her bright half-moon eyes, but although Hyw's heart is melting, he will not stay and for some unknown reason, and will not consider abandoning Mynddy there.

"We must go!" Hyw says without any explanation and he kicks at Sarn's sides.

"Wait…wait a moment!" The old woman calls, but Gwion steps forward, interrupting her words.

"Māthōg and his men have been seen riding to the north, but not all his paths are known to us…the warriors of Gododdyn follow where he leads them, but Māthōg is fickle in his ways!" Hyw looks back at Gwion who has stepped forward towards him and he nods his approval.

"Stay… I was wrong!" Gwion begs Hyw, but Hyw's mind is set as Sarn steps forward and up and onto the trail. The old woman perseveres and walks after Hyw talking as she does so.

"Do not trust the Warriors of Gododdyn…not all seek after thy safety!" Hyw pulls at Sarn's reins and she comes to a halt again. Turning in the saddle, the woman continues to speak.

"I have heard of Geddyn's respect for you, but not all his men share in his feelings. Some murmur against him, and thee. Geddyn has ridden north seeking Māthōg, but some of those who remain have set their hearts against thee and thy companion!"

"It is the second time thou hast warned me of danger and I thank thee for thy words!" The old woman turns to go, but Hyw is lost in a familiar feeling and he goes to talk again.

"I keep my friends and pay my debts unless the sky falls down!" There was no need to swear an oath between them, but something had compelled him, what? Hyw doesn't know, nor can he tell.

The old woman turns to Hyw on hearing his oath and her words are softly spoken.

"The sky had yet fallen…and it is we who owe the debt. No word or thought or deed can repay thee for all thou hast done. Go thy way in peace and may the Gods bless thee!" The old woman smiles up at Hyw, but he has already turned to go and whether he heard her words, or not, the woman cannot tell.

She calls after him again.

"As Gwion said…Māthōg's ways are fickle, guard thy footfall well!" She bows her head as she turns away with the sweet tears of joy welling in her eyes.

Mynddy looks back to where Angharydd and Gwion stand with Rhyannon. Rhyannon breaks free from her parents and runs towards where Sarn walks. The child stops and squints as she smiles. She looks down towards Mynddy and Hyw, raising one arm above her head; her fingers extended up and her hand tilted back as she waves. Leaning her head to one side, Rhyannon calls out.

"Annon 'bye now, Annon 'bye." Mynddy looks back at her and then turns away with tears welling in her eyes and closing them, a single teardrop breaks free onto her face.

Chapter Thirteen

The morning is young as Sarn ambles along the narrow path by the river. Skirting its banks, Hyw leads them to the east to disguise their path. It is apparent that some of the people of the valley have divided loyalties and cannot be trusted. Once out of sight of the village, Hyw turns Sarn to the south, then into a valley leading westward. They follow yet another tributary of the river as it cuts its way through the rugged, but beautiful landscape. Walking in its borders, they follow a track through a mixture of thick woods and meadows as the river tumbles ever on. From time to time its waters cascade over small falls, hidden among the trees.

"We must follow this valley and then climb back over the mountains… it is a good walk and night will be upon us before its end!" Hyw's words drift out into the woods and over the river, but Mynddy gives no sign of recognition. The sound of Hyw's voice brings her some comfort though, but her melancholy weighs heavy on Hyw's mind.

Thinking back to the old lady's words, he understands not all the Warriors of Gododdyn can be trusted. If Geddyn were there, their passage would be safe, but he is not, and so their journey back to the shelter would be long and arduous.

Sarn is tired and saunters along the path at little more than a walk. Her thoughts are for the stallion, her stricken companion they left to fend for himself. Her master would have to hurry, but they seemed to be going in the wrong direction. She understands the journey they face but is tired and hungry.

'When will my master ever stop his wanderings?' The question was a pointless one and Sarn knew she would willingly follow wherever Hyw led her. In the short time she had been with him, she had grown fond of Hyw. Gentle and considerate to her, he never asked more than she could bear.

The woods begin to grow thick around them, but they eventually climb out into the broad green pastures of the upper valley. Long fields stretch out from the banks of the river with low clouds drifting across the gathering skies as the mountains push their tops up towards their covers. Hyw looks up at the skies, suspecting rain but not for some time.

Stopping for a while, Hyw scans the valley and distant woods while Sarn drinks. Eventually, he helps Mynddy down and she too scoops water from the river with her cupped hands. When all have had their fill, Hyw helps Mynddy back into the saddle and walks on holding Sarn's reins. Mynddy had seemed to come alive when looking after Rhyannon, but in the quiet of their journeying, she seems to sink back in herself.

High in the heart of the valley three ribbons of smoke gently rise into the day, their fires set amid a small huddle of crofts. Not wishing to encounter more strangers, Hyw leads them up by the edge of a great wood that stretches along the length of the valley as far as he can see. The trees grow thick in the woods whose borders are overgrown with last-years bracken, tangled up in brambles. Their path becomes more difficult and Hyw is forced to lead Sarn along the edge of the pasture, but in doing so, he knows they risk being seen. Walking on into the afternoon, Hyw anxiously peers towards the huddle of crofts and along the valley for any sign of trouble.

Furtively skirting around the crofts, he can see a man cutting wood near the first building and beyond its slate-rock walls another is tending a flock of small brown Soay Sheep. An unseen dog barks and a child runs out from behind one of the other crofts with a stick in its hand. The child pretends to draw an arrow back across the centre of their imaginary bow.

Pausing for a moment, Hyw is reminded of his childhood games. The young child reminds him of his sister, Bayr, although at the distance, Hyw cannot make out whether it is a boy or a girl. The child halts its fanciful attack as despatching some unseen evil that has dared to attack its home. Hyw is lost in his childhood memories and the guilt he feels for his sister's death bleeds through him. A woman's voice calls out and an old man answers her; somewhere amid the two crofts, a baby is crying.

Two buzzards circle high above the woods as they soar on the back of the sun's warm rays and Hyw studies the distant billowing clouds.

If they follow the woods their path will take them close to the crofts, but there seems to be little other choice. Even if they managed to penetrate deeper into the woods, their sides are sheer and unrelenting, hiding rocks and cliffs, and Hyw can see where they must climb the valley's steep sides beyond the trees.

Sarn comes to a halt as Hyw scans again. Unusually nervous, he can see nothing. The crofters may become a problem, but any problem they presented would not be insurmountable. Looking down into the centre of the valley where the river meanders through the pastures and flat fields, Hyw, for one moment, thinks he can see movement amid the trees; possibly cattle and he dismisses what he sees, but lets his eyes linger for a while to see if he can confirm his suspicions.

The river has become little more than a gently flowing stream, lined with trees. As the line of trees meanders along the banks of the stream, it gives way to more substantial woodlands. Straining his eyes as he looks, he scans the opposite tree line with quiet concern as he imagines movement again. Unsure, something or someone is concealed in the shadows on the opposite side of the valley.

Walking slowly on, he tries to gain a greater vantage point to view the opposite tree line, but his senses are numb. The rush of blood inside him has little effect and he is tired from his lonely night's vigil. First, he sees something and then there's nothing and he begins to wonder if there is anything there at all.

Sarn's ears have pricked up, but her gaze is set further along the edge of the wood; in the direction, they are walking. The far tree line is quickly forgotten as Hyw senses something in the trees ahead of them. Mynddy sits with her brother's bow held loosely in her hand; two arrows lay across its handle. She gazes blankly out in front of them, staring headlong into her awful memories.

Hyw lets go of Sarn's reins feeling the animal's growing concerns. Beginning to stalk through the trees with an arrow notched into his bow, trusting Sarn's acute senses implicitly. Sarn quietly follows her master.

Hearing something move further along the tree line, Hyw stands motionless, not daring to move. Sarn is silent and Hyw knows she has come to a halt close behind him. Slowly Hyw becomes aware of someone just in front of them, in the shadows beneath a large beech; he can't see what or who it is yet, but there is a shadow within a shadow and he knows someone is there.

Looking back up at Mynddy, Hyw can see her gaze has settled on him. Signing up at her with one finger placed over his lips, he indicates for her to be silent. Then pointing with the first two fingers of his right hand, he indicates to his eyes then he loops them around the string of his bow, letting the bow hang loose. Holding one finger in the air, he then points into the woods in front of them, indicating below the huge old tree.

The man cutting wood near the crofts has seen Hyw and has stopped swinging his axe. Standing with the axe upright between his legs with its head on the ground, both his hands rest on top of its handle. Calling out, another man appears at his side, but Hyw cannot turn to where they stand, his attention is firmly fixed on the shadows beneath the tree line. Every muscle and sinew in Hyw's body is poised, watching and waiting.

Something moves and the silhouette of a man steps out from under the tree as a lone archer breaks cover thinking the men are pointing up at him. Hyw recognises the Scotti Slag and in one long, smooth, precise movement, he bends his bow. The Grot is shaken, as his wits stir inside him and he looks up at Hyw sensing his impending doom. Quickly turning, he frantically bends his bow, but it is too late. Hyw's feathered warrior thrashes through the air, puncturing his breast. There is a low thump and the power of Hyw's swift shaft forces the archer to stumble back; his bow falling and his body slumping to the ground. Without thinking, Hyw is running towards the crofters.

"Rally thy men…Māthōg is attacking!" He screams as he runs and points to the opposite tree line. Māthōg is not in sight, but Hyw knows he is near, he can sense his presence as the breath of the dragon chases down his spine. The one man grabs at his axe, but is confused and hesitates over defending himself against Hyw or turning to where his presumed attacker is pointing.

Changing the emphasis of his charge he tries to place himself between the crofters and Māthōg's imminent attack. As he does so Māthōg and several of his men break the far tree line. They look up towards Hyw's chase with some confusion. The thunder of Sarn's charge vibrates through the ground. Hyw looks, and to his surprise, Mynddy is guiding his sturdy champion. Her face is contorted with rage and her long hair flows freely in the rush of Sarn's gallop. Staring incredulously, he cannot free himself from the image. Mynddy has an arrow notched into the string of her bow, which she has brought to bear. She is a fearsome sight and for one fleeting moment all her senses return and they are bent towards the death of Māthōg and his men.

Hyw's head is pounding and he forces great gulps of breath into his lungs, but all his fears are forgotten as he watches Mynddy. She rides like the wind, with her dress and hair billowing out; she bends her brother's bow as steering Sarn with her legs. Hyw is mesmerised and wonders who she is and what powers she possesses. She rides as if born in the saddle and she wields her bow as if it were part of her arm; with her whole being fixed on one purpose.

Quickly coming to his senses, and knowing the danger she is in, Hyw sprints towards Māthōg. On seeing Sarn charging across the field, Māthōg and his men turn in a panic, riding back through the trees. Māthōg knows his desperate enemy's only care is his death and a whole army of men could not prevent Hyw's swift blade from piercing his heart, but in the heat of the moment, he has mistaken Mynddy for Hyw. Māthōg disappears from view, but Mynddy continues her deadly flight.

"Mynddy!" Hyw calls out, running full tilt towards her. She continues unabated.

"Sarn!" Hyw calls out for his gentle beast to cease her gallop. Sarn, in turn, struggles under Mynddy's persuasions to continue. Finally, Sarn slows and turns back towards Hyw as he rushes to Mynddy's side with his eyes constantly scanning the far tree line.

Looking up Hyw can see a fire in Mynddy's eyes he has not seen since that first day by the lake. Smiling up at her, her eyes soften towards him, but she still makes no sound.

Running to where Māthōg rode, Hyw looks beneath the low branches of the trees and into the shadows of the woods. He can hear Sarn following. Māthōg and his men are riding hard at the side of the river. They cross its slow meandering currents, splashing and spraying water as they flee. Hyw stands watching as they disappear into the distance.

Suddenly a shock of thoughts runs through him and he trembles in their wake. Suddenly, he finds himself standing on the rock of his family's throne looking through Bayr's frightened eyes. In his waking dreams, he views Māthōg's hungry onslaught towards his sister and he can still hear her cries in his head. In the same instant, the terrifying vision ceases, but it has pierced through him, like a blade.

Hyw can hear Sarn behind where he stands, but there is another sound at the edge of the trees. The young child who had been playing with the stick stalking her imaginary prey has run after Hyw and Mynddy's attack. In its innocence, the child has not recognised the danger. Mynddy has seen the young girl, but Hyw can only hear her approach as awful memories choke his mind. In his visions, the frightened child he once was, stares down through the shadows beneath the trees of the Jingles as Māthōg's lone archer once more creeps towards him.

Hyw panics as he hears the child's footsteps behind him and he turns in his nightmare, bending his bow. The frightened screams of the child's mother shatters the silence; her helpless cries look on as a feathered warrior falters in its attack. Hyw is staring into the frightened eyes of his sister Bayr. The young child is the spit of her and Hyw's heart shatters as if it were made of glass. The young girl, still has her stick held in her hand, but her game has turned against her and she is frozen in her fears. Hyw's honed and shafted blade has picked out the child's heart and it is still bent towards that one deadly intent.

A calm familiar voice breathes words into Hyw's ears as ghostly hands reach down into his broken heart. His eyes stare into those of his sister, but his deadly intentions have been set in motion and cannot easily be deflected.

"Save thy sister Hyw Bach, save thy sister!"

A mother trembles in the sum of all her fears and a second guttural cry empties into Hyw. He cannot get the picture of his sister out of his head and nor does he want to.

Another ghostly hand carefully reaches out, touching him on the shoulder. It is slowly cupped around the top of his arm as another hand gently touches his lips and yet another, his face. Others grip at the string of his bow and yet more at his forearm. Sarn looks quietly on as one by one the Standing Sentinels step forward, reaching out with their lips and mouths, their hands and hearts until the sum of all Hyw's rage and anger has been assuaged. Gradually relaxing the strain from his feathered warrior, the ghostly guardians stand between Hyw and the frightened girl. One of the celestial warriors gently pushes at his bow and it slowly moves to one side. Without any discernable thought sparking inside him, the bow eventually relaxes between Hyw's hands.

Sarn watches her master as he sinks to his knees, with tears clouding his eyes. The frightened mother rushes forward, snatching the girl up into her arms, crying out as she does so.

One by one the sentinels back away into the shadows of the trees.

Mynddy cradles Hyw's head in her lap, stroking her fingers through his hair. There are tears in her eyes, which fall onto her cheeks, rolling down her face. Mynddy's long hair reaches down to cover her shame and only that one, most beautiful Sentinel, remains to wrap both their broken hearts in the warmth of her loving arms.

For the first time, Mynddy recognises and understands Hyw's pain, and at that moment their hearts beat as if they were one. Sarn looks down the hedge of trees and along the banks of the small river where the ghostly guardians keep their silent vigils.

Still shaking and trembling, Hyw slowly comes to, watched over by the crofters who have gathered around where he has fallen. They can barely believe what they have just witnessed and they whisper one to another.

Sarn continues to watch as Hyw jumps and rouses. Looks quickly up at Mynddy, Hyw then stares at the small crowd of people who have gathered, but He is weak from his visions and there is little will inside him. Finding his feet, Mynddy struggles as she tries to get Hyw into the saddle. Silently climbing up behind him she pulls on the reins and coaxes Sarn to lead them away with the crofters unable to comprehend the day.

The afternoon presses endlessly on towards the evening's fading light. The three companions remain silent as Sarn slowly saunters up the mountain. A chill is in the air and the dusk of the evening's lengthening shadows grow, as darker clouds drift across the skies. Before they reach the lake below Hyw's winter shelter, the first rain begins to fall.

Hyw remains quiet; Sarn has led them back over the mountains. The image of Bayr is still mixed up with that of the young girl whom he had almost slaughtered. He has managed somehow to keep his bow in his hand, but Mynddy has continuously cradled him in her arms on their long journey. She draws her mother's fur cape around them, but in the rain, Sarn struggles on the path and Mynddy has to lead them up to the shelter.

Looking up in quiet anticipation, she scans the shelter for any sign of life. Her want to see the crippled stallion fills her with dreadful anticipation. There is also the sinking anticipation of Geddyn's men being there. The stallion's head is protruding over the gate of the stable, but to Mynddy's dismay, it seems subdued.

Suddenly in the dim light of the evening's rain, Mynddy hesitates, seeing a silhouette of someone standing at the stable door. All arrayed in their battle garb they are standing by a huge warhorse. The warrior steps out of the shadows and Mynddy freezes.

Chapter Fourteen

A fearsome sight dressed for battle, the warrior is wearing a burnished helmet, with the image of a wolf's head set over its crest. It has a wide post, which reaches down from the bottom of the wolf's snout like a tongue extending down over his nose with what looks like two metal jaws reaching forward over his jawline. His long braided hair hangs from the rear of the helmet, into the centre of his back. On what little Mynddy can see of his face there is dry and cracked blue woad daubed on his skin, but it is streaked with little rivulets of his sweat and rain. A brown hardened breastplate of leather covers a suit of mail protecting his shoulders and arms, but the breastplate is almost black from the rain. Mynddy jumps and freezes, as Blaidd steps forward expecting a warm welcome from his friend.

"They have come over the waters in greater numbers than ever…Damn the Scotti…Damn Māthōg…we have been unable to find him my friend, but have done battle with many of his cohorts!"

Blaidd's words break into the silence and he forgets to ask for a blessing on Hyw; stumbling headlong into his purpose for coming. There is no considered thought behind what Blaidd says and his coarsely tempered words, maul at Mynddy's nightmares, but for a moment they seem to stir something inside Hyw.

Looking up into the vacant expression in his friend's eyes, Blaidd immediately realises there is something wrong. Stepping forward he helps Hyw down. Mynddy's heart and mind recover slightly and she is taken aback by Blaidd's insight, as he immediately recognises Hyw's melancholy. Recovering some sense of composure, Mynddy assists Blaidd in walking Hyw to his shelter. Trembling, as if lingering in the cold of winter, Hyw is lost in his nightmares.

Blaidd tends to the horses and then sparks a fire in the hearth as Mynddy tends to Hyw. She fetches water and begins to wash him down; first his face and then his hands and arms. Helpless as a baby, Hyw sits motionless on a stool looking into the fire as flames lick at his mind and the image of Bayr burns like kindling in his head.

Blaidd leaves and returns a few moments later with more wood for the fire. He makes two more journeys into the horse's stables before there is enough wood for the night. Making a further journey, he returns, this time carrying a roll of bedding for the night. Ducking in through the doorway, his eyes meet Mynddys'. They both stare for a moment; each one suspicious of the other. Pulling at Hyw's arm, Mynddy tries to lead him to his bed, but he is lost in some dark realm.

"Come, my friend, sleep is what ye need!" Blaidd takes Hyw's other arm and together they coax him onto his cot. As doing so Blaidd's eyes find Mynddy again. She looks back at him. Blaidd smiles awkwardly, trying to discern through Mynddy's silence. Although looking into her eyes, it is the secret desires of her heart he seeks, but Mynddy is suspicious of his intentions. Sitting, Blaidd looks at her and she turns from his intrusive eyes.

"I must talk to him!" His words are softly spoken and Mynddy can hear the love he holds for his friend and her concerns ease slightly.

"There are those things I must say unto him before I go to battle again!"

The sound of the rain grows heavy on the slates; its waters drip in a steady stream above the doorway as a torrent of drips turns into a waterfall. The horses graze on fresh hay on the other side of the wall and as Mynddy looks up at him, Blaidd holds her gaze, but, growing uneasy, she looks away and begins to lay Hyw down on his bed. Placing a pillow under his head, Blaidd throws a blanket over him, with Mynddy climbing over Hyw, lying next to him. She shivers while looking back up at Blaidd unable to free herself from the prying questions in his eyes. Trying to smile again, he turns to stoke the fire, placing more wood on its growing furnace.

Standing, Blaidd unbuckles his breastplate, then leaning forward he pulls the suit of mail over his head. In doing so his shirt rides up, revealing his upper torso. He is leanly built and the muscles of his stomach and chest are clearly defined. Turning slightly, he reaches up to pull his shirt down and Mynddy jumps in the darkness of the shelter as she catches sight of his battle wounds; a thin scar, possibly a stab wound, just above his hip and two longer scars extending up his back. One of these extends up under his shirt and the other is rough and wide.

The floor of the damp shelter provides little room, but Blaidd finds a space to lay out his bedding and, blowing out the single beeswax candle, he pulls his blanket over him. Mynddy lays in her own melancholy and silence as she wonders what horrors Blaidd has encountered in battle.

Shadows from the fire flicker and dance on the shelter's roof and walls as the rain outside eases slightly. Mynddy places an arm over Hyw's chest and lies on her side, cuddling up next to him, feeling for his warmth. It is a mutual arrangement. Blaidd rolls over and in the flickering light, he stares past his friend to Mynddy. They both look for a while and then Mynddy looks down to Hyw whose eyes are open, staring blankly at the bare slates on the roof. Water slowly gathers at the corner of one of the tiles forming a small droplet; the dewdrop of rain grows larger, dripping onto the floor and the process starts over again.

Blaidd breaks the silence.

"The Scotti are coming, my friend!" Mynddy shies away at his words, but he continues unabated.

"We have slaughtered one band of raiders, but more will follow!" Silence reigns in the darkness of the shelter as Blaidd ponders on his words and whether Hyw understands them.

In the silence, Mynddy begins to run her fingers through Hyw's hair, parting it and then she combs its damp rat's tails off his face. Hyw continues to stare up at the roof where another droplet of water is forming

"The king has instructed Geddyn to gather all the Warriors of Gododdyn!" Blaidd seems to muse over a thought and then speaks as if to himself.

"Māthōg is the key!" Mynddy looks straight into Blaidd as he utters the name.

"Yes, Māthōg is the key," He says as if confirming the thought to himself.

"Cut out the heart and the body fails!"

Mynddy calms her thoughts and slowly leans towards Hyw, kissing him gently on his brow. Her lips breathe fire onto his skin as she kisses him again and again. Tears begin to well in her eyes. One drops onto her cheek, but she wipes at her face before it can fall. In the darkness, Blaidd tries to make out her every move.

"I must be away to battle in the morning, but before I go..."

His words are for Mynddy and they both pause in their differing thoughts.

"I rode with his father…and his grandfather against the Romans, against many who came to do battle with us. I was there when they found his mother…I was there when we…" Blaidd's words falter and he looks up at Mynddy, suspecting so much and knowing so little.

"I know of the islands of the sea!" Hyw's words erupt into the hearts of both, Mynddy and Blaidd. They are slow, to begin with, but they gather in strength.

"Hello my old friend, it is good to have thee back," Blaidd whispers as Mynddy smiles and for a moment things seem bright.

"I know of the islands of the sea!" Hyw repeats his words and Blaidd muses over them before he speaks.

"But dust thou know of the covenant, Hyw bach?"

"I know of the holy man and his teachings. I know there were promises given and promises made, but of their substance, I know not, save only my grandfather would have died to keep their secret sacred!" Blaidd looks straight into Mynddy's eyes as though his words are for her as much as for Hyw. Mynddy cannot look away, understanding the nature of those things of which they speak.

"Many people have died keeping those words sacred Hyw bach, but I have been commanded to speak with thee. Do not ask me how or why or by whom, I cannot say." There is a silence, during which Blaidd appears to gather strength from somewhere deep inside him.

"We were commanded to prepare our people for that day when they would hear the word, but were forbidden to give the word unto our people."

"What word?" Hyw asks.

"I am forbidden to say more of our promises," Blaidd says, still looking at Mynddy as he speaks.

"Search those things thy parents and grandfather have taught thee and thou wilt understand… There are those in this land who yet keep the word. Many travelled with us and some have yet to take their voyage, but I fear thy grandfather's brother has journeyed into the next life and so my purpose has a greater urgency."

At Blaidd's words, Hyw turns towards his friend, but instead of looking at Blaidd, he appears to look straight through him. Hyw's eyes shine in the darkness and he stares, as if through the wall, over the mountains and lakes; over the seas to where the wild horse's thunder onto distant rocky shores and as he stares, he whispers half to himself.

"He yet lives!" Hyw's words are quietly spoken, but Blaidd is left in no doubt of their surety. Blaidd tentatively reaches his hand up towards Hyw. Mynddy, who has been caught away in the magic of their puzzling conversation, jumps at the movement, becoming sceptical of Blaidd's intentions, but does not shy away.

Reaching under Hyw's smock, Blaidd brings out the arrowhead, holding it away from Hyw's chest, so he can see it in the flickering light. It is dirty and in the darkness, Hyw's eyes struggle to focus, but eventually, he makes out the binding and the pattern sewn within it. Blaidd speaks, slowly and quietly.

"Those who made their oaths vowed to die before they would reveal its word."

"Yes, but what is the word?" Hyw asks.

"Why it is the word of God Hyw bach…the word of God." Hyw's understanding is mixed up with his shattered memories, but Blaidd brings him some comfort as he ponders his life.

"Why me…what dust thou want with me?" Hyw asks, still puzzling over Blaidd's purposes.

"Not I, but he…he has a work for thee Hyw bach." Hyw is silent.

"He has a work for thee. The King shall come…"

"Yes, yes, my grandfather's words!" Hyw interrupts.

"No not his words; the word of God revealed to us while on the islands of the sea. All who were present there were blessed and each of us was given a task to perform. We were chosen to prepare the way and told that if we accomplished our tasks we would be blessed beyond our wildest dreams. We received all at the hands of that holy man and each of us heard the blessings the other received." Blaidd looks at Hyw, making sure he has his full attention.

"Thy grandfather, father and mother were all given the same blessing…" Hyw stares deep into Blaidd's eyes, hanging on every word as it falls from his mouth.

"They were all charged with the protection of thy life Hyw bach…and that if necessary they should sacrifice their lives for thee!" The tears well in Hyw's eyes and he cannot speak. Blaidd continues to hold his gaze.

"They begged to know for what purpose and were told that ye, Hyw bach, had a purpose of thine own to fulfil, but of its substance, they were not told. I rejoiced when I saw thee and have tried in my way to help thee. Thy people were forbidden to tell thee of this covenant, but I have made no such promise."

With his message delivered, Blaidd relaxes in the silence of the night, but tears run uncontrollably down Hyw's cheeks. Making no sound, his mind is caught up in memories of his mother's love and care; his father's hard work and dedication and his grandfather's ever-present words of guidance. After some time, Blaidd breaks the silence.

"It would seem God has a purpose for thee to fulfil in this life, Hyw bach." Hyw seems to relax slightly, but the complexities of his memories and thoughts trouble him. Mynddy continues to stroke his hair, her hand moving down towards where the arrowhead has fallen onto his chest. She takes hold of it in her hand and studies it carefully. As she does so, she feels in the pocket of her dress for the arrowhead plucked from her sister's breast. Her finger finds its honed edges and she is confused and frightened, but she knows, Hyw is the rock on which she must build her life.

"Māthōg was in the valley to the south of us today!"

"Ye did battle with him?" Blaidd asks, trying to hide the surprise in his voice.

"No, he ran like a dog with his tail between his legs…with Mynddy riding after him." Blaidd is confused at Hyw's words and wonders what has become of him.

'If he has not fought Māthōg…why does he linger in such melancholy?, but his eyes smile up at Mynddy, recalling her heroic charge.

"I think he is looking for a place to make his own; a place where he can build defences." Blaidd is quiet at Hyw's thoughts and he mulls them over and over in his mind.

"I am uncertain of what ye say Hyw bach. We have heard a rumour that he will ride to meet others who are journeying over the seas as we speak. I ride for battle in the morning. Geddyn has asked if thou wilt join us…we have need of thy strength in arms, but he has told me to tell thee, it is not a command and he asked me to remind thee of the promise he made unto thee."

The silence waits for Hyw's word. Mynddy waits. She would willingly ride with Hyw into battle, but she did not wish to ride with the Warriors of Gododdyn and they would, in no way, tolerate a woman in their company.

"I give thanks to thy master for the trust he gives unto me…I am unworthy of it. My intent with Māthōg is known, but I long to ride to the west…no… I am compelled to ride west. I must search…" Hyw's words fall silent, but Blaidd knows his thoughts wander to the sacred islands of the sea and Blaidd's mind journeys with him.

"Ye know I cannot travel with thee…although my heart longs to be at thy side. This much I can give thee…when ye first see the island, Hyw bach, thou wilt be standing on top of a small hillock; unless ye spy it from a great distance. On the shores of the sea below thee, thou wilt see a small fishing village. Above the village are a smithy's shelter and stables. The old man who keeps the stables journeyed with us; he will help thee if he can. I will tell my Lord of thine intentions; he will understand or at least I shall plead thy wishes before him. If all else fails I will tell Geddyn that thou art mad."

Hyw smiles at Blaidd's words and they both begin to laugh. The rain continues to fall on the roof and there is a continual dripping onto the ground where their waters relentlessly seep. Blaidd stirs again, fuelling the fire.

"I will see thee again, Hyw bach. We will be riding to meet the Scotti. Our paths lie in the same direction." Mynddy leans forward and kisses Hyw's brow again.

"Shall I take the crippled stallion? He would be fed and watered in my stables and would want for nothing." Hyw looks at Mynddy at his side, but he knows the answer even before she shakes her head.

"No…we will take him with us." Blaidd is lying on his side propped up on his elbow. Shaking his head in some dismay he bows it slightly, knowing the troubles his young friends would be facing and the handicap the crippled horse would present to them. Looking around at the weary band of orphaned followers, Hyw has gathered around him, Blaidd's fears settle slightly, sensing it must be.

With the sun streaming in under the curtained doorway, Blaidd wakes with its intrusive light. The ground outside is still damp and its vapours rise in the early morning's misty blaze. Looking at Hyw, he is still fast asleep on his bedding, moaning in dreadful remembrance.

Mynddy is missing. Rolling up his bedroll, Blaidd makes his way out into the day. The horses are gone from the stable. Looking down at the lake; thin plumes of mist ribbon out over its surface, but the bright sun is quickly burning its vapours away.

Mynddy is watering and bathing the stallion; the other two horses are standing close by in the cold refreshing water. Blaidd watches Mynddy, with his eyes moving in close. She is dressed only in her lace petticoat, which does not hide her modesty. Her dress is laid out on a rock. It has been washed and cleaned and is drying in the sun's rays. The stallion seems to nuzzle up to her, placing its snout between her breasts as she scratches the horse's forehead and around its ears.

Looking down at the quiet scene, his eyes follow her every movement. Each shape and curve of Mynddy's body is open to his view. Resisting the temptation to go down to her, he allows his eyes to linger longer than he should. Mynddy steps away from the horse, tugging at her petticoat. She pulls it over her head and as she throws it onto the rock, next to her dress, she slips under the water. Swimming a short way out from the shore, she turns to swim back. Blaidd can hear the disturbance of the water and he can hear her short sharp breath as she pants with the waters cold fingers clutching at her. The morning's sun seems to dance and sparkle on the surface of the lake around where Mynddy swims. His eyes move in closer still, but eventually, Blaidd turns his gaze away from her unadorned naked body.

Busying himself in the stable for a while, Blaidd returns to the shelter to raise a fire for some food. Hyw rouses and then wakes with a start. Immediately realising it is only his friend, he still searches for his weapons; feeling naked without them at his side and he finds them where Mynddy placed them at the foot of his bed.

"Mynddy is tending to the stallion at the lake," Blaidd says stoking and coaxing the logs in the fireplace, and as he does so, he tries to purge her image from his mind. Eventually, he gets down on his knees and starts to blow gently at the ashes. A small plume of smoke emerges as a small spark glows in the grate. Slowly building the fire, its flames begin to take hold.

"Art thou beholden to her…the girl, I mean…Mynddy is it?" Blaidd stumbles over his words and betrays a distant longing deep inside him, a memory perhaps, but he is a stranger to those delicate feelings, having lived a savage life for so long.

"I feel beholden to her if that is what ye are asking," Hyw says cautiously, not because he understands or sees into Blaidd's longings, but because he is unsure himself of how he feels.

"I am not given to her, or she to me…if she could talk, she would say I saved her, but I feel the death of those she loves tugging at my soul and they weigh heavy on my mind." Tears begin to well in Hyw's eyes and he fights to prevent their waters as his waking dreams flicker and he is once again standing in the darkness of Mynddy's home amid the horrors, decisions and indecisions. Mynddy's sister looks up at him, pulling the Grot onto her with his arrow piercing her heart, and with that image fixed in his mind, his nightmare fades with her life.

Hyw tries to gather his thoughts as his mind tumbles in turmoil. Thinking of Sián and the way he left her; he is filled with an overwhelming longing for his home and part of that feeling is mixed with those uncertain feelings he has for Sián.

"There is someone else." Hyw almost chokes the words out feeling guilty somehow, as though he has betrayed their love. There is a long silence before Blaidd leaves the shelter and goes out into the stable. Hyw can hear him rummaging in his pack and moments later he returns with a large flat pan. He places the pan on the floor close to the fire. Inside it, are several large hen's eggs and almost a dozen smaller eggs, but in the light and the haze of his tears, Hyw cannot make out their type. There is also a large slab of cured pig's belly and Blaidd starts to cut it into thin strips. Next to the slab of meat are two small, flat loaves of bread.

Breakfast is already sizzling in the pan when they hear the sound of the horses and Mynddy outside. Stabling the horses, she tentatively ducks her head through the curtained doorway. Hyw smiles up at her, remembering the promise he has made and he wonders how he can fulfil it. Mynddy slowly smiles back.

She is wearing the dress with the lace petticoat showing at its neck where the dress has been left undone. Her hair is still wet and hangs down over her shoulders. Mynddy has combed it, but where it hangs over her shoulders and dress, it is becoming tangled again. There are large damp patches on her dress where her hair has gathered and her body is clearly outlined beneath its scant coverings. Blaidd's Hungry eyes rummage through her, but he turns his head in shame as Mynddy sees his intent and quickly turns to go.

Hyw busies himself; with plates and forks, tearing at the bread. Blaidd is a practised cook, but his practice has not necessarily made him a good cook, but giving thanks for the food, he tucks into his large plateful. Mynddy does not return to the shelter and Hyw goes out with her plate of food.

He finds her in the stable, tending the stallion's wound. It is healing well; there is a little swelling, but the actual wound is beginning to seal over. Hyw hands one of two plates to Mynddy and they both sit just outside the stable door.

Before they have finished Blaidd emerges from the shelter, dressed for battle. Taking his horse from the stable he begins to place the tack and armour over its head. Mynddy and Hyw continue to eat quietly as he saddles his horse and secures his pack. Checking his sword and blade along with his bow and quiver full of arrows, he works in silence.

When Mynddy is finished she gets up and taking the empty plates with her, makes her way down to the lake, having no wish to be present when Blaidd leaves. Hyw remains, watching his friends' preparations for war. When he has finished, Blaidd turns to Hyw.

"Well my friend I must be away, but we shall meet again…if not here, we shall ride together in the eternities." Hyw smiles and stands as Blaidd climbs into the saddle.

"May he keep thee in his tender mercies, Hyw bach, until we meet again?"

With these words, Blaidd turns, but he cannot leave. Gazing out over the lake, Blaidd looks to its far shores, over to the small croft. Hyw knows the croft well and the shepherd and his small family; he had often made their acquaintance over the long winter months.

His eyes are bright with tears and Hyw wonders where his longings roam. Blaidd seems to bow his head slightly and he mutters words under his breath, but of their content, Hyw cannot tell. Slowly Blaidd turns in the saddle and gently coaxes his horse along the path.

Watching Blaidd's huge warhorse picking its way down through the boulders, Hyw stands at the edge of the great rock on which his shelter is built. Following every movement of his friend, Blaidd sets out along the path that leads up through the valley, but the warhorse turns down towards the lake.

Hyw looks to where Mynddy is sitting on a rock near the shore. The plates are long since clean and dry. She sits as if in some trance. Her arms folded around her knees, with her knees pulled into her chest. On hearing Blaidd approaching, Mynddy jumps nervously. Quickly scrambling down from the rock, she backs away from Blaidd's advance. Hyw grows concerned by what he sees, but holds his ground, trusting his friend.

The huge horse comes to a halt a short distance from the rock. Mynddy has shied away to the water's edge and turns, standing with the lake lapping at her feet. Her arms are folded, half crossed over her chest and even from where Hyw is standing he can see the uncertainty etched on her face.

"I have frightened thee…it was not my purpose…I have made thee feel awkward and for that I am ashamed!" Blaidd bows his head as he continues.

"Forgive an old man's memories in the sight of such beauty." With these words, he turns to go, but then he stops and turns in the saddle.

"I have heard my brethren speak of thee; they will not touch thee while I yet live." Blaidd bows his head again and spurs at his horse and moments later he is gone.

Hyw settles slightly as he senses Mynddy's fears subsiding. Sitting on a large rock he looks down towards the lake.

Blaidd rides off into the distance of its shore line. Mynddy stands looking out across the lake. Her hair is beginning to dry and a soft breeze caresses its long tresses. Hyw watches. Mynddy stoops and cupping her hand she scoops at the water, drinking. She scoops again, throwing a handful of water onto her face and she begins to wash. Hyw's eyes miss nothing and his heart breaks, knowing the sorrows she suffers. She strips to the waist, splashing the cold water over her skin, rubbing and cleaning herself for a second time. Staring down at her, his thoughts are off and away, thinking of Sián.

Chapter Fifteen

The afternoon grows heavy as clouds ride high above the mountains. It had taken them the best part of the morning to prepare for the journey. The stallion is unable to carry anyone but has a small bundle tied to its back. It still limps along but seems in better spirits. Hyw walks in front of Sarn with Mynddy riding. Still quiet, she too appears to be brighter in herself.

They follow the river through the valley, managing to skirt around small clusters of crofts without incident. Mountains rise on every side. During the winter's long months, Hyw had climbed high on their backs and seen where their path must lead. The problem is finding his way when walking in the depths of the valleys. He knows the general direction, but whether the best path lies to the north or the south of given mountains, he would have to discern as they meandered with streams and rivers flowing ever on. There is a way to the south, over flat lands, just before the sea or they could travel further north from mountain to mountain.

At the far end of the valley, the way west is blocked by a series of mountains running from north to south. The river they are following joins a larger river, which in its course runs south of the mountains. A small collection of crofts stands in their way which they need to pass, but whether they should go over the mountains to the north or take the flat lands to the south, Hyw cannot tell. While they are still a little way from the village, Hyw turns to Sarn.

"Come, my old friend...which path should we tread, hey, Sarn bach?" Sarn looks deep into Hyw's eyes, and nods her head at the sound of his voice, but doesn't move. Hyw waits awhile, but still, his gentle friend only stares back at him. Suddenly Mynddy points towards the river. Hyw looks around and sees the stallion has already half-crossed its playful flow and is standing waiting at the end of its tether. Turning to the stallion, Hyw smiles.

"Okay my new friend, we shall follow after thee." Walking to the edge of the river, Hyw jumps out onto the first rock looking for stepping-stones across its tumbling flow. Looking back to where Mynddy is coaxing Sarn to follow him, Hyw calls out to his faithful friend.

"Consider thyself sacked, Sarn bach." Hyw lifts one arm in the air and tugs at an imaginary noose around his neck. Sarn whinnies and shakes her head; first up and down and then from side to side. Mynddy leans forward, hugging Sarn to save the Sarn's feelings and looking across to Hyw she smiles, a soft warm smile, the type of smile that fills a man's heart. Pausing, Hyw smiles back, pulling harder on the imaginary rope and cocking his head to one side, contorting his face as if he has been hung on the gallows.

They follow the river to the south and re-cross its tumbling flow further down stream. The shadows of thick woodland and forest cover their movements. The trees spread their moss and fern-drenched branches above them. The sounds of the river tumbling over its rocks are accompanied by a continual trickle of water as it drips, oozes and seeps from every twig, branch and rock. The differing fragrances of the ever-changing forest haunt Hyw's mind as it stirs forgotten memories of home.

The river's stream calms as it meanders out of the trees and into the low flat lands to the south. Studying its course, Hyw can see where it spreads and seeps into bogs and marshes. Sheep and cattle graze on the lush pasture, and a hawk chases and swoops across the skies towards a dove, but both are quickly lost in the wild blue yonder. Continuing south they stay close to the tree line as it backs up against the mountains, but eventually, the mountains subside and the trees give way to the continuing quagmires and salt-marshes.

From the tree line, Hyw looks out over the flat lands spreading to the west. To the north, there are hills and further mountains. The other side of the valley blocks Hyw's view to the south, but he knows there is a range of hills and mountains with, he assumes, the sea beyond them. To the west, there are low-lying marshes and beyond them the sea.

Hyw's secret longing to see the sea addles his senses. Wise or not, he plans to see their wild horses before the end of the day. A single track leads to the west, following the northern perimeter of the swamps. Tracking the line of some distant hills, Hyw figures he can cut down towards the sea from there.

The afternoon forges on towards the evening's dwindling light. The track is well-defined and well-used by shepherds, craftsmen, miners and quarrymen, walking to or from the mountains. Those they pass pay scant attention to Hyw's small band. One old man scurries quickly back to a small croft hidden in the trees, but their encounters pass without any drama.

As evening approaches they begin to climb out of the valley up to the brow of one of the higher ridges. Breaking the crest of the hill Hyw looks out over the dark, slate-grey flatlands of the sea. Sitting for a while, he looks out and over the long bay in front of him; its wide sands stretching into the distance. His heart soars as he strains to hear the distant roar of wild horses.

Sarn is tired and the stallion is walking with a pronounced limp. Hyw looks up at Mynddy; her eyes staring out over the same deep blue-grey sea. Looking briefly up to the higher ground, where Hyw knows they would be safe, he turns from the safety of the hills and leads his forgotten band of cast-offs down towards the sea. They approach a wide field bordering a tufted string of grassy dunes stretching along the coastline to the distant headland. Beyond the headland is the finger of land his grandfather had spoken of.

The evening is fast falling as Sarn saunters across the wide field towards the dunes. The darkness spreads rapidly and the need for shelter is becoming more urgent. Hyw knows he cannot afford to hide in the dark. Looking for a way through the dunes he climbs the sandy banks to search for a suitable place to camp. Mynddy pulls Sarn to a halt and climbs down, gathering both horses together. Moments later, Hyw appears above them.

"Come…over here!" Hyw points between the dunes where he is standing, to a larger dune to the west. Calling to Sarn, Sarn immediately climbs up as Mynddy follows leading the limping stallion. They drop into a large gap between five different dunes, the hollow being large enough for even the horses. A gap lies between a large dune to their rear and a smaller dune to the west, wide enough for the horses to walk through and low enough to be out of sight of passers-by. It offers them an easy escape route to the beach and Hyw cannot quite believe their good fortune, but as Mynddy lays out their bedding, Hyw scouts out the different dunes. Climbing to the top of the middle of three dunes separating them from the sea, he lays on his stomach looking to the south.

In the dying light, Hyw looks out across the beach, over a wide bay. The sands seem to go on forever. The sea is some distance away, with wave upon wave rolling into the endless bay. Beyond the long flat sands stands a hill, behind which tiers of mountains stretch out along the coastline. On the hill, he can just make out a collection of buildings, behind which he picks out the outline of a fort, but in the meagre light, it is difficult to be sure. Several ribbons of smoke climb high into the sky from the side of the hill three of which seem to come from within the ramparts of the fort.

Hyw continues to watch for some time. 'There is no smoke without fire and no fire without a guard. But have they seen our hiding place?'

After some time pondering their situation, Hyw turns his attention to the west. He can make out only one croft set high on the headland, with a single stack of smoke rising from its stone chimney. However, beyond the headland on a further hillock jutting out from the distant coastline, he is convinced there is another fort, a little closer than the first, but both a good distance away. This second fort is set on what looks like a hill of rock that appears to be slightly smaller than that of the first, but both are too substantial for Hyw to ignore their presence. The forts look out across the bay, each to the other and standing on their battlements a sentry could survey all the land between.

'I have set my camp in the very jaws of Annwn' Hyw thinks.

Not being aware of the politics of the different tribes, or their claims on the land, Hyw cannot discern the danger he is in. He knows of the Painted Men of the North, the Warriors of Gododdyn, and their claims, but he does not know how far their influence or power has reached. Blaidd had told him of their plans to ride to the west, but of whether they were riding to strange and dangerous ground or not, he does not know.

'I will have to keep guard during the night!'

After making camp and feeding the horses, Mynddy slowly crawls up the side of the dune to lie next to Hyw. With their bedding laid out and food prepared, Mynddy looks across the vast bay and assesses her safety for herself.

At that moment a fire erupts to the west; something is burning to one side of the fort. It is larger than a campfire, but what purpose it serves, Hyw cannot tell. Another fire erupts close to the first and Hyw can just make out the outline of a croft silhouetted in the first blaze. The smoke from its thatch is rising high into the night. A flare arches into the sky; a flaming arrow shot from the area of the fort, but it has been shot out to sea, where its only purpose could be to signal some calamity or danger and a second arrow is sent the way of the first.

Mynddy and Hyw look to the south as the flaming arrows arch through the sky. Laying on the dune for some time, watching, there are no more signals. There seems to be some activity at the fort to the west, but of its substance, Hyw cannot tell.

If they had to flee during the night the horses would need water. They had crossed a small stream a little further back from the dunes; it wasn't ideal, but it would be enough.

"The forts are too close for comfort!" Hyw whispers to Mynddy.

"If we need to leave in a hurry…we must prepare the horses…but our camp is well concealed!"

They eat some food after which Hyw crawls up the side of the dunes again. Fires still burn to the west, but in the darkness, he can see nothing more. Straining his eyes to the south he looks for riders but sees nothing. The continuous roll of the waves sounds in his ears, calling to him, but he dare not answer their call.

Mynddy crawls up the dune beside him, having grown nervous waiting in the dark. Within the shadow of the mountain to the south a faint light flickers for a moment and then dies. To the west, even the smoke has eventually been shrouded by the night.

"I must water the horses." Whispers Hyw as though they were camped just below the walls of the forts. They both slip back into the safety of the dunes. Hyw waits awhile, listening to the night, before leading the horses to the stream. Mynddy follows him. Each carries their bow, with arrows at the ready. Walking in single file, Hyw leads his trusted friend and Mynddy follows with the Stallion.

Beyond the dunes, they walk through the flat field. For the most part, it is good pasture, only occasionally giving way to bog. At its far end, where the stream runs, it gives way to softer ground. They all drink their fill. Hyw constantly scans around them, with both his ears and his eyes. They are out in the open and passing guards would easily see them, even in the shadows of the night. He knows each of the guardians of the mountain paths above his home, he knows them by name, and they are friends, but these are strange lands.

"At first light, we must search out secret paths that will lead us on our way!" Returning to the dunes, Hyw cannot settle. Checking their camp, he looks out through the darkness of the night, again and again.

Eventually, he lies down on the bedding and Mynddy cuddles in at his side. An owl screeches and cries as it hunts overhead; a fox yelps somewhere in the distance and a single frog croaks from its watery hole somewhere behind them. The frog is joined by another, then another and soon there is a gathering chorus. The fox yelps again, only a pup, but it is getting closer. Hyw listens as Mynddy's lifeblood beats at his side. An owl swoops as it cries and the frogs are silenced for a while. The creeping creatures of the night sound amid the continuous roll of distant waves, but it is the waves that hypnotise Hyw's mind, dragging him off into the restless dreams of forgotten nightmares.

Chapter Sixteen

Sarn's soft lips nuzzle at Hyw's face and ears. The warm waft of her breath flows over his skin as he wakes with a start and his trusted friend backs away. Feeling for his bow, he can see the sun is above the dunes although its blaze is masked behind hazy clouds. They have slept too long.

Alien sounds are coming from beyond the dunes. Something isn't right and looking up at Sarn's uneasy countenance, he knows all is not well. Both horses remain still with their heads half raised and their ears pricked back.

"I thank thee, my old friend," Hyw whispers to Sarn. Mynddy is lying in his arms and Hyw pulls her up towards him.

"Shush." The gesture is as quiet as Hyw can make it and slowly Mynddy rouses. Hyw places a finger to his lips, although he cannot think why; he had scarcely heard a sound from Mynddy since the day he found her. Recognition of their situation is instant and both get to their knees with bows in hand. Through the gap in the dunes come the sound of horses and the clank of armour. The almost static clatter sounds in their ears, with the beat of horses and men busying themselves for battle. Knowing he cannot be seen, even if he stands erect, for some reason he squats as he scurries from one side of their camp to the other. Hyw moves towards the dunes that separate them from the marshy field and he crawls up towards their small summit.

Looking through the wind-swept grasses of the dunes; Hyw can make out an army of men gathering in the field behind them. Keeping himself low, he tries to gain a greater vantage point and fingertip by fingertip he edges through the dune's sparse grasses.

Four lines of warriors are ranked across the field; seventy to eighty men, all on horse back. Hyw looks closer and his heart jumps as he sees Blaidd and Geddyn at the head of the Warriors of Gododdyn, with Māddrōg and old Dynōg sitting next to them. Not breaking cover, Hyw strains to see further. Preparations for their impending battle are well under way, but he cannot make out their foe.

Suddenly, he sees movement through the dunes, to the west. First one then another archer drops into the hollow next to their camp. Hyw instantly recognises the dress of the Scotti archers. Turning to Mynddy, she has also seen the bowmen. How someone hasn't stumbled across their camp, Hyw cannot quite make out, but as he scrambles back to Mynddy's side, he catches sight of more of the Scotti. They are too close for comfort, but all their intentions are engrossed in the imminent battle.

Hyw notches an arrow into the string of his bow as he assesses the duty before him. He could despatch one of the two Grots, but it would then be a race against time to silence the other.

Just as he's mulling the problem over in his mind, Mynddy stands at his side. Looking momentarily at her, she nods with an arrow notched into her bow. Hyw cannot know, nor can he tell Mynddy's capabilities. Her first foray that he witnessed, she seemed unable to shoot, but her charge towards Māthōg and his fleeing men was different again. Riding like the wind, as though she were born in the saddle, with her bow bent toward her enemy, but she had not engaged them and whether in her melancholy she could rise above her fears, Hyw cannot tell.

There is a moment between them and for some reason, Hyw's mind settles as his confidence grows and he trusts the determined expression on Mynddy's face. They both bend their bows and as they do so, Hyw can hear movement on the sand behind them. There is no time to lose; he releases his feathered warrior, which is swiftly followed by Mynddy's. Her aim could not have been more certain and they both turn in the same instant, notching arrows into place to guard their rear.

The sound of footsteps moving through the gap in the dunes fills their ears with their hearts racing down hill out of control. Hyw is ready, but something nags at his mind and, in his madness, he quickly scans behind where they are standing to make sure that he is the first thing anyone will see. A Grot appears through the gap in the dunes. An old man compared to the first two archers, but he is an experienced bowman, walking with purpose; his feet placed firmly on the ground, with his bow bent ready.

Hyw is still scanning the dunes behind him as the Grot steps into view. The rush of an arrow through the air followed by a low thud quickly turns Hyw's head, as an arrow from Mynddy's bow rips into the Slag's chest. A second archer steps into view, oblivious to the fate of his comrade. His head is slightly bowed as Hyw's feathered warrior slams into him, almost taking him off his feet. Mynddy's arrow is moments behind his and a third Grot dies without ever seeing them.

The battle has not yet commenced, but it is near and there is no time to waste. Hyw and Mynddy are more reckless in their movement and observations. Hyw scurries up the dune and looks over to where he presumes their enemy should be. In the distance, he can just make out their ranks and his heart sinks. Their numbers are far more than a hundred, maybe as many again, and more Scotti archers are secreting themselves amid the dunes. This is no party of marauders; this is an army fit for a king, an invasion force. Hyw searches for Māthōg amidst their ranks, but cannot see him or his men.

There is more activity from the direction of the beach as Hyw and Mynddy make their way through the gap in the dunes to assess their situation. Things couldn't be more desperate. A band of Scotti Slags on horseback, two score, maybe a little less, are preparing to attack Geddyn's men from the rear. Archers are still walking along the beach and secreting themselves, in pairs, between the dunes.

Beyond this band of assassins, to the southwest, across the expanse of sands in the estuary, Hyw can see a large band of warriors. They are riding hard through the shallow waters of the sea, their horses kicking up spray as they charge, but they are a good distance away and will be too late. A second and smaller group, behind the first, are again riding hard. Hyw scans them, but cannot make out whether they are friend or foe, but he presumes they are not the Scotti.

Rushing back to their camp, Hyw grabs at Sarn's tether. There is no time to saddle her up. Mynddy is at Hyw's side and as he jumps onto Sarn's back, she looks up at him as if for inspiration.

"Stay here. I will try to draw them away, but I need thee to cover my attack!" Mynddy smiles and nods her head. Hyw is ready and kicks at Sarn's sides. Sarn bursts out of the gap in the dunes with her heart racing. Giving out a cry that would wake all the forces of Annwn, he turns his faithful friend towards the coming fray.

The dunes seem to disappear from his side as the colour drains from his vision, but he cannot turn his gaze from the large band of assassins. Although Hyw is screaming with all his might he can barely hear his voice. Everything seems to be closing in around him and he remembers the fear he felt as a small boy, racing through him. Taking a deep breath, Hyw fills his lungs to bursting and lets out another piercing yell.

Hyw's guttural cry reaches the ears of the battlefield. Blaidd and Geddyn both turn towards its call.

"Aye, it wid seem yon Phantom made tha Fecht Eftir all. Geddyn smiles at his comrade, searching for Hyw, still not realising the dangers they are in. Looking towards the dunes, an archer breaks his cover to loose an arrow at Hyw, first one, and then another.

Suddenly the dunes erupt as the stallion bursts high onto their banks with Mynddy sitting astride Sarn's saddle. Her bow is bent towards the first archer and he is despatched in an instant. She spurs the stallion on, as her bow bends again. A roar goes up from the battlefield as Geddyn's men cheer her on.

"Dinae sit there ye fools a whit...eftir them!" Geddyn's voice booms out his orders as scanning the dunes and he sees the archers as the outer ranks turn toward them.

Hyw continues his cry as Sarn charges towards the Scotti assassins. The leader of the group points and cries as four men separate themselves from the rest, to meet Hyw's advance, but one is instantly silenced by a feathered warrior from Hyw's arsenal.

"Kill tha whelp!" Their leader cries, charging towards the dunes having been forced into battle prematurely and the thunder of war commences.

Hyw despatches a second Grot but is advancing on their swords. Turning Sarn, he heads out towards the sea, drawing more Grots after him. They all favour their chances against the one as opposed to the frenzy of battle. Hyw turns on Sarn's back and fires and then turns Sarn back towards the fray.

The band of Scotti has been stifled by the dunes and as they breach the sandy hillocks they are met by Geddyn's rear guard.

Seeing the battle commence the main Scotti ranks begin their assault, but are hesitant with their leader being drawn too easily. The Scotti have miscalculated both the distance and the terrain. Geddyn waits, sitting at the head of his Warriors. His rearguard has all but dealt with the impetuous Scotti assassins, their numbers depleted by Hyw's advance.

Another small band of Grots are assembled at the far side of the field and on seeing their comrades attack they too enter the field, but are met with as much force from their rear as faces them on the battlefield, as more Warriors of Gododdyn join the battle, shredding through any hope of a surprise attack by the Scotti.

The Painted Men of the North are still outnumbered, even with reinforcements, but Geddyn and his men know the ground and the Scotti have been unable to survey the field. They continue their charge, but as the ground beneath them gives way to hidden bogs and water holes, their horses fall. As one horse falls it fells those behind it. The Scotti struggle to keep their line as a host of shouts and screams call out.

Mynddy continues her charge across the top of the dunes. She has despatched three more archers with another being charged down by the stallion. It is a magnificent animal and the Warriors continue to cheer at her advance while waiting for their orders to attack. With each arrow, she looses a roar goes up as the warriors build the frenzied delirium of battle within them. Most of them turn towards Mynddy's continued assault standing in their saddles, thrusting their swords to the skies as their cheers fill the air. Some even stand on the rear haunches of their horses screaming and shouting as Mynddy despatches yet another Grot.

One warrior, standing on the rump of his horse, rips a hardened leather breastplate from his chest, revealing his tattooed torso. Every muscle and sinew in his body seems to flex as he slams the hilt of his sword against his stomach. Saluting Mynddy, she is oblivious to the great honour the warrior gives her, then he turns to the charging Scotti; screaming and yelling; slamming the flat of his swords-blade against his stomach and chest; pulling at his braided hair, as he builds the delirium and turbulence of the coming fray within him.

Yet more warriors climb onto their horses spurred on by the young girl charging down and despatching the Scotti Archers. Geddyn sees and feels the clamour of battle all around him, but holds his men. Yet more of the Scotti horses fall as the thunder of their hooves shakes every heart.

The last Grot falls from its horse, as Hyw speeds past his crumpled remains, back towards Mynddy's position on the dunes. He cannot see the battlefield and neither do those gathered to do battle see his clamour to arms. The rear assault has failed and the last of the fleeing assassins bridges the dunes in his hasty retreat. Two feathered warriors hit him simultaneously, one in his eye and the other rips through his throat; he is instantly unhorsed, with one of his feet caught in its stirrup and he is dragged out across the hard flat sands.

Hyw looks up to Mynddy, his comrade in arms, as Sarn charges towards her. They each catch sight of the other and Hyw can see that her eyes are once more full of fire.

Looking out across the ranks of warriors straining as they wait for battle, Hyw raises his bow high in the air as his cry reaches the ears of his friends. The stallion rears up with Mynddy in the saddle and the warriors roar their appreciation, cheering and shouting as the clarion calls and Geddyn finally orders his men into battle.

With one deafening cry, all the Sons of Gododdyn scream after him, save only Blaidd who lingers to salute his friend and then he too joins the pursuit. The ranks of the Scotti have been broken by the terrain and victory is within Geddyn's grasp.

An arrow whistles past Mynddy's head and they both turn. Further along the dunes, Scotti archers have ceased the battle and have fixed their intent on Hyw and Mynddy. Immediately turning, they both ride down the dunes onto the beach as Sarn and the stallion pursue their new quarry. Five or possibly six archers are running towards their position along the beach. One stops to loose another blade, but his aim is wild and the arrow passes between Hyw and Mynddy who continue their charge.

The others scatter and run. A feathered warrior from Mynddy's bow cuts the first down before he can notch another arrow into his bow. One by one the Slags are chased down and despatched by either Hyw or Mynddy. Only the last Grot was brave enough to face them and his courage was met with two arrows, which both hit him centre mass almost simultaneously.

The foray of battle can be heard from beyond the dunes. Hyw looks out across the sands for the chasing bands of warriors, but they are still a long way off. Riding hard, Hyw and Mynddy reach the top of the dunes and again survey the field. A frenzy of flashing blades; clanking armour and splintered war-boards meets their eyes and ears. Cries and screams echo from every quarter.

Win? Lose? Who can tell? Death stalks the field, like a plague of bare-faced crows. Hyw longs to ride headlong into Annwn, but this is a battle for lance, sword and shield; not a battle for the bow. His strength lies in surprise and a continued aggressive attack, but a hunter who stalks his prey could not survive this battlefield.

Hyw remembers his swordplay and searches for its steel amid the fury. Blaidd is in the heat of battle; Hyw can see his helmet glint in the sun.

'Geddyn cannot be far away!' Hyw thinks to himself and his eyes scan to and fro, finally resting on Geddyn with Cilydd at his side. They are both in the midst of the fiercest fighting. The day would be theirs, but the battle is far from over.

Suddenly Cilydd's horse falters and he falls to the ground. Hyw cannot make out what has happened and amid the battle, he does not see him rise again. The fighting escalates, but still, Hyw cannot see his young friend. Hyw turns to Mynddy in an instant.

"Wait here!" The words are curt, but Mynddy understands their urgency, although her promise goes unspoken as Sarn charges the field. The battle is spread out and Hyw soon finds himself advancing on his friend's position. Cilydd is lying on the ground at his father's feet. Geddyn is in mortal combat with two Grots, one of whom looks like a dragon spitting fire; the other is a 'man mountain'. Hyw's blade is swift and cuts down the fiery dragon, leaving Geddyn a fighting chance against the other giant.

Blaidd is protecting Geddyn's rear with Māddrōg and Dynōg flanking his other side; all sitting high above Cilydd's body, which is lying motionless between their frightened horses. Blaidd's horse rears and as its hooves fall, and with a blow from his sword he decapitates yet another Scotti Slag. Another of Hyw's arrows tears through the air and the man mountain crumbles, but Hyw has no time to help Blaidd with his foes. Geddyn turns as Sarn comes to a halt.

"Can ye no git Cilydd from tha feld?"

Jumping from Sarn's back, Hyw bends over his friend; his helmet is badly dented where a blade has crashed down on it and blood is pouring from an unseen wound, but Cilydd is stirring. Hyw grabs at him, pulling him to his feet, while Geddyn and Blaidd guard his rescue. Struggling, Hyw stands Cilydd next to Sarn. He pushes from one side and Geddyn pulls at his son from the other, until he is full across Sarn's bare back. Jumping up behind him, Hyw spurs Sarn back towards the dunes.

Sarn is quick and wastes no time and Hyw's bow works just as hard as his trusted horse, but as he reaches the dunes, he is notching the last of his feathered warriors into his bow.

Mynddy has kept her promise, but she has not been idle, and neither has her bow. Hyw can hear the charge of a warhorse close behind him and the screams of a Scotti Slag cut into him. An arrow from Mynddy's bow halts the Scotti's cry.

Unceremoniously dropping Cilydd from Sarn's back, he slumps onto the sand but is almost fully conscious. Taking his helmet off, he begins to dap at his wound.

The battle is almost at an end; those left to fight another day sink to their knees, exhausted. Severed limbs, blood and bodies are strewn everywhere. Men raise themselves slowly up to their knees only to faint back to the wounded earth in exhaustion.

Mynddy watches as one of the Warriors of Gododdyn tries to make his feet. A little distance in front of this warrior, two Scotti Slags are struggling to gain their senses.

Mynddy suddenly recognises the old warrior, whose eyes had hungered after her. She watches, thinking on his life and remembers the intentions of his heart. The warrior sinks to his knees, too weak to stand. One of the Scotti Grots falls to the earth in a faint, but the other has made it to his feet. The Grot raises his huge sword as the helpless Son of Gododdyn can only watch and wait for the Grot's merciless intentions. Mynddy bends her bow; her aim is sure. The arrow pierces the Slag, just above his breastplate and he crumples to the ground. The helpless Son of Gododdyn looks up at Mynddy and then collapses in a faint.

Fully roused, Cilydd has a want and it is all Hyw can do to stop him from re-entering the battlefield. Slowly the fray ceases. Horses and men sink in exhaustion; scattered in endless confusion. There are thirty or more men still on horseback and ten or more on foot. Several of those on foot are still charging the battlefield, making sure all the Scotti are dead. No one is spared.

Cilydd is standing, although a little dazed. Next to him, Hyw and Mynddy sit high on Sarn and the Stallion. A small group of warriors ride over to the dunes and each salute, both Hyw and Mynddy, bowing their heads to the hilt of their swords and then raising them to the heavens. Hyw looks to the field beyond the grateful warriors; he scans the ground for his friends, but he cannot see them.

Scouring the area where he had rescued Cilydd, a small group of warriors is huddled over something or someone. In an instant, Hyw recognises both

Blaidd and Geddyn's horses near the silent huddle. His reaction is instant and Sarn charges the battlefield for the last time.

At the same moment, Mynddy and Cilydd seem to see and understand. Cilydd races down the dunes, but in his daze, he almost faints again. Pausing at the bottom, Mynddy offers her hand to Cilydd as she takes one of her feet from her stirrup. Cilydd looks up at her, still in a daze, but he takes her hand and climbs up behind her. Immediately, she becomes uneasy as he leans against her, wrapping his arms around her waist. Eventually, she kicks at the stallion's sides.

Hyw jumps from Sarn's back and instantly dives between the huddle of warriors at Geddyn's side and they both bend over Blaidd's broken body. Lying on his back, his helmet on the ground next to him, blood is flowing freely from a wound on Blaidd's shoulder and another wound on the inside of his leg, which is spurting with bright red blood. Two warriors are fighting to stem the wound, with another tending to the wound on his shoulder. Blaidd is barely conscious, but he manages a smile for his friend.

"Aye, it would seem thy madness did not keep ye from battle after all." Blaidd seems to choke on his words and he struggles with a glob of blood at the back of his throat, but he manages to raise another smile. Looking through the warriors gathered around him, Cilydd drops at his side, but he is not whom Blaidd's eyes seek.

His eyes eventually settle on Mynddy as she stares down through the crowd of warriors. Looking straight at her, his finger slowly moves across his chest, beckoning her closer. Mynddy hesitates as warriors make way for her. The three Warriors who are working on his wounds also back away, realising the futility of their labours. Blaidd beckons again and Mynddy climbs down from the stallion.

She is slow and hesitates, but Blaidd is insistent and she bends closer to him, kneeling at his side. Struggling to move his hand, he finally finds the leather thong at his neck. Too weak to move, Hyw pulls at the thong and hands it to him.

Blaidd holds the arrowhead in his hand and beckons Mynddy closer still as holding his token out. Mynddy goes to take hold of it, but as she does so, with the last of his remaining strength, Blaidd grabs hold of her hand and wraps his token tightly inside it. Mynddy jumps and holds back, uncertain and nervous about the old warrior's intentions, but Blaidd continues to beckon her closer.

A sudden calm seems to enter her and settling her mind, she slowly bends forward. Using all his remaining strength, Blaidd lifts his other hand up behind Mynddy's head and he gently pulls her in towards him. Mynddy submits to Blaidd's hand and he raises his head to her ear. He begins to whisper, but the blood in his throat chokes his words and he turns his head, coughing it out. Using the last dregs of life within him, he holds Mynddy to him and this time he manages to whisper clearly. Tears begin to well in Mynddy's eyes and as he finishes his words, his body slumps lifeless to the ground.

Chapter Seventeen

Silence pervades as all battle ceases. Even the moans of those who are wounded cease or are brought to an abrupt end. The two chasing bands of men arrive, too late for battle and can only gather the spoils of war. Throughout the battlefield, Men and warriors seem to raise themselves from the dead, having fainted or collapsed in their exhaustion. Those who chase the dead, move quickly from one body to another.

Hyw hears one of them call out.

"Life yet sparks in this one!" Another voice calls out.

"Aye an here!"

Geddyn orders his men as Mynddy and Hyw turn from the awful dross of battle, to attend to what is left of their lives. The stallion's wound has ripped open in his exertions and Mynddy tends to the horse's needs with tears in her eyes. It had seemed strong and capable in the fray, but its struggles are over and its limp has returned. The saddle is changed and Hyw gathers their meagre belongings together.

As they emerge from the dunes a shout goes up. The Sons of Gododdyn have gathered and salute both Hyw and Mynddy, along with their horses. Geddyn walks over to the clamour of warriors, but Cilydd tends to Blaidd. Before Geddyn can speak a shout goes up.

"Sheltie, Sire!" Everyone looks to the far end of the field, where a dozen or more riders are heading towards them. They are not charging the field, although every warrior girds himself and draws his weapon in preparation.

"Can ye nae see wir een braithren?" Geddyn calls out as he waits for the approach of yet more of the Sons of Gododdyn. The leader of this band of men is taller and leaner than Geddyn if a little younger; although in looks, the similarity is striking. The band of warriors come to a halt in front of Geddyn and their leader dismounts.

"Fit ken ye ma Bráthair?" The two warriors walk off, finding a private space in the field to talk.

Hyw looks over the battlefield, with his concerns growing for his fallen friend. Most of the warriors will be buried where they have fallen. Blaidd's body has been covered in a shroud, but no plans have been made for his burial. Looking at some of the Scotti, Hyw can see they are mainly young lads and old men with just a few experienced warriors amongst them.

Several of Geddyn's men are constructing a large fire. They are cutting down large bushes and small trees, which their steeds drag to the blaze. Others are gathering the Scotti dead and they throw them into the flames. More trees and bushes are felled and the fire is kept well stoked with both bodies and tinder; the smell of the flames licking at their flesh is sickly sweet and it drifts over the field.

Hyw looks at Geddyn who is still deep in conversation with his brother. His brother had held the hill fort to the west. The Scotti had attacked them the previous morning, taking them by surprise. Many of the crofters outside the fort had been killed or worse. They had impaled two children on the opposite hillside in full view of the fort and had raped and decapitated both their mothers'. No mercy or consideration was shown as they laid siege to the fort, but unbeknown to Geddyn's brother, the Scotti had withdrawn during the night.

Another warrior walks over to Cilydd and whispers to him, handing him a bundle of arrows. Cilydd in turn walks over to Hyw.

"I dinna ken if all are guid, but ye can choose fur ye sel." Cilydd places the arrows on the ground between them and Hyw bends to inspect the feathered warriors. Mynddy, on seeing the bundle, climbs down from Sarn's back and begins to sort through them. A second warrior approaches and drops another bundle of arrows onto the pile. There are many Scotti blades, but they are too cumbersome for Hyw or Mynddy's needs; with heavy shafts and thick fletches that would drag in the breeze.

Moments later, one of the youngest warriors, brings a handful of arrows he has collected from the far side of the dunes. Washing their tips in the sea he has hurried back through the dunes and brings them to Hyw and Mynddy. Hyw takes them thanking the young warrior as he does so. The warrior smiles, knowing his place in history is fixed with Hyw's gratitude.

They search through the pile for Ywel's old arrows. Mynddy helps and she secures them one by one in either her own, or Hyw's quiver. Something seems to spark in Cilydd and he sidles away unnoticed. Quickly returning, he is carrying Blaidd's quiver.

"Dinna fash yersel," Cilydd says, handing the quiver to Hyw, who takes it and pauses, looking at the familiar blades; wrestling with memories of his friend.

"Nae Bother," Cilydd goes to say more as Mynddy takes the quiver and walking over to the horses, she ties it to the rear of Sarn's saddle without further thought. Something has changed inside her and she seems more certain of her life. Whatever Blaidd had whispered to her, it has sparked somewhere deep inside her, she is different; she still does not speak, but somehow she is different.

Two more riders enter the field from the west. They make their way to Geddyn and his brother. Hyw watches the four men as they talk. One of the two riders points out to the west and then to the north, tracing the line of the diminishing mountains westward and then he re-indicates further to the west.

Hyw approaches Geddyn, who seems to be deep in thought. Looking up at Hyw, he says.

"Wilt tha nae allow us ta rid with thee Laddie, at least as far as the fort, it will gie us time tae blether an thank ye afor yer courage een battle…Māthōg has been seen tae tha north an he and the Scotti are travelling westward…Ah hav reason to believe these Scotti Slags are his min…An army fur him t'tak the lands westward…He has support from the Triad of Druids…thon faa sought refuge on Gaelic shores…Ah have ordered men to take care of Blaidd an they ken tha desires of his heart."

Geddyn is still exhausted from battle and his words are concise, almost curt, and he seems to gather strength before he talks again. When he does, his voice is different; he is quiet and subdued.

"He wast one of tha greatest min ah haft eer ken." Geddyn stops and takes Ywel's arrowhead from around his neck, holding it out between them.

"Oh thon ah cud ken tha pwer this wields; Oh thon ah had a hundred such as he…and ye my fren…enough, we shall ha teem t'spik on tha trail, let us be away. And faa is thon wild lassie with thee? Ye must spik me, thon ah ma Ken."

Geddyn shouts orders to his men as they gather altogether to make preparations. There are many Scotti horses, which the warriors have tethered in pairs. Geddyn sends some warriors back to the fort to the south, but the greater portion of men he sends to the fort, west across the headland. Yet more men wait on Geddyn's word. Two by two he sends out scouts; his most trusted warriors.

Geddyn is quiet and circumspect in what he says to each pair. Briefing them in seclusion, so only they know his orders; all that is except Hyw, who for some unknown reason Geddyn allows close enough to hear. Hyw hears and sees all, but struggles at times to understand Geddyn's strange tongue.

It is obvious by the way he talks that Geddyn intimately knows and understands the lie of the land westward and he sends out each pair to watch over separate quarters. It also becomes apparent, that Geddyn believes Māthōg is responsible for the army of men they have just massacred, but neither Geddyn nor Hyw can figure out why he had not been at their head. Although if he had been, the battle may well have swung the other way.

Geddyn keeps sighing and muttering to himself occasionally.

"It's a mess laddie…a real fash." When he is finished only a hand full of men are left on the field, two of Geddyn's guards and five others, including Cilydd with Six warriors surrounding Blaidd's broken body. Hyw can see them wrapping it in fine linen and eventually all six carry him to his horse.

Mynddy is eager to leave and Hyw can sense her impatience, but he looks steadily up at her, sat a stride Sarn and she knows her patience will have to last a while longer.

"Cam laddie!" Geddyn walks over to the six warriors who are placing Blaidd over his horse's saddle and Hyw follows a short distance behind him. Geddyn turns to the oldest warrior.

"Div ye ken ma command?"

"Ah wilt take him t'tha lake Sire…" The old warrior then looks at Hyw and hesitates.

"Go on then…" The warrior starts again.

"Ah wilt take him to where Hyw kept his watch through the winter, above the lake," The warrior hesitates again as his words attract Hyw's full attention. Geddyn turns to Hyw.

"Hit wast Blaidd's desire to be buried aroon tha lake…ahin his home." Hyw turns to Geddyn.

"Hit wast his home ower fit ye kept thy lonely vigil…his wif and bairn are buried there…at least they are buried on tha far shore of tha lake…They were…" Geddyn's words fall silent.

"Hit was his wish t'be buried far ye built thy watch twer, sut he cud keep a watch ower those he loves more than he!"

Hyw realises the irony of the awful coincidence and he turns to the older of the waiting warriors.

"Destroy all I have built there and throw it into the lake. Dig and line a funeral barque fit for his voyage to the celestial shores and then build an altar over him, fit for a king."

"Ah tha auld ways, we ha need of them noo, more than e'er…ye heard the laddie, spare Nithin. He wast tha greatest among us, see ye do him honour…I send thee, Gyrant, in my stead!" The old warrior acknowledges the honour Geddyn has given to him and Gyrant turns the men back towards the mountains.

Geddyn still has hold of the old arrowhead in his hand and brings it up in front of him as they both walk back to where Mynddy and his men are waiting.

"So laddie, dost this represent tha auld ways or has it brought tee us new ways. Ah have heard spik of a new religion eftir the order of the Romans… or at least eftir their Christian ways. Come now laddie, spik all an' tell us wit ye know!" There is a silence between them and Geddyn stops walking a moment, causing Hyw to hesitate.

"I know very little… My grandfather would have allowed his life to be taken before he revealed the secrets his token represents and I know too little of their secrets to tell thee anything for sure. He spoke of the old ways, of good men he had known, but he said the Druids have perverted what was once held to be true. He taught me of a God of love…my heart was hard and I did not hear his words until it was too late. I did not believe…but now…now I feel something…a familiar presence sometimes, a still small voice in my heart and my mind, but I cannot be sure of anything. He spoke of the Christian God; the God of the Romans, but they too have all perverted his ways." Hyw then mutters under his breath.

"The king shall come." Geddyn hears his words and turns to him in silence, looking deep into Hyw's eyes as he remembers the first time he saw Geddyn all those years ago.

Geddyn nods his appreciation for Hyw's words, but has little understanding, although he senses the same power he knew in Blaidd, in Hyw, and he longs for Hyw to pledge his allegiance to him, just as Blaidd had.

"Thou art strange laddie, but ah wid trust thee with ma life." Geddyn turns to where Mynddy is sitting astride Sarn and then looks back to Hyw.

"Thou hinnae a steed to bear ye hence." The Warriors of Gododdyn have gathered many horses in the spoils of battle, and at Geddyn's words, they clamour to give, not the gathered horses, but their horses to him.

A warrior steps forward and kneels in front of Hyw, holding the reins of a wild-looking black stallion in his hand. He bows his head in front of Hyw and holds the reins out and up. Hyw pauses. Mynddy looks uneasy recognising the warrior; the same warrior whose wanton eyes had lusted after her; the same warrior who had been saved from a certain death, by Mynddy's swift blade.

Looking at Mynddy, sensing her unease, Hyw looks back to the warrior still kneeling before him, unable or unwilling to raise his stare, but Hyw takes the reins and smiles up at Mynddy. The warrior immediately gets to his feet and turns towards Mynddy, still with his head bowed in shame. Raising his sword high into the air; he salutes her.

Chapter Eighteen

They soon reach the hill fort to the west, but Hyw does not wish to approach its battlements, uneasy at what Mynddy may witness. Geddyn orders two of his men to ride with them, to point out the way over the hills. They follow their lead into the afternoon when they turn to the north and then to the west again, skirting a larger settlement and then two smaller villages. The two warriors know the trail well and whisper to Hyw the way he should follow.

"Ye wid be safer doon by tha sea laddie…Aye, tha dunes back on tae thick mire!" but the warriors are circumspect in what they say in front of Mynddy.

"Och ye ken tha Scotti are coming…Aye laddie, een their droves…why then do ye ride headlong in t'their advance?"

Mynddy is uneasy in the warrior's company and is glad when they turn to go. For some reason, Hyw hands back the stallion, telling Geddyn's men to thank the old warrior for its loan. Turning to Sarn and taking hold of her reins, he begins to lead his old friend south, towards the low lands and the sea.

The way ahead circumscribes a small headland, then it drops down between its sheltered watchtower and the thick marshes. The sea comes into view, with endless rolling waves drifting slowly into the bay's continuous shoreline. Hyw pauses, looking out, checking and rechecking for signs of danger. The long continuous bay curves out to the horizon where a larger headland rises as it reaches out into the sea. Looking up at Mynddy, Hyw wonders about her thoughts.

"We must take our rest in the dunes tonight. The warriors have said it will be safe!" Mynddy smiles and begins to stroke Sarn's neck, and behind her ears, as if to tell the beast it wouldn't be long. She seems brighter, but they are both feeling the strains of battle and they stand exhausted, not wanting to move. Eventually, Sarn steps forward nudging Hyw to move and they all saunter down the grassy slope above the bay, watching the wild horses of the sea. Huge waves tumble, crashing and roaring towards the shore. Some of the waves are taller than Hyw himself, but still, he longs to wade into their cooling waters, despite a hesitant fear of their toppling towers.

    Exhaustion hungers inside him as he leads his band of orphaned pilgrims over the fine sands towards the dunes. Occasionally he climbs their grassy battlements to check for a place for the night. Mynddy climbs down from Sarn and leads both horses, following Hyw as he flits from one dune to another. The evening is fast approaching as Hyw spies a suitable place to hide up, not as perfect as their camp the night before, but the two warriors had assured him the Scotti would not ride this way.

Undoing Sarn's saddle and taking the bundle from the stallion's back, he slings them, one over each shoulder, and carries them into the heart of the dunes. Mynddy turns towards the sea and leads the horses over the sand while Hyw lays out the thick blankets. Light clouds are beginning to drift over the sky and Hyw checks for rain. Deciding it probably won't, he still strings out a blanket above the bed, just in case. When camp is set, he climbs up and sits on top of the dune just above their bed, looking out over the crashing waves. The moment chases through his head as a wave of exhaustion hits him and he struggles to keep awake.

The two horses gallop along the shoreline, Sarn leading the stallion as it tries to keep up; hobbling in Sarn's wake. They turn and run back in front of Mynddy who is half turned away from Hyw looking out to sea, watching the horses as they frolic in the shallows.

Hyw smiles to himself as he looks at Mynddy, searching for every detail. She is half-turned from him, but he can see the side of her face and the shape of her body through her dress. Her hair and dress are blowing in a strong breeze. She grabs a handful of hair at the back of her head, trying to keep it under control. Clasping her hand around something at her chest, one of her breasts is clearly outlined against her arm. He remembers Blaidd's token and realises, she is holding the arrowhead, which she has strung around her neck and he wonders on Blaidd's secret words.

Search further, Hyw watches as Mynddy walks closer to the sea. Gathering her dress up at the front she paddles into the water. Hesitating slightly, she steps deeper into the spent waves. Sarn and the stallion canter towards her. Wave upon wave of wild horses seems to gallop, charging towards her with their spindrift manes floating free in the breeze. Mynddy begins to bathe the stallion around the area of its wound, splashing the salt waters over the horse's side. Sarn moves in close. The two horses seem at ease with each other and Sarn nuzzles up to the stallion as Mynddy is lost somewhere between them.

Hyw thinks of Sián, he can see her now; he can see her bright eyes, see her smile radiating out towards him, but slowly her image fades as Hyw drifts away into his dreams.

Waking with a start, Hyw looks uneasily around him. Sitting bolt upright, his head brushes against the blanket spread out above him. Quickly searching for his bow, the roar of the wild horses of the sea and the smell of their salty waters seem to fill his head.

Yet again Hyw and Mynddy gather what is left of their lives and rolling it into three bundles they tie them onto Sarn and the Stallions' backs. The stallion's wound is struggling to heal and the horse is limping again. They walk slowly out onto the sand and turn towards the headland at the far end of the bay. Mynddy cannot bear to see the horse limping and before they have taken a handful of paces she jumps down from Sarn's back, stripping the stallion of its load and placing it all on Sarn.

Her melancholy seems to have eased and she smiles at Hyw who is looking on with some amusement. Picking her brother's bow up from the sand, she takes the reins of the stallion and sets off along the beach, leaving Hyw to lead Sarn. Following for a while, Hyw takes the lead as they begin to climb up onto the back of the headland to the west. Its summit is covered in bracken with only one indistinct path running around its top as it looks out over the wild waters of the seas.

From its highest point, Hyw can see a further smaller hill off in the distance. Huge white clouds billow up in a brightening sunny sky casting their shadows onto the undulating landscape. The warbling of Skylarks can be heard all around; summer will soon be upon them and Hyw breaths the passing seasons in as his eyes continuously study the surrounding hills.

From the summit of the second hill, a small island is visible out to sea, smaller than Hyw imagined and he doubts whether it is the sacred isle he had often seen in his waking visions. A second smaller island lies close to the first, but it is little more than a large rock sticking out of the water.

They quickly climb down from the back of the hill, to avoid being seen and not before time. On a distant ridge, a small band of men on horseback are riding to the west. They are quick, but Hyw takes no chances and they hold up for a while in the thick bracken, laying both horses on their sides. The rest gives Hyw time to think and plan. On the distant shoreline close to the small islands lies a cluster of crofts and he wonders if it is the village Blaidd spoke of.

Hyw is sure they are close but has no way of knowing how close, other than the uncertain shadows of his visions. They would have to circle the village and come back to the shores of the sea further along the coast. From their hiding place, Hyw makes a mental note of every croft and stack of smoke. There is no way of knowing whether they are friend or foe; Geddyn and his men were uncertain of the loyalty of the people on the westernmost part of the peninsular and Blaidd had only given reference to one person of whom Hyw could demand trust.

The afternoon presses endlessly on as the sun climbs high into the sky. Hyw and Mynddy step from shadow to shadow as they keep to uncertain hedgerows and walk in the dips and valleys of the rolling fields and hills, keeping rocks, hills and even large trees between them and any sign of life.

Slowly their journey leads them up to the headland beyond the small village. They had seen several small groups of men, off in the distance of the day, some riding in pairs, but one group numbered about ten or twelve. Three riders had ridden down towards the village and had been met by two others, but from the distance, Hyw could not say if they were Scotti or not; but he assumed they were.

They follow an obscure trail that leads them high above the village. Mynddy has walked all day and Hyw can see she is tired. The stallion is lame and needs to rest more than Mynddy does, but if they stop they will be found. The Scotti seem to surround them and Hyw trusts his feelings more than his sense.

They break the crest of the hill just as evening falls. A large red sun is quenching itself into the sea to one side of the sacred isle; its light bouncing off clouds that straddle the horizon with Hyw's heart soaring at its sight. The island looks like a great fish breaking the surface of the dark blue sea, its humped back rising high into the air.

Pausing awhile, Hyw seems to search through his feelings, and slowly, back through all the years, the image of Ywel's brother comes flooding into his mind and he knows…he knows as surely as if Old Dwyr were standing in front of him. Hyw breathes a sigh of relief, but his journey isn't over.

A path leads down through the ferns and bracken, to a small croft and sheltered workings some distance away, just as Hyw had imagined from Blaidd's description. Beyond the croft, the dark blue-grey sea and beyond that the sacred isle sits waiting for them, but the seas around the island seem to swirl with treacherous currents and Hyw has no idea of how he will make the haven of its rocky shores.

A kindly light burns through a crack in one of the shutters of the croft, but with so many Scotti blades and bows afoot, Hyw cannot be sure of a friendly welcome. The shadows of the evening are falling fast around them as they step out onto the path which is bordered by large clumps of bracken. Keeping to one side of the path, again moving from shadow to shadow, they slowly make their way towards the low wind-swept buildings.

Up a small incline towards its brow, Hyw can see its ridge runs out to both sides of the track, with its path leading through a small thicket of bushes and trees; a perfect place for an ambush. Hyw stops as his eyes scan to and fro, picking out every shadow, bush and tree. Signalling for Mynddy to stay, he slowly moves forward with his bow in hand, a feathered warrior notched securely into place.

Inching forward, every shadow potentially hides a Scotti assassin, but his eyes penetrate the empty darkness as slowly and surely he places one foot after another.

Hyw despairs as he hears Sarn and Mynddy on the path behind him, but above their silent clatter, a muffled cough chokes out of the thicket, not a thick gruff cough, but a young innocent cough. Its noise is almost at Hyw's feet and he turns, bending his bow. Just a little way off in the bracken, next to a clump of bushes, he catches sight of the child's frightened eyes, but as their eyes meet, the child's mother steps out of the bracken with a bow bent towards Hyw's heart.

There is a look in the young mother's eyes that tells Hyw she would sacrifice all for those she loves. That self-same look stares back through Hyw's memories, back through the years, and Hyw is once more sitting in the fear and trepidation of the dry cave, staring at the tears draining from his mother's frightened, but determined eyes and he immediately flounders in the deep seas of his waking visions.

Sensing Hyw's hesitation, Mynddy steps out from behind him with her bow bent towards the frightened young woman. The young mother gives out a long guttural cry.

"Giffydd..." Everything seems to happen at once. Hyw drops his aim; relaxing the grip on his bow as Mynddy steps wider, keeping her brother's bow bent towards the woman. Children begin to cry as the bracken erupts with the screams of those the woman is protecting. Somewhere, out of Hyw's sight, the door of a croft flies open as a young man charges into the gathering shadows of the evening. The mother quakes in fear as Giffydd, her husband, races to her, wielding his blade.

The mother drops to her knees and her bow falls to the ground with her three children running into the sanctuary of her arms. Hugging them to her breast, there is another hidden in the shadows of the bushes. Slowly a pale slim young girl steps out from between two bushes, into the evening, where both Hyw and Mynddy can see her; she is exquisitely beautiful, with long fair hair that reaches down to the top of her legs, but she is little more than a child herself; maybe fourteen or fifteen.

Mynddy relaxes her aim as Hyw turns towards the young man who is still charging up the hill. Breaking the crest of the small incline; the young man's eyes search the dying light for the Scotti Slags that supposedly have found the hiding place of his family. Catching the sight of Hyw standing with his arms to his side, his bow held limply in one hand; Giffydd is unsure of Hyw's intentions as Mynddy turns her deadly blade towards him.

The children's cries subside on hearing their father's approach and Giffydd slows his charge on seeing Hyw standing at his mercy. Stopping, he stares at the strangers, standing only a short distance from them. First, he scrutinises Hyw and then at Mynddy, who looks more than capable with the bow she still has bent towards him. It is all the woman can do to prevent her children from running to their father, but her young sister steps up to give her a hand, lifting the youngest boy into her arms.

Hyw stares across at Giffydd.

"We are friends…" Hyw says quietly.

Giffydd doesn't relax at Hyw's words and Hyw senses his hesitation.

"We have been sent by Blaidd." At these words, the young man begins to relax. Slowly Hyw raises his hand to his chest and taking hold of the arrowhead, he pulls it out from behind his smock. Giffydd stares, almost in disbelief and turns his eyes to Mynddy almost expecting her to reach up to her neck, but she remains silent with her bow bent towards him.

Giffydd raises his arms in submission and Mynddy relaxes her grip on the string of her bow. Stepping forward, he smiles at Hyw who smiles back. Giffydd reaches out taking hold of Hyw's token and he examines the arrowhead. Then extending his arm forward, he shakes Hyw by the hand

and as they shake, Hyw grips his new found friend by the arm, as is the custom of old friends.

"Thou hast come in perilous times my friend…we must be careful," Giffydd says, almost in a whisper, but his wife Seryn interrupts him, unable to keep her silence.

"Ye have seen Blaidd…he is here?" She asks with some excitement in her voice.

"Blaidd is dead," Hyw says with reverence etched into his words, but his they cut deep into her flesh, as surely as if he had fired an arrow into her heart. She drops to her knees in her tears and her sister falls into her arms as they both mourn the death of their uncle.

"It is grave news ye bring," Giffydd says as his head bows and he moves to comfort his wife and family and in her grief, Seryn cries out.

"Who will keep our people in the hearts of Gododdyn now Blaidd is gone?"

"He died a hero…saving Geddyn and his son. They will remember and could not ever forget…he has taken his journey before us, but he will watch over our footfall with those who look on!" Hyw's words surprise even him, but they do not impress Seryn whose tongue is sharp as she speaks out again.

"Ye speak of the old ways…"

"Seryn!" Giffydd tries to silence his wife, but she will not halt her words.

"The old ways are dead…where is thy God now?" Giffydd lifts his wife up, pulling her into his arms and cradles her head on his shoulder. Whispering into her ear, she continues to cry.

Hyw is silent, thinking about her words and looking back through time, he can see the author of his thoughts, Ywel. Thinking on the old man and all his words, Hyw has reason to doubt more than most, but somehow their seed has swollen inside his heart.

"The old ways have been reborn and their light has been rekindled…I am Hyw the son of Bryn, who was the son of Ywel, a son of Bryn Ywel and the people of the Mountain of Tears; these are my words and I stand in need of thy help."

Hyw speaks with power and majesty as every fear is silenced and all their eyes rest on him. Even the children have stopped their sobbing and look up at him, as though he were a Guardian of the Gates of Annwn itself. Every name he mentioned had touched their ears before; all heroes to them. Blaidd had told them of his travels and of those he had travelled with. He had rehearsed many stories of Hyw's grandfather and father and had even told them of Isobel. Each name Hyw had mentioned was a hero in the sight of those present and it showed in the faces of the children. Even Seryn's heart is full as she attempts to control her tears.

"What is it ye want from us? Pray to tell…and if it is ours to give, it shall be thine." Giffydd's words are spoken almost in a whisper, but their might strikes a cord in every heart. Hyw cannot talk for a moment as he gathers his thoughts amongst his racing feelings. Giffydd is impatient.

"Speak and it shall be thine."

Hyw cannot seem to find the words he needs; he is overwhelmed by his feelings as tears well in his eyes. Sensing Hyw's hesitation, Mynddy steps forward placing her hand on Hyw's shoulder. Her touch seems to wake him, but still, he is silent. Giffydd speaks again.

"Ye wish to see the old man…ye wish to see Old Dwyr?" Hyw's heart is racing.

"He has been waiting for thee…he has seen thee in his dreams…his waking visions…he says that ye…!" Giffydd's words falter and he lowers his voice again.

"He says thou art a man of…!" Giffydd cannot utter the words, but Hyw knows their meaning.

"Come, we have much to prepare and the time is far spent."

Chapter Nineteen

The young family gather in a huddle close to the door, just inside the croft; waiting for Hyw and Mynddy. The oldest child, a boy, is standing on a stool looking out through a small window next to the door. Suddenly he jumps down and with a rush of excitement in his voice he says in a forced whisper.

"They're here." The door swings open and Hyw and Mynddy step inside, ducking under the doorway.

The croft is small and lit only by one candle. As Hyw and Mynddy walk into the room, Giffydd steps forward, again taking Hyw by the hand.

"I am Giffydd and this is my wife Seryn." Seryn smiles at Hyw and he sees her face clearly for the first time. Her complexion is moon pale, with long braids of hair tied in a large bunch at the back of her head.

"This is her sister, Cayr..." Giffydd indicates with his hand, to where Seryn's sister is sitting on a stool almost at his feet. Hyw looks at Cayr.

She is the light of beauty itself, or at least, one day would be. Perhaps a little younger than he first thought...fourteen, maybe even thirteen. Giffydd then turns to his children. The boy first, who is perhaps only six or seven.

"This is Ywel, after thy grandfather, maybe?" Hyw is slightly shocked by the words, not understanding how a stranger could know such intimate details about his family.

"He is still young, but his eyes and ears are keen and he is strong for his age." The boy smiles up at his father, supposing it is a good thing for him to say, but then he looks at Hyw. Hyw smiles down at the lad, who stands in awe, but is still a little uncertain of the hero who stands before him.

"Thou hast a noble name, guard it well," Hyw says as the boy turns back to his father.

"Go now...gather thy things and watch the windows," Giffydd says as shooing him to his work. The boy hurries over to the window, climbing onto a stool. There is a small bow in his hand and a tiny bone-handled blade on a belt at his side, similar to the one Hyw keeps on his belt.

Giffydd turns to his daughter next. She is fair in complexion, just like her mother and Cayr. She cannot be any more than a year younger than her brother, with straw-coloured hair, falling in waves over her shoulders. She is standing half-hidden behind her mother, with one of her hands resting across her mother's shoulders, her fingers playing with her mother's hair. The other hand is held up to her face as she sucks at her thumb.

"This is Steryn, our only girl and here is our youngest, Gwion." Giffydd indicates to Gwion, who is lying across his mother's arms as she rocks him from side to side. He looks two or three and seems to be getting too big for his mother to cuddle and carry continuously.

A short silence prevails as all eyes rest on Mynddy. Hyw feels slightly awkward and is lost for the right words, but he manages to speak.

"This is Mynddy…sadness has taken the words out of her mouth…her family are lost…" Hyw begins to stumble but recovers enough to say.

"She has seen much!"

His words seem to light a fire inside Seryn who gets to her feet placing Gwion on the floor. Studying Mynddy's face, looking deep into her eyes, Seryn's questions are directed to Hyw.

"The Scotti…?"

Hyw bows his head slightly.

"Yes."

"Māthōg and his assassins?" Seryn hisses with venom in her voice.

Hyw raises his head at the mention of Māthōg's name.

"Yes, it was Māthōg." The venom is in Hyw's throat, but Seryn continues.

"Thou wast there?"

"I came too late," Hyw says with the poison almost choking him.

"But ye saved her?" Hyw drops his head as if in shame as the memories of that awful day sear through him. Seryn steps forward with open arms towards Mynddy.

"My poor child!" Seryn takes hold of Mynddy and cradles her to her breast.

"My poor sweet thing!" Seryn caresses Mynddy holding her close, running her hands over and through her hair. The tears well in Mynddy's eyes and roll out onto her cheeks, but still, she makes no sound. Something breaks inside her and Mynddy cannot cope with her feelings as she too remembers her sister's sacrifice as she rests in the gentle arms of this stranger.

"Come now," Seryn says quietly, pressing Mynddy closer to her breast and Mynddy's tears flow freely.

It is then that Hyw notices Seryn's sister Cayr with tears rolling down her cheeks, falling onto her smock. Seryn looks down to where Cayr is sitting and indicates for her to move closer. Cayr rushes to her sister's side and all three girls drown, each in the arms of the other.

Giffydd looks at Hyw.

"She was little more than a babe in arms when the Scotti visited their home. Seryn was with me…we were newlywed. They are the only two that remain of six sisters in all…" Giffydd cannot continue, but Seryn comes to his aide.

"We must go…we cannot stay here… we should have left days ago…the Scotti are all around us, it is only a matter of time." Seryn is still standing with both Mynddy and Cayr in her arms.

"It is a little more desperate than ye could know." Giffydd continues.

"The Druids have formed an unholy alliance with the Scotti and they intend to claim this land for their own." Silence falls in the dim light of the croft. Giffydd looks over to his son who seems ill at ease on his perch.

"What do you see, bach?"

"I'm not sure Da…it may just be shadows.

"Let me see!" Giffydd moves to the window, lifting his son to one side. Hyw moves to a small window further along the adjacent wall and looks out into the shadows of the night as Seryn blows at the candle.

Two shadowy figures emerge at the stables; one on horseback, the other on foot, having climbed down to look into the stables where Sarn and the stallion are resting.

"What can ye see, Hyw bach?" Giffydd's intimate words shock Hyw.

"Two at the stables…one still on horseback."

"I have one, just off to the left of the door," Giffydd says, gripping the hilt of his sword. The croft erupts into quiet commotion as Mynddy grabs her bow and the two youngest run to their mother's side.

Hyw looks across at Mynddy. She is ready, knowing she will be protecting Hyw's attack on the two warriors near the stables. They move to the door as one and Giffydd steps forward as third in line. He would take the warrior at the door if Hyw's first arrow does not find its mark. Cayr and Young Ywel have their bows ready; they will protect the doorway from inside the croft. One last look around to check everything is ready and Hyw slowly moves toward the door. In one swift movement, he is out into the shadows of the night and directly tracing his footsteps is Mynddy.

Hyw's eyes search the silent darkness for the first Slag, whom Giffydd had said was to the left of the door. Hesitating, he bends his bow, still searching and finally, he finds the shadow of the first Grot, still sitting on his horse.

"Hyw!" The shadow calls out in the darkness.

"Wait!" Hyw calls out recognising the voice.

"They're friends!" His words frantically call into the night as he relaxes the grip on his bow.

"Wis tha thee, Hyw?" The voice calls out again.

Giffydd inches forward.

"Over here!" Hyw calls out and the warrior climbs down from his horse and walks over. It is Māddrōg, Geddyn's second in command.

Out of the shadows behind where the warrior sat on his horse, step a further two horsemen. The two at the stables approach cautiously having heard the commotion.

"What news Hyw?" Māddrōg asks.

"Giffydd can tell thee more than I!" Hyw says indicating to his new friend.

"Come inside where we can talk freely!" Giffydd turns towards the door, calling inside the croft.

"We're coming back inside…everything's alright…Cayr?"

"Okay," Cayr calls back, easing the grip on her bow. Still Giffydd waits.

"Ywel bach?"

"Yes, Da."

"We're coming in, they are our friends!" Giffydd says, still a little uncertain about his son's understanding of the situation, but young Ywel has already lowered his aim. Ywel grows a little impatient with his father's uncertainty, but Seryn calls out.

"It's fine…come on in!" She smiles over towards her son with warm patience and understanding. A candle is lit from the dying fire and its light flickers at the windows again.

Māddrōg turns to his men who seem to be growing in numbers by the moment. He sends some out to watch the paths and others to guard the croft, and then he turns, ducking as he walks through the doorway.

"We know many of the Scotti are in the village over yonder. We sent the old man down with…" Māddrōg's words come to an abrupt halt as he sees the small throng of faces waiting for him inside.

"Hello, there mar wee bairns!" The children all gasp as he comes into view. The two youngest run to Seryn, hiding behind her, peeping from around her dress. They look up at Māddrōg in fearful-awe, while still holding onto their mother's legs through her smock.

Māddrōg is dressed in his full battle regalia, with dried woad daubed on his face cracking slightly as his face moves as talking. He is wearing a burnished helmet, which has been fashioned in the shape of a dragon's head with his face showing out of the dragon's open mouth. His long beard is plaited and then divided in two and plaited again; hanging down, out of the front of his helmet like a snake's tongue.

Seeing a smile on the warrior's face and sensing his security, Gwion steps out from behind his mother and looks up at the warrior.

"Art thou a dragon?" Māddrōg roars with laughter, which doesn't ease the tension in the dim light of the croft, but his laughter dies and a rye grin spreads across his face. Both Mynddy and Cayr are uneasy in his presence and Māddrōg can see their unease.

"Nay laddie...Ah am nae a dragon, I'm Māddrōg, one of the Sons of Gododdyn, second in command to Geddyn of the king's Triad!"

"Ye were saying...?" Hyw questions again, just as eager to hear news from Māddrōg.

"Aye as ah wis saying, we sent tha ol'man deen tae tha village wi a cart full o' grog... the Scotti beat him a little, and robbed him o'tha cart. He's all reet. Two o' m'best men are wi him...they'll tak him home when he's feeling up to it..."

Māddrōg can sense Hyw's unease at the news of the old man.

"Ah the ol'man is sprite fur his age...he escaped thaa bows and blades ...they'll be drinking well in ta tha wee hours...The Scotti wi be drunk by noo."

"Good!" Says Giffydd.

"This is just the opportunity we need Hyw bach." He turns to Seryn.

"We must leave…prepare the little ones…we will be travelling light…take only that which is essential." Seryn gives him a questioning look.

"We cannot stay here, can we? Ye said it thyself."

"Where are we to go then…?" Seryn asks with a perplexed look on her face.

"The island of course?" Giffydd says almost as though his wife isn't thinking straight. But Seryn cannot contain herself.

"Thou art off thy head…I think ye have been on the grog thyself…The boat is in the harbour and the Scotti are in the village…how dust thou propose to get us to the island and if we get there…the old man's mad…look at all his wives now…"

Seryn stops her words, but it is too late and Hyw hesitates in his thoughts with his heart reaching out across the waters. Nodding to himself, as if confirming it, Hyw says nothing of his feelings. Seryn speaks again, but this time her words are more calculated and although spoken to Giffydd, they are meant for Hyw.

"Ye know the Druids have vowed to rid the island of 'blasphemers'." Giffydd pauses for a moment looking at his wife. It is a loving look; a look of patience with just a hint of frustration.

"But we are part of that blasphemy are we not?" Giffydd's words are quietly spoken, but all who are there hear them, as if they were the tolling of a bell. After a moment, Giffydd turns to Māddrōg.

"When will thy men be here?"

"T'feet?" Māddrōg asks but then doesn't wait for the answer.

"I cannae be sure, that'll depend on whit ye can tell me of the Scotti." Giffydd interrupts him.

"Days or weeks?" Giffydd grows impatient in his excitement.

"Ah rid to meet Geddyn afore tha dawn laddie…he waits wi ma braithren: an when ah bring him word we shall attack…afore dawn if all is well."

Giffydd smiles at his wife.

"It's perfect…I will fetch the boat…the tide doesn't turn till just before dawn…all the Scotti will be fast gone in the stupor of their grog…Ye can take the children to the far rock and I will pick thee up there." Hyw is excited at his friend's words, but Seryn is still not convinced.

"What if the Scotti are on the trail?"

"Mynddy can go with you," Hyw says quickly without thinking. Looking across at her, knowing he has spoken out of turn, Mynddy smiles back at him.

"But what of the horses?" Hyw asks, thinking of everything. There is a spinney not far from here…I have spent some time there watching for the Scotti…there is an old forgotten barn…they will be safe, at least for a time…Cayr knows it well…there is time."

"Aye, hit would seem tha hae tha makings of a plan," Māddrōg says as his concerns settle slightly.

"Now what can ye tell me of the Scotti?" Giffydd begins to explain the movements of Scotti he has seen that day.

"I have heard rumour of Māthōg, but no one has seen him…I would estimate no more than forty or fifty men in the village…with perhaps a dozen more on the hillsides keeping watch."

"Show ma." Māddrōg stands and heads for the door, with Giffydd and Hyw following after him. Mynddy is close behind.

Hyw may be the only person she trusts, but if she is to lead the family, without Hyw, she wants to see and hear the plan for herself.

Giffydd points out the positions of the distant Scotti guards, explaining how many men he had seen in each position. The night is thick around them and the hills and mountains are little more than shadows, but Māddrōg knows the lie of the land. In pointing to the last, and closest, position, Giffydd says.

"Hyw and I will be going past there; just before dawn…ye could leave them to us if thou wirt of a mind!"

Māddrōg looks at him and nods.

"Aye, it's set then…I will send riders with news for Geddyn and I will remain to take the others!" Giffydd nods his appreciation, then continues.

"I have not seen the Triad Druids, or any sign of Māthōg, although as I say, his name is on their lips."

As they turn back to the croft, Māddrōg calls out into the darkness.

"Dynōg."

In the same instant, the name falls from his lips, the old warrior appears from a scrub of bracken close to the doorway.

"Aye Sire!"

"Ye ken all?"

"It wouldnae surprise ma if the Scotti didnae hear thee Sire." Dynōg smiles as Māddrōg gives him a stern look and then smiles himself. Māddrōg walks towards Dynōg and places an arm over his shoulder as they talk. Hyw's heart warms to the warriors once again; especially Māddrōg, the way he speaks; his dry sense of humour and the way he is with his men. Both warriors whisper together. Two other men join them, with three horses at the rein. Eventually, the three mount up and slowly ride off into the shadows of the night.

Giffydd and Hyw return to the croft followed by Māddrōg as Mynddy sidles through the shadows. The door closes behind them and inside the croft, all are busy, preparing what they need for their journey. Cayr is ready with a bow in her hand and smiles up at Mynddy. She has never seen a woman treat and be treated as an equal to men before.

Hyw moves close to Mynddy and whispers

"If I spoke out of turn, I'm sorry…art thou happy with what has been said?" Mynddy turns to him, understanding his concern and nods her agreement.

There is a knock at the door and it opens slightly. A young man dressed for battle peers around the doorframe. He looks straight at Cayr and Mynddy. He has heard of Mynddy's heroic charge in the battle of the dunes, but the exquisite beauty of Cayr takes all his attention. Cayr looks up at him and smiles. She knows the young warrior; his name is Gwydn, after his father.

The young man lives in the North Country, close to the sea, but when the Scotti attacked, he joined Māddrōg and his men, to fight. Gwydn is a farmer and appears uneasy in his battle garb. Knowing how to use the plough and a scythe, he is not comfortable with the sword in his hand. There is a bow strapped across his back, with which he could display a little more expertise, but he is nonetheless uneasy as he smiles back at Cayr.

"What is it, laddie?"

The young man pushes the door fully open.

"Riders sire!" Gwydn says and he turns to go.

"Stay a wee while laddie, ah hae an errand fur thee…dae tha know these people?" The young man nods as he turns again and stands in silence.

"With thy permission Hyw and Mynddy, I would like the laddie to go with thee, tee tak tha horses. Ah may need to know their whereabouts, if ye ken my meaning?" They understand that if anything happens to them, the horses would be taken care of and they nod their approval.

"Fit tha stallion's wounds?"

"Not good I'm afraid," Hyw says in a subdued voice.

"Ye hear thon laddie…tak fit ye need…!" Māddrōg says, but then sensing Gwydn's nerves, he adds.

"Tha hast nee need to fear, the lassie will protect thee." Māddrōg laughs and the young warrior bows his head slightly, looking down at Cayr who smiles up at him, warming his heart.

"Hurry then laddie, the lassies are waiting on thee."

The youngest is asleep; he will need his rest before dawn breaks. Gwydn returns with all he needs to tend to the stallion's wounds. Mynddy and Cayr pick up Hyw and Mynddy's bedrolls of blankets and they hand them to the young warrior.

Mynddy looks over to where Hyw is busy in conversation with Giffydd and Māddrōg. Mynddy, Cayr and Gwydn slip quietly out of the door without any recognition from Hyw. They hide in some bushes and wait awhile as their eyes get used to the dark. The door opens behind them. It is Hyw.

"I will go with you." He whispers as Mynddy's heart smiles to the night.

Plans have been made and remade, and the night passes by. Those who remain, settle down to wait for the dawn's slow grey light. None, but the youngest can sleep. All the talk of battle and Druids, Scotti and mad-old-holy-men has excited their minds.

Māddrōg senses their excitement and begins to tell them stories. Before he starts he undoes the buckle from under his chin and takes his helmet off, placing it at his side. Regaling them, he recounts Mynddy,s heroic charge over the dunes. Roaring with every arrow she loosed and cheering as all the warriors of Gododdyn built the frenzy of battle within them.

Māddrōg seems good with words and he builds great suspense into his tales.

"Aye, an hae ye heard o' tha Phantom of Annwn?" He makes the actions of some dragon or demon as he breathes the words out. Even the youngest has woken and he sits mesmerised in his mother's lap, burying his head into her chest as the suspense gets too much for him. Māddrōg talks of their chase and of how the phantom had circled behind them. Telling them of the killing of the wild hog and of…

The door opens and Cayr and the young warrior walk in followed a few moments later by Mynddy and Hyw. Māddrōg looks up waiting on Hyw. Hyw nods over to him and Māddrōg turns back to his tale.

"Aye ah almost killed him with a reckless shot from my bow, but he ducked an is here to spik o' the tale himsel." Māddrōg beckons to Hyw and the children's eyes follow as they gasp up at him.

"Aye do tha remember ma first well-placed arroo, Hyw? Tha one that made ye duck?" Hyw nods at Māddrōg's question, remembering having to duck from the blade.

"That was ma blade laddie." Māddrōg looks straight into Hyw as he continues, slowly and quietly with all ears bent towards his words. But Hyw remains quiet, knowing Māddrōg was sitting right in front of him on his horse.

"Ah widdae killed ye given the chance," Māddrōg holds Hyw's gaze.

"Aa wouldha killed many fan ah came to this land." Māddrōg's voice becomes serious, speaking quietly, but with full purpose and meaning.

"Ah saw tha people as somehow tainted. As ye know, oor people once came fae these lands, but the Romans destroyed what we both held precious, but noo…noo…" He hesitates.

"Noo yer people hae touched our hearts; Mynddy and y'sel; yer grandfaither and many more. We cam to conquer, t' tak back what once was oors, but we hae bin shown greater ways. We are one people if tha can be said wi any surety eftir tha treachery o'tha Romans. Thy people are noo oor people and tha name will always be on ma lips, Hyw."

Giffydd leans across to where Hyw has sat near him and whispers so only Hyw can hear.

"Thou art the Phantom of Annwn?" Hyw smiles and Giffydd nods as he smiles back having heard only rumours of the legend.

Chapter Twenty

The slow grey light of dawn begins to seep into the distant horizon and it is time.

Māddrōg to his feet and one by one everyone rises and prepares to follow him. It will be sometime before the dawn is upon them and their battle is over.

Weapons have been checked and rechecked continuously during the night, but as everyone gets to their feet they check their weapons once more. Māddrōg replaces the helmet on his head and touches the hilt of his sword to make sure it is still in its scabbard and, as he does so, almost simultaneously Giffydd touches the hilt of his blade. They can both feel the weight of their swords hanging at their sides, but still, an unknowing urge within them forces their hands down. Hyw and Mynddy check their bows in the dim light, and each feels for the fletches on their trusted feathered warriors. Watching carefully those around them, Cayr and young Ywel feel at their sides for their arrows. One of Māddrōg's men is waiting with his horse.

"We shall no need steed's t'nicht, Dynōg. T'nicht we walk in t' battle."

Their plan has been played and replayed in their minds countless times during the night; everyone knows their part and each part is imprinted on that individual's mind.

The air is chilled, with only a slight breeze; the mood is sombre with everyone checking their position, looking all around them. A hunters-moon peeps from behind high clouds that drift effortlessly across the expanse of the night, like shadows within shadows.

Walking in single file the silent procession wends its way along the path leading down towards the village. Hyw scouts out in front, followed by Māddrōg. They walk a little way down the path and somewhere in the darkness, a voice calls out, in no more than a whisper.

"Here sire!" A warrior slowly rises out of the shadows of the thick bracken and walks up to Māddrōg taking his place behind him in the line.

"Here sire" Another warrior calls out to the night and he too slowly rises out of the shadows. A further six warriors join them before they have walked an arrow's flight from the croft.

They walk for some distance before Hyw pauses at the first path where he knows the women must leave them and head off towards the 'far rock', but something is wrong and Māddrōg whispers Hyw's name. One of his men takes Hyw's place and Hyw works his way back through the line of warriors until he gets to Mynddy. She is standing with her eyes fixed on the path down towards the village. All her intentions are set on Hyw and his destiny, and now the time has come, and she cannot bring herself to leave him. Her wish is to follow the young man she has grown to love and he sighs slightly as he smiles at her, knowing something of the desires of her heart.

"Ye agreed to the plan Mynddy," Hyw says, in a very matter-of-fact way, as though Mynddy had been discussing the plan all through the night, but he holds no hope of recognition for his words and Mynddy continues to stare down towards the village. In the dark shadows that gather in her melancholy, the love she holds for Hyw is the only light she has found to guide her.

'This could become a problem.' Hyw thinks to himself.

"They need the protection of thy bow Mynddy." Mynddy looks straight into Hyw's eyes as tears begin to well in her own. Taking hold of Hyw's shirt, she moves her hand up to where the arrowhead is hanging around his neck. Her hand folds around it and tightens its grip as though she would never let go. Hyw sighs again, looking into her dark eyes as they flash in the moon's silver glow.

In the catch-light of the moment, he realises her wants and wishes, and they flood into him, overwhelming his senses for a while. She cannot bring herself to leave him, no, there is something more, something deeper than want, or need, or even desire; there is a vow between them that no words have ever uttered.

Hyw places his hands gently on either side of her face, cradling her head inside them. Mynddy looks straight back at him as she tries desperately to rein in her feelings. She is not afraid to die, she has faced death before and cheated the hangman, and she would face it again if that is what is needed, but Mynddy has vowed to walk at Hyw's side. Pulling her from the jaws of Annwn he had rescued her, and no matter what; she cannot bring herself to leave him.

"I will see thee at the 'far rock'; I promise!" Hyw pauses as all his life is laid bare, with tears blurring his vision as he whispers into her ear, with Giffydd standing close.

"Unless the sky falls down!" His oath is enough, but Hyw places a soft kiss on Mynddy's lips and as he pulls away he smiles; a warm soft smile that melts all the fear in Mynddy's heart and she turns to her path, quietly walking out to take up her lead, guarding their new friends.

Hyw thinks for a moment of Sián and his thoughts bring an ache to his heart; an ache for his home, but Hyw can taste Mynddy on his lips and it is Mynddy's image that continues to play in the pictures of his mind.

Hyw watches as Mynddy walks off into the deepening darkness, followed by young Ywel with his small bow held ready. Seryn, carrying her youngest with his head over her shoulder, is walking close behind her. Cayr takes up the rear, constantly checking around her. Before they disappear into the gloom, Cayr takes one last look back at the warriors; her eyes search for Gwydn. Hyw can see the woman in the child that stands before him; so can Gwydn and Gwydn's heart follows after Cayr.

When they're all out of sight, Hyw again takes up his position at the head of Māddrōg's men, but before moving off, they hear the rush of an arrow and the dying groans of a drunken Grot who has stumbled from his watch in the haze of his stupor. Mynddy's arrow finds his heart before he can find his feet or his blade. Hyw runs back along the path; so does Gwydn.

One of the children cries out but is quickly calmed by Seryn. Hyw pauses and listens. Seryn comforts her children, but her words are fading into the distance as they continue along the path undaunted. Turning back to his path, Hyw is confident in Mynddy's abilities. Gwydn looks across to where Māddrōg is standing. Māddrōg turns to him and pauses.

"Gee on then laddie, go tee her; ah free thee from yer ooth." At these words, Gwydn turns and follows after Cayr.

Their separate ways lead them further from each other and Hyw wonders if what they are doing will be worthwhile as he questions his need to see his grandfather's brother. Blaidd's family could have escaped over the hills to the north; they didn't have to march into the jaws of Annwn and his mind ponders over the power his grandfather's words and tokens hold.

After walking for some time the path eventually leads down past a thicket of bushes; beyond which Hyw remembers the main track runs. The path there would be more substantial; a track, wide enough for oxen and carts. It is a way the Scotti would be watching. At the crossroads ahead, their paths would split with the warriors taking the trail to the east; Hyw and Giffydd then making their way down through the village.

According to what Giffydd had said they would soon encounter the first Scotti watch. Approaching the thicket with great caution, Hyw can see it is perfect for an ambush. The warriors stand waiting for his signal to continue, but Hyw can hear something off in front of him.

Standing, listening, Hyw cannot hear sufficiently to make out what it is; possibly the sound of a sick animal. Creeping forward, he makes no discernable sound. Stopping again, he listens.

'Someone is snoring!' Hyw can hear someone snoring.

'This is outrageous.' He thinks to himself.

'The grog has certainly done its job.' But there is something more; another sound, but again, Hyw cannot quite make it out. A trickle of water maybe; then, someone sighs, as both sounds seem to mingle.

Suddenly a Grot walks out from the thicket of bushes to Hyw's left; he is fastening the front of his pants after relieving himself. The Grot's eyes focus on Hyw, but Hyw's feathered warrior tears into him in the same instant. Rushing towards the crossroads, Hyw notches in another blade, his eyes constantly scanning for more Grots. In the commotion, he hears a second grot rousing, but he cannot see him. Running to the other side of the track, he frantically looks into every shadow, checking every silhouette.

Māddrōg's men are straining at the leash, wanting to join in the chase, but Hyw raises his hand to the square, holding them back.

"Watch an learn…aye my wee laddie's, watch an learn," Māddrōg says as the first Grot staggers out onto the path in front of them, falling to his knees and then forward onto his face.

"Hae ye nae heard of 'The Phantom of Annwn'?" At these words he turns to his men, just to see the expression on their faces. Their eyes follow the fleeting shadows of Hyw's chase; their ears straining to hear his feathered warriors thrashing through the night; some of his men know Hyw as the Phantom, but the others look on in disbelief having only heard whispers of the legend.

Finally, Hyw sees the second Grot where he has fallen asleep under a small tree. The Grot never makes his feet. Hyw doesn't rest and stands as still as a statue, he continues to survey every shadow and silhouette to make absolutely sure these were the only two Grots at the crossroads.

Suddenly bushes further down the narrow lane erupt as their branches shake and quiver and a frightened shadow jumps out onto the track. Seeing Hyw the Slag runs for his life. Hyw takes careful aim. If the Slag were to escape all their plans would be brought to nought. Arching through the air, his arrow cuts the shadow down. Walking up to the dying Slag, Hyw retrieves his blade paying little regard to the Slag's dying groans.

In the rush of his hunt, Hyw has moved out of Māddrōg's sight and his men wait with bated breath for his return. Walking back into their view, there is a collective sigh of relief. Wiping the blood off his arrow onto a tuft of fern, he places it back into his quiver. Reaching the first grot, he bends down to retrieve the last of his arrows, but it is of no more use to him; its shaft broke as the Grot fell. Hyw forgets the arrow and approaches Māddrōg.

"Gentlemen, tha Phantom of Annwn!" He announces to his men.

"T'think ah once almost killed him ma sel!" Whispering, he laughs in the darkness; he wasn't the type of warrior to bandy with his words, skulking in the shadows, but his dry wit raises the spirit of his men. Hyw remains silent, but his new friend, Giffydd, just looks back at him in utter bewilderment as every warrior turns to their Gods thanking them that Hyw is on their side.

Nodding, only once toward Māddrōg, Hyw turns to the path. Giffydd follows him and the warriors peel off onto the lane behind them.

The sky is brightening slightly to the east where the dawn will be, but the sun's rising is still far away. The moon is hidden behind a small cluster of clouds, but it will not be out of sight for long. The first of the crofts is clearly in sight, but the second Scotti watch is closer still. Giffydd points to where it should be; on the top of a small outcrop of rocks, but Hyw can't see anyone there.

A muffled cry breaks the silence somewhere behind them. Maddrōg and his men have found their first kill, but one of his young warriors has been clumsy.

Just below the Scotti watchtower, a voice echoes out of the shadows.

"Shush. Did ye hear that?"

"Hear what? Keep thoi mind on what thou art doin'. Hold her still…hold her still I say!" A second, impatient voice calls out. The muffled cry of a girl is heard and Hyw's blood begins to simmer on the fires of his rage. Wasting no time and quickly advancing on the Scotti position, knowing they are too occupied to hear his approach.

One Grot is leaning back, drinking from a jug and Hyw can see a second kneeling at the head of a third. The second Grot has a young girl's arms pinned to the ground. She is lying, struggling and moaning with the third Grot on top of her. There is a tearing of cloth and the girl cries out. Another voice calls out.

"Free up darling, be good for moi, an' woi'll spare thoi throat." Finally understanding what atrocities are unfolding, a short distance from where

252

they stand, Giffydd tries to move past Hyw, but Hyw has been here before and he holds him back with his arm. Without making a sound, he moves to within a few paces of the Scotti Slags. His aim is true and the first Slag sinks to the earth, dropping the jug of grog as he falls. The second Grot calls out, thinking the first is just too drunk to stand.

"Moind our grog!" But words are silenced and he collapses on the ground next to the girl. Wasting little time, in an instant, he is standing over the third Grot. He has dropped his bow and in his hand, Hyw holds his small blade. Grabbing at the Grot's head, Hyw places his open hand firmly over the Slag's mouth, so he cannot call out. Pulling at his head, Hyw sees the young girl's face for the first time. She is young, very young and too petrified to scream out, not knowing or having any understanding of who Hyw is.

Wrenching at the Grots neck, and pulling him into his own body wrapping his legs around him, Hyw rolls onto the ground, freeing the petrified girl as he does so. Tightening his grip on the Slag, he drags the small blade across the Grot's throat for the first time. The Grot struggles and Hyw tightens his grip further, almost choking the life out of the wretched Slag as he slashes at his throat, over and over again. The Slag becomes frantic, but Hyw does not loosen his grip or let the knife rest in his hand. Finally, the Slag stops struggling and Hyw lets him fall limp to the ground.

The girl is trembling and quaking looking up at Hyw unable to move. He is covered in blood and so is the girl. Hyw scrambles to her side and takes hold of her chin raising her head away from her neck. The girl jumps as he moves towards her as she begins to shake uncontrollably. Checking her neck and arms for any wounds, he leaves her be, only when he is certain she has no hurt.

Giffydd falls to his knees at her side and pulls her dress together. Quickly and quietly he talks to her.

"Ceri…Ceri…listen to me Ceri!" The girl is petrified.

"Ye must listen to me, carefully…The Sons of Gododdyn are here…they are about to attack…dust thou understand? Thou must find a place to hide…dust thou know where I live?" The young girl continues to shake uncontrollably.

"Dust thou know where I live?" He says more forcefully. She remains silent. Giffydd shakes at her; the girl nods as she sobs.

"Art thou sure ye understand?" She nods again her tears falling onto her face.

"Go to our croft…no one is there, but it is open…there is food and shelter and a place to hide. Run now, run and don't stop till ye get there."

The girl turns to run up the track, but then she stops and looks back; almost as though she is waiting for someone. She watches and waits. Giffydd shoos his arm after her and as he does so, the girl turns and runs up the path, out of their sight.

Turning back to Hyw, Giffydd can see him bent over, what he thinks is one of the Slags. Giffydd looks again, but this time the awful realisation hits him. Hyw is covering Ceri's older sister with a blanket; blood from the open wound at her throat is smeared down her naked body. Giffydd's heart breaks and his feelings tumble in confusion as trying to come to terms with the awful scene before him. He wonders about his new friend, but his wondering doesn't last for long as his thoughts turn to Ceri.

'We should have kept her with us.' But his thoughts argue in his head as revulsion turns his stomach and he doubts his ability to continue. Hyw kneels at the dead girl's side; she is one of Cayr's friends from the village and Giffydd's mind shudders as his concerns grow for the safety of his family and he fights an overwhelming urge to run after them.

They flit from croft to croft, down towards the harbour. They have to wait at the side of one croft, hiding in the shadows, as a large group of Scotti, walk up through the village towards the upper track, where Hyw and

Giffydd have just come from. Giffydd prays for Ceri's safety, but his prayers soon turn to his family.

There is a commotion coming from the direction of the sea wall, near the quayside; somewhere unseen, people from the village are struggling and crying, but Hyw and Giffydd cannot save all his friends.

They soon find their way past the last of the freestanding crofts, dropping down towards the quay. Hyw constantly scans the area where he can hear voices, but he can see nothing. Masts from the luggers are swaying and bobbing in the harbour and Hyw can hear the lapping of the water, but the tortured innocent cries of children infest his mind as he realises Giffydd cannot hear their muffled cries.

Giffydd takes the lead and drops over the quayside, climbing down a small rope ladder into a large sailboat, with a dipping lug rig. It is quite large; as large a boat as one man could handle by himself. Giffydd begins pulling at ropes, untying others, pulling the sail part way up the mast, with the sheet ready. Finding the ores, he places them down the side of the boat. Hyw is halfway down the ladder and Giffydd calls to him in a whisper.

"Jump down!" But Hyw's attention is fixed elsewhere. There is a door to a croft that forms part of the seawall, where Hyw knows the muffled cries in his head are emanating from and the suffering of those beyond its stone walls will not let him be. The raucous laughter of drunken Slags erupts from behind the door, for all to hear and both Giffydd and Hyw know what is taking place beyond its solid board. Giffydd calls again.

"We must go."

"I can't leave them," Hyw says as he hesitates.

"What about thy promise to Mynddy?" Giffydd asks.

"The sky hasn't fallen yet," Hyw says with an awkward smile etched on his face and he begins to climb back up the ladder.

The door opens with a clatter and Hyw ducks down behind the quay. The door slams shut and Hyw slowly raises his head back up. An old Scotti Slag has dragged a woman out of the croft; he has her pinned against the wall, with a blade at her throat. She pleads with the man.

"Let the girls go. I will give ye what ye and thy men want."

Hyw's mind is made up and he jumps out onto the quayside, followed quickly by Giffydd who is scrambling from his boat. Hyw's bow is bent towards the Grot and he quickly advances on his position. The woman catches sight of Hyw's swift advance and his presence immediately shows in the expression on her face, but his purpose will not be checked. Sensing his impending doom, the Grot releases his grip on the woman, but he is too late and Hyw's arrow splinters through the grots neck.

Turning immediately to the door, Giffydd struggles to keep up with Hyw's advance, and his stomach turns in the wake of their impending battle he wishes he had taken his family over the hills to the north as he prays for the day to come, bringing his sword to bear.

Approach the door, it is quickly dragged open again. The emerging grot staggers back with the force of Hyw's arrow ripping through him. Hyw doesn't allow his attack to stall and he quickly storms through the door. The two remaining Slags are little more than boys and they freeze in their fear on seeing Hyw with his bow bent towards them; his feathered warrior's brightly honed talons keep them pinned to a sidewall and they begin to quake and tremble.

Giffydd enters the room and cannot quite believe what he sees. Most of his friends and neighbours are bound and gagged along the far wall, piled in a heap, like sacks of grain; men, women and children all blindfolded, thrown one on top of the other; some of the children are crying, but most are too petrified and just moan in their fear. A girl lies in the centre of the room, bloodied and bruised with her dress ripped open at the front; her naked body, open to the world.

Giffydd recognises her and then sees her father lying on the floor close by, his blindfold has been ripped off and it is lying on the floor close to his head. They had forced him to watch as they brutalised his daughter. Tears are falling from the man's face, onto the hard stone floor, but the girl is rousing. Giffydd cuts him free and hands him his sword, but the blade is immediately dropped as the man falls to his daughter's side. Pawing over her, he lifts her into his heart.

Giffydd has finally found the stomach for battle and plucking his sword up from the ground, he unleashes his rage on the two Scotti Slags. They cower from his charge, his anger honed into every ounce of his crashing blade as its bright steal splits one of their skulls, cleaving it in two. Thrashes at the air, over and over again with every fibre of his body tearing at the two boys. One of their heads rolls to one side as it is severed from its body, but he does not relent, continuing to hack at their mutilated corpses until his rage cannot sustain him anymore and he drops to his knees. Kneeling on the floor, Giffydd is unable to take in the carnage in front of him. Hyw cuts at the cords, which bind his friends and neighbours speaking almost in a whisper.

"The Warriors of Gododdyn are attacking at dawn. Take the women and children and hide in the boats…quickly." Gathering themselves together; everyone makes their way to the door, with some of them moving across the quayside towards the boats.

Hyw drags at Giffydd's arm, but he will not move.

"The boat awaits…thy family…!" At the mention of his family, Giffydd seems to stir slightly. Looking up at Hyw and still dazed he says.

"Has the sky fallen yet?"

Giffydd tries to smile with his words.

"No, not yet, Giffydd bach, but if it did we would storm Annwn itself and with the dragons breath chasing after us, we would free all the dead"

Giffydd slowly gets to his feet and they both walk out onto the quayside. One of the men whom they have freed is standing at the corner of the quay, looking up into the village. His wife is standing near the boats; two other women are comforting and consoling her. Giffydd moves over to the man and putting his arm around him he turns him back to his wife and the harbour. As leading the man back, Giffydd talks quietly to him. Hyw watches and waits. Halfway back to the boats, Giffydd whispers something to the man and he collapses in some sorrow or grief.

His wife rushes to his side, but as she does so, she looks up at Giffydd. He is unable to speak and she collapses onto her husband's neck in a rage of tears. Hyw moves across to where Giffydd is standing over them.

"We need to get them in the boats…if the Scotti hear them…!" Both Hyw and Giffydd drag the man to his feet and two women rush over to console the man's wife. Hyw is the last to climb down and as he jumps into the fishing lugger, he can see a small armada of sailboats, slipping out of the harbour.

A shout goes up, from somewhere across the quay and two Scotti Slags begin to run along the seawall towards where Giffydd and Hyw are rowing frantically. They are the last boat to leave and there is still some way to go before they are safe. Looking at the running men, Hyw can see neither of them has a bow, but there are three more, who have joined their chase. They are still a little way off, but Hyw readies himself as Giffydd takes both oars.

Standing astern he bends his bow towards the chasing Slags. They have seen the carnage Hyw and Giffydd have left behind and their chase falters. The two Slags at the front call the bowmen forward, but they are reluctant to move. The eldest Slag draws his sword and marches back to his archers, threatening them with his blade. Hyw looses his feathered warrior and it arches through the air, striking the remonstrating grot in the middle of his back. Falling onto the quayside, the others quickly drag him out of Hyw's range, concerned only for their own safety.

As the boat clears the harbour wall, Giffydd raises the sail. There is only a slight breeze, but the sail fills and the boat heels to his promptings. There is a rumbling clamour and roar from the hillside above the village as the dawn's battle commences.

Chapter Twenty-One

The Lugger seems to slice through the water. The sea had been calm and clear inside the harbour wall, but as they race out into the bay, the waves swell around them. The sun rises over the top of the distant mountains, bleeding its burning colours into the scattered clouds above their rocky crags.

Looking down at the sea, with its wild horses rushing and splashing past the helm of the boat, Hyw gazes into its depths. He can see nothing as an ocean of deep dark blue-green water carries them aloft. All his life Hyw had longed to see the sea, to feel its power, to ride its wild horses, but in all his life he had never felt as excited as he does in the moment and closing his eyes for one wild moment, he is lost in the crashing miasma of all his childhood wants and dreams.

A large wave roars and crashes into the boat, waking Hyw with a jolt, as it tosses its salty spray high into the air, spitting and hissing at him as his mind clears and the dangers become all too obvious around him.

Opening his eyes, the fishing boat has found its way out into the bay and the sacred isle soon comes into view. It seems to glow, bathed in the sun's radiant early morning light and Hyw's heart leaps in anticipation. Soon he would have the answer to all his childhood fears; he would finally meet the man who knew all his fears and the answer to his waking dreams and that thought rode on the crest of the waves with him.

Giffydd is more at home on the sea than he is with a sword in his hand and he busies himself with the tiller and sail, turning the boat, tacking through the wind, back towards the shore. The villagers are following his lead, although they have no inkling as to his purpose. Hyw moves up into the prow, confident in Giffydd's skills and feeling a little in the way. Giffydd fights with the sail they tack one way and then the other.

Further along the coast, out towards the headland, Hyw can see someone standing high on a rock jutting out above the sea's crashing white waters. Although a long way off, Hyw knows it is Mynddy. Waves are crashing on the rocks at her feet, catapulting huge plumes of white sea spray high into the air. She has her brother's bow in her hand with an arrow notched into place.

They draw nearer, and Hyw can see Cayr standing at her side. Their hair is blowing in the breeze, one coloured like ripened barley; the other dark as autumn's burnished leaves. Standing behind Cayr is Gwydn; one of his hands is placed, almost casually, on her shoulder. On seeing the small fleet, Cayr runs back to her sister, who is looking after the children. Gwydn turns to follow her, but Mynddy remains motionless.

Beyond the rocky shoreline is a small inlet with a tiny sandy beach. Giffydd points to it, but Mynddy remains high on the rock. Hyw looks up at her.

'She is beautiful.' The thought races through his mind; he has seen her beauty before; watched her and yes in quiet moments he had wanted her, but as he gazes at her standing on the rock he is tempted by the moment and longs to lose himself in her silent ways.

She is wild and free with her hair and dress blowing in the sea breeze. All her pain and sadness are open to him, but he looks for the girl whom he had watched bathing in the lake. Remembering her laugh, her smile, the way she had played with her sister and the light that shone in her eyes as she had looked across the lake towards him.

Scrutinising her fragile life, she can feel his gaze upon her. After her life had been torn apart, she had followed after him, she had walked at his side, rode like the wind and fought as a warrior and in the euphoria of both their thoughts, they cannot imagine life, each without the other at their side.

Mynddy watches as Hyw sails beneath where she is standing and she remembers Blaidd's words and reaffirms her silent vow to him. They each smile at the other. Mynddy can see the blood of Hyw's battle which has been spilt on his smock. Looking out over the small flotilla, she knows; deep inside, she knows; just as surely as if she had been standing with him that he had pushed at the promise he made, but it does not matter; she does not care and in an instant she forgives him; she would always forgive him, now and forever. In her broken and silent world, all her love and all her cares are wrapped up in her feelings for Hyw and soon she will be at his side once more.

One by one the small fleet touches the shore; Mynddy runs towards Hyw. Watching her running over the sand, her hair spilling into the breeze, her dress flying up, her brother's bow held tightly in her hand; he can see a small patch of blood on her dress and he prays it is not her own. Mynddy slows as she approaches, with the last of the boats reaching the shore. Hyw smiles up at her, holding out his hand for her to join him. Mynddy falls into Hyw's arms and hugs him as though she would never let him go.

Giffydd briefs the villagers and then turns back towards his boat. The men help his family up into the Lugger, led by Gwydn. They turn it back out to sea and Gwydn wades out up to his waist in the waves, holding fast to its keel. Cayr is standing over him, looking over the side of the boat. Giffydd raises the sail, but Gwydn will not let go. He is dragged along and his feet leave the sand as he holds onto the boat with one hand. Cayr drops to her knees, leaning over the side and helps to pull him up. Struggling, Mynddy steps forward to help her new friend and together they manage to pull Gwydn over the side of the boat. Cayr looks over to her sister. Seryn smiles and with that tacit permission, Cayr throws her arms around Gwydn's neck.

In the distance, beyond the sea and shoreline, the villagers clamber over rock and fern. They hurry to rescue what is left of their lives and the lives of their precious children huddled in the darkness and fear.

The boat heels as the wind fills the sail and they are swiftly drawn further out to sea. The Sacred Island comes into view, still bathed in the sun's glowing light. A thin veil of mist on the sea surrounds the island, making it look as if it is floating above the water. The sea becomes quite rough and Giffydd sails further out to avoid the strong currents that run between the mainland and the island. Tacking, first one way, then the other, the island seems always to be floating towards them.

Lower at one end, the island rises to a large hill as it tracks further away from the mainland. They draw closer still. Hyw is sure he can see someone on top of the hill. Giffydd is forced, by the strong currents, to sail around the back of the island moving in close so the top of the hill is out of his sight. Hyw watches the rugged rocky shoreline and can hear the waves crashing onto its treacherous rocks. Anticipation bubbles inside him but he manages to smile at Giffydd and Giffydd smiles back.

"Not long now Hyw bach," Giffydd says, seeing Hyw's apprehension.

"See…look…just over there!" Both Hyw and Mynddy turn to look.

"That small gap," Giffydd says, pointing again.

Hyw's heart begins to race and its beat thumps inside his head. Standing, he looks out to where he can make out a small gap in the rocky shoreline. Mynddy stands at his side and takes hold of Hyw's arm. They look at each other, smiling and Hyw places his arm around her. Everyone in the boat looks up at them. Mynddy buries herself in Hyw's side as Hyw wraps her in his powerful, but gentle arms.

They turn into the shoreline, towards a hidden pocket of sand spread between the rocks. The beach ahead is smaller than the one they have just left. Giffydd draws in the sail and lets the boat slow as it approaches the island. Gwydn pushes past Hyw and Mynddy and perches himself on the prow, waiting for the boat to hit the sand. As it does, he jumps down into the sea, pulling at the boat with a rope.

Looking around them, Hyw has a limited view of the island but can just make out the top of the hill. There is something on its crest but h is unsure of what it is. Looking back to the mainland he can see the distant mountains covered in clouds. The entire coastline stretching to the east is open to his gaze as his eyes follow its distant coastline south.

 Jumping from the boat, Hyw turns and helps Mynddy, carrying her onto the sand; gently setting her down. Everyone drags the boat up the beach. The children are excited and they continue to chatter and play together.

"Welcome Hyw bach!" A soft voice calls out. Everyone looks up to where the voice has come from and standing at the end of a path leading up onto the island itself is an old man dressed in drab robes. His long white hair is blowing free. He has a fine wispy bead just like that of Ywel, his brother. The old man's eyes seem to sparkle as he stares across at Hyw.

He is taller than Hyw remembered; taller than his brother Ywel and although very old and slim, his body isn't bent. Hyw recognises him instantly and holding out his open arms, Hyw is drawn towards him.

"How art thou Hyw bach?" Dwyr asks as he takes a step down towards Hyw. Taking hold of Hyw, cupping his head in his hands, Dwyr gently bends Hyw's head forward, kissing him on the top of his hair.

"Let me look at thee then!" Dwyr steps away slightly and grips Hyw by the shoulders, just as Ywel used to when Hyw was a child. Looking straight into him the old man's eyes begin to well up, but Hyw cannot control his own feelings and he falls into Dwyr's arms. Overwhelmed, Hyw's tears splash onto the old man's robes and Dwyr gently pulls him into his breast. Holding each other, all the pain of Hyw's life and journey seems to ease, but he cannot bring himself to speak. Eventually, they both separate, but Dwyr still holds on to Hyw's shoulders.

"I have long awaited this day Hyw bach," Dwyr says as he rubs at his eyes, clearing his tears away, enough for him to see, but Hyw is still overcome by the moment.

"The time is far spent and we must make preparations." Suddenly Hyw notices a small throng of people standing on the path behind Dwyr. The group consists of three men and several women, all much older than Hyw, but none of them as old as Dwyr, except for one old woman with plaited long grey hair that has been wrapped around the back of her head into a bun. There is a small throng of children, some of whom are quite young, but others are almost fully grown. Hyw is surprised, although he does not understand why, to see all the people of the island carrying bows, with all the men wearing swords, including Dwyr.

A young man stands near the front of the group, a little younger than Hyw, with a mop of deep red hair splashed over the top of his head. It is tightly curled and the curls at the front of his hair fall over his face, partially hiding his eyes. A young girl stands close to him, whom Hyw instantly recognises as the young man's sister. Their likeness is quite extraordinary, although Hyw cannot make out if they are just brother and sister, or whether they are twins; he finds it impossible to differentiate their relative ages. All those present seem to stare at Hyw with a certain excitement caught up in their eyes and that excitement glows in every countenance.

The old woman's eyes sparkle just like Dwyr's and although she is slightly bowed with age, Hyw can see, when she steps towards him, that she too appears to be as sprite as the old man.

"It is time!" The old lady says to Dwyr, almost in a whisper.

Dwyr speaks quietly, but quickly to Hyw.

"It is time…we have much to do and say and so little time remaining. The idolatrous High Priests and the Scotti have formed an unholy alliance and they will soon be upon us. Māthōg's treachery has conspired against us." Hyw is quick to interrupt.

"The sons of Gododdyn have attacked the village, they will rout the Scotti!"

Dwyr pauses as his head bows.

"Yes, Hyw bach, we have a great ally in the power of their arms, but although the village is free, we have not rid the land of their evil," Dwyr speaks as though he has seen all the battle that morning and much more.

"Māthōg yet lives and many of his men too. The unholy alliance still has many who follow after him and he seeks thy life and the lives of those around thee…His rage is bent towards thee and he will not rest until he has spilt thy blood!"

Hyw had forgotten his friends for a moment, but at their mention, he turns to them. Mynddy smiles up at him and steps forward with Hyw taking her under his arm.

"Ah, Mynddy!" The old man says to Hyw's astonishment as he marvels over the clarity of the old man's visions.

"Our father has witnessed thy struggle and soon thou wilt be whole again. Come we have much to do and so little time."

Dwyr beckons to the small crowd who wait on his command. The women step forward and the old lady holds out her hand towards Mynddy. Mynddy hesitates slightly, looking up at Hyw. Smiling, he nods at her and she smiles back and any concern seems to vanish. Placing her hand in that of the old lady's, all the women gather around her. They walk off into the island. Some of the other women walk down to Cayr and Seryn and her children, and they too walk up the path leading into the heart of the island. Dwyr organises the men and boys. Two of them, a young boy and one of the men, stay with the boat. One of the men tries to get Gwydn to take his duty at the boat, but Dwyr intervenes.

"No, no, we have need of Gwydn and I believe Gwydn has need of me." Gwydn smiles awkwardly, not understanding Dwyr's words.

Placing his arm around Hyw, the old man leads him up a winding narrow path. The plain splendour of the island comes into view. Every mountain and hill of the distant coastline is open to his eyes and he looks to the mountains and imagines his home far beyond their rocky crags. He wanders in his dreams; over the hills and far away, but he is dragged back to reality by Dwyr's words.

It is quite apparent that the old man has seen both Mynddy and Hyw's struggle and his words and understanding pour a soothing balm onto Hyw's heart. At times, as Dwyr speaks, tears well in his eyes, but every word he has prepared is too precious to fall unheard, so he is careful with his feelings. Dwyr speaks of his visions and dreams, but to Hyw's dismay, the old man gives him little comfort saying only.

"It is a gift from God, Hyw bach, guard it well!" Hyw pursues him in their conversation, but Dwyr will not be persuaded to say more, other than.

"Thy visions may not be as clear as mine, but ye must study their meanings out in thy mind, no one can give their meaning to you, except God himself."

Time passes and still Dwyr talks quickly and quietly to Hyw. Eventually, his words fall silent, although he does not take his arm from around Hyw's shoulder and he seems to wait for Hyw to speak. Uneasy, Hyw has only one question remaining.

"What of the word, what of this truth Ywel spoke of?"

Dwyr smiles.

"My brother has taught thee well…what dust thou know of this truth?" Dwyr asks.

"I know of thy journeys to the sacred islands of the distant seas…I know of the old man who blessed thee and gave to thee a promise."

Dwyr interrupts him.

"Ah, but dust thou know of the promises we made?"

Hyw is silent for a moment.

"I know of the promise, but of its substance, I know nothing."

Dwyr smiles and looks up to the sky as though he is in prayer, but his words are addressed to Ywel.

"Thou hast taught him well my brother, but know he must be strong." The words bring Hyw no more comfort and he wonders in what way he could be stronger. Turning back to Hyw he says.

"I have little power and no authority I can pass to you…the word is the truth and if thou art strong thou mayest find a place for it in thy heart. It is like thy dreams; ye must find the meanings for thyself. The word of God does not change, but many seek to change it for their own perverted ways. God gave us his word, but we rejected it and killed his son whom he sent to save us. Look to the pit from whence ye are dug, Hyw bach and guard those things ye know to be true…search my brother's words, for he has taught thee well…I will give unto ye all I have left to give."

Dwyr again pauses and he reaches inside Hyw's smock taking hold of the arrowhead and he brings it out for all to see.

"This is the token of the promises we made, the power it holds will fade with the lives of those who keep its word sacred. Its word or power cannot be passed to you, although ye may see the truth it holds, so guard it well…the king shall come and gather his people…watch and pray, Hyw bach, watch and pray. The time may come when thou art called to defend the word, but until that day ye must watch and pray."

The old man steps away from Hyw, bowing his head. Walking a little further, he appears to cry, but the prayer he utters is for Hyw's continued strength.

A strong breeze is blowing and the long grass on top of the hill bends and ripples under its breath. Hyw is drained with his continued concentration and he bows his head as the breeze blows through him. There is a faint chill in the wind and he looks up and over the sea. Storms are gathering on the horizon and the high clouds of the morning's dawn are joined by a threatening, billowing armada, the early morning sun brings glowing colours to the distant storms.

Hyw looks around him. While caught away in the puzzle of Dwyr's words, they have reached the top of the hill at the far end of the island. Close to where he is standing is a stone table, with what looks like a stone step on either side. The table is built like an altar with small rocks laid on each other to form the base and a large flat rock laid across it to form its top, which is about waist high. The men are gathered at the far side of this stone table, apparently waiting, although Hyw cannot discern what they are waiting for.

Suddenly Hyw is aware of others walking behind him. He turns to see. The women have joined them again, but his eyes rest only on Mynddy and her appearance takes his breath away. She is dressed in a long plain calico dress reaching to the ground with a thinly woven gold sash tied around her waist. Her hair has been plaited on either side of her head and tied at the back. Woven into the plaits are small white flowers which circle her head like a crown. Hyw is transfixed as Mynddy smiles up at him. She moves in closer, but Hyw cannot speak.

"Art thou ready Hyw bach? Art thou ready for thy blessing?" Hyw can bring himself to do nothing more than nod his head, still caught in Mynddy's perfect symmetry. Someone or something guides him to the stone table. Mynddy kneels on the step on one side and Hyw kneels on the step on the other side. Dwyr stands at their head, taking them both by the right hand. Joining their hands together, he gently lays them across the stone table, but all Hyw can see and feel is Mynddy and his eyes cannot be drawn from her sight.

Dwyr raises his arms, looking up to the heavens and then places his hands, one on each of their heads. He speaks in an ancient tongue, but Hyw knows he is calling for the choicest of God's blessings to be poured out upon Mynddy and himself. Eventually, Dwyr's words cease and he looks down at Hyw and smiles.

"Ye may kiss thy bride, Hyw bach!"

The shock of Dwyr's words seems to enter Hyw and pierce his heart, but in his shock, he leans forward and Mynddy kisses him.

'Bride?' The word echoes in Hyw's head.

'Bride?' Hyw searches for the word's meaning in his mind and he checks it over and over again. The spell of Mynddy's beauty has been broken.

'A blessing' he is sure; it was just a blessing; for strength; for courage; for the journey ahead; 'not marriage!'

'There I have said the word.' Everything is tumbling inside his head and in the commotion, he hears Dwyr say.

"What God has joined together let not man split asunder."

'There has been a mistake.' The words are still in Hyw's head, but thoughts of his forgotten love for Sián nag at him and he cannot bring himself to look at Mynddy.

Giffydd is congratulating him and the entire congregation of women crowd around Mynddy. She smiles, her heart bursting. Both Mynddy and Hyw are drawn together in the tumult of the crowd. Mynddy hugs Hyw's side and Hyw places one arm around her shoulders, still unsure of his feelings.

'How could I have let this happen?' The thought haunts him.

Dwyr calls out.

"Shush, silence now!" Everyone settles and it is then that Hyw notices Cayr. She too is dressed as Mynddy, her long fair hair braided and plaited with a crown of white flowers. She is angelic in her appearance and could have been mistaken for one of the sentinels standing at the throne of God himself. Seryn is standing behind her, with her hands placed over her sister's shoulders, both looking into Giffydd's ashen face.

"Well?" Seryn says to her husband.

"Well, what?" Giffydd asks in utter bewilderment; failing to see what everyone else present has long since realised; including Hyw.

"If her father were here he would give her away, but he isn't!" Giffydd still looks back at them confused.

"Thou art the only one who can give her away; the only one she would have to give her away, can ye still not see?" Gwydn steps forward to the altar and finally the paradigm shifts.

"No…No…definitely not…look at them? They are too young…they…!" Giffydd's words fail him.

"Time is running away from us…yes and we live in strange times. Let them take hold of love while they can. Yes, they are young…young and in love." Seryn pleads.

"Now take her hand before I do thy duties for thee!" Seryn gives Giffydd, a certain look, and without further compromise, he steps forward, smiles at

Cayr and holds his arm out for her to hook her hand inside it. Leading her to the altar she kneels across the table from Gwydn.

Hyw watches Cayr's face as she stares across the altar at the man she loves. It is full of joy and her happiness seems to radiate from somewhere deep inside her.

'She is young, very young!' Hyw thinks to himself, but somehow he knows they will make it. Dwyr raises his arms and then pronounces the blessing. Mynddy hugs at Hyw's side and Hyw draws her into him, his arm still wrapped around her shoulder. What he is doing, Hyw can't quite be sure, but he feels a calm thought radiating through him.

When the ceremony is finished and everyone has congratulated both couples, Dwyr approaches Hyw and Mynddy. His eyes are full and his breath seems low and calm as though he is at rest after some great battle.

"I have looked to this day, through all my years; I have seen it in my waking visions, since before ye were both born…my promise is complete…I have kept my covenant and my work is done."

Chapter Twenty-Two

A shout cries up from the boat. Everyone looks. Those set to guard it are waving up the hill and one points out to sea. Hyw looks and just off the mainland, he can see three large sea-going vessels, two of them full of men. The third is further away and it is difficult to tell how many warriors there are onboard.

"Quick, thou hast no time to waste!" Dwyr shouts to Hyw and Mynddy as he orders his people.

"Take the children to ground!" He calls to the women, but Hyw intervenes.

"We can take them…they only have one place to land, if indeed they are coming here at all."

"Oh they are coming here...and they can land anywhere!" Hyw looks up at Dwyr.

"Dwyr is right Hyw, they will put men ashore one by one along the rocks...we cannot defend the whole island.

"Then what are we to do? We cannot all sail in one boat!"

"We will be fine...we are safe here...they will not find us where we hide." Says Dwyr, as he reorders the women to take the children to ground.

"Giffydd, try to draw them through the straits; the wind is increasing and..." Dwyr calls up to the skies as if the storm will obey his will.

"Flaming chariots ride on its storm." Suddenly as if in answer to his prayer, a flash of lightning forks down with a crash of thunder. The fork of lighting dances among the wild horses of the sea.

"Thy family will be safe here, Giffydd...ye must ride the waves and thy family will only weigh down thy boat...but Hyw and Mynddy must escape before the night falls"

Dwyr looks across at Hyw while giving the command and he knows it is true, but Giffydd looks across at Seryn's stern face; her hair blowing free in the wind with her children huddled around her.

"He is in thy care, Hyw bach..." She calls after them and Hyw knows Giffidd's life has been trusted to his hand. The sun darkens as a cloud rolls by, another fork of lightning flashes across the distant skies and a long roll of thunder rumbles and bounces off distant hills. Cayr turns to go with Gwydn, notching an arrow into the string of her bow.

"Cayr...not thee as well!" Seryn cries out after her sister. Cayr runs back and kisses Seryn on the cheek.

"The time will come when I am with child and its safety will order my life, but until that day I will stand at Gwydn's side." Her words are softly spoken and the love she holds for her sister shines in her eyes, but still, she turns to go, with two fingers securing an arrow into the string of her bow.

Everyone runs down the hill towards the boat. Hyw hadn't realised how far it was and Dwyr struggles to keep up with their pace. When they arrive at the beach, he is lagging some way behind. Hyw cannot leave and he runs back towards the old man, but Dwyr shoos him on and Hyw turns again to go. He is the last one in the boat, but he orders them to wait for Dwyr. The old man is out of breath when he finally gets to them, but he wades out to the boat, through the gathering waves.

Hyw bends down over the stern and Dwyr talks quickly to him.

"Geddyn, will guard thy rear…his men are waiting for you, but ye must ride the winds of the storm…save thy sister Hyw bach…save thy sister!" The words cut deep into Hyw and he can hardly speak.

"How do y'…?" Hyw does not ask the question, knowing Dwyr has seen all, in his visions. Tears are welling in both their eyes.

"We have no time for tears Hyw bach…there may come a time when ye choose to give thy life for that truth ye seek, but that time is not here or now. Look to the living, Hyw bach…only seek that kindly light the dead have seen fit to leave us…it wilt guide thee on thy way…I know our people walk with you; I have seen them and so have you…search thy dreams, Hyw bach, search thy dreams."

Dwyr's words lift Hyw's spirit and he wants to question the old man further, but Giffydd shouts to him.

"We must be away…they are upon us!" Dwyr lets go of the boat, but calls after Hyw as Giffydd and Gwydn pull at the ores.

"Follow their kindly light, Hyw bach!" Dwyr then points to the sails of the Scotti ships.

"Cut the heart out…cut the heart out and the body will die!"

Dwyr is standing up to his breast in the water. Waves roll in on him, as Hyw looks back, but the old man seems to sway up and down with their swell and eventually, Hyw sees him wade back to the beach. When he is sure Dwyr is safe, Hyw turns his attention to his friends, wiping his eyes as he does so.

Giffydd and Gwydn are both rowing their hearts out. He hadn't realised the peril they were in. The storm is increasing at a phenomenal rate and Hyw takes over from Giffydd so he can raise the sail, but he can't raise it until they are clear of the rocks. Hyw pulls with all his might. Finally, Giffydd raises the sail, jumps into his place at the tiller and begins to tac away from the approaching Scotti. Mynddy is riding high in the prow and Hyw moves forward to join her.

The sea is rough and the small boat is tossed to a fro. Lightning from the approaching storm flashes across the sky as a constant roll of thunder fills the air.

"Hold on, it's going to get worse!" Giffydd calls out as his small fishing boat is thrown up into the air off the back of a crashing wave, hitting the sea with a loud thump.

"I will try to come about between them, but it will be difficult and if misjudged we will have an almighty scrap on our hands."

Hyw studies the three boats bearing down on them. The first is full of Scotti Slags, but at their head, Hyw recognises the robes of one of the idolatrous Druids. The boats are lined with Scotti war boards, their lances and swords drawn at the ready. The second boat is a little way off, with the third barely making headway in the chase.

Hyw watches the distant boat and wonders about its progress; the first boats are struggling in the waves with their cumbersome loads, but the third ship isn't packed with as many warriors and it seems to sit higher in the water. Each of the chasing Scotti ships is rigged in much the same way as Giffydd's humble craft, but they are at least five or six times its size.

The third ship should be the fastest and Hyw fears it is waiting to cut off their escape. Turning back to Giffydd with Dwyr's words still ringing in his ears.

"Can ye cut in front of the first boat?" Hyw calls out above the strengthening winds.

"I can try, but it is madness!" Giffydd calls back.

"We will pass too close to the ship and Scotti lances."

"Do it…there is some method in my melancholy!" Gwydn and Mynddy are standing on either side of Hyw with Cayr just behind them. Hyw calls Cayr forward and whispers to all of them in turn, as though the Scotti can hear every word he utters. The rain begins to fall as Giffydd brings the boat about. The storm's winds fill the sail and the boat heaves over as it cuts through the waves. Hyw positions them along the side of the boat, with the girls in the centre as both he and Gwydn stand on either flank.

"Not until I say!" Hyw calls out.

The Scotti Slags at the front of the approaching ship see Hyw organising his archers and they pick up their shields, but as Hyw suspected, they cannot resist watching what Hyw and his comrades are doing. The Druid in the prow organises them positioning their shields; constructing a wall for both his and their defence, but the Scotti are undisciplined and push to look for the approaching danger; peeping from behind their war boards.

Giffydd is pulling on the sail with one hand and pushing the tiller with his other. The boat is heeled over with its sail bending low. It is difficult for his crew of archers to hold their positions, but they manage somehow. The ship comes into range and the Scotti at the rear of the boat begin to jeer.

"Hold thy aim!" Hyw calls out as every bow bends towards their enemy. The wall of shields tightens, and the Scotti Slags peer through the gaps. The Druid at their centre shouts for them to hold their position.

"Hold thy aim!" Hyw calls again!" A lance is launched from somewhere in mid-ship, but it is woefully short of its mark and another jeer from the Scotti Slags cries out.

"Hold!" Hyw calls again. Giffydd is straining with the rudder and sail, but he has judged their speed and distance perfectly. Their small boat passes just under the prow of the Scotti ship.

"Now!" Hyw calls out as he and Gwydn loose their feathered warriors; one to one side of the ship and the other to the opposite side. Their blades arch through the air, watched intently by the Scotti shield men. There is a clamour on the boat as shields are forced out to meet the path of both arrows. But the Scotti are too impetuous and as they raise their shields a gap appears and Mynddy and Cayr are left with a clear shot of the Druid.

"Now!" Hyw calls out and a second pair of arrows arches through the air, skewering into the Druid's breast.

Hyw has notched another arrow into the string of his bow and Gywdn is not far behind him. The Scotti are in disarray, and as the Druid falls to the deck, their shields weaken, with some being dropped altogether. Another gap appears, Hyw takes aim and another Grot falls; then another, from Gwydn's bow and yet another from Mynddy's.

"Enough!" Hyw calls out before Cayr can chance her aim.

For all their skills with the bow, Giffydd is the hero of the day. His prowess with his small Lugger is just as honed as anyone's ability with the bow. Hyw smiles over at him and he nods his head in appreciation as Giffydd smiles back.

"A good plan, Hyw bach," Giffydd calls out.

"Cut the heart out and the body dies!" Hyw calls back.

"We are not in a position to do that again!" Giffydd says, but maybe the storm is with us…?"

"Aye and the old man's prayers!" Hyw points up to the billowing storm. Giffydd brings the boat too and eases up on the sail, tacking towards the second Scotti ship, although he could never turn into its path.

"What art thou doing?" Hyw calls out.

"Let the dogs see the boar!" He calls back.

Hyw smiles, trusting his friend.

The first Scotti ship is in total confusion, but it manages somehow to turn after them. The second boat changes its tack to intercept them and the chase is on. The third Scotti ship may become a problem; it is further back, closer to the coast, and if it is sailed by a skilful hand, it could catch them, but Giffydd is confident and he keeps a smile on his face. Lowering the sail, Cayr scrambles over to shorten it, tying in the reefs.

"What is in thy mind?" Hyw calls above the howling wind, but Giffydd just continues to smile.

"Hold on!" He eventually calls out as he finally brings their boat about, turning the sail into the wind again. The mast strains as it bends and the boat heels over under the immense pressure. Gwydn goes to help Cayr and Giffydd. The rudder and sail are their only weapons and Giffydd will need the aid of those who are able. All three of them fight to control the wind, sail and boat. The Lugger picks up speed and rides on the crest of the billowing waves. Hyw watches the wild horses of the sea as they race the little craft into the straights.

Looking back at the Scotti ships, the first is picking up speed, but is heeled over too far and with its crew in a panic; no one has trimmed its sail. The Slags on board are struggling to hold on. Two of them end up in the water, with no hope of rescue. One flounders and then sinks beneath the waves. The other manages to keep his head above the teaming waters a little longer; thrashing at the buckles on his armour, but its weight soon drags him down.

The storm is gathering pace and the skies open up. Torrential rain hammers down on them, wetting the sails and rigging, but the Lugger is buoyant with Giffydd at its helm. Lightning flashes across the sky and thunder booms, rumbling all around them.

The second Scotti boat is sluggish in water with its heavy load, but whoever guides its helm is pushing the ship to its furthest limits. The waves batter at and over its stern. The ship heels over dangerously and waves start to spill over its deck. Finally, there is more water inside than out and it slowly begins to sink. Men rip at their armour; some manage to strip it off, but most do not. They struggle and thrash at the water, but the boat sinks out of sight under the weight of their weapons of war.

The first boat seems to be doing slightly better, but it is at an awkward tack. From beyond its desperate struggle, Hyw can see a cluster of huge waves crashing towards them. Calling to Giffydd he points to the waves. Giffydd takes a long look behind them, but as he turns back, Hyw can see a determined smile etched onto his face.

The first of the big waves hit the Scotti ship turning it to one side. The helmsman struggles to turn it back to its course, but the second wave is soon upon them. It seems to swamp the ship, turning it on its side. Most of its men are catapulted into the sea, with some clinging to the mast. The third wave is devastating and its roar signals their end; completely covering the ship there is no further sign of its hull or crew.

The first wave is almost upon Giffydd's little craft. The wild horses are gone, but in their place is a mountain of water, which dwarfs the tiny boat. To Hyw's surprise, the boat rides up on the wave and he looks back to the next mountain of water. Its wild horses are also calling off their charge and Giffydd smiles up at the Gods, but the third wave is unrelenting.

"Hold on!" He calls out. Giffydd fights with the rudder while Gwydn and Cayr pit themselves against the rope that pulls the sail too. As the wave approaches, they have almost matched its speed. The boat rises into the crest of the wave, with its wild horses crashing and galloping all around them, but somehow the wave forces them along with its power. Giffydd shrieks out in the exhilaration of the moment as they begin to ride the wave. Eventually, its wild horses call off their charge and the small boat rises and falls as the mountain of water slips underneath them.

The third Scotti ship is making good headway, but the power of the waves has forged a good lead for Hyw and his friends. Studying the Scotti boat, a huge warrior is standing on its prow with several other warriors around him. Hyw is unsure, but it can only be Māthōg. Whoever it is, they begin remonstrating with the Slag at the ship's helm. Shouting at the crew, his words are lost in the torrent of the storm. Hyw watches as he marches up and down on the deck of the ship, throwing shields and armour into the sea to make the boat lighter.

The giant warrior comes back into the prow of the boat shouting and pointing towards Giffydd's little fishing boat. Finally, he turns back to the crew and in a fit of rage begins to throw young Scotti grots overboard. The young lads remaining, begin to unbuckle their armour so they can swim for it, but for many, it is too late. The unfolding scene is outrageous, but in its madness, Hyw knows and recognises their tormentor. It is Māthōg and that confirmation stirs Hyw's rage, but he is still a long way ahead of them.

Rounding the headland, the small bay comes into sight. The storm's rage eases slightly in the lea of the cliffs and headland.

"I must take the boat back for my family," Giffydd says as they approach the small bay.

"Take Gwydn and Cayr; their bows will aid thee."

"We will be fine…thy need is greater than ours, but art thou sure ye can weather the storm?" Hyw asks. Giffydd just looks up at Hyw and grins. Hyw regrets asking but continues.

"Ye know where we will be?" Giffydd nods.

"And ye know my home beyond the mountains?" Giffydd nods again.

"I thank thee, my good friend!" Hyw turns to Gwydn and Cayr and smiles. Cayr throws herself at Mynddy and hugs her; both with tears in their eyes.

"Set us on the rocks…it will save thee dropping the sail!"

Mynddy does not want to leave Cayr's arms, but Hyw calls to her. Eventually, as they approach the rocky shoreline Hyw has to pull at Mynddy's arm. Giffydd judges the waves perfectly and calls for them to jump.

The rocks are wet, but they manage to keep their feet. Turning around, they watch as Giffydd tacks out into the bay. They look for Māthōg's ship, but it does not appear. The worst of the storm is over as Mynddy and Hyw turn to go, bowing their heads into the torrents of rain.

Chapter Twenty-Three

Moving cautiously, Mynddy takes the lead as they make their way to the hidden stable, where the horses are hidden. The spinney comes into view and they hide in the bracken, surveying the trees for any sign of Scotti.

"Here Sire!" Dynōg's whisper is barely discernable above the wind. Hyw looks deeper into the bracken, off to his right, and catches sight of the old warrior's hiding place. Shrouded over with a thick woollen blanket, he is still soaked through to the skin as he keeps his vigil with pride.

"Ma master has nae arrived yet, but it is safe for ye t'go inside…call to the laddie an tha will let thee in." Just as he speaks Māddrōg appears on the path behind them with several of his men.

"Ah, good of ye tae turn up when yon fray is over!" Māddrōg says with a large grin spread across his face. Hyw smiles back.

"How tha mighty hae fallen…who wis at the helm of tha wee boatie?" Māddrōg grins again and it is obvious that he had watched the chase through the storm.

"Māthōg canna put ashore…an we win no be facing his sword for some time yet!" Hyw smiles, but Mynddy is tense. The warriors have grown accustomed to her hesitation, even though she is a heroine to each who had witnessed her battle.

"Cam then laddie, we hae nae time tae spik!" They all make their way into the spinney; all, but Dynōg, who slowly sinks back into his clump of bracken.

"Art thou asleep in there laddie?" Māddrōg's voice bellows out just as they approach the tumbled-down barn. A young lad jumps too as they enter, walking past a wooden door that is mostly in pieces on the ground while what remains of its board rots on its woeful leather hinges.

At the far end of the barn, the roof is mostly intact with stalls where the stallion and Sarn have kept themselves warm and dry. Mynddy immediately goes over to the horses. Placing her bow against the wall, she climbs over, girding her dress up above her knees. Sarn is beside herself and cannot contain her excitement as Mynddy throws her arms around the horse's neck. But the stallion is quiet, both Mynddy and Sarn move over to him. Mynddy caresses its head and slowly works her way down the animal's wounded side. It has healed well, but there is still some poison around it. Someone has been tending the wound.

Māddrōg becomes serious and talks quickly and quietly to Hyw as Mynddy begins to saddle Sarn and the stallion. The attack had not gone well. It had all gone to plan, but most of the Scotti had left before it had begun. Two of Geddyn's scouts had seen them leave and not knowing how many remained in the village Geddyn had split his men the best he could. Giffydd and Hyw had put pay to all, but a token resistance there.

"Aye it wist something o' a rout laddie." Māddrōg seems to have a constant grin on his face, but his amusement is short-lived as he continues to explain their position. Geddyn and his contingent had engaged the Scotti as they left, but most of the Scotti escaped. "Dinna be doon hearted laddie, my Lord has sent us to aid ye in yer escape, an ma braithren'll root oot what remains o' yon Slags." Hyw remains quiet, listening carefully.

"We canna take ye further than 'The mouth of Anwnn'," Māddrōg says as a perplexed look spreads across Hyw's face.

"The Mouth of Anwnn?" Hyw asks.

"Why aye laddie the bay the two warriors brought ye to on yer journey here." Everything becomes clear and Hyw turns to prepare himself, helping Mynddy with the horses.

"They canna o'got fair…two scouts hae combed the area an haenae foond hide nor hair of them… most have fled t'tha north!"

Mynddy has gathered their belongings together and Māddrōg briefs his men.

It is mid-afternoon as they make their way from the barn. The rain is steady, but the worst of the storm has passed. Sarn carries both Hyw and Mynddy; wrapped up together under their blankets and furs, both holding their bows at the ready.

Mynddy feels behind her and finds Hyw's free hand on her hip. She pulls it in around her waist. Tentatively, Hyw allows Mynddy to place his hand on her belly, but his feelings calm as she leans into him and he pulls her close.

The stallion walks quietly behind them; its limp is barely noticeable, but Hyw still doesn't want to over-exert the beast unless it becomes absolutely necessary. Māddrōg's men take the lead and Hyw is happy to relax in their care. Dynōg is left to bring up the rear.

Hyw watches the old warrior; perhaps the eldest of all Māddrōg's men, but he seems one of the most capable. Indeed, by the way, Māddrōg speaks and by the respect, he shows him, Hyw surmises Dynōg is the most trusted of all his men. As well as keeping their rear, Dynōg constantly checks on both Hyw and Mynddy's welfare; pointing out their way and explaining the best paths to follow when they part. He doesn't seem to have confidence in the capabilities of the two scouts.

"Tis nae a wee area fur two men tae cover!" Hyw hears his warning and changes the plait on both his and Mynddy's bows. Checking their arsenal of arrows, he replenishes his dwindling supply from those in Blaidd's old quiver.

The rain begins to ease as evening draws in, and has stopped altogether by the time the sun is setting beyond a blanket of clouds draped above the horizon. Looking to the west, across the sea to where a deep red glow embellishes the clouds, he knows the skies will clear during the night. Catching sight of the island behind them, he wonders about his friends and checks his waking visions for their safety, but can see nothing.

They reach the headland leading to 'The Mouth of Annwn' as evening falls and they find the path, which circumscribes its outer edges, high above the sea. The clouds cover any hope of seeing clearly, but Hyw and Mynddy must continue alone. The warriors turn to go, except for Māddrōg and Dynōg. Their goodbyes are little more than a long look and a nod from Dynōg. The only words spoken are those of Māddrōg.

"Ah shall meet tha ageen laddie…hold t'tha path…an mind tha blether o'Dynōg's!" With that, he turns to go. Hyw has already climbed down from Sarn's back, bracing himself for the walk. Mynddy takes the stallion's reins but keeps her bow at the ready. Mynddy is still silent, but her spirit is lifting. The stallion nuzzles up to Hyw's arm and nudges him from time to time. Hyw turns to the horse.

"Well my new friend, we have neglected thee…a name…we need a name for thee…now let me see!" Hyw mulls the thought over in his mind as he scratches at the stallion's ears.

"Hyraidd…yes Hyraidd…thou art my longing for home!" Hyw looks back up at Mynddy and then corrects himself.

"No…thou art our longing for home!" And with that, the horse shakes his head up and down snorting his approval as Hyw scratches its nose. Sarn joins in, rattling her head around as she whinnies her approval.

Hyw turns to the path and in the silence tries to divine a way through the thick bracken in the encroaching night. Thinking about the day's turbulent events, he finds it hard to concentrate. The Scotti treachery weighs on his mind, the two girls they had defiled; his long-awaited meeting with Dwyr and his unforeseen marriage to Mynddy.

Hyw grieves at how little he sees in his waking visions and how menacing their shadows have grown. Dwyr had taught him little of their meanings, there is so much he needs to know, and yet, Hyw is somehow content.

'If Dwyr does not think it necessary for me to know then I don't need to know.' But for some reason, he still grieves to himself but not for his marriage to Mynddy. If he searches his feelings, he knows it is right.

'I will spend the eternities with her,' No, his grief is for the uncertainty of their future and maybe they would walk the eternities before their lives together have begun.

They walk for some distance before the bay comes into view; it is little more than a faint outline through the murk of the night, but Hyw can see the thin plumes of its waves endlessly rolling towards its sandy shore. They walk on, keeping to the path above the bay. Wet bracken clings to Hyw's leggings, soaking through to his legs and he is soaking wet almost up to his waist. The steep sides of the headland allow no room for manoeuvre. The clouds are thinning, but the moon has not yet risen or is hiding in some other quarter of the crystal sphere.

Sarn hesitates slightly; so does Hyraidd, the stallion. They both hold their heads aloft with their ears pricked up to catch every sound and Sarn refuses to take another step until her master has noticed those same dangers she can sense.

Pausing and listening, Hyw can hear nothing, but looking back towards Sarn, he knows something is wrong. Hyraidd begins to scrape one of his hooves on the ground. Looking around, Hyw moves back towards his trusted companions, recognising their insecurities. Gazing across at Sarn, he slowly takes Hyraidd's reins from Mynddy. Smiling, he looks up at his bride; she is like some phantom, ghostly white in her dress. It is gathered up around the top of her legs so she can ride as a man. Taking hold of her leg, Hyw can feel her trembling, but her brother's bow is still held securely in her hand.

"If we get parted, I will see thee on the sands…Ye know where!" His words are less than a whisper and Mynddy struggles to hear their meaning, and by the time she does, it is too late.

"Yargh!" Hyw cries, striking Sarn with the flat of his hand, straight across her rump.

"Sorry old girl!" He says under his breath, but Sarn understands the dangers they are in and submits herself to Hyw's command. With Hyw's cry, the bracken erupts into a flurry of screams and shouts. Sarn charges along the path, with Mynddy struggling to gain control of the reins.

A silhouette breaks the skyline above the bracken to one side and she despatches a swift blade on a devastating course towards it. Another racing silhouette cries, running into their path, only to be trampled under Sarn's stampede.

Hyraidd jumps in all the commotion as Hyw heaves himself onto his back and bringing his bow to bear, he kicks at the stallion's sides. The huge warhorse begins its thunderous charge without further encouragement from Hyw's heels. Hyraidd has his mate in sight and he exerts all of his might and power to catch up with Sarn.

Two more silhouettes appear from the shadowy horizon of the bracken. 'Druids!" The recognition flashes through Hyw like lightning, but his charge is carrying him away. An arrow thrashes through the air, passing close to Hyw's head, from where? Hyw cannot tell. Another arrow whips towards him, but its flight is swiftly brought to an end. Thrump. Hyw hears the low thump as it hits something, possibly the trunk of a small tree or bush by the path.

The stallion stumbles slightly but forges relentlessly on. A shadow jumps out onto the path in front of them. Another idolatrous Druid, but this one is wielding a broad sword. Hyw's swift blade rages into the night, but the Druid is dangerously close.

Thump. The arrow finds its target and the stallion's stampede crashes through its victim. There is a clamour of shadows all around them as the night comes to life. Thrashing silhouettes race towards the galloping ghostly stallion, but Hyw's new steed is swift and soon the dangers are far behind them. The moon finally finds a hazy patch of thin clouds, but its meagre light helps only a little and Hyw must trust Hyraidd's galloping heart.

The path leads out and onto a wider track which in turn, bends down towards the beach. Mynddy is riding hard; knowing Hyw and the stallion are only a few paces behind her. Sarn's hooves sink into the soft sand and finally the spray of the sea splashes around them. Hyraidd is slowing his charge and Mynddy turns Sarn back towards them. Hyw coaxes at Hyraidd's sides, but it seems to have tired quickly; 'the wound maybe?'

Mynddy draws in close; riding up to Hyw. Her eyes settle on him, but an awful realisation hits as her world hedges in around her. In horror,

Mynddy's eyes focus on Hyraidd. She desperately wants to scream out, but as she opens her mouth, not one sound escapes from her lips. There is a huge sprawl of blood splattered across the stallion's front, coursing from a large wound at its neck. Mynddy jumps down from Sarn's back and runs over to the helpless steed. Only as Mynddy approaches does Hyw realize that something is wrong.

Jumping down, he beats Mynddy to the front of his gallant friend, but he cannot stop Mynddy from pushing past him. A large Scotti arrow is protruding from the horse's breast alongside a gaping wound from the Druid's broadsword. Both Hyw and Mynddy instantly realise the situation is beyond their control. Bright red blood is spewing from the horse's neck and the arrow is close to Hyraidd's heart. There is nothing they can do.

Hyraidd whinnies and snorts as he struggles to stay on his leg. Blood is pouring down the steed's legs and a pool of blood gathers around its hooves. The animal's head drops and blood starts to drip from its mouth. It coughs and staggers then whinnies again. Dropping to its knees; life is draining from the horse's eyes.

Overwhelmed, Mynddy cannot control her emotions. She is helpless. Sarn moves in closer, pushing her head up to the stallions'. Their eyes meet, but Hyraidd is fading fast. Collapsing to the sand, a wave washes in around its neck and head; the water turning crimson as a stream of blood foams around them.

Lights are sparking high on the headland as torches are lit. Hyw can hear shouts in the commotion they have caused. The torches flit back and forth, but eventually, they find some semblance of order.

Sarn is still nuzzling at the stallion and Mynddy turns from the horse into Hyw's arms; her tears are inconsolable, but still, she makes no sound. Hyw is fighting a burning deep inside, as his rage begins to sear through him with his longing for home lying broken in the surf and wake. Taking a long, but slow deep breath in, Hyw whispers to Mynddy.

"It is time…the torches are coming…the Druids will soon be upon us." Taking her by the shoulders, he gently wipes at a tear with his finger. They both turn to Sarn, but she will not be drawn from Hyraidd's side. Hyw coaxes his old friend, but no matter how he tries she will not move.

Mynddy pushes past him. Sarn's head is down and she gives no sign of recognition of Mynddy's presence as the horse continues to caress and nibble at her dead companion's ears and head. Taking hold of Sarn's mane, she begins scratching and stroking up and along her neck towards the horse's ears. Placing an arm over the horse, Mynddy hugs Sarn's neck.

Finally, Sarn looks up at her and Mynddy pulls her head into her; there are tears in Mynddy's eyes. Scratching and caressing, she pours her love, like a balm, onto the animal; Sarn can sense Mynddy's care and devotion seeping into her and she turns, until eventually, they are face to face, staring, each into the other's eyes. Mynddy cannot control her tears and she rests her forehead against Sarns' as the balm soothes into the great mare.

The lanterns are quickly descending towards the beach. Hyw whispers into Sarn's ear so both the women in his life can hear him.

"Look after my bride Sarn bach…I will be, but a trice!" Hyw disappears up the beach towards the dunes. Small waves lap at Sarn and Mynddy's feet, but Mynddy continues to caress the horse as time seems to slow.

Somewhere an arrow arches, unseen and unheard, through the air. There is a muffled cry as one of the pursuing torches is dropped and another Druid's life melts into the Mouth of Annwn.

Moments later Hyw is back with his grieving companions. Mynddy is sitting on Sarn's back and his old friend is ready to carry her wherever Hyw leads.

"They will only be delayed a short while…we must go!" Mynddy smiles down at Hyw; with her bow ready.

"Art thou ready my friend?" Hyw asks Sarn. She seems to warm at his words and raises her head, pricking her ears back at the thought of their flight.

"Come, my Friend!" Hyw calls as he turns, running along the shoreline in the shallow waters. The moon escapes from behind the thinning clouds and its torchlight finds their retreat in its brightening silver blaze. The idolatrous Druids see their prey and the chase is on.

Sarn seems to find renewed strength. Hyw leads them up and out of the water, running up the beach at the far end of the bay. The torches of the Druids are swift over the sands; their meagre light sways and flickers as if performing some ritualistic dance as the Scotti Slags relentlessly follow their masters.

Slowing his charge, Hyw scans the dunes ahead of them. The pathway between their hillocks is made for an ambush, and there would be too many of them for Hyw and Mynddy to fight alone.

Sarn watches her master as he steps off the beach and between the dunes. The path continues straight back with some bracken at the edge of a large area of mire and swamp. Sarn moves up behind her master, but she can sense a presence on either side of the path. Pausing; she listens again. There are humans, lying in wait on either side of the path. Lifting her head high into the air, her ears spark upright so she can hear the very breath of the moment. Her master moves dangerously close to where the assassins are lying in wait. Sarn whinnies out a warning to him; he is in grave peril. Mynddy nudges at the horse's sides, but Sarn will not move.

Suddenly, the most beautiful of all the sentinels is standing at Sarn's side. She smiles at her old friend as she takes hold of Sarn's reins and leaning forward, she whispers into the horse's ears.

"Come Sarn bach, it is safe!" Although Sarn cannot feel the sentinel's touch on the reins, some power moves inside her as she takes a step forward.

Hyw has come to a halt in front of two thickets of bracken, one on either side of the path. Something is wrong, he can sense it, feel it, but the sound of the chasing Druids is close behind them.

Eventually, that most beautiful of all the sentinels moves forward, seen only by Sarn. The ghostly apparition turns, and raising a flaming sword out in front of her, she stands ready. Beaconing to Sarn, Sarn hesitates.

"Here Sire!" Dynōg's low whisper breathes out of the thicket to the left of the path.

"There are nae many of us…but ye can leave em t'oor swift blades laddie!" Dynōg is a swordsman, not an archer and Hyw knows the odds are stacked against his friends, but he turns and beckons to Mynddy; Sarn is still cautious in her advance. Quickly leading them past the two thickets, Hyw turns Sarn back to face the beach.

"Stay here!" Hyw whispers to Mynddy.

"Stay here and let them see you!" Hyw smiles up at Mynddy who understands his thoughts and plans and watches as he turns, disappearing into the thicket where Dynōg is hiding. Preparing herself, Mynddy places several arrows in her hand at the handle of her bow.

Sarn looks for the sentinels, but she can only see the one most beautiful of all the spirits, who is slowly walking back along the path towards the beach, her flaming sword aloft. Sarn watches with a quietly troubled heart, when, from either side of the path, a ghostly throng moves out to cover the opening to the beach, barring the way. They seem to move in unison out into the dark shadows that veil the Druid's approach and they fade into the gloom of the night as one by one they draw their flaming swords, bringing them up to the ready.

The Druid's clatter can be heard from beyond the dunes, shouting and cursing at their Scotti minions.

"Through there…they are, but two…get thy yellow livers' through that gap!"

One by one, four Scotti Slags move cautiously between the dunes, towards Mynddy's position.

She sits ready.

There is an older warrior at their head who moves with some caution and stealth; a bow held at the ready with an arrow notched into place. The Scotti warrior has been tutored in the course of many battles and is more than proficient at his trade, but his three companions, who each have a sword drawn, are less than confident and they all appear nervous.

One of the Scotti swordsmen sees Mynddy astride Sarn at the very moment the archer draws her into his sights. They both seem to pause slightly as they check she is alone.

"He's left her to us, lads!" The swordsman cries back to his waiting comrades as the archer bends his bow ready. Everything then seems to happen in one continuous rush. There is a call and cry from the beach as the rest of the Scotti Slags charge forward, the young Slag with the sword begins his charge to gain their prize.

Thrump. An arrow from Hyw's bow rips at the archer's neck and in the shock, he releases his own blade, but the Scotti swordsman has run into his sights. The arrow skewers his impetuous cohort, hitting him in the back of the head. There is little force in its blade, but it manages to puncture his flesh; stunning him. Crying out in his agonies, the grot throws his arms wide. Thump. One of Mynddy's blades smashes into his chest.

The thickets and dunes on either side of the path spring into life, but it is too late to recall the rash and impulsive Scotti Slags. Trush, thump; thump. Arrows speed to halt every Scotti blade as Dynōg and Hamish step out to protect Mynddy and Sarn, but they have to race her towards the fray. They both scramble towards a fearsome-looking Scotti grot who leads their attack, but Mynddy's shattering shaft beats them to the kill. Hyw is stood on top of a dune to cut off any retreat as the ambush turns into a massacre. Hamish and Dynōg's swords finally taste Scotti blood and their rage is quenched.

The carnage of their slaughter is short-lived and Hyw turns his attention to the Idolatrous Druids, but to his amazement, they are shrieking and crying, running in every direction as if the baying hounds of Annwn were biting at every heel. Those Druids who have 'the seeing eye' look on the awful apparitions of the standing sentinels, but they cannot quench their swords in the blood of the dead.

Hyw's amusement subsides as a familiar presence grows at his side and he is a child again, wrapped up in the comfort and warmth of his mother's arms.

The rolling thunder of warhorses can be heard galloping across the sands towards them. It is Māddrōg and the remainder of his men. The Druid's horrified screams are soon quelled and the slaughter is quickly over.

"We have nae got them all Laddie…aat least one of their holy men has escaped…Hamish and Dynōg willna return until he is deed or drowned in the mire!" Māddrōg says to Hyw as he organises and gathers his men.

"Had I known tha peril, ah widdae followed after ye mae sel." Māddrōg continues. "We intercepted two o' oor scouts who had followed the Slags in tae tha area we left thee… Dynōg raced a heid while I tried tae follow eftir ye."

Dynōg returns with a smile on his face.

"Tha holy man wilnae bother them on their trail!" Both Hamish and he are dressed only in their plaid skirts, with a sash over each of their shoulders. Hamish is the larger of the two warriors, but it is Dynōg who has the blood of the Scotti splattered over his shoulder and breast and he looks up at Mynddy who is sitting silently on Sarn.

"Lassie, ah wouldnae hesitate t'follow ye in tae ony fray!" With his words, he salutes her and raises his sword in front of her, he then turns to Hyw. Hyw nods his appreciation turning to watch the warriors as they build a fire to burn the criminals.

Chapter Twenty-Four

"Māthōg hae-his guard aat his sid and they are only a few...tha idolatrous Druids an a few o'tha Scotti Slags abide, but aa scattered tae tha winds...they willnae bother ye!" The scout's report is half speculation, but it is uncannily close to the truth.

"Nae bother, ah willnae loose tham...they are cornered on yonder heidland; they willnae escape...ma hoonds are closing in!" Māddrōg says as they part for the second time that night.

Hyw walks for most of the night, leading Sarn, as Mynddy sleeps on and off. Their progress is slow; stopping at every shifting shadow and waking sound. Hyw's eyes search through the silhouettes of trees and thickets of bracken and heather that line their way. Exhausted, his eyes grow heavy in the thick of night. Sarn snouts and nibbles at the side of his face, then she nudges him in the back and step upon step they stumble forward.

Sometime in the small hours, Hyw looks up at his bride and he is overwhelmed as he drawers her beauty and spectacle in. Caught in the silver blaze of the moon, both Sarn and Mynddy glow like some terrible, but beautiful apparition of Annwn. The shimmering blaze of her dress, the crown of flowers in her hair and the fire burning in the catch-light of her eyes, sears into him and he is lost in the magic and growing fantasy of his redemption. Their eyes meet as Mynddy's slow, but certain smile soothes into him and in that moment, all his life, all his loss and all his pain are purged from him.

The night slips slowly by as both Sarn and Hyw follow the silver ribbon of the track, but before they reach the end of the great finger of land, the slow grey light of morning begins to appear in the sky before them.

Sometime just before dawn, exhausted from walking, Hyw climbs up behind his bride. Tentatively holding her close, he folds his free hand over her hip and then slowly moves it across her flat taught stomach. Mynddy takes his bow and places both bows across her lap. Hyw leans his head against her back, and in an instant he is gone, drifting somewhere between death and the dawn. Mynddy can feel him jump and flinch in his nightmares as she holds his arms firmly wrapped in her own.

After the sunrise, Sarn is left to struggle alone, with her sleepy load secure on her back. Time passes slowly by as a big sun climbs high into the sky, chasing thin veils of mist from the bogs and marshes by the river. Walking forever on, Sarn occasionally stops, waiting in the shadows as dangers pass.

The day is hot and eventually, it burns into Hyw and Mynddy. They both wake with a start as Sarn ambles between the mountains. It takes a moment for Hyw to recognise where they are.

'We must find a safe place to rest!' Hyw thinks to himself.

The trail winds up through the trees as its stream trickles and splashes at Sarn's feet. They climb out of the woods and up into the foothills of the mountains. Hyw's eyes take in all the beauty around him, as though he is seeing the mountains for the first time, with their cascading rivers falling over the edge of the world.

Wending her way up towards the wild waters, Sarn leads them to the secret pool, where Hyw had rested before the winter. The endless torrent of water streams down as if it gushes from the branches of the few trees and bushes that hide the crystal-clear pool from the prying eyes of the world above.

Every muscle and sinew of both their bodies ache as they climb down from Sarn's back.

Hyw looks up at the teaming waters as each detail of their secret climbs clamours in front of him: the short sheep-shorn mountain grass that had cooled his feet and the small ledge where he had rested all simmer in his mind. The incredible wonder of the cascading waters seems to light in Mynddy's eyes as she struggles to take in the full splendour of the scene before her.

Offloading their bundles and climbing up to the grassy ledge above the pool, Hyw unfolds his life, laying it bare before him. Stretching a blanket above them he forms a shelter and returning to the bundles, he lays his father's wolf-skin-coat over their woollen blankets, for a bed.

Deep in thought, Mynddy climbs down and stands at the edge of the pool. Crouching on a large smooth rock, which slopes down into the pool. Slowly leaning forward, she cups her hands, scooping at the surface of the pool.

Hyw stops his life to watch as she drinks from her hand and scoops again. When she has finished drinking she splashes her face and begins to wash, but something seems to light inside her and she too pauses her life. Kneeling, at the edge of the pool little droplets of water spark in the sunlight as they drip from her lips.

Mynddy stares down into the deep waters and her eyes catch sight of her shimmering reflection and for the first time, she sees her crown of flowers platted in her hair. Some of the flowers are gone, lost in the storm or on the treacherous trail, but Mynddy stares in awe at her reflection and she smiles back at herself.

Slowly she drags herself to her feet and carefully steps, rock-to-rock, picking her way across the rushing waters. Climbing back up to where Hyw is lying on their bed, she smiles, and then crouching at his side, she rummages through her open bundle of diminishing rags she has tried to keep from their squalid life. Clasping her hand around something hidden at its centre, she slowly brings out a small earthenware jug, with a stopper in the top; it barely fills the palm of her hand. Smiling again, she picks her way back down to the water's edge and kneeling, Mynddy places the jug at her side.

Sarn munches on the crushed oats Hyw has placed for her and she seems to pay no attention to her master and his bride, but Hyw cannot stop his gaze from following after Mynddy. Reaching up to the back of her head, Mynddy slowly undoes the plats in her hair. First one, then another flower falls onto the surface of the pool as she unties each braid. Watching as each petal and stem tumble onto the mirror of the pool, Hyw is transfixed; each flower rippling and glistening in a sparkle of the sunlight as they drift off and over the rapid waters; down to the edge of the world.

 When both plats are undone, Mynddy stands. Gently shaking her hair the last few flowers fall free as her hair curls down the centre of her back, like the stream spilling over the mountainside. Her hair, the flowers and the sparkle of the water, all ripple across the surface of Hyw's mind and he is lost in the uncertainty and frailties of her emerging beauty. He watches the reflection cast into the upside-down world of the shimmering pool.

Hyw's eyes continue to follow after her, just as they had done, the day he first saw her, playing with her sister, in that other time, that other world, that other life. Hyw's heart breaks as he thinks of all she has lost and he pours out only the gentlest of feelings towards her.

Remembering his washing in the lake, in another life, another dream; another nightmare and in a start, he looks down at his hands, his legs and the dirty blood-soaked rags he wears. In a moment of shame, he strips his smock from his body and throws it to one side. Climbing down, he squats on a flat rock by the pool just below where Mynddy stands in some muse or trance

Tentatively, leaning forward, Hyw spies the blood and dirt caked into his face and he feels shame. Mynddy had come to him, clean and pure, dressed in a calico gown; a vision fit for any dream. How could he have stood by his bride drenched in the blood of assassins; the stench, the filth and the dirt tear at his soul? There is a longing, deep inside him, a longing to be clean; a longing to be free; free of the squalid life he had led and he begins to wash in a clamour of all his disgrace.

Above him, Mynddy reaches for the ties down the front of her dress and she pulls their first cords. One by one their knots fall open. Placing her hand over her shoulder, she cups her arm around her breasts as she holds the dress up and she slips her arms from their sleeves.

Transfixed, with the dirt and shame dripping from his face, Hyw watches her. Looking up, he sees all her beauty, her majesty, her waking spender and her hidden dignity. The river, the falls, the breeze through the trees and all the tumbling world around him seems to pause.

Turning towards him, Mynddy smiles as her dress begins the escape her clasping arms. Its coverings slip from her body, falling silently to the rock at her feet.

A need, and a want, fill Hyw and from somewhere deep inside he feels an overwhelming hunger.

Stepping over her dress, Mynddy spreads it out on the rock at her side. The white lace petticoat glows in the sunlight as the tresses of her hair fall over her face and shoulders. With her head slightly bowed, she parts her hair with a single finger holding it back from her face.

Searching every fold of the petticoat's scant coverings an uncertain sun blazes through its materials, silhouetting the curve and shape of her body and Hyw's eyes grow wide as the want inside him grows.

Mynddy tips her toe into the pool as a tremor of cold shocks through her. Dipping again she is ready and she carefully picks her way into the water's edge. Holding her hair back with her forefingers, her elbows form scant coverings for her dignity. Stepping into deeper water the cold pool again shocks into her, but she continues her downward path until the hem of her petticoat is touching the surface of the pool.

Looking down at Hyw, Mynddy smiles as her eyes invite him to bathe. Feeling caught in the moment Hyw does not want to disturb the dream unfolding before him, but the hunger inside him tentatively urges him to stand.

Holding her hands out in front of her, Mynddy pushes out into the centre of the pool as her hair falls onto the surface of the water. She turns and stands, her breasts and nipples are clearly outlined beneath the thin material of her slip. Mynddy's face and hair are reflected in the surface of the water as her long hair drowns in its depths.

Transfixed, Hyw seems unable to move and he struggles to hold onto his feelings as a strange wanton urge fills him.

Standing, Mynddy looks across at Hyw and raises one hand, holding it out towards him, but he still seems incapable of movement as he stares back in wonder at the unveiled beauty of his bride. Slowly raising her other hand, she holds them out towards him, her eyes inviting him to move and piece by piece he falls toward her.

Reaching the edge of the pool, Hyw again hesitates, not knowing or understanding her wants and fears and he falters at the water's edge.

Looking deep into Hyw's eyes, holding his gaze, Mynddy leans back, and spreading her arms out, she floats across the pool. Her arms waft slowly back and forth; her hair billows out and into the depths of the water; her breasts surfacing as her legs part slightly and Hyw can see the dark hair between them showing through the white material. Searching through a miasma of dancing colours and reflections, he gazes at her ever-changing shape beneath the pool's shimmering delights.

Smiling, Mynddy's gaze sidles up to Hyw and standing, she opens her arms towards him.

Mynddy can see the muscles of Hyw's powerful arms showing beneath his gaunt flesh and his whole body seems to flex and tighten with each move he makes. Sitting down at the edge of the water, Hyw pulls at the string around his waist and as he slips into the cold water his pants eventually fall free. The cold instantly freezes into him as he gulps and pants in the freezing water.

Wading out into the depths of the pool towards Mynddy, she opens her arms out towards him. Hyw is still panting and shivering as he falls into her. Spluttering and shivering, he smiles at the girl within her, who has found a place to explore her life again.

Mynddy takes the earthenware jug from the rock and pours some of its oily contents into her hand. She begins to rub it onto Hyw's chest and arms as they both soap and wash each other. Their hands touch and caress, but they are circumspect in their movement.

Hyw can see Mynddy's body beneath her petticoat; the curve of her breasts; her cold nipples showing through and the shape of her body under the wet garment.

Eventually, Mynddy places the jug back on the rock; she waits for a moment, almost as though she is going to say something, but she just smiles and pushes past Hyw, swimming out to where the river falls from the mountain above. Pursuing her, Hyw longs for her touch on his body once more Catching her just before the falls, placing an arm around her waist; they both immerse themselves in the stream with its immense power all around them. Its forces pour through them. Splashing and spitting, its cold fingers clutching and biting into them. Surfacing in the middle of the rivers crashing world, the thrashing waters pummel at their half-naked bodies.

There are large smooth rocks below the waterfall and Hyw climbs up on their seat and he sits with a torrent of water crashing around him as he fights, gasping for every breath. Mynddy grabs at his leg and he reaches out, taking hold of her hand, and pulling her up beside him. They both sit, with the power of the water thrashing endlessly around them.

Mynddy is the first to slip back down into the pool and she swims back through its cold waters. Starting to climb out at the far end, she pauses when she is still up to her waist in the water. Hyw follows her but stops to watch his bride with the power of the stream still rushing and crashing all around him. Standing up to his neck in the pool he is caught up in the vision of Mynddy glowing and dripping in a dazzling silhouette of bright sunlight.

Watching and waiting, Mynddy pulls her hair back into a ponytail. Twisting it back in on itself, she lays it up and over her head. Holding it in place with one hand the sun and the day seem to soak into her. Hyw can see and sense her pain and melancholy, but he can also see and sense the beautiful vibrant young woman trapped by all her fears.

Scooping at the surface of the pool, she splashes the crystal clear waters over her neck and shoulders, as if it were a sweetly scented balm. Not one drop escapes Hyw's eyes and he catches each spit and spray of water as it trickles down her back splashing and shattering across the surface of the pool. The sun flickers and dances on the rippling waters as Mynddy drowns in a halo of dazzling sunbeams.

Looking, Hyw can see the wild, but magnificently beautiful creature that lives somewhere deep inside her and within the rise and fall of his uncertain feelings he rides the wave of his crashing thoughts towards her.

All in one sudden moment Hyw finally recognises the beautiful swan of his waking dreams, in the maiden before him.

Stopping a little way from where Mynddy stands, still in some dream, with the day drifting through her; every curve and shape, ripple and crease of her body shows through as Hyw waits. Suddenly, Mynddy wakes her thoughts and turns to him. Something softens inside her and reaching down she peels her petticoat from her wet body.

A shudder of uncertain feelings runs quickly inside him, like the cascading waters pouring from the mountainside. Continuing to pull at the petticoat Mynddy works it up to her shoulders and Hyw is helpless before her. His eyes stray to places his heart longs to follow, water dripping and rolling from every curve and hollow. Mynddy smiles again looking straight at him and then pulls the petticoat over her head, throwing it onto the rocks.

Leaning forward she sinks into Hyw's arms and they kiss as they slip beneath the mirror of the pool. They are trapped in a phosphorescence of bubbles, caught amid the brilliance of sunlight, as it blazes around them. Bubbles glisten and dance on their endless meandering journey to the world above. Their hair floats free, framing their perfect symmetry as they each look longingly at the other and they kiss; along slow kisses as if they could breathe in their underwater world.

Each moment seems to struggle into the next as every bubble stalls in its meandering path. Even the waterfall slowly gathers itself in, as time stands still, waiting patiently for the moment to end. Mynddy is wrapped up in Hyw's arms, and she, in turn, wraps herself around Hyw.

Moving his arms lower, he takes hold of Mynddy around her waist, his thumbs finding the hollow of her hip bones. They wallow there for a moment, but then he lifts her from their watery bed. Mynddy breaks the surface of the pool as Hyw pulls her close to him and presses his lips against her belly; he wants to smother her in his kisses, but can only curse love for its shortness of breath and easing his grip, he too, returns to the world above.

Kissing, over and over again as though their kisses could extinguish all their pain, they pursue, each the other's wants and needs. They move closer as if they could climb inside each other. Never wanting their feelings to end, they continue. Their kisses become more frantic, as though the moment might suddenly end leaving them empty and alone.

They succumb to the cold before their kisses are exhausted. Trembling and naked, arm in arm, they climb up to the ledge above the mountain pool. Wrapping themselves up in the blankets and each other, their cold bodies begin to warm beneath the furs. Cold wet hair is draped in a tangled web between them, clinging to their bodies, arresting the warmth as it tries to thaw through them.

Their bodies touch as they move closer; falling into each other. Resting her head on Hyw's arm, Mynddy tentatively smiles, warming the space between them. Hyw parts her hair with a cold finger, gently teasing its mass of wet tresses from her face. For all the crashing feelings inside him, Hyw can only smile through his fears; a fear of wanting too much and of losing too much. His desire burns inside him, but his fear is that of someone who has loved and lost and as they each stare at the other, they seem to understand, but will love overcome all their fears.

Trembling slightly, Mynddy settles beneath Hyw's touch as he traces his finger down her side, watching as it rises and falls from her shoulder to her waist and then over her hips. Relaxing in the last light and warmth of the sun, her hand finds Hyws' as he slowly traces the line of her soft warm breasts.

Moving lower, Mynddy pulls him in close. The sun drops below the facing mountains as Mynddy rolls towards him; eventually sitting astride him. Dragging a blanket up and over her shoulders, she leans forward with her breasts touching and teasing his chest as they drown under the cover of their blankets and furs.

Caressing and pulling, each at the other, they begin the hold and move, kissing and caressing; making love deep into the night. Hyw whispers continuously of her beauty, breathing his soft words over and over again as he sinks inside her; resting on her; kissing her breasts and he drowns in the hollows of her hips.

Chapter Twenty-Five

Hyw wakes with Mynddy wrapped in his arms; her naked body soft and warm under the blankets and furs. Slowly rousing and opening her eyes, Mynddy smiles as she gazes up at Hyw. She moves her hand over his face, her fingers caressing his jaw and chin. Pressing a finger against his lips, Mynddy traces the line of his mouth then strokes her finger lightly across his lips. They begin to kiss again, but Sarn nuzzles her hairy snout underneath their blankets, with her soft lips nibbling at both of their necks and faces. Hyw pushes his old friend away.

"Not now Sarn bach…can ye not see I am busy?"

The sun has pushed high into the sky but is hidden behind the gathering clouds. Sarn will not let them be and finally, after playing and fighting for some time, they are forced out of their bed.

Once more, Hyw and Mynddy gather their lives together and bundle them up into two rolls, which they tie at the rear of Sarn's saddle. They stand for some time looking back at the pool before they turn down the trail. Crossing over the ford at the foot of the mountain, they take one last look up at the waterfalls as memories of the night brush through them.

Walking eastward Hyw turns Sarn for home. With the lengthening days, if they had risen with the dawn, their journey would have been complete before the sun set, but it is late and with a billowing storm rising high on the back of the mountains it would probably take well into the following morning, even if they travelled through the night.

The rain begins to fall before they reach the far end of the valley; a fine drizzle at first, but as they begin to climb towards the pass, the skies open. Mynddy pulls her wrap and a thick woollen blanket up around her head and it drapes down over both her and Sarn. Untying the bundle further, secure in her shrouded world, Mynddy hands Hyw a blanket and his father's wolf skins, but it is not enough. Pulling them over his head and bow, he continues to walk in front of Sarn.

Glancing across the lower lake, Hyw looks up to where his winter shelter had been. In its place is an altar of rock covering Blaidd's broken body; a huge platform, with rocks jutting out and up to the heavens. Remembering his old friend in the heat of battle, Hyw ponders on his life.

'Why would a man fight with such vigour and venom for those who came to conquer?' The question burns inside him as a need to worship at his friend's grave grips his heart, but time will not permit and searching his waking visions, Hyw is content with the preparations his kinsmen made for Blaidd's voyage beyond the stars.

'There is still so much I do not know or understand!' The thought haunts Hyw's mind as the rain bounces and pounds onto the trail around him. Their way meanders up the steep sides of the valley with the towering rain splashing and spraying from the rocks of the mountainside onto the track. Rivulets of the pouring torrent seem to spring from the mountain, the track becoming a stream, which, at times flows around Hyw's ankles. The rain increases and soon Hyw is fighting against the rivers of water cascading off the mountainside. He is tempted to take refuge in a small incline at the side of their path, but his longing for home is too great for him to tarry there. Looking back across the lake, the words are spoken soft and low.

"Till we meet again my old friend" His whispers wake the heavens and a flash of lightning cracks through the clouds as its thunder bounces and crashes from mountain to mountain as if the heavens had heard his prayer.

As they round a corner, close to the top of the valley; two of Geddyn's men come into view, both on horseback wrapped up against the torrent. They recognise Sarn to begin with, but on seeing Hyw and Mynddy, they dismount and bow as Mynddy rides past. One of them salutes her, drawing his blade, holding the hilt of his sword up to his forehead. They walk on, but the one who saluted calls back.

"Have ye news of the battle?"

"The Druids have been put to the sword and all, but a few of their Slags, but Māthōg yet lives!" Hyw's words are very matter-of-fact, as though what he is saying has no meaning and it seems as though the battle and their escape were in another time or place, but the warriors seem pleased with the news.

Wondering about his friends, he mutters a prayer for their safety; for Dwyr, Giffydd, his wife and family. He thinks of Cayr and Gwydn and of his marriage to Mynddy. Smiling, Hyw looks up through the rain towards her. He can see a warm smile radiating out from under her snug, safe wraps. His love for Mynddy is the only thing that matters anymore and he holds that thought close to his heart.

Trudging through the rain, the two warriors have set Hyw thinking and his thoughts run to Māthōg. With his heart beating the advance, further questions perplex his mind. Māthōg had been in the last of the Scotti ships, Hyw is sure of it, but he had not seen him clear the headland. Māddrōg had stated they would not face his sword for sometime, but surely he would return. Things had become a little confusing in all the rush. Pausing, Hyw reaches out with his heart.

'Yes!' The thought races through him and he can sense Dwyr's safety, and the safety of their friends,

'But what of Māthōg?' Fear suddenly enters his thoughts.

'He may have drowned in the storm?' Searching through his thoughts and feelings, yet again; Hyw cannot see and he curses his feeble visions.

The rain continues to beat down on his sodden shroud, its teaming waters chilling through in places, but he feels snug and protected as he trudges on with the storm crashing above them unabated. They begin their journey along the high path, past the pools and lakes as the path picks its way through the quagmires of the valley. Looking across to the pass; the mountains are shrouded in clouds, with streams of white water bleeding from their sides. Their gushing veins are a magnificent spectacle.

Thoughts of Ywel bring Hyw's mind back to his dreams of home as their walk continues towards the crossroads and the Sacred Birch Woods beyond. Thinking of Hefyn and Olwyn and what he might find on his return. Eventually, Hyw's thoughts find Sián and pangs of guilt ride on a wave of feelings that crash inside him. Hyw smiles awkwardly up at Mynddy; she can sense his hesitation but smiles back as he looks away.

'How can I face Sián?' The question boils inside him and there is an ache in the pit of his stomach that will not let him be.

Hyw can remember little, if anything, of his leaving; he remembers pain, a pain so strong it addled his mind; he had woke up sitting on Sarn as she toiled up past the Shade of the Mountain; all else Hyw could only guess at, but on the trail he had remembered Sián; through the midst of the fog that had clouded his mind, he had heard her calling after him and bit by bit his visit to Olwyn's that night had come back to him.

"Shall I wait for thee, Hyw bach?" Sián's words track Hyw's guilt and the pain in the pit of his stomach grows.

Climbing up behind Mynddy, Sarn carries both their weight as she ambles by the old man's croft, just past the crossroads. Hyw hugs Mynddy close as she settles back into his arms.

The pain in Hyw's stomach instantly eases. Turning back in the saddle, Mynddy looks longingly at Hyw. She leans toward him and they begin to kiss, long slow kisses and Hyw longs to make love, again and again. He can feel Mynddy's body pressing into his and she turns in the saddle to face him. They wrap themselves up in each other with the rain pouring down their bodies, but eventually, their kissing gives way to the rain and the trail.

They follow the path along the river as it meanders and then falls into the valley below. By the time the afternoon is upon them, they are approaching the small huddle of crofts in the Sacred Birch Woods. The rain is still heavy, but soon they would be warm and dry, resting at the ease of good friends.

'Our journey can wait till the morning!' Hyw thinks to himself.

Sarn saunters down the path as Hyw whispers to Mynddy, words of home,

'Our home'; cut into the mountain, overlooking a valley. He whispers of good friends, but, as he does so his heart breaks for the loss of his family and he realises his lonely mountain home is empty and bare.

Sián once again enters his thoughts and suddenly his journey home doesn't have the same urgency. With his stomach churning, Hyw cuddles Mynddy to him in the hope of some relief.

Rhyannon is standing in her usual position watching the valley from behind the stable door of their croft. Her keen eyes catch sight of the movement and shrieking with joy, the door is flung open and before her mother can stop her she is running along the path.

With her arms open, she carriers towards them. She cries out, seeing her small friend, Mynddy can barely contain herself as she jumps from Sarn's back and discards the warm dry covers as she runs to greet her young friend. Crouching on the path, with her arms flung wide, Rhyannon almost bowls her over in a flood of tears and kisses and smiles.

"'Annon 'appy…'Annon 'appy!" Mynddy hugs her to her breast and smiles through her own tears while holding her young friend securely in her arms.

Angharydd is hurrying along the track, running as fast as she can, after her daughter, but she struggles to keep up and is out of breath as she approaches them, although she manages a broad smile for both Mynddy and Hyw.

"'Annon 'appy now!"

"Yes, I am happy too, Rhyannon," Angharydd says when she has caught her breath sufficiently to speak.

"Ye must stay…!" The invitation is instant and without hesitation.

"We have food and shelter…enough for all!"

Hyw steps forward; his feelings are uncertain, but he looks at Angharydd, studying the weary look on her face; remembering the first time he saw her and his eyes still, for some reason, follow after her beauty.

The rain is beginning to soak through her clothes and hair and Hyw can see a swell in her stomach, her face glowing with a certain radiance that somehow draws him in. Smiling, Angharydd stops only a few paces from him, staring up into his eyes. There is something between them, although Hyw does not quite understand his feelings, it is that same feeling that broke his will and sent him out to look for Rhyannon. Hyw is secure in his love for Mynddy, but still, his eyes stare back at Angharydd.

"We were hoping for a cot for the night…or somewhere we can lay our heads!"

"Come…we have been expecting you…two of Geddyn's men have been here asking after you; asking if we had seen you…they told us to expect thee and make ye welcome…But thou would always be welcome here!"

As Angharydd speaks she does not take her eyes from Hyw. Gwion is walking along the trail behind her. Smiling, he waves.

"It is good to see thee…we have been expecting you!" Gwion says reaching for Hyw's hand. They all walk back as though it were a perfect summer's day. Mynddy holds her covers up to shelter Rhyannon. Angharydd stoops down to pick up her daughter and she walks at Mynddy's side with Mynddy holding the cape over her head.

"Have ye not found thy tongue yet?" Mynddy bows her head slightly and shakes it slowly from side to side.

"I am sure it will return soon…ye must stay as long as ye like!" Angharydd's words are full of genuine concern and her offer of shelter is driven by greater feelings, which neither of them fully comprehend. Angharydd continues to question Mynddy, but Rhyannon is impatient and pulls Mynddy's face towards hers, talking as she does so.

"Annon appy now!" She says, over and over again. Angharydd continues with her own questions.

"Hyw makes thee happy?" Mynddy looks at Angharydd and dips her eyes away from the question.

"Thou art lovers yet?" Mynddy is embarrassed at Angharydd's forthright question and again drops her eyes from Angharydd's eager stare. Sensing Mynddy's awkward feelings, there is something more in Mynddy's hesitation and Angharydd asks again.

"Thou art married?" Mynddy hesitates, but with her head still bowed she side smiles up at her friend.

"Thou art married?" The question is asked, but it is more a statement.

"Thou art married!" Angharydd says out loud as Mynddy's heart jumps at her friend's brash ways.

"Ye hear that Gwion...they are married!"

Gwion nods his acknowledgement but goes quickly back to his conversation with Hyw. It could barely be described as a conversation. Hyw had said very little as Gwion organised their stay. It transpires that there is an empty croft, just behind Gwion and Angharydd's small home, an old smithy. The girls follow Rhyannon's lead. She has wriggled out of her mother's arms and is pulling Mynddy by the hand to the door of their croft.

The two men lead Sarn up to the Old Smithy, which has been built at the foot of a great step in the mountainside. It has two distinct sections, joined together, but running at right angles to each other. The section that protrudes out towards there approach is made up of three different annexes, each stepping down the side of the steep path. The first two sections have stable doors. Gwion opens the second door.

"Thou wilt be comfortable here for the night!" He says with Hyw not quite understanding whether he meant, Sarn or, Mynddy and himself.

Leading Sarn into the small stable, it has been recently cleaned out with fresh straw strewn across its cobbled floor and two nets of hay hung from the back wall. Two earthenware pots stand on the floor, one containing water and the other containing a cereal of crushed oats. Cobwebs garland the walls and hang from the roof beams. Hyw can see it has not been used in a long time, but he is happy to be in the dry and works quietly around Sarn, stripping the saddle and their load from her back as Gwion stands in the doorway, watching.

Knowing Hyw's work is almost finished, Gwion turns and runs through the pouring rain to the door of the croft. Kicking at the door, on his second firm boot, it swings open.

Fussing around Sarn before he leaves her, Hyw makes his way to where Gwion is standing in the doorway of the croft. The ground is set with widely tiered cobbled steps and as Hyw climbs past the third annexe he peers inside and sees an old forge which, in the shadows, looks as though it had not been worked in many years.

The main section of the croft is made up of two rooms with a big beamed fireplace at its centre to heat both rooms at once. A fire simmers in its hearth and a stock of wood lies to one side. The croft is warm and Gwion lights two candles with a spill from the fire, but it is all that he does. There are logs on the hearth and the fire needs stoking, but Hyw thinks it rude to throw a couple of logs on its blaze or rake at the glowing embers. A table is set in the main room with three stools around it.

A smaller stool is set near the fire; almost identical to the stool his mother used when preparing his meals as a child. Hyw stares down at the imagined face of his mother. She smiles back at him and he longs to sink into the comfort of her arms. Isobel's image fades only to be replaced by the image of his sister. She too turns and smiles at Hyw as his heart breaks inside him and he turns from their fading reflections.

The front of the croft has two windows, one in each room, with window seats set in the thick stone walls beneath them. Both windows look out over the valley and Hyw stands at the one in the main room, gazing out through the towering rain. The whole valley is open to his gaze. Looking around in the dim light and through the open doorway between the two rooms, Hyw can see a large cot with fresh bedding filled with straw. A small wooden table of some skilful construction lies close to the cot, in the centre of which stands a large round bowl and inside the bowl an earthenware jug full of fresh spring-water.

Someone has made much preparation for their coming, but, looking up at Gwion who has returned to stand, almost awkwardly in the doorway; Hyw doubts it is his work. Gwion seems a good person, but Hyw wonders on a sense of absence he feels from him. Taking one of the bundles under his arm, Hyw steps towards the door and the other croft, where the girls are waiting. Gwion hesitates in the doorway and their eyes meet.

"Someone has been troubled at our coming and for that I thank thee!" Gwion nods in recognition of Hyw's words. Stepping down and out of the door, they share the wolf-skins as they walk down the path. Half way, Gwion seems to snap out of some mild melancholy and he talks to Hyw, in his new found clarity of thought.

"Geddyn's men brought the hay and some food for thee…Angharydd prepared the croft with a little help from Rhyannon of course!"

The smell of the food is wetting Hyw's lips and the warm waft from the fire hits them as they step inside the dim light of the croft. Mynddy is sitting on a stool near the fire, with Rhyannon on her knee. Rhyannon's excitement has quelled slightly, but she still holds Mynddy's gaze saying

"'Annon 'appy!" For about the hundredth time. Mynddy points a finger to the centre of her chest and raising both hands to her face she exaggerates a smile, flowering her hands open as she beams at Rhyannon.

The croft itself is large compared with the handful scattered at the foot of the mountain side around them. It is well constructed with three rooms. Puzzling over its construction, he can see it is clean and tidy which again he doesn't put down to his friend Gwion. The roof is made of slate and although open to their view, it does not have a leak anywhere. Again the fireplace is a big beamed opening between the first two rooms and on a spit roasting over its flames is the rear quarter of a wild hog. Set into the wall, on either side of the fireplace, are what appear to be oven doors and the grate is built up with little ledges where pans are placed over the fire. One of these pans has a lid which is rattling and the boiling water inside is bubbling and spitting at its edges.

Angharydd is busying herself with preparations for the meal; Mynddy is in some distant world playing and signing with Rhyannon; Gwion sits at a large table, set at the back of the room as Hyw places his bundle on the floor just beyond where Mynddy and Rhyannon are playing. Mynddy looks up at Hyw and smiles then she looks at Rhyannon and places one finger to her lips. Picking up the bundle, Mynddy stands and, taking hold of Rhyannon's hand, they walk to the door. Looking over to where Angharydd is toiling with the spit and fire and the baby in her belly Rhyannon says excitedly.

"'Annon come, 'Annon come with Indy!" Angharydd stops her work, but only enough to nod her approval at Mynddy and Rhyannon. Mynddy opens the door and steps out into the rain with her young companion grasping at her hand. They disappear towards the second croft as the door closes behind them.

Gwion steps up to where Angharydd is still toiling over the fire; it would be some time before the meat is cooked, but he takes a small blade from its scabbard on his belt and cuts at the meat. Angharydd stops her work at the spit in some frustration. Carving a small piece of crisp crackling, Gwion takes a large piece of fat and meat with it. Holding the meat between his thumb and the blade, he lifts it to his mouth. First he blows then he nibbles with his lips. He blows again and waits a moment, before popping the meat into his mouth. It is still hot and Gwion huffs and puffs as he chews. Angharydd takes the knife from Gwion and gives him a sharp look. He grins. Angharydd wraps the back of his knuckles with the flat of the blade.

"We have guests…where art thy manners?" Angharydd places the blade on the hearth so Gwion cannot steel any more meat and goes back to her work, checking the trotters boiling in one of the pots over the fire.

"No wonder I haven't made an honest woman of thee yet!" Gwion snaps in a playful way. Watching and listening in silence, Hyw sits on one of the stools near the table. There is a hunger growing in his stomach and his want to do just as Gwion had. His eyes rest on Angharydd and he senses a growing frustration in her. Gwion steps behind his wife and pulls her up and away from her work. Standing behind her he pulls Angharydd close to him, working his arms around her belly. She struggles and squirms in his arms. His hands find her swollen stomach and he gently caresses her, working his hands up as he does so. Angharydd leans her head back next to Gwion's and she kisses him on the cheek. One of Gwion's hands moves higher and he cups it beneath one of her breast. There is a squeal and Angharydd fights to free herself from his grip. Hyw is slightly embarrassed and Angharydd slaps Gwion's hand as she goes back to her work.

The door opens. Hyw is expecting to see Mynddy and Rhyannon but is not surprised when the old man and woman walk in; Angharydd's parents. They stand in the open doorway, both looking across, to where Hyw is sitting at the table. Getting to his feet, he smiles as they enter the room. The old man steps forward, taking Hyw by the hand, and says.

"It is good to see thee safe and well, Hyw bach…!" He shrugs his shoulders and then throws his head back as though scoffing at what he is about to say.

"The Phantom of Annwn…well, well!" The old-man tuts then smiles, and makes out he is spitting on the ground, although no spittle passes his lips and he curses the growing intolerance and ignorance of his people under his breath.

The old woman is close behind her husband and as he lets go of Hyw's hand, she steps forward. Staring up at him, she is silent, as her eyes begin to well. Placing her hands, one over each ear, she cups Hyw's head in them and tilts it forward, kissing him on his hair. There are tears on her cheeks as she pulls away, but she takes hold of his hand and encourages him to sit with her at the table. Sitting back down, the old lady keeps hold of his arm.

It is sometime before Mynddy returns. They hear Rhyannon's laughter inside the croft, before the door swings open and they both bundle into the warmth. As the door closes, Mynddy strips the cape from Rhyannon and hangs it at the rear of the door. Everyone turns to look at them. Mynddy has washed, changed and braided her hair, in a similar fashion to how the women on the sacred isle had plaited it, but without the flowers. Mynddy has also braided Rhyannon's hair and Rhyannon is standing with a big smile glowing in her eyes.

"Oh, don't ye look a dream!" Angharydd exclaims, stepping towards them and bending down she hugs and kisses her daughter.

"Ye look just like Mynddy!" Angharydd says as Rhyannon's heart swells. Rhyannon thinks Mynddy is the most beautiful maiden she has ever seen and they both laze awhile at the compliment Angharydd has paid them.

The smell of rising bread is almost suffocating and the hind quarter of the hog is more than enough for the family and guests. Angharydd opens one of the oven doors to a rush of heat and fumes that intoxicate Hyw's senses, dragging him back to his childhood as he stands alone in the kitchen of his mother's wants and dreams.

The day drifts into the evening as one visitor follows another and every mouth in the small huddle of crofts is fed, and more. Hyw and Mynddy watch as everyone comes and goes, mostly old men and women.

Sometime in the evening a young couple pay a visit. The girl is perhaps two tears younger than Mynddy and the young man about Hyw's age. The girl is so heavily pregnant, Hyw grows concerned in case she has the child there and then. He has visions of her grasping at her stomach as she doubles over in her pains, with Hyw having to clear the table and then being kicked out into the rain with all the other men. The young woman finds it difficult to move and waddles like a duck over to where Angharydd is standing at the range, but it is while Hyw is watching her that he becomes puzzled.

There is something amiss with the people who visit them, or maybe it is the absence of someone. Hyw cannot quite work it out, but his mind ponders over something which eludes his understanding.

'Where are the people?' Yes, visitors come and go, but people are missing. Hyw sees it in his mind before he understands his thoughts fully and he questions again.

'Where are the people…? Where are the men and women…? Where are the warriors…?'

Both Hyw and the old woman watch Angharydd as she fusses over the girl, helping her down onto a stool by the fire; Hyw still has a picture of her, in his mind, giving birth on the table. The old woman leans towards Hyw, and in a soft low voice, almost as though she understands his thoughts and questions, she curses.

"Damn the Romans!" Hyw remembers his grandfather cursing them in the same way.

"Damn them all to Annwn. It isn't enough to strip a people bare, to leave them lonely, to let them dwindle and die without a care in their old age!"

There is venom in the old lady's words, but she trusts Hyw enough to speak freely. Maybe she was secure in the oath he had sworn to her and Hyw thinks back to his words, but he is still confused by his own thoughts.

"First the Romans strip us of a generation…then Gododdyn comes to claim its rule…and now the Druids seek after the innocence of our children for the perverted rituals of blood sacrifices!"

Finally Hyw sees clearly through the mists that have clouded his mind, but his clearer vision makes him shudder. People were missing; a whole generation had been lost. Hyw looks around the room at the people gathered there as a sudden light is turned on in his head. They are all old; a dying people. Everywhere Hyw had been he had seen old men and women with only a few young families and those families had little direction.

Turning to the old woman at his side, Hyw looks at her. He had thought her to be Rhyannon's grandmother, but with a stark realisation he can see she is of much greater age. She is Rhyannon's great grandmother. The old woman can see Hyw's understanding grow. For some reason it wasn't the same in his valley; warriors still watched over them.

"We took them into the woods…our young ones…as the Romans raped our lands. There were those who wished to leave with them…those who believed they were Roman…and even though they had never seen that distant land, they longed for that home they called Rome." The quiet rise and fall of conversation in the room drown the old woman's whisperings.

"Where art thy sons and thy daughters?" Hyw asks.

"They have been taken. Some of our children were servants…even our little ones and when the Romans left, they took many of them away. Angharydd's sisters' were taken…to what end we cannot say…our son and their mother went after them with sword and spear, but they never returned…many did not…but we live in hope!"

It is a familiar story to Hyw's ears and he feels the growing pains of his people.

"The croft is theirs…?" The old lady bows her head. Hyw is silent in his thoughts. Maybe he understands Gwion's depression.

'But what of Mynddy's people…where are they from…? What blood runs in her veins?' The way she was on some occasions, her clothes, and even the way she holds herself at times, indicates a statelier upbringing.

'She has been taught skills with the blade that would indicate a lower station in life…unless…? She rides like the wind, as if her station was higher, but wields her bow as if born to it…!' Hyw's thoughts are confused.

After some time the old lady continues.

"I look to the Gods for a new light, but they are silent in the shadows of our darkest nights!"

Hyw remembers his grandfather's words, but instead of feeling his old impatience, Hyw's heart has mellowed and the message Ywel once bore, echoes deep in his heart.

"I have heard a breath in the stillness of the night and it whispers of thee...Hyw bach!" The old lady continues.

"It says thou hast an inner sight!" Hyw bows his head and sways it from side to side as he takes in a long deep breath.

"Do ye...dust thou have an inner sight, Hyw bach?"

Hyw remains silent for a while, caught up in the intricacies of her conversations.

Rhyannon is playing at the hearth with her mother. Mynddy has freed herself from Rhyannon's grip and has sidled up behind them and she too awaits Hyw's reply. Hyw is silent for some time as the chatter of conversation raises with yet more guests.

"I do not know if I have an inner sight, as ye call it...and what I see is not clear, but my grandfather knew the things of which ye fear...he saw the lament of our people and he told me of the light which ye seek...the light of truth!"

The hustle and bustle of the room's activities subside as Hyw speaks in little more than a whisper, but unbeknown to him every ear is bent in his direction.

"My grandfather feared for our people...he said, for some it will be too late...that they have already lost their way. My grandfather spoke to us of, but one God, who has set the brightest star of the morning for us to follow in his way. That star was the son of God, but his light has been taken from us for a season and we must walk by faith. Speaking of the Druids, to some of whom he showed great reverence, but of others, he said 'they draw near to us with their mouths, but their hearts are full of treachery'. Instead of sacrificing their hearts, they make idolatrous sacrifices of our people whose innocent blood defiles their altars."

Hyw's words fall into the silence of the room as he realises everyone has been straining to hear his words, but the silence is broken with a sudden knock at the door. It is not the usual knock of a friend or neighbour, who would, straight way walk in and a stranger waits in the darkness, in the pouring rain.

All eyes are pinned to the door and as Hyw senses the unease of his friends, he gathers his bow to him. Angharydd tumbles Rhyannon into the back bedroom and her young heavily pregnant friend waddles after her. Gwion pulls at the door with Hyw and Mynddy on guard, but as the door opens they both relax.

Standing in the rain and darkness and the dim light of the doorway is Māddrōg, a grin painted on his face as he stands alone in his battle garb. Hyw knows that others will be waiting on him. The woad of war on his face has all but drained from him, but he recognises the fuss his presence has caused as Māddrōg's eyes search for Hyw

"Argh, Hyw laddie!" His gruff voice shudders into the croft, but it is the old woman, who calls out.

"Let him in, let Hyw's friend see the fire!" At the old lady's words, Gwion moves to one side and ducking through the doorway Māddrōg steps in.

"Ah hav brought someone to see thee, laddie!" And following Māddrōg through the door is Hefydd.

"He did nae fancy facing the sharp end of thy bow so 'ee made me knock een his stead!" Māddrōg laughs and Hefydd smiles at Hyw while shaking his hand, but pausing a moment he throws his arms around his friend and hugs him, smiling as he does so.

"Aye, it is good to see thee, Laddie!" Hefydd says while breaking away from Hyw's grip.

Everyone is somewhat taken aback, firstly by the familiarity of Māddrōg and then by the respect both Hefydd and Māddrōg show to Hyw. They both turn to Mynddy and bow towards her with every face shocked at the sight of it.

They then turn back to Hyw as a hush falls over the room.

"We ha com fur thee Laddie!" Mynddy is uncertain of Māddrōg's words, but Hyw remains silent. Everyone in the room is stunned. The old lady is the only one who regains charge of her senses enough to bustle through the crowded room towards the fire; pushing her friends and family gently to one side as she does so. Beckoning at the two warriors she says.

"Come, warm thy selves by the fire, there is food for all!"

With this, Angharydd springs into life, emerging back into the room with two wooden dishes in her hand. Hyw grabs a third platter and as Angharydd serves their new guests, Hyw fills the third plate.

When his plate is full, Hyw turns to Māddrōg who is staring at one of the two plates in the old lady's hands.

"Whit noo laddie?" Māddrōg says impatiently. Hyw points to the door with a nod of his head.

"There is nae anyone oot there!" Māddrōg protests, but Hyw continues to look him in the eye. Māddrōg relents and begins to smile.

"Okay laddie, but donae disturb his duties then."

Throwing a dry blanket over his head, covering the plate, Hyw leaves his bow by the door as he steps out into the stormy night. The wind is howling through the valley with rain pouring and funnelling from every leaf and slate, roof and bough.

"Dynōg!" Hyw calls out, his voice only just managing to permeate the squall.

"Dynōg!" He calls louder. Hearing nothing Hyw steps into the path and moves towards the top croft. A thicket of bushes is huddled to one side of the path; it is a good place to keep guard over his master. Closer to the bushes, Hyw calls out again and Dynōg slowly rises from the centre of the young yew trees, looking like some dark demon with a blanket draped over his head. Hyw looks around for their horses, but cannot see them.

"Come with me!" Hyw says quietly. Dynōg follows Hyw up the path to the doorway of the croft that has been prepared for Mynddy and himself. Discarding their coverings at the door, Hyw moves quickly towards the fire, placing the platter of food on the table. Stoking at the dying embers in the hearth, Hyw throws three large logs onto its renewed blaze. Turning again he pulls up a stool for his old friend.

"This is the best place to perform thy duties…here…Look there is a window seat which affords a view of the whole valley and ye cannot be seen, enjoy the food. There is a stable for thy steeds!"

Hyw points to the stable door and then turns to go, but Dynōg calls after him.

"Tha art a good friend, Hyw bach" Hyw is surprised by Dynōg's words, not for what he says, but in the way he says it; mimicking Hyw's tongue as though they are old friends.

"We ha the play of life a'tween us…there is nae a greater bond laddie!" Dynōg moves towards Hyw and shakes him by the hand.

"Unless the sky falls down!" Hyw says, looking Dynōg straight in the eye. "Aye laddie…unless tha sky falls doon."

Slipping out of the croft into the storm, Hyw hesitates then, looking to one side, he sees a dog rose growing beneath the lea of the croft's roof. Thinking to himself, he picks several young rose-heads from the bush. Returning inside, much to Dynōg's puzzlement, he scatters the rose petals onto the cot, and then leaves in silence.

Pausing with one hand placed against the door, Hyw listens. Laughter is coming from the people gathered beyond its solid board and Hyw can hear Māddrōg's voice above his friend's merriment. Pushing at the door, he enters, as the merriment stops momentarily. Every eye follows Hyw as Māddrōg begins his tales again.

"Tee think ah almost killed him…eye, he is a fly adversary alright" Hyw has heard Māddrōg's tales before and he knows it was not Māddrōg's arrow, but he lets his friends enjoy the warrior's words as they laugh, or cry and with the croft in stunned and reverent silence, they listen in utter bewilderment as Māddrōg recalls Mynddy's gallant charge along the dunes.

Hyw moves over to Mynddy, who has found a stool and is sitting at the far end of the fire with Rhyannon fast asleep on her cot. It seems Hyw has to move around everyone in the room to get to her. Pulling up a stool, he sits next to her and wraps her in his arms. She seems tense and is still uncertain of Māddrōg and Hefydd's purposes. Kissing her brow, he whispers to her.

"All will be fine!" Hyw's words are comforting although he wonders about his friend's purpose himself.

"We ha come for thee, Laddie!" Māddrōg had said, but it is Hefydd's eyes that flit to them and he moves through the rise and fall of conversation in the room until he is sitting beside them. Pulling up a stool, Hefydd sits by the fire, facing them. His voice is barely more than a whisper and they lean toward each other so no one else can hear.

"Māddrōg was nae prudent wi his words…we hav nae come for thee, but we do ha need of thy skills, Hyw!" Hefydd hesitates, thinking of how he may continue as Mynddy relaxes slightly.

"Ye ken we are far from oor hames!" Hesitating again Hefydd seems to change direction both in thought and word.

"Māthōg has nae succeeded een his plan and he has goon back t' Scotti shores t'lick his wounds, but he will return…and we must be ready for him!"

327

Hyw ponders on the truth he can see in his friend's words, but remains silent.

"Ma men ha need of rest and tha weapons of war art in need of thy skills laddie…we ha wandered far from our hames and there are nae many left with thy skills…damn the Romans!" Hefydd curses, but quickly returns to his purpose.

"Could ye no bide a while Laddie and see ma men reet…I ha never seen such work as ye wrought on that Scotti blade ye gave t'oor Cilydd…if I must travel to tha hame, I win, but tha time it win waste is valuable and ma warriors need tee guard against Māthōg's return!"

There is an extended silence between them. Hyw had so wanted to take Mynddy home, but his thoughts had turned away from the idea as thoughts of Sián and the way he left had filled his head.

'What if she has waited all this time for me?' The thought quakes through him as Hefydd continues.

"I will supply thee wi all tha need and ma men will pay thee for tha skills!" Unbeknown to the three of them, Gwion has seen them talking. Moving around to their rear he has been listening and he interrupts.

"Thou mayest stay as long as ye want, Hyw bach…" He too hesitates as he looks down at Hyw waiting on his word. It is as though Gwion had been waiting on a thought all his life, but had finally realised his thoughts have been brought to nothing.

'They will not return!' Gwion grieves to himself.

'They are gone forever!' His thoughts cut into him, but coming to the eventual realisation seems to lighten something inside him. His sisters and his parents would never return and are swallowed up in all the treachery and violence that is Rome.

"Ye must stay…we have need of thee…if only for a season." Gwion almost begs and with his crumbling thoughts, Hyw nods his head as Mynddy smiles.

Chapter Twenty-Six

Three days pass and in those few fleeting hours Mynddy silently cleans and clears the croft. It is more than comfortable for their needs and in her silence she builds a home around them.

Hyw's work isn't quite as straight forward. There are few, if any tools. A large quenching tank stands in the centre of the forge, hewn from a huge block of rock. Beyond the quenching tank the forge is in a sad state of repair and Hyw has to concentrate all his energies on servicing it; bringing it back to a workable state.

There is no anvil, no tongs, no paring knife, no stand, no pritchel, no pincers and no mandrill. There are two hammers, one a small shoeing hammer and the other a larger cats-head. Amongst a pile of twigs and leaves in the corner, Hyw finds a few unfinished shoes, whose valuable metal has somehow been over looked. If anyone brought work to him, there would be little he could do.

In the early morning of the fourth day, six of Geddyn's men arrive with a large cart pulled by two huge oxen, in which is a selection of tools adequate for Hyw's needs. The old lady is at the cart before Hyw can get to her. Recognising the majority of workings as being stolen from the forge by Hefydd's men on a previous visit when they had not been so hospitable. She says nothing, but there is some disquiet and shame between Hefydd's men and the old lady.

Hyw's presence serves to quell any rising feelings on both sides. Gwion helps to offload the tools and soon all are ferrying its contents up to the forge. Gwion offers to help Hyw put some order to his workshop, but his help consists mainly of watching Hyw work.

Hyw had set Gwion the task of finding or making charcoal, but Gwion's efforts are slow. Part way through the afternoon the cart returns, this time the old man from the croft at the High Cross is in charge of its load. It is full of charcoal with some more tools stacked behind the old man's seat.

Later in the day, Gwion takes Hyw into the woods to check on his charcoal burners which, Hyw thinks, are somewhere between poor and useless. However between them they establish two large covered and simmering fires with a substantial amount of wood beneath them. Hyw works as hard as ever, but where ever he goes he keeps his bow at his side.

Both return to their crofts as darkness falls. Walking back through the woods; Gwion catches sight of a large roebuck grazing in a small clearing. Hyw allows Gwion the honour of the kill, but, as he draws the arrow back across his bow, Hyw knows his friend is not up to the task. Gwion's blade drops just below the animal's stomach; grazing one of its front legs. Hyw is quick to react, but not as swift as the deer and the smell of venison on the spit teases their minds as they approach the village.

The following day Hyw takes Gwion out onto the fields that lead down by the river. A huge old oak stands in the centre of one of the long fields and Mynddy strings up a sack full of straw beneath its boughs. To begin with they all practise, but Gwion's practice becomes a tad frustrating. Hyw tactfully coaches him as the villagers gather around to watch. There are old men, some with their wives, all with bows in their hands. One old lady gathers three more sacks of straw and ties them to the tree.

The young couple, who had been there on that first night, come down, the young man with a bow in his hand and the young girl waddling a short distance behind him. Angharydd watches as she waddles through the meadow and she runs to fetch a high stool for her friend to sit on. Soon a host of villagers have gathered around while Hyw instructs Gwion on the finer arts of the bow.

Some of the old men are reasonable archers and are eager to practice, but some of the younger lads have much to learn. Eventually, the lower branches of the tree are cluttered with sacks swinging to and fro as arrows hit or skim past them. Hyw instructs as Mynddy moves between them, holding, moving and demonstrating, in a vain attempt to correct the error of their ways. Hyw again ponders on the missing generations of his people and the skills the Romans had taken with them.

Rhyannon has a small bow of her own, one of her father's which has lost some of its power and been paired down and stripped so she can draw an arrow down its full length. Mynddy sets a target on the ground, out to one side, a short distance away from the others, and she begins to coach her young friend. Within a short space of time, Rhyannon begins to close her arrows in on the sack.

Everyone is engrossed in their new work and all, but Mynddy and Hyw miss the approach of Hefydd, Māddrōg and Dynōg. They sit astride their steeds on the track above, watching with interest and growing amusement at some of the old women trying to outshoot their men.

The cart again trundles along the track with the old man sat in the centre of its plank. Loaded onto its boards are old spears, javelins and a variety of Scotti and Gododdyn blades, war boards, helmets and breastplates. Under where the old man sits is a stack of thrown shoes and pieces of mangled metal.

The games come to a halt as the villagers help to stock the old smithy, but they pause their practice at the butts only as long as it takes to empty the cart.

Mynddy continues her silent tuition, but Hefydd gathers Hyw to one side and leads him down the track and along the path by the river.

"Have ye enough for thy needs laddie…?" Hyw nods and it is some time before he speaks again. Hefydd walks with his arm placed over Hyw's shoulders as they move closer to the river; its ripples and currents bobbing and stumbling over the rocks and boulders in its way, but the tune of wild waters begins to sing in Hyw's ears.

"Have ye the art to take the sword from the stone Laddie?" There are perils; both in the question and the answer and Hyw ponders how he can avoid both without breaking the oath that exists between them. Working the iron is one thing, but having the art and science to take the sword from the stone is something different; something that in the same breath is both precious and treacherous.

The Romans had taken all, but a few with such knowledge. Hyw pauses in his thoughts, realising why the forge had lain empty for so long and in his ponderings, he thinks about Gwion's apparent lack of enthusiasm to become involved in its re-establishment.

"It cannot be done here!" Hefydd sees and senses Hyw's hesitation and does not pursue the matter further with Hyw leaving him to presume.

'Ah, he could then…if he were elsewhere…maybe an his een home?' And it is Hefydd who is eventually left to ponder. Hyw's home is too far for his men to travel; they could do it, but it would mean delays that would cost them dearly. The Scotti would return and Geddyn needed to keep his eye fixed on the west.

"Is all ready for thy work then Laddie?" Hyw nods and they turn back towards the village and his labours.

"Thy Lassie has a way with the bow that I've n'er seen in a woman afore...I wonder Laddie, could I no send some o' mee young laddies' to be instructed of her?" Hefydd looks straight into Hyw, waiting for a response. Hyw thinks about Mynddy's uncertainty around some of his men and he gives the only answer he can.

"Ye had better ask Mynddy how she feels about that!" Hyw says not wishing to upset either his friend or his wife. Walking up towards the forge, Hyw looks back into the valley, where he sees Hefydd talking to Mynddy. She seems slightly unnerved to begin with, although she has increasingly begun to trust Hefydd, and as Hyw watches, she nods in agreement.

Hyw passes by Māddrōg and Dynōg who both smile and then try to gain Hyw's attention with greetings and smiles. Dynōg is standing between his gelding and Hefydd's warhorse, while Māddrōg is still astride his monstrous black stallion. Talk together, Hyw takes the reins of Hefydd's horse and examines each of its hooves in turn. Without saying a word he leads it up to the forge and secures it outside the door, which is still in need of some repair.

Stoking up the forge, Māddrōg joins Hyw. By the time Hefydd joins them, Hyw has removed one of the shoes and is already cleaning and preparing the hoof. Māddrōg smiles awkwardly and then asks if Hyw can check his horse. Smiling up at his friend, he nods. The following days are full of work and sleep.

There is a passion between Hyw and Mynddy. At times it threatens to overwhelm them. Their lovemaking continues long into the morning, sometimes even until the slow light of dawn appears. Hyw is constantly tired and aches in the dreams of his sleep, but he always finds time for Mynddy. Often they walk up into the High Woods, to be alone. Hyw talks of his hopes and dreams and his home.

Sometimes they make love, but Mynddy remains silent, other than her sighs and moans in her love and passion for Hyw.

Making signs with their fingers Mynddy and Rhyannon begin to talk in silence with their hands. Their friendship grows and they become inseparable; Rhyannon often following Hyw and Mynddy on their walks up the mountain and with the strain of Hyw's work and their little friend, their lovemaking, at times, becomes a little awkward.

One night, Hyw and Mynddy are lying; each in the other's arms, after making love, when a frantic knock at the door suddenly wakes their thoughts. It is Gwion, in great agitation. Angharydd and her mother have gone to her friend's home as her time has come, but things are not going well with the birth and the old lady wished to know if Mynddy has any experience in such matters. She doesn't, but both she and Hyw dress and make their way to the bottom of the village, down by the river, where the young couple lives.

The moon is bright and a myriad of stars shine above them, but as they approach the small croft the darkness of the young girls suffering becomes apparent. The door flies open and the old lady looks straight into Mynddy, but Mynddy can only shake her head. A single candle burns behind where she stands and she turns back to the room. Mynddy follows the old woman and Hyw follows Mynddy. The old woman halts Hyw's approach with an open hand against his chest, but he insists and pushes past her.

In a moment he recognises the hopeless plight of the young girl; Hyw had learnt little of these things, but he had watched Hefyn at work with cattle and sheep. The young girl is lying with her legs apart on a wooden table. There is a mess of blood and a single small foot protruding from her. She is covered in sweat and her whole body is taught as she strains and pants in her agonies.

The old woman mutters something under her breath, which Hyw cannot make out as she ties a cord around the tiny limb. The girl raises her head up as if it would be her last and dying breath and she looks long into Hyw's eyes. No words fall from her lips, but Hyw knows and understands the faith she is placing in him and he turns on his heels and runs.

Sarn is saddled almost in an instant and she is ready. Hyw has not the knowledge or the power the young girl needs to save her and her baby, but he knows someone who has. Sarn is quick over the ground and soon Hyw is approaching the small croft again.

Gwion calls to him and the old lady walks out as he comes to a halt. Even in the darkness of the night, Hyw can see the tears on the old woman's face and the lifeless bundle of rags in her hands.

"It is too late Hyw bach!" She says as placing the bundle on the ground just out side the door. The young man runs in through the door and cries out as his eyes meet the sight of his love as she lies, lifeless and bleeding on the table.

Jumping from Sarn's back, Hyw runs to the bundle of rags, gathering it into his arms, but the old woman turns back to the room.

"Our fight is for the living, not the dead Hyw bach!" And with her words, she closes the door behind her.

Opening up the little bundle of rags, he gazes down at the listless red and purple little fellow. On more than one occasion, he had watched Hefyn with sheep; trying to blow the breath of life back into them. Sometimes it worked and sometimes it didn't.

. Hyw's thoughts are racing inside him and he can do nothing, but place his mouth over the little one's nose and mouth and blow gently. Blowing again and again, pressing his fingers against the baby's chest with Gwion looking on in disbelief. The taste of blood and bile on his lips is sour and he wants to retch, but he fights to control his stomach, as he continues in the darkness of the night.

Time refuses to move forward as all of Hyw's efforts are brought to nothing. The door opens for a last time and the old woman emerges, her head bowed in her grief.

"It is finished!" And with those words, she wanders off up the path and out of sight; her breast heaving with bitter tears.

Hyw sits on the ground out side, listening, as Mynddy cleans and dresses the body and Angharydd consoles the young man. Gwion paces up and down outside, but eventually, he too, enters the shadows that have gathered inside the small croft.

A small circle of friends gathers around the funeral barque cut in the side of the mountain for the young mother and her baby. Part way through the spoken word, Hyw notices two riders coming from the west. Māddrōg and Dynōg with a third horse under rein that they are leading towards the company. It is no time for work and Hyw wishes with all his heart, but with some understanding, they wait a short distance away.

When the spoken word is finished the young man leaves and walks down to his croft. Opening the door he leans inside and takes up a large bundle and throws it over his back with his bow in his hand. Walking back out, he makes his way over to where Māddrōg and Dynōg are patiently waiting and he climbs up into the saddle of the third horse and they turn to go.

Time presses slowly on as days blur into weeks. The summer is warm and gathers its crops, but as the summer wains, Mynddy seems to suffer from some sickness. Some mornings, she struggles to perform her instruction at the butts, but whatever ails her seems to settle without too much hindrance.

People from far and wide begin to join her daily practice; crofters, labourers, woodsmen and their wives. Hefydd's young men, including Cilydd, all behave with the utmost respect for their master at arms and Mynddy begins to realise the power her influence wields.

Angharydd gives birth early one morning. She had fallen into her labours the day before and had suffered throughout the night. Gwion paces up and down, beside himself, but all goes well and Gwion is presented with a son; Dafydd. They are overjoyed, but none more so than Rhyannon to find she has a baby brother.

In early autumn, with leaves beginning to turn, Mynddy's belly starts to swell. On one of their walks, Mynddy turns to Hyw cupping her hands under the small bump of her belly, but it still takes Hyw some time to recognise what she is trying to tell him. Then, like a gush of water off the mountainside, a smile breaks onto his face and he cradles her in his arms, constantly whispering to her of his love and care for her and the unborn child.

They stay all afternoon on the mountainside as Hyw makes his plans for their future, but Mynddy is uncertain of his longing for home. She has grown content, even though she has always understood their stay would be temporary, but she has been able to visit her own home and the graves of her family and thoughts of moving again unsettled her. Then, thinking about Hyw, she knows she will follow him wherever he goes.

Hyw's workload is easing. The Scotti had not returned in force. A few families had arrived in small boats to settle and Hefydd's men left them to their own. They were working people, people of the land, not marauders.

Discussions with Hefydd, for Hyw's return home, go well and he is not met with his anticipated opposition, so they began to pack and prepare to leave before the end of autumn.

The day before they are due to leave it begins to snow and it does not stop for almost a week. The snow remains and thoughts of leaving are put on hold for a time as Mynddy ripens.

In the cold of winter, Hyw cuddles in behind his wife. He cups his hands and arms around her stomach and feels as the little life quickens inside her. Everything is as it should be, with Hyw and Mynddy finding a certain peace together.

Chapter Twenty-Seven

Hyw pets Sarn's nose and scratches around her ears. She is tired. There is an understanding within her that her master has been busy during the long hot summer and the cold winter months, but he had still found time to pet her whenever he passed her stable door; though her upkeep had been left to Mynddy.

"Art thou ready my old friend?" Hyw asks with his usual softly spoken and caring words. Sarn is ready, she would always be ready. Ever since her master had rescued her from the cruel clutches of the Scotti, she had carried him where ever he needed. In his malady of mind, she had been his ears and eyes, protecting him; quickly baring him from danger and she had indicated to him, passing dangers; carrying him into battle and leading him through wild countries. She had borne his love and they had both been a blessing in her life, but in all, she had kept her oath to that one, most beautiful of all the Sentinels.

Sarn looks up at Hyw, with an ache in her bones. The weather is cold and she suspects a change in fortunes, besides, she is growing tired, too tired and she knows it will not be long.

Placing a saddle over Sarn's back, Hyw pauses. Staring down he looks at the girdle and then at Sarn's girth; her belly is swollen, but Hyw's eyes seem blind and his mind is clouded with eager thoughts of home.

"The summer has fed thee well my old friend…Mynddy has been spoiling thee!" The signs are clear, but Hyw cannot see and he patiently alters the girdle. Walking Sarn out into the cold dark morning, she sees the packs intended for her back and almost quakes with dread at the sudden realization of Hyw's plans, but she trusts her master and cannot refuse.

The morning is crisp and cold. Winter had been long and hard, but the weather had brightened continuously since the beginning of the week and Hyw's mind is set on their journey home.

Mynddy steps out from the doorway of the croft and walks down to where Hyw is securing the large bundles of their belongings. Placing both her hands on her hips, she forces them around into the small of her back as she stretches and heaves. Sarn looks back toward her and Mynddy smiles, a little awkwardly.

Petting Sarn, Sarn nuzzles into Mynddy's side and couches in her love and care. Nibbling at Mynddy's neck, Sarn moves her head down placing it next to Mynddy's swollen belly. Neither of them is fit to travel, but wrapped up in Mynddy's arms and spurred on by her master's quiet determination, Sarn resigns herself to the day.

Standing next to Sarn, Hyw waits to lift Mynddy into the saddle; he heaves and Mynddy groans slightly, but then smiles down at Hyw. Her belly is as plump as a Giant Puffball and she holds onto it as Hyw looks quizzically up into her pale but beautifully radiant face.

Checking with her, concerned with her strength to travel, Mynddy relented. knowing and sensing how much he wanted their child to be born in his land, amongst his people; people he knows and loves; she had nodded her approval, submitting to all his requests.

Mynddy is strong, but all her strength is concentrated on the unborn child and the fierce warrior she had once been is being helped into the saddle and watched over constantly. It is still winter, even though the snows have thawed and the last few days have been warm and sunny.

Following the tragic events of the summer, with their pregnant young friends, Hyw's thoughts had turned to Olwyn and he accepts that she is his real longing for home. In all his imaginings, he cannot trust his child being brought into the world by any other hand and there is no other he would trust with that sacred duty.

The sun is not yet up although the sky is beginning to brighten; there isn't a cloud in sight. The day is crisp and cold, but clear. Both Hyw and Mynddy wrap themselves up against its bite and with God's speed, they would make Olwyn's before the sun sets.

Although their goodbyes had been said the night before, Gwion has woken with the dawn to pay his final respects.

"I owe thee more than my life, more than I can ever repay…May God go with thee and guard thy path, till we meet again." He does not know, nor can he tell how much Gwion's prayer will guard them on their way. Gwion walks a little further down the path as they amble towards their long journey.

The sound of a gate clattering somewhere behind them sparks in Mynddy's mind and she turns in the saddle. Rhyannon is running along the path towards them. Screaming and shrieking as she runs, with all her horror and pain splashing out onto her rosy red cheeks. Gwion stands out with his open arms and catches hold of his daughter, throwing her high into the air. Unable to contain her feelings, Mynddy jumps from Sarn with no regard for her delicate condition; opening her arms, Rhyannon buries herself in Mynddy's neck.

"Annon no want go, no go Indy…no go!" Mynddy kisses Rhyannon, through her tears, and tries to stand, but Rhyannon has her gripped tightly and will not let her go. Angharydd, who has followed her daughter down the path, bends towards her and Rhyannon turns to bury herself in her mother's arms crying and sobbing.

"Indy no go…Indy no go!" Angharydd comforts her, leaning forward to kiss her dear friend and Rhyannon grabs at Mynddy's neck again.

"Annon love Indy…Annon love Indy!" Mynddy breaks free hesitating as though she is about to say something, but pointing to the centre of her chest, she then crosses her forearms over her breasts and points towards Rhyannon. Climbing back into the saddle, Mynddy struggles to tear herself away from her friends and when she turns, she knows she cannot look back. Hyw coaxes Sarn to walk as Mynddy allows her tears to fall freely.

"There will be new friends," Hyw says quietly, but Mynddy does not hear his words as her mind struggles to free itself from the grip of Rhyannon's love; Hyw feels helpless in its wake.

Angharydd's struggle is more physical and eventually, she relents to the fray. Rhyannon screams as she cries and once again runs down the track towards her friend, but Sarn is carrying Mynddy away and sinking into the roots of a great beach, Rhyannon explodes in her grief.

After a few moments, she manages to control her feelings sufficiently to stand on the tangled roots of the old tree. Rhyannon calls out, but her frustrated and garbled words cannot be understood and all Mynddy can do is cry as Rhyannon hugs her heart and points back toward her friend.

Hyw catches hold of Mynddy's leg and reaches his arm up to her back in a vain effort to comfort her. Smiling, Mynddy smiles back through her tears. Moving back out in front of them, there are greater hands than his guiding them on their path.

Cupping his hand around his old friend's head, Hyw comforts Sarn, knowing the journey they face. They walk through the main part of the village, following the track down to the Romans Way.

"Art thou alright my old friend?" Asks Hyw.

"Ye seem a little tired today!" Sarn whinnies as she walks, wishing she too could talk, but after some time, they begin to climb up and out of the valley toward the high moors. The sun starts to take some of the chill from the air, but the day is still cold. Hyw checks again on his old friend, with some unseen trouble gnawing at his mind, walking before the two loves of his life, coaxing both to follow after him.

Mynddy tentatively smiles as they climb quickly up to the high moors. The undulating ground seems unrelenting. The track is sparse in places and quite boggy in the hollows, but it winds its way forever up and on, circumscribing ponds and lakes, picking its way between swamps and bogs, marsh and mire.

The wind picks up to a blustery breeze and on the high ground it tears into them and the afternoon's sun isn't enough to warm them. Taking a blanket from their roll, Mynddy wraps it over her. Sitting like some royal princess, huddled up in her mother's fur wrap, Hyw's father's wolf-skin coat and a thick woollen blanket. It has the desired effect and Mynddy settles, into her draft-free, warm and cosy world.

Slightly apprehensive of their journey into the unknown, she had travelled the high moors before with her family. They had fled their land and moved west in search of security; leaving their comfortable life behind them, but all had been brought to nothing and Mynddy grieves for the loss of her family.

Still fresh, Hyw's pace is quick over the ground, but Sarn is beginning to tire. Looking around, he estimates they are over halfway, but whether they will make it before nightfall is doubtful. Taking hold of Sarn's reins he begins to run, slowly at first, but when he tries to increase the pace he looks up at Mynddy and stops.

It is Sarn who is most grateful for the rest. Walking backwards on the trail, Hyw studies Mynddy and smiles. Returning a warm soft smile, Mynddy sets a fire in Hyw's heart, but looking down at Sarn he can see she is not herself. Sweating and frothing a little at the mouth, he studies his old friend, and suddenly the paradigm shifts.

'How could I have been so blind?' The thought shocks him and he looks up to the heavens as greater concerns meet his eyes. Climbing high into the sky above the mountainous horizon are billowing thick grey clouds, chasing behind them, stretching out as far as Hyw can see. Their billows rise in differing shades of dark blue and grey, but they are swept over with swathes of white at their edges.

'Snow!' The word rages in his mind and the thought shudders through him, looking back at Sarn he can sense her pain.

"Come my old friend?" On hearing Hyw, Mynddy wraps her hands and arms around her own swollen belly; the way she had done to show Hyw she was pregnant. He is beside himself and sinks to his knees in front of his old companion.

"Forgive me Sarn bach, I did not know…I was blind, please forgive me!" Sarn nuzzles up to him and he cradles her head in his arms. Tears begin well in his eyes, but he fights to control his tumbling thoughts. In a moment Mynddy is at his side and she pulls him up into her arms and smiles. Hyw turns to her and utters one word to take the smile from her face.

"Snow…snow is coming!" And Hyw points to the mountains behind them. Gazing back at the billowing clouds climbing high into the sky,

Mynddy turns back to Hyw and tentatively smiles. It is a smile that covers a host of sinking reservations. Hyw's heart softens and he begins to prepare for the worst.

Taking the quiver of arrows from off his belt he stows them in Sarn's already heavy-ladened pack. Handing Mynddy his bow, she notches an arrow into place, and placing the bow across her lap she girds her wraps around her, securing them at the front. Mynddy knows they must be swift. If the snow catches them on the high moors there would be little hope, but they have begun their descent and she can see what looks like a valley ahead of them.

"It will be with us soon!" Hyw shouts against the gathering wind as studying the path ahead. The skies are already beginning to darken and soon they will devour the sun.

"Half a watch, at most" He speaks in hope of bringing Mynddy comfort, but she can see how close the clouds are and it would take the wings of an eagle to escape their wrath.

"We must try to make the tree line, down yonder. It may afford us some cover… maybe even shelter?" Mynddy kicks at Sarn's sides although Sarn doesn't need any encouragement with Hyw running out in front; she too understands the urgency of their flight.

The snow begins to fall before they make the tree line. It blows in a flurry of frozen tentacles, but then larger flakes begin to fall. The storm towers above them, blotting out their view of the small mountains across the valley, where Hyw knows his home lies. He had not reckoned on being out in the night and certainly had no thought of snow. The wind begins to howl around them and Hyw almost has to shout to make himself heard

"We must try to continue best we can and only stop if we have to…let me know if things get too much!" Mynddy's smile fades, but she is still warm and snug in her wraps and as she attempts a smile again, it belies a growing foreboding. Only her face can feel the cold, but soon the large flakes of snow are falling into her eyes, making them sting. Hyw knows if they follow the tree line it will take them down into the valley and from there; it would be a relatively short climb up between the mountains and through to Olwyn's where they would rest from the storm.

The snow is heavy and within a short time, it is lying thick on the ground. Their path soon becomes indistinct and both Hyw and Sarn begin to struggle with their footings. First Hyw would slip and then Sarn, not being able to see any detail around them. The woods to one side of him are nothing more than passing shadows in the wind and snow. The raging storm is unrelenting, cutting straight through Hyw's clothes. He stops.

"I must wrap up and tend to Sarn or none of us will make it!" Mynddy nods her approval from beneath her shroud. Digging into the pack on Sarn's back, he brings out two more blankets. Spreading one across the rear of his faithful friend, he wraps himself up in the other.

Looking up he can see Mynddy; the smile on her face fading slightly, but she nods at Hyw and he quickly turns to Sarn. Face to Face with his old friend, looking deep into her eyes, he speaks softly amid the buffeting winds.

"I have done thee wrong my old friend, but we must fly. Art thou up to this Sarn bach...I'm sorry?" Sarn looks back into Hyw's eyes, but he is not the only person holding onto her reins and looking out past Hyw to the ghostly figure of that one terrible but heavenly apparition, Sarn remembers her oath as a host of ghostly wraithlike figures takes hold of her mane, leading her forward. Waching, Sarn follows the procession of white spectres into the coming night. The guardians have gathered but not all wait on Sarn, some forge their way along the path, pointing the way home.

Turning to the trail, Hyw feels a flush of warmth and a familiar presence, but it is soon forgotten in the storm.

Trying to run for a time, he soon realises he is in danger of stumbling or even falling with the chance of losing his way or maybe even losing those more precious to him than life itself. They make good progress, to begin with, Hyw constantly holding a leash he has tied into Sarn's reins.

"It wouldn't do to lose thee my old friend…hey Sarn bach" Hyw stumbles again and again and on his second fall to the floor, he decides to give more caution to his footfall.

'If I walk a little slower I will be able to keep better guard of where we are.' But Sarn somehow knows the way, and from time to time pulls gently in the right direction.

The afternoon is disappearing into the darkening grey of the skies and the storm's shadow spreads its menace into the blind wanderings of the night. There is no dusk or evening light, only the billowing darkness of the storm as it howls around them.

The snow lies deep before them and in places, it has drifted up to Hyw's knees and still, it continues to fall. Hyw can feel the cold seeping through to his damp feet and his toes are growing numb. Forced to walk slower and slower, the cold bites into him.

The storm eases slightly as they descend into the valley. Snow is lying thick on the trees, but the path is so indistinct that it is difficult to tell where they are other than the shadows of the mountains in front of them. A distant kindly light flickers in the darkness on the distant slopes of the mountains ahead of them, but the storm comes back with a greater ferocity and extinguishes its faint glow.

Slowly they begin to climb, winding their way up through the snow-bound meadows. Everything is thick and dark and cold. There is no let up in the raging storm and Hyw looks for shelter; anything that will bring them some rest from the freezing wind. Sarn is struggling and Hyw is aware of her tedious pace. She whinnies at times but seems to regain some semblance of composure and continues.

"It's almost done!" Hyw whispers to her, but his words are swallowed up by the howling winds. Freezing cold, Hyw rests a moment from wading through deep drifts strung across their way. His want to climb in behind Mynddy pulls at him, but he knows Sarn hasn't the strength.

"If we stop, we'll freeze!" Hyw shouts out, almost bellowing his words to the storm itself, but Mynddy remains silent as they wander somewhere between death and dawn.

Sarn pauses. Hyw feels her neck and between her front legs and knows she is slowly freezing.

"Come Sarn bach, we cannot loiter here…we must keep moving."

Mynddy wakes from a lingering trance and leans forward, stroking Sarn's neck. The warmth of her hand seems to raise Sarn's spirits and Mynddy pats the horse's haunches as they once again walk on. The climb is long and difficult, over the frozen landscape of the threatening night. Nothing is moving, but the storm. No lights and no shelter. They pause for a few moments behind a high dry stonewall, which affords them some respite, but the snow has drifted up around it and they cannot gain its heart without digging and reluctantly they have to move.

On and on they walk, into the swirling haze.

The shadow of a familiar mountain rises beside them, but how familiar it is, Hyw cannot say. Instinct is a poor guide and Hyw cannot be sure of his direction, but a familiar air takes hold of his senses as he forges blindly on. Sarn seems to guide him along an indistinct path, but her intuition and strength are fading fast and she is unsure how long she can continue. There is a pain inside her belly and she can feel the distress of the little foal inside her. Struggling again and again they continue to climb.

"Not long now, my old friend and ye shall rest!"

The hillside has a sharp slope and both Sarn and Hyw stumble forward. Mynddy hangs on, tightening her grip on the reins. The constant buffeting as they move and stumble is causing her too much distress. Moaning in her pain, Hyw is instantly at her side.

"What's wrong, Mynddy; art thou in pain? Is it the child? What can I do? Tell me what I can do?" Mynddy winces as she smiles, but she cups her hand over the side of Hyw's face and nods at him as the warmth of her touch drains into him.

Hyw stares into Sarn's sad face as she begins to shiver and quake.

"Ye can make it, Sarn bach? Come on old girl!" Sarn can barely raise the strength to whinny, but she begins to stumble forward once more and as they continue climbing the snow begins to ease. It quits altogether and for a time their spirits soar with Hyw looking all around to orientate where they are. The snow seems to have fallen heaviest over the mountains, but he thinks they are heading in the right direction. They are about to skirt over The Dragons Back and if he is right, they would soon be resting in the warmth of Olwyn's secure home.

Hyw continues wading through the deep snow on the crest of the mountain as Sarn plods listlessly behind him. Looking out and down towards the valley, he knows they are heading in the right direction. The tree line is indistinct, but something calls him home.

Sarn struggles forward and Hyw can see the strain in every step she makes. Doing his best to encourage her, she stops for a rest, twice more, before they start the descent into the valley. The silhouette of the tree line comes into view, but, as Hyw dares to hope, the snow begins to fall again and within a few short paces the storm is upon them wreaking its vengeance on Hyw's impatient stupidity.

Faltering he falls. Heaving on his arms and legs he manages to stand. Staggering forward, The Druids White Woods and its familiar paths come into view, but Sarn seems in great distress. Making the tree line, Hyw begins to recognise where they are, but Sarn refuses to go further. Hyw whispers in her ear.

"Not far my old friend and soon ye shall rest in the comfort of Olwyn's stables!" Sarn cannot raise her head or even give any sign of recognition to Hyw's words.

"It's not far Mynddy, I know where we are!" Slowly, Sarn begins to move but is shivering uncontrollably. Hyw looks up at Mynddy. There is a pained expression on her face and he knows he cannot ask her to walk, but Sarn's life is teetering on the brink. To have come so far in such a condition is a miracle, but the miracle may not hold and Hyw wallows in the despair of his guilt.

Leading them between the branches of the first trees they begin to descend into the valley, down by the river, across the stepping stones and up into the Black woods that back onto Olwyn's. Sarn's pace is torturous, the snow is still thick beneath the trees, but at least the path is discernable under the firs.

Sarn's steps become pitiful to watch and with the storm gathering again she seems to give up all will. The wind howls around them like a prowling wolf as the icy blizzard freezes through them. Somehow, Hyw manages to keep them moving. The trees become thick around them, which offers a little shelter, but takes all light and sense of direction from him.

Hyw presses on, but the ice and snow seem to gather around them, barring his way. Certain he is close to the edge of the woods, he pushes forward. Stubbing his toe, crying out in a rage of panic and despair he screams to the heavens.

"I can't see Taid…I can't see anything!" There is real panic in his voice as the child in him remembers his grandfather's lesson in the darkness beneath the trees.

"Calm thyself and look Hyw bach!" Ywel calls out as if he were there, fighting against the storm alongside his grandson.

But with no hint of surprise, Hyw calls back.

"Look at what?" His frustrations show in his memories.

"There is light Hyw bach, but ye must search it out. Calm thee now and look…look for the light…the light, Hyw bach!"

Taking a deep breath, trusting in his grandfather; through the storm and freezing snow, gradually Hyw's eyes become accustomed to the dark. Off in the distance of the woods, he can just make out a minute glow and he sees the glimmer of some small light in the distance.

"What can ye see Hyw bach?"

Hyw's eyes are full, but he fixes his stare on the pinprick of light. Crying out to Mynddy he beckons her on.

"I can see a light…look!" He points as he turns back to them, but as he does so, Sarn falters, falling onto one of her forelegs. Desperately trying to gain her feet, it is some time before she finds the strength to stand. On stumbling a second time, Mynddy climbs down and stands next to her as they both shiver in the freezing wind and snow.

Mynddy wraps her arms around Sarn's neck and talks softly in her ear, but Sarn sinks onto both her knees and, even with Mynddy's soothing words, she cannot coax her to move and all seems lost. Sarn is slipping away in front of them and there is little they can do to ease her pain. Crying out again and again, as her pain drags her down. Kneeling in front of her, Hyw begs her to rise.

"Come now… please Sarn bach…Rest is just over yonder…just beyond the trees, please…Sarn bach!" Tears fill his eyes, but no matter what Mynddy or Hyw do or say Sarn's head drops and she can do no more. Hyw takes hold of the bit in her mouth and drags at her. Sarn shakes her head slightly but doesn't have the strength to stand.

"Come now!" Hyw cries out.

"Ye cannot die here, I forbid thee to die!" Mynddy moves over to where Hyw is standing and places one arm over Hyw's shoulders. Tears are welling in her eyes and as Hyw looks at her, they brim over.

"No!" Hyw cries out again, tears gushing onto his cheeks.

"I will not leave her here" Dragging at the bit again and again. Sarn looks up through her fading eyes, but her master's desperation is disappearing in the haze. Even the guardians appear to be drifting as they look helplessly on, but the one most beautiful of all the guardians steps forward and takes hold of her son's arm as he tugs at the bit and eventually Sarn seems to find some strength and slowly struggles to her feet.

They are tired and cold, but Mynddy and Hyw walk on either side of Sarn as they cradle her head between them. Mynddy is struggling with twinges of pain and winces and moans from time to time, stopping occasionally to catch her breath. There is something wet between her legs and she fears the worst but says nothing. Only her face had suffered on the trail, but the cold seems to claw at her legs reaching down to her toes.

Sarn still finds it a great effort to walk. The distant glow brightens and Hyw can see the field above Olwyn's farm through the storm and the snow-clad branches of the trees. Staggering forward, they can see a light glowing at Olwyn's window. Even through the strength of the storm its warmth calls out to the three lonely strangers.

"Look Mynddy…a light…it is Olwyn's!"

Mynddy looks up, but then drops to her knees in pain. Hyw ducks under Sarn and catches hold of her just before she sinks into the snow. Cradling her head in his arms, he kneels to support her on his lap. Mynddy rouses slightly and tries to smile, but no matter how much she exerts herself, she cannot extinguish the pain from somewhere deep in her belly.

"Come on, just a few short paces and we shall rest!" Hyw helps her to her feet and supports her as they hobble forward.

"Come Sarn bach, thou hast earned thy rest my old friend!" But Sarn cannot move another step and she sinks to her knees rolling onto her side and all is lost.

"No!" Hyw cries out, but the storm swallows his lament. It seems the fires of Annwn are set to devour one or the other of the two women in his life or maybe even both and Hyw is desperately torn.

"Art thou alright for a moment?" Hyw asks Mynddy. Hyw quickly wraps Sarn in a blanket and gently strokes her neck. She has done all she can, and she seems to be fading fast before his eyes. Struggling, she tries to lift her head but fails. She tries to whinny at her master, but no sound comes.

"Hold on Sarn bach, Hold on!" Tears stain his cheeks as he talks softly and quietly to his truest friend.

"I will come back for thee…hold on!"

With his words emptying into the storm, Hyw jumps to his feet. A sharp stabbing pain bites at his legs and he winces as he fights to stay upright. Looking back to where he had left Mynddy only a moment before, she is nowhere in sight. Hyw rushes to the edge of the woods and catches sight of her wading through the deep drifts of snow strewn across the field. Faltering slightly, she takes another tentative step and falters again falling into a deep drift.

Attempting to stand she falls again. Making her feet, she seems to compose herself but sways slightly. Taking another step, she stumbles and faints into another large drift of snow. The cold quenches her swoon and she struggles to her feet once more but falls before she can take another step.

Hyw bounds through the snow, rushing to her side and lifts her from the deep drift. Looking back towards the woods where he left Sarn, he sees her head slowly sink into the snow. Unseen by Hyw, all, but one of the guardians gathers around his trusted companion.

Hyw cradles Mynddy in his arms as a mother's love guards her children from the tempest. How he makes it to Olwyn's door, he does not know, but he lowers Mynddy's feet to the ground while pulling her into his side. Hammering on the door, he screams out with Mynddy leaning on his bow. She falters again and Hyw cannot hold her weight as she falls forward against the door.

"Olwyn…Hefyn!" Hyw cries out again, hammering against the thick wooden board as trying to support Mynddy, propping her up against the door, straining to keep her on her feet. She is fading fast and he can feel yet another life slipping through his fingers. The snow is piled up around them, almost to Mynddy's waist and he can feel her shivering in his arms. He bangs louder on the door with his fist hammering until the door bounces on its catch.

"Olwyn!" Hyw cries out in the night, but all his strength has gone and his cries are lost in the squall of the storm.

Chapter Twenty-Eight

There is a sudden commotion as the door opens with Mynddy falling onto the drift of snow and snow, in turn, falls through the doorway.

Olwyn's robust figure is silhouetted in the dim light of a lamp that is held aloft somewhere behind her. Hyw looks up into his old friends face; Olwyn appears old and tired, but she is wielding a large sword and looks more than capable of using it. Quickly stepping to one side, Olwyn backs out of sight and Hyw's eyes fix themselves to the point of Hefyn's deadly arrow. Relief turns to fear as Hefyn raises his bow, drawing the arrow back through its full length as he takes aim.

"No…Hefyn, it's me…Hyw!" Hefyn is flanked by his older brothers, Pwyll and Oglwyn, each with swords in their hands. Māthōg and all his men would be hard pushed to storm this doorway. Still there is another figure lurking in the shadows, with her bow at the ready.

'Megan!' Hefyn pauses, still on aim as his eyes study the stranger at his door. The boy who rode off in his anger has returned a man. The faint light of recognition flickers in his eyes.

"Hyw bach…well, well…is that you then Hyw bach!" A large grin spreads across Hefyn's face, but Hyw is already bending over Mynddy as she moans in some delirium. Almost immediately Olwyn is crouching at her side.

"Lantern!" She calls out.

"Help me…help me get her to a cot…Annwn preserve us!" Olwyn works quickly, checking her over. They both lift Mynddy from the floor as she groans and Olwyn calls out.

"Sián…the cot in pallor-bach." Hyw looks up, straight into Sián's eyes. She has a lantern held up in one hand and her other hand is cupped under her swollen stomach, which is large with child. Sián smiles awkwardly at Hyw, but there is no time for questions as she leads the way. But Olwyn questions at Hyw, somewhat incoherently.

"Hyw bach…how? where? good grief boy…have ye walked in this…? We heard they had been…Māthōg? The storm…Hyw bach," The whole entourage follows them into the parlour as Hyw's memory sparks inside him.

"My horse has collapsed out on the path in the woods, just above Pen-y-cae!" Hefyn immediately turns seeing a way in which he too can help and one of his brothers turns to go with him. Olwyn calls after them.

"Take blankets and lanterns with you…Good grief child, what where ye thinking…travelling on a night such as this?"

"I think my horse is...?" Hyw cannot bring himself to tell of his fears and in helpless resignation he looks down at Mynddy's listless body.

356

"Not to mind now…Hefyn will sort it!" Olwyn says, turning her attention to the girl, feeling at her forehead, holding her arm at the wrist and rubbing Mynddy's frozen hands in hers.

"What about the baby?" Hyw asks sheepishly?"

"Ye should have thought of that before ye started out in such weather," Olwyn snaps, but she smiles warmly at Hyw and speaks again.

"She seems to be fine… fainted quite likely and no wonder at it then."

"Is she going to have the child?" Hyw asks.

"Yes I think she probably will, but not just yet," Olwyn places her ear over Mynddy's lower stomach and listens for a while; she changes position and listens again.

"We should have heard more than moans and groans if she were about to drop Hyw bach."

"Is it…?"

"Everything seems fine. She seems to be made of stern stuff, but she will need her rest now."

Olwyn looks up at Sián who is standing in the corner of the room holding the lantern, watching, listening and wondering, but with the attention of Olwyn's eyes, she places the lantern on the side.

"Sián, the child needs rest and warmth; get some more blankets and see to her?" Sián nods and turns to go.

Mynddy wakes and looks up into Olwyn's tired eyes. Smiling, she is still a little faint and uncertain until she sees Hyw standing at the stranger's side. Looking up she smiles again, realising all is well, but she has little idea of what tragedies await them, in the snow-covered woods outside. Hyw leans over her.

"This is Olwyn…I told thee of her." Olwyn cracks her stern face into a smile. Hyw turns to Olwyn and tentatively says.

"And this is my bride, Mynddy." Sián steps back into the room just as Hyw says the words and they both look at each other; Hyw's eyes find her swollen stomach once more. There is an awkward silence until she walks over with a blanket and spreads it over the bed. A tear, wells in Olwyn's eye and looking down at Mynddy, Olwyn goes to say something but seems to change her mind.

"Well, well, well…plenty of time for questions later I suppose…rest now Mynddy bach."

A draught blows through the house as the main door opens and Oglwyn's voice calls out.

"Mam we need thee…Hefyn needs thee…quick now!" Oglwyn's voice is urgent, but it pauses.

"Thou shouldst follow as well, Hyw bach!"

"Thou shalt stay here with thy wife," Olwyn says sternly, but Mynddy looks up at him and then to the door and their fallen friend.

"Ye go I'm sure Mynddy will be fine with me, it will give us chance to get to know one another." Sián smiles at the thought of finding out all that has gone on as Oglwyn calls out again.

"Hefyn says, bring blankets and more lanterns!"

Olwyn is in the hallway putting on a heavy fur coat. There is a pile of three blankets next to where she is standing and two lanterns already trimmed and lit. Hyw picks up the blankets and heads towards the door with Olwyn following close behind. The furious storm howls around them, as they struggle back up the field.

"It's a wonder ye are not all dead!" Olwyn calls out, above the storms buffetings.

Hyw sees, what looks like Pwyll, walking down to the stables, a low flickering light guiding his way.

'Megan!' Hyw recognises her slight outline. Pwyll is carrying something wrapped up in a blanket, but Hyw is half blinded by the blizzard and cannot make out what it is, but by the way Pwyll is walking whatever it is, it is heavy.

Lights flicker just inside the woods and Hyw does not dare to hope, but lifting his lantern higher, he begins to run. His hands and feet are still numb and torn apart with sharp stabbing pains, like needles pricking at his fingers and toes. Stumbling, he falls.

"Take thy time!" Olwyn calls after him, but Hyw cannot hear a word she says and getting to his feet, he begins to run again. Slowing his pace as he enters the woods with his path lit only by the dim lamplight. There is a stain of blood in the snow by the path and Hyw fears the worst.

Drawing in closer, he sees Hefyn's lantern flickering through the trees. Sarn's motionless body comes into view. Hearing her whinny and cry out in pain, his heart races as he rushes to Sarn's side. Dropping to his knees he exclaims.

"Thou art alive Sarn bach… she's alive…!" But Hefyn quells Hyw's euphoria,

"Yes, but she might not be for long if we don't get her to the barn." Although Hefyn is the youngest, he takes charge of his brothers at such times, having inherited his mother's way with life, having 'the healers touch'.

Sarn is covered in blankets, but on seeing Hyw she begins to struggle, trying to raise her head up. Hyw kneels at her side, cradling her head in his lap. There is a lot of blood on the snow for some reason and Hyw is frantic.

"How? Where is she injured?"

Hefyn talks as he works quickly around her.

"She's not wounded Hyw, she's a mother. She's just given birth to one and there's another on its way, if she has the strength?" It takes a moment for the news to sink in, but when it does, Hyw drops his head in shame. Olwyn kneels on one of the blankets and looks towards Hefyn who speaks quickly.

"She has given birth to one, but it is not her due time. The foal is weak but alive." Then he adds gravely.

"For now!" There is another waiting to come, its front hooves are out, but the mare is too weak, we may have to pull it free, and even then, none may live through the night. She is bleeding badly and I'm afraid it will all be over if the foal isn't out soon."

On hearing Hefyn's matter-of-fact words there is a low, sick, sinking feeling in the pit of Hyw's stomach and he is silent in his guilt. 'Oh why could I not have waited?'

Olwyn talks quickly to her son.

"Dust thou have the twine?" She asks. Hefyn nods.

"Then what are we waiting for?" Hefyn moves around to the rear of the horse and Olwyn joins him. Hyw cradles Sarn's head as he looks down into her sad eyes

"I was so caught up in my impatience, I did not notice Sarn bach? How I have neglected thee? Forgive me, my friend!" Sarn winces and jumps, moaning in pain and a few minutes later, it is done.

Olwyn drags the foal quickly onto a waiting blanket, wiping around its head and mouth, but there is no life inside the tiny creature. She works quickly and quietly as Hefyn tends to Sarn. Olwyn has her hand in the poor foal's mouth and is clearing out its throat. Hyw watches unable to speak, but Sarn is impatient to see her newborn and she struggles against Hyw's arms.

"Can we get her to her feet…?" Hefyn calls to Hyw.

"She needs to be in the barn…she is half frozen and weak as a kitten!"

Hefyn's words spur Hyw into action. Pulling at her head and at the leash, he encourages Sarn to stand and slowly she struggles to her feet. Hefyn throws blankets over her, but she will not leave her newborn. Looking down at the lifeless foal, she nuzzles and nudges it with her soft snout. Olwyn clears something from the foal's nose and then presses gently on its stomach. She keeps pressing slowly, but firmly and then listens at its mouth, but can hear nothing in the storm.

The newborn foal is a dappled, beautiful blue-grey mare, identically coloured as Sarn, except for a few dark black or brown polka dots on its hindquarters; Hyw cannot make out their true colour in the darkness. It is the stallion's colouring and he looks up at Sarn, wondering for an instant.

"Take her to the barn…quickly now!" Olwyn says, listening to see if the foal is breathing again.

"What about the foal?" Hyw calls.

"Hefyn and I will bring it… get her to the barn!"

"Come Sarn!" Hyw pulls at the leash, but Sarn ignores his promptings, still nuzzling at the dead foal.

"She will not leave without the foal!" Hyw cries out as the fury of the storm blasts between them.

Olwyn is still working frantically to put some life into the poor, helpless animal. Clamping its mouth shut with one hand and holding the other hand over one of its nostrils, Olwyn places her lips to its nose. Blowing gently, her efforts fail.

'Nothing!' Olwyn pulls at the foal's head leaning it back and blows again. Air escapes from under her hand as the foal's soft lips pucker and bellow open. She clamps a finger over where her breath is escaping and blows again. Hyw can see the foal's belly rise and fall as Olwyn breathes for the wretched creature. Again and again, she blows.

Stopping to listen at its chest, eventually Olwyn gently pushes down on its stomach again. She looks up at Hyw, her cheeks stained with tears; it is a long, cold, hard look, but on seeing Hyw's pained expression, Olwyn says nothing.

Nodding at Hefyn, he bends down and quickly scoops up the fragile foal, wrapping her in a blanket and his arms. Starting back along the trail, Sarn follows behind as Olwyn and Hyw light the way with their lanterns.

The barn is bigger than Hyw's entire home and is lit by several lanterns hanging from hooks set in the thick wooden beams over head. There are three main stalls set down the furthest wall where several horses gaze at the strangers in their midst. An old disused fire place is set in the end wall and Pwyll is crouched next to its dusty hearth trying to spark some timber into life. There are a further two stalls down the near wall, one of which is empty. Eventually Pwyll sparks a light and feeds its flame to more kindling and tinder in the giant grate.

There is an abundance of hay in the last stall, where Oglwyn is tending to the firstborn foal, rubbing it all over with the dried grass. It is shaky and trembling, but standing on its own four legs. Its colouring is almost identical to Sarn and Hyw's heart jumps as his eyes rest on the fragile creature.

Hefyn walks into the stall, followed closely by Sarn, Olwyn and finally Hyw. Hefyn places the second fragile life on the hay and, with Olwyn, sinks at its side. Hyw is frozen in his guilt and can only look on as Sarn nuzzles at both fragile lives. The first foal walks at the side of its mother as Sarn begins to groom and tend to its simple needs. Nuzzling under Sarn's belly, it begins to suckle from her.

Slowly Hyw moves closer. There is another flurry of activity around the weakest foal and this time Hefyn begins the pumping on its stomach as Olwyn breathes for the wretched animal. Some time passes and they rest as the foal breathes again. They move away so Sarn can encourage it to stand, but it is far too weak.

A fire eventually rages in the grate bringing much needed warmth to the old barn. The door opens and in walks Mynddy and Sián.

"I told thee to rest and I told thee to look after her, which includes keeping her in bed!" Olwyn calls to both girls from the stall where she is still on her knees.

"Mynddy is fine," Sián says with a hint of impatience in her voice.

"Ye could have told me she does not speak though…we just couldn't stay there…hey Mynddy…with thee all out here."

Olwyn looks up at Hyw with some concern. He is shaking uncontrollably and doesn't appear to know where he is or what is happening around him. Oglwyn moves over to where he stands and placing a large woollen blanket over his shoulders, he ushers him to a stool by the fire. Olwyn looks back to the girls.

"Well there isn't much to see here and it will be a long night, so if thou art staying make thyself comfortable." But there is something to see. Mynddy is overwhelmed; she hadn't expected to see Sarn alive, but gazing over the two foals her heart almost bursts; all the efforts Sarn had made weigh on Mynddy's shoulders. She moves into the stall watched closely by Olwyn.

Moving in front of Sarn, Mynddy cradles her head in her arms stroking and kissing her dear friend.

"Ye shouldst not be here Mynddy… go and tend to Hyw," Olwyn says softly, wondering what tragedy has befallen her to rob her of her tongue.

Mynddy moves over to the fire and pulls Hyw into her arms, kissing his face and frozen fingers. Warming herself into him they snuggle up by the growing blaze. Hyw looks over to where the second feeble foal lies as if asleep and his heart cries up to the heavens. Praying, his lips begin to move. His broken heart calls out to that God of love Ywel had spoken of…for his angels to aid the foal's desperate struggle.

Looking around Hyw can see his good friend Hefyn watching over the poor creature, with Olwyn's watchful eyes fixed on both of them.

Pwyll returns with the last of Hyw's packs and Megan soon finds his side, but her eyes rest on Hyw with a mountain of questions forging through her. There is a silence between them. There is still a lost look about her and Megan's questioning eyes search through Hyw's thoughts.

They all pick over the desperate scene in front of them, wishing and praying, but as Sarn looks up through her sad eyes a different scene increasingly troubles her. Hyw cannot see all before him, but that other troubling scene is open to Sarn alone. The Sentinels, who have remained at her side throughout their journey, gather around her; touching, caressing, and reaching out to her broken heart. Looking down to where her crippled foal lays in the arms of that one most beautiful of all the guardians. The Sentinel strokes the crippled creature's neck, quietly whispering in its ear. Slowly the ghost-like apparition cups the foal in her arms and scoops it from the hay. Sarn watches with a growing clamour as her sad child is carried away.

Hefyn and Olwyn both paw over the foal, Olwyn trying desperately to breathe life back into her, Hefyn working at her heart. They struggle on and on, Olwyn checking for life time after time.

"Come on!" Olwyn cries out in her frustrations, but goes instantly back to her work. It is Pwyll who moves between them and quietly says.

"It is enough... thou hast done all ye can, it is time." Olwyn looks up through eyes, drained of all their tears and then goes back to the lifeless creature.

"It isn't time!" And she thumbs on the dead foal's chest.

"Come on!" She cries.

Hefyn kneels back from the foal.

"Enough Mam...we've done all we can." Olwyn looks at Hefyn, her eyes stained with tears and slowly getting to her feet she walks out of the stall. Pausing only an instant, she looks into Hyw with Mynddy wrapped in his arms.

"We did what we could then, sorry Hyw bach!"

Tears splash onto Mynddy's face, but Hyw is silent in his guilt. Olwyn says nothing more as she bows her head and walks from the barn. Hyw gets quickly to his feet and goes after her.

"Leave her... she has struggled on the edge of life too often...she'll be fine, give her time!" Hefyn calls out, but Hyw pays no heed. Catching up to her with the snow is still thick in the air.

"Olwyn!" Hyw calls out. Olwyn turns to him and stops; the tears are still falling onto her face, but she is not sobbing or crying out loud. Hyw speaks slowly to her.

"Olwyn, this is my doing...I know what it takes from us...from you...I have stood on that edge, cursed God and yearned for my life to end, but this...this here is my doing...all mine...it is not thine to carry"

Olwyn smiles through her tears and steps towards Hyw. She cups her hand around his cheek and then at the back of his head as she pulls him into her, and cradles him their.

"I am sorry," Hyw sobs. Pulling away from her he continues.

"I have cursed God in the night…I have cursed the passing of life in his hands…maybe, like a child, our curses brush over his heart, but he has given unto me a little light and in the darkness he whispers to me. The ghosts of those I love still stalk my sanity, but he has sent the stars to guide me; they are, but a few in the dim darkness of the night. At first they shone in her eyes and then in her smile. They shine in the warmth of thy arms…yes, and in the love of good friends, but the brightest of them shines in the love Mynddy has brought into my life. I will follow that light where ever it leads me. When Māthōg…!" Hyw struggles in his thoughts.

"When he came…" Hyw again struggles and cannot bring himself to say the words, thinking about his family's lives and he changes direction.

"For all life's treachery…for all its pain, I have still found love and that love will lead me on. And when he comes…for come he will…I have seen it…It will not matter, live or die, it is all the same. For God has shown me his mercy and my life is in his hand." They fall into each other, hugging and crying together.

"I have come home and if it is God's will, I will make a home here!"

Chapter Twenty-Nine

Two days slowly drift by with Hefyn constantly tending to Sarn and the foal. Mynddy is exhausted and Olwyn confines her to bed, but her love for Sarn pulls at her and eventually, Olwyn relents, letting Hyw make up a cot in the barn. Sarn is quiet but determined. Suckling at her mother, the foal, gains in strength.

Sián fusses over Mynddy, wanting to be her friend, but Mynddy's silent melancholy does not make it easy and Hyw does not leave Myddy's side. There is another and from the shadows of the barn, Megan's watch is constant.

During the summer months, Hyw's dreams and visions had faded; his heart was still and his fears subsided, but with the arrival of winter storms his Waking Dreams had increased. Nothing clear or certain; mainly shadows through the trees and fear of their meanings mixed up in all his longing for home.

Rumours of Māthōg's treachery had reached Olwyn's ears. Hyw had spoken to her on that first morning and Olwyn asked about his journey, but he had not said much. Telling her of his finding Mynddy and their journey to the sacred isle. With some surprise, she listened to how they had been married and their flight and delays on their journey home.

Megan sits, listening to every word, hoping for news of her savage torturers, but hears little to assuage her own sufferings.

It is strange at first, Hefyn and Sián, Mynddy and Hyw, but things seem to settle slowly as though it were all part of some great plan running its natural course.

When the time is right, Hefyn and Hyw walk down the old track into the valley and Hyw looks out to where he knows his home is nestled between the trees. A shiver of excitement and apprehension spark inside him as he catches sight of the small rock face with its capstone; The Rock of his Family's Throne. The top of the chimney is just visible, peeping out above the trees. A mixture of strange feelings stirs Hyw's mind as he remembers the endless stack of smoke spewing from its funnel, calling him home at the end of his childhood adventures, like a chicken gathering her chicks.

Hefyn is quiet as they walk, with Hyw leading the way, his bow in hand and it is he who breaks the silence.

"How art thou and Sián?" Hyw asks, looking back at his old friend to gauge his response. But what he is really asking is.

"How is Sián?"

"Okay I guess." Hefyn's answer is deliberately slow and carefully considered, which Hyw takes as hesitation. There are still uncertain feelings in his heart for his childhood sweetheart. There is a long pause before Hefyn speaks again.

"When ye left...!" A lump gathers at the back of Hefyn's throat and he swallows hard on his words.

"She was quiet and restless for some time. I had comforted her that first night...and was the only person she would trust with her feelings. I had lost Bayr and nothing could replace what I felt for thy sister, but in the weeks and months that followed something grew between us and I was able to reach out to her and Sián to me. She is still quiet at times and that frustrates me if ye understand my meaning?" Hefyn looks across at Hyw, who, more than any other, knows and understands Sián's melancholy.

"She is beautiful..." He looks up at Hyw and finds no discernable change, light on his face, he continues.

"Her body is full and warm..." Hefyn pauses only slightly, but when he continues his voice has changed and there is a light in his eye Hyw has never seen before.

"I love her...I love her more than life itself...she is fun and warm and exciting...she will make a good mother and all that, but sometimes..." Hefyn stops walking for a moment as Hyw turns to him. Half of him wants to hear; no, he has to hear, even longs to hear.

"Sometimes..." Hefyn continues.

"Sometimes she is quiet and withdrawn...off and away somewhere, somewhere I cannot follow." Hefyn looks at Hyw for inspiration, but he is disappointed.

"What can I say? What can I do? I want to be there for her...to help her, if that is possible?"

Hyw takes a moment to gather his own thoughts, knowing Sián's distance is like a gathering storm. They were friends, childhood sweethearts even, but they would never be more than good friends, because of those gathering storms that cloud the mountains of both their hearts. Looking deep into Hefyn's eyes, Hyw can see the quiet frustration there. Wanting to say the right thing, he thinks long and hard before speaking.

"Thou art the one who has a way with life…not me. Death is all I have seen and it yet stalks me in the night…be patient and things will work out; I'm sure of it!"

Hyw remembers Ywel's words to Blodwen.

"Seen and suffered much, he has then!" And he remembers old Mordda and his suffering.

"She has seen and suffered much, but things are now as they should be!" Hyw pauses again thinking on his fruitless journey.

"It takes time…It took me a long time to realise hunting down Māthōg and his blood red Crows is not the answer I seek!" Hyw turns away.

"I regret now, ever having walked that path and wish…"

Hefyn interrupts.

"But thou hast gained so much…ye rescued Mynddy and ye have found love together; thou art given to her with a baby on the way… Mam says Mynddy is big enough for two. Dust thou have twins in thy family?" Hefyn asks making light of their conversation.

But Hyw's mind is busy. He had not rescued her as people seemed to think, and he feels responsible, in some way, for her sister's death, which still weighs heavily on his mind. Leaving her, he had ridden off up the track, away from the village; they had been married before he knew what was happening. His life had run down hill, out of control, for too long and talking to his friend, who has taken his childhood sweetheart to bride, serves only to confuse Hyw's feelings more and he doesn't quite know what to think. Part of him wants to take Sián in his arms and live out his childhood dreams, but another part of him looks into the fire of Mynddy's bright eyes and he knows everything is as it should be.

They cross over the track, but it isn't until they are walking up the path to his home that his mind wakes again.

"She had a twin sister…at least I think they were twins!"

Hyw falters as Hefyn smiles in a knowing way.

"When is Mynddy due…?" He doesn't wait for an answer.

"Mam says it won't be long." Hyw counts back in his head and on his fingers without Hefyn seeing what he was doing. There is just under a month to go; he counts again.

"Yes, nearly a month." He says as if he is confirming it to himself but their lovemaking had been so often, at the time, he could be sure of nothing.

"When is Sián due?"

"A little over a month," Hefyn says with a sparkle in his eye.

"I can't wait…but imagine Hyw bach…twins!" But all Hyw can think off is Sarn and the foal that died.

"I didn't know horses could have twins," Hyw questions almost to himself.

"They don't usually…at least Mam says it is rare…"

They set to work.

Hefyn had looked after the old place, barricading the small cave to keep vagabonds out. Having taken all the tools away, he had sealed up the main part of his friends home with nails and great logs leant against the old oak door. There is much work still to be done. Cots need straightening and

371

mending in places. They bring fresh bedding and mattresses down and hitching up the cart they return with the anvil and all the tools. The following day they cut wood and a large fire burns continuously in the hearth bringing much needed warmth to Hyw's neglected home.

In the afternoon of the fifth day, Hyw brings Mynddy down to check on their progress. Not intending them to stay, on seeing her new home, Mynddy smiles and insists. Reaching over to him, they walk, arm in arm, up to the door with Hyw carrying her over the threshold.

Standing behind her, he places his arms around her, cupping his hands and arms under her swollen belly. The little life inside her jumps and kicks. Mynddy turns her head back to his and they kiss as placing her hands over his. Turning and standing in front of the fire, Hyw continues to hold her belly in his hands, gently caressing, and feeling as the little life inside her rests for a moment. They fall asleep, wrapped up in each others arms as Hyw whispers constantly of love and the life they will build together.

But Hyw's sleep is plagued by dark visions and he wakes in the night. Wrapping himself up against the cold winter's night he takes a brand from the fire and sits out on The Rock of his Families Throne. Building his blaze his waking dreams still won't let him be and he finds himself lost in some dark wood with shadowy figures tracking his every move.

Straining to see through the gathering shadows, Hyw's eyes rest on a small shaft of light; a pinprick or maybe just a leaf or sprig of leaves off in the distant shadows of the night, and he fixes his stare to that anchor.

 Wrapped up in his father's wolf skin coat, Mynddy steps up behind him. She has grown accustomed to Hyw's restless nights and taking him in her arms the vision fades as Hyw calls out.

"Taid!" Leading him back to there cot, she holds him in her arms constantly soothing the balm of her love into his troubled brow.

In the morning, Hyw hasn't the heart to wake Mynddy and he eases out of the cave, moving silently across the clearing, stepping towards the lean-to shack.

Staring down through the hole in the seat of their toilet, he remembers his fear from all those years ago, but that fear, no longer cripples his senses, and the warrior within him stares back at the child, he once was, quaking in the darkness below.

Watching his memories, he guards over his sister; the broken arrowhead held firmly in his hand, but he is calm, as calm as he has ever been and Hyw smiles back at his sister's image. The toilet door bangs behind him as he makes his way towards the rock.

He is glad to be alone with his thoughts. Sarn will be staying at Olwyn's for the foreseeable future; the foal is making good progress but is still weak.

'I will have to take work on immediately!' Hyw thinks to himself. People are already approaching Olwyn to see if he has stoked the forge yet.

'My family's art and science will be much in demand!'

With those thoughts, Hyw thinks on his father and his heart sinks, but he manages to smile as memories of happier times ripple through him.

'I miss my old friend!' Sarn has been his constant companion on the trail; his friend and confidante; a warrior in battle and his guide in the darkness of the night.

'I need her close as soon as she is able!'

Hyw's heart tumbles like the wild waters of the stream as he catches sight of Sarn in the valley below. Olwyn is leading her and the foal is draped over Hefyn's saddle. Behind where Hefyn's gelding picks its way between large swathes of snow, Sián and Megan are walking with there heads bowed to watch their feet as they talk to each other. Sián is doing most of the talking with Megan quiet at her side, her bow in hand.

They intended staying only for the morning, to make Sarn and the foal comfortable in the stables, but as Mynddy pets her old friend, her waters break and she 'begins her labours'. Hyw is beside himself, thinking on Sarn's misfortunes, but Olwyn's quiet strength pours into him. Sián flits in and out while Megan takes up a position on the rock, keeping a watch over the valley.

The pain is shallow to begin with, but it quickly builds. Sitting at Mynddy's side, Hyw holds her hand, and with each throbbing spasm, she grips onto it as though she would crush it.

Sitting on the rock across the small clearing, Megan listens for Mynddy's struggle, but Mynddy suffers in her silence. Megan had hoped for children herself, but following her brutalisation by the Scotti and the still birth of her first child, she fears she is barren and her heart breaks inside her.

Sweat pours from Mynddy's brow as Olwyn tries to make her comfortable. The contractions grow in intensity as the fire of the pain burns into her, but still, Mynddy does not call out. Sián fusses, mopping her brow. Olwyn checks again and again, but all seems well.

"Ye are doing well Mynddy bach…soon then…very soon now!" Olwyn says as Mynddy fights the agony of another deepening spasm. Hyw constantly whispers of his love for her and Mynddy manages a smile, but it is short lived as another spasm sears into her. The afternoon struggles on into the evening as Mynddy is sapped of all her energy, but the fearless warrior inside her, fights on into the gathering night.

"Ye had better leave now, Hyw bach!" Olwyn says.

"This is a time for women to bear their burdens alone!" But Mynddy holds onto him and Hyw smiles down at her.

"We have stepped into Annwn together, and struggled through the cauldrons of fire; conquering every phantom and demon it spat at us…I will not leave her side; not now, not ever!"

The pain is almost unbearable, but Mynddy does not cry out; only her breathing is laboured as she quickly pants and then struggles to fill her lungs, before the next contraction starts.

"When I say, Mynddy bach…I would for thee to push!" Mynddy nods her understanding. The contraction begins.

"Push, Mynddy bach… Push!"

Gripping Hyw's arm as if she would rip it from his body, Mynddy grimaces and she pushes down with all her might. The contraction eases.

"Hold Mynddy don't push!" Mynddy pants until the contraction begins again.

"Push Mynddy push for all ye are worth!" Her body screams out, but her mouth is silent with little more than a low grunt or groan passing her lips. Looking down, Hyw can see the top of the babies head and its hair, but cannot make out if the hair is red or if it is coloured over with blood.

"I can see him…her…our baby…it's…!" Hyw splutters in his excitement as Mynddy pants again.

"Push Mynddy…push!" Olwyn says as cupping the babies head in her hands, and with all her strength gone, Mynddy pushes one last time.

"It's a girl, Mynddy bach…a beautiful little girl!" Olwyn says, placing the child in Mynddy's arms.

The child cries out and, still sitting on the great rock, its cries reach Megan's ears. A tear breaks out onto her face and she breaks down as climbing from the back of the rock.

Smiling down at the delicate, blood soaked baby in her arms, Mynddy's joys are complete, but her euphoria is short lived.

"There is another little mite waiting to come out Mynddy bach!" And on hearing the news, Sián takes the child and wraps it up in a shawl, cleaning the blood from its face and dark hair. Hyw is beside himself and although she is weak as a kitten, Mynddy seems to find the strength from somewhere. There is a grimace that spreads out onto her face as she pushes with all her dwindling might. Everything seems to happen in one movement and before Hyw realises, their second child is in Olwyn's secure arms.

"It's a boy…!" Olwyn declares, handing it to Mynddy. She is overcome and reaches up for her other child as they both cry out in unison.

Olwyn remains busy and although she is exhausted, she washes and cleans, first Mynddy and then the babies. Wrapping them both in shawls Olwyn hands them to Hyw. Stunned in his joy, Hyw cannot take his gathering euphoria in as he cradles them, one in each arm. Smiling down at Mynddy he gazes back at both his children. Looking deep into his daughter's eyes, he looks up, as if for inspiration, then looking back at Mynddy he smiles.

"Rhyannon!" He half breathes their little friend's name, and Mynddy smiles her approval with a tear in her eye. Placing Rhyannon in her mother's arms, Hyw turns to his son. There is a moment of silence, as if Hyw is struggling with some inner torment, but he smiles and nods.

"Bryn Ywel!"

"A fitting name Hyw bach!" Olwyn says as Hyw hands the baby to Mynddy and she raises them both up to her breasts, each in turn.

After some time, Hefyn manages to drag Sián away and they make their way home on Hefyn's young gelding, but Megan will not leave the rock.

Some time passes before Olwyn has done all she can and slowly gathers herself together.

The door opens and Megan peeps in around its sturdy framework. Mynddy is the first to see her and she smiles over at her quiet new friend. Megan hesitates. Her cheeks are still stained with tears, but with Mynddy's bright smile inviting her forward, Megan steps a little closer. Holding her babies out, Megan steps closer still. Olwyn is silent and watches with growing unease, knowing Megan's wants and needs, but as she cradles both babies in her arms, Olwyn's fears ease.

Megan takes a long slow deep breath, as though she is breathing in her whole life. Her tears begin to flow freely, but through her tears she manages to smile, looking down at Mynddy and then up at Hyw. Mynddy smiles back and slowly nods her head.

"Thou mayest come here when ever ye wish Megan bach!" Hyw says with Mynddy nodding her approval.

"Come now Megan we must be away child…our work here is complete!" But Megan stands cradling the babies as if Olwyn had not spoken.

"Come Megan we must go…Pwyll will be waiting!" Waking her senses, Megan leans forward and places Rhyannon and Bryn Ywel back in their mother's arms.

The night is full of babies suckling, mothers smiling and father's crying; unable to take in the wonder of it all, but sleep soon overcomes them.

Sometime just before dawn, Hyw falls into a restless sleep. Suffering in his dreams, he fixes his gaze on the small pinprick of light off in the haunted woods of his nightmares. The night is thick around him. Alone, he has somehow concealed a wound at his side and he struggles along the paths of his nightmare.

Suddenly a menacing shadow jumps out in front of him, raising a sword above his head. Even in the darkness of the night, Hyw recognises his father's sword in Māthōg's hands, but as it falls towards him he wakes and a sudden realisation hits him; it is not his own eyes through which he sees.

Chapter Thirty

Both babies are snugly wrapped in a cot next to where Mynddy lies safe and secure in her own dreams. Staring down through the dim light of the cave, Hyw pauses. Anxiously listening for their breathing as he catches sight of the gentle rise and fall of their covers and he smiles to himself as hugging their delicate lives to his heart.

Stepping towards the door, Hyw turns again and his eyes search through the shadows to where his young family are softly sleeping. Both babies are lying on their sides, each facing the other, smiling and content, each in the others presence. Exhausted from her labours, Mynddy had only stirred once during the night to feed her children as Hyw kept his loving vigil over his family.

With his heart full to overflowing, he turns again to the door. As passing the fire he bends and delicately rakes at its smouldering embers, placing three huge logs on its renewed blaze.

'There…It will last till the end of the morning with little more attention.' Lingering again, his life pours through him. Thinking quietly to himself, for several long moments, Hyw listens for signs of Mynddy rousing, but only silence rains down amid the slow rise and fall of his children's breathing.

Hyw so wants to stand on The Rock of his Family's Throne, just once before the start of their day; he longs to sit in the warmth of his mother's ghostly arms, to feel her love and care. To share his joys with the ghosts of all those he loves.

Fumbling at the curtain, Hyw presses his hand through the gap and touches the solid plank of the thick oak door, but as he pushes through the gap, it is as though he steps from this world into Annwn as his recurring vision hits him like a charging bull.

Instead of the cold grey light of the morning, Hyw is instantly blinded in the shadows and the night of some strange wood. Stumbling forward he tries to gain his senses and searching for the light, he falls onto the twisted roots of a distant woods crowded trees. Feeling his side, Hyw brings his hand up and can only stare at the blood dripping from his fingers. Managing to find his feet, he tries to shake the torturous vision from him, to no avail.

"It is not my vision…!" Hyw cries out, struggling against the forces of Annwn that seem to have him bound. Looking down, he is dressed in long robes. The awful realisation hits him. It is Dwyr's eyes through which he sees; Ywel's brother is hurt and alone and as that understanding hits him, he is released from the clutches of Annwn.

Week as a kitten, Hyw has fallen at the base of the great rock, but his mind races forward, scouring his thoughts for some understanding.

'The night was thick around me…do they warn of the future or tell of the past; it seemed so real!' Panicking in his thoughts, his desperate feelings of Dwyr's plight burn inside him.

The fresh morning sunlight breaks over the distant mountains casting a bright halo over the rock's smooth surface. Scrambling to his feet the nightmare threatens to overwhelm him again, but he manages to stay in this world, at least for the moment, although ghostly memories seem to surround him like shadows on every side. Raising himself up fully, his mind clears and the shadows of his Waking Dreams flee.

It is quiet; not even the birds disturb the slumber. Spring is in the air; the morning is crisp and cold with the last of the late snow, still clinging to the ground, but only in the shadows.

Something stirs Hyw's mind, but he doesn't see Sarn's ears prick back or hear her quiet discontent. Everything seems to gather in around him as a guttural cry screams out, shattering Hyw's heart.

"Hyw!" Mynddy shrieks in horror, but before he can turn the sight of the Scotti Slags sat astride their warhorses in the valley below hits him. There is no time to think as some wild commotion gathers a storm behind him. Six Scotti Grots are waiting at arms in the common below, but Hyw has no time to stand and stare. Sarn cries out kicking at the stable door and the stampede of Hyw's unseen foe shudders into him.

Turning in an instant Māthōg's giant warhorse is charging towards him from the far end of the clearing. His twisted face bellows out his hungry war cry as he brandishes the great blade high into the air. A matted, tangle of dirty long grey hair hangs over his face and shoulders and his beard, thick with spittle, hides the twisted contortions of his mouth. All his fury empties into Hyw, who has been caught off guard. The scar on Māthōg's face is clearly visible, but his one-stone eye appears distorted, with its bottom lid drooping down onto his cheek.

Hyw freezes with all his childhood fears gripping at his throat, but something jumps inside him; a familiar tremble he has felt before. It is Mynddy. Hyw cannot see her, but somewhere just out of sight, Mynddy is suffering in the same nightmare, but this is no dream; it is real. Māthōg's attack is quickly bearing down on him cutting off any possibility of retrieving his bow.

Letting out an almighty roar, Māthōg goads his stampeding stead on. The horse squeals and cries as sharp spurs puncture its sides and Hyw is trapped with no hope of escape.

Mynddy cries out again. "No…"

Hyw looks across to see the heavy curtained doorway explode; the oak door slams aside and Mynddy runs out into the clearing. She has found Hyw's bow and is frantically trying to notch an arrow into place, but in the commotion the arrow falls to the ground. Mynddy's attack does not falter and throwing her arms wide, she runs headlong into the path of the charging stead.

The horse rears up with Māthōg snatching at the reins. Throwing her arms high into the air, screaming as she does so; Hyw's bow clatters against the stallion's snout. Māthōg is thrown from the stead with the great blade being catapulted high into the air. The horse's hooves thunder down on Mynddy's head and she collapses, lifeless to the ground.

Hyw cries out as each rapidly fleeting moment seems to struggle into the next.

"No…Please No…!"

There is a thud as Māthōg hits the ground, but Hyw cannot sustain himself as he stares on in disbelief. Blood is coursing from a wound on the top of Mynddy's head, but it is the only sign of life within her. Sinking to his knees; all Hyw's hopes and dreams lie broken on the ground in front of him. The sound of a baby crying for its mother empties into him, but Hyw's ears are barred.

The honed and deadly tip of the tumbling sword impales itself in the dirt of the clearing. Standing upright, it wavers like a flower blowing in the breeze just a few paces in front of him. All is lost as his eyes focus beyond the great sword, to where Mynddy's lifeless body is face down in the dirt. A baby's fractious cries scream out again as Rhyannon wakes her brother. This time Hyw hears his daughter calling and the sum of all his rage curdles in his gut.

The blade is still swaying back and forth goading at Hyw's mind as he dares to dream. Beyond where it stands, Māthōg is struggling to his knees. Leaping forward, the sword rings clearly as Hyw pulls it free from the rocky earth, extending it up to the heavens.

Over the years, Hyw had forgotten how perfectly his father had formed the great blade and it seems to fit his hand as though it were made for him and him alone. It is light and its balance is perfect as he swiftly brings it to bear. Goaded on by memories of his father, Hyw widens his stance.

Māthōg has finally managed to get to his feet, but there is something wrong. His stallion has stopped a little distance behind him and Māthōg appears to limp, dragging one of his feet across the ground. The horse is nervous as he stumbles back and it shies away, but eventually, the old warrior snatches its reins and brings it back under his control.

Drawing a second blade from a scabbard on its saddle he turns to face Hyw, but the old warrior is awkward. Māthōg's free arm is strangely buckled and appears stiff and useless. The warhorse jumps and turns crashing into its master. Māthōg stumbles, but he manages to keep hold of his blade. Falling to his knees, he is forced to use his new sword like a walking stick. For some reason his left arm will not work, as if it is lame. Old and decrepit, his movements are mechanical and forced, and he struggles to find his feet once more.

Hyw watches the pathetic sight of his once barbarous foe struggling in front of him and his anger is tempered slightly. Lowering his father's blade; the image of a wretched face flashes in Hyw's mind. One image merges into the next as the wretched vision quakes through him. Helpless, the rolling wave of his nightmares crashes inside Hyw as the sword purges all the good it has betrayed in the hands of its evil master. The face of every child Māthōg has cut down; every man he has run through and every maiden he and his men have ever defiled, flash in Hyw's mind, blinding him. Their cries and screams fill his head until he can take no more. Struggling to take control of his senses, his debilitating visions have him caught in their snare.

In one fleeting moment, Hyw manages to focus on Māthōg, but then as quickly as the moment appears it disappears as another image flashes before him and by the time Hyw focuses on Māthōg again, he has found his feet. Another image and Māthōg is wielding his blade. Another wretched image and Māthōg is advancing, with his deadly blade flashing before him. Hyw swings out blindly with his father's sword, but he finds no magic within its bright steel.

Māthōg bellows out, but Hyw cannot understand his words as he flounders in the dark seas of his visions. Māthōg's voice is somehow stifled as if his tongue is in the way of his words.

"Urgh skoi's arout to fall, 'ung whelp?"

Another image plagues Hyw's mind and Māthōg is quickly upon him, bringing his sword swiftly to bear. Hyw struggles to raise his own blade in front of him in an attempt to parry the attack; there is a sudden clash of metal and in a flash, Hyw's vision clears as he stumbles back with the force Māthōg's attack.

Gripping the handle of his father's blade, Hyw finally takes full control of his senses. Māthōg advances as Hyw brings his father's blade up to the ready as it seems to sing as it slices through the air.

Wielding his father's might through the steel of his blade, Hyw steps into the fray, but as he does so, Māthōg's mouth seems to erupt with a volcano of blood spewing from his lips. Spilling every last drop of energy into his arms, Hyw lets out one long guttural cry, but as the blade slices through the air, Hyw sees an arrowhead protruding from Māthōg's mouth. The force of Hyw's crashing blade snaps his neck, as the sword's honed edges cut into his poisoned flesh. Māthōg's head flies up into the air. Tumbling to the ground, there is an arrow embedded into the base of his severed skull and his headless body momentarily staggers before joining his head in the dirt.

Standing behind where Māthōg stood is Megan, her bow still held up on aim. She is trembling in her memories and struggles to hold onto her rage. Hyw smiles at her as her anger turns to tears and her pain shatters any hope of a smile. The agonies she bares are too much and she cries out.

Pwyll is at her side in an instant, but she struggles free from his arms and rushes forward snatching Māthōg's head by its hair. With one giant leap, she is astride the rock shrieking out as holding the filthy fiend's head high above her with its blood dripping down her arm.

A ripple of dread quakes through the Scotti Slags still sat astride their steeds in the common. The sight of their master's head held high with thick dark blood oozing in great clots from his severed neck is too much for the youngest of the warriors and he slowly bows his head.

Hyw drops to his knees next to Mynddy and Olwyn is only a pace behind him as Hefyn guards the path to their rear. Grabbing at Mynddy's waist Olwyn heaves it from the ground. She splutters, but still is not conscious. Spluttering again, she rouses and smiles up at Hyw. Trembling uncontrollably, Hyw is overwhelmed as he smiles back, but the danger has not passed and he quickly shouts his orders.

"Get her inside…we must prepare for their attack. Go…go now; they will be upon us soon!"

"She will be fine!" Olwyn cries out.

Sián and Olwyn, help Mynddy to her feet as Hyw turns to the impending battle. It is then he sees him for the first time, a blade in his hand and a large patch of blood on the side of his robes. It is Dwyr. Their eyes meet, but there is no time for greetings and Hyw can only smile.

"I tried to warn thee Hyw bach!" Dwyr says but then seems to faint slightly.

"Thy wounds!" Hyw says quickly.

"Olwyn will tend to thee!"

"I'm fine!" Dwyr quickly regains his composure.

"Let an old man die in the frailties of his battle!"

Turning in an instant, Hyw takes three paces and leaps onto the back of the rock as Megan shrieks out like some crazed animal, hurling Māthōg's head down into the valley.

Gazing down at Māthōg's men, Hyw's blood runs cold, but he looks again and wonders about their waiting. The young lad, whom Hyw had spared the day they attacked Mynddy's home is sitting at their head.

On seeing Māthōg's head bouncing and tumbling towards them, the lad's head bows again, but then he saunters slowly forward. Five other riders wait on him, but Hyw is uneasy and searches the valley for signs of any other riders as he checks the shadows of the trees for archers.

Holding out his hands and letting the reins of his horse fall, the young man kicks at his stead's sides. It eventually comes to a halt just below the cliff. The lad looks up at Hyw, his arms still open wide. With his sword still in its sheath, placing himself at the mercy of Megan's bow.

Hyw is confused, as he stares back at the lad. He had once had him in his sights, but spared him; for what reason, he did not know. The lad gets down from his stead. Tall and slim, he is perhaps taller than Māthōg with long dark hair. Bending he picks up his father's head and places it in a sack. When back in the saddle the lad looks up and drawing his blade, salutes Hyw and Megan.

Standing with the confidence of his father's bright steel held firmly in his hand, Megan is beside him, her bow firmly bent towards this Blood Red Crow.

All eyes are upon him, but instead of placing his sword back in its scabbard, he drops it into the grass at the side of his horse, its point sticking in the ground with the sword standing upright. The lad then turns to the path leading up to where Hyw stands. Three further Slags break free from the others and each, in turn, takes their blades from their scabbards dropping them to the ground at their sides as they follow the lad towards the path.

Running back across the clearing, Hyw is met by Hefyn's smiling face; he is standing in the shadows of a tree, partway down the path. The lad and his three companions slowly approach their position and both Hefyn and Oglwyn bend their bows towards them.

"Let them be for now!" Hyw says.

The lad still has his arms spread wide; his hands open with his palms forward. Hyw's eyes quickly scan the bushes and trees. There is no sign of anyone else with them. Oglwyn has backed up into the clearing with Hefyn finding a position among the trees; both have their bows bent towards the heart of the trebling youth. Megan is standing at Hyw's side, but her bow isn't bent towards the lad.

It is still bitterly cold, but there is a bead of sweat that tracks a path down the lad's forehead. Smiling nervously his horse continues up the path as Hyw backs into the clearing. The lad has dark features but is not dressed for battle and apart from his sword the only other sign of a weapon is a small cutting blade on his belt. He is probably a little younger than Hyw, but is thin and looks like he hasn't eaten in days. Staring straight into Hyw he says.

"I am Pebyn son of Māthōg!" The words enter Hyw like a bolt of lightning. The very name seems to fill him with rage and he struggles to control his feelings.

'It is over… Māthōg is dead…!' Hyw has to remind himself, but all his soul wants to tear at this wretch, ripping him limb from limb. Remaining still and quiet, Hyw does not show his feelings in any way.

"Come moi auld friend…" Pebyn starts again, but Hyw stops him before he can say another word.

"Thy father once referred to my father as his 'old friend'; shortly before he killed both him and my mother…so be quick with thy business before we despatch thee and thy comrades, and we will be done with thee."

Instantly regretting his familiar words Pebyn swallows hard.

"I come for my father and then we shall leave in peace…if it be thy will."

Hyw backs further into the clearing constantly holding the great blade out towards where Pebyn sits. Looking down into the valley he counts two men, waiting patiently, still sitting astride their horses. Walking forward, he nods and with that tacit permission, Pebyn's horse steps into the clearing.

Pebyn is quick but careful as he dismounts. From the rear of his horse, he gathers a large sack to him. Māthōg's body is slightly more problematic than his head and he positions the stallion close to where Māthōg has fallen, but no matter how he tries he cannot pick his father's huge body up from the dirt.

Hyw watches him struggle. Hefyn and Oglwyn both look across to Hyw not knowing what to do. Stepping forward, Hyw bends to help Pebyn with his pitiful load. A cover is placed over Māthōg's body and they both begin to heave the sack up and over his lifeless body.

The three Grots waiting on the path have dismounted and they step into the clearing, but as they do so, they freeze with Megan instantly bending her bow towards them.

Checking them over, she slowly lowers her aim not recognising any of them, but they have sparked something inside her and she runs to the path, followed swiftly by Pwyll, but before he can catch her, she is gone. Jumping on one of their steeds, with her bow in hand, she is off, riding back down the path. Pwyll runs back to the rock and watches as Megan gallops out into the common towards the two remaining Slags. Circling wide and looping around them, they both hold their empty hands out to their sides. Slowing her charge Megan approaches.

"Hyw!" Pwyll calls and he is there in an instant, leaving Māthōg's body to Pebyn and his men.

Hyw stares down into the common as Megan approaches the first rider.

"Are either of these Māthōg's men…did they ride with Māthōg?" Hyw asks impatiently.

Looking up, Pebyn is silent.

"Did they ride with Māthōg?" Hyw bellows in a tone that leaves Pebyn in no doubt as to the urgency of his words.

"One of them did!" Pebyn says reluctantly as he leaves his work and steps over to where Hyw and Pwyll are standing, but Pwyll leaps from the boulder and dashing across the clearing, he runs headlong down the path. Hefyn follows after him.

"Is it Scarface?" Hyw's words almost explode into the chasing air.

"No…it is…!" Pebyn has Megan in his view.

The first grot keeps his hands held firmly out to his sides as Megan rides in front of him, but the second appears uneasy and there is a moment of recognition between them and in an instant, he reaches for his blade. Megan's arrow rips through his throat, but he manages to stay astride his stead. A second arrow smashes into his face and he falls to the ground. There is a third arrow instantly notched into Megan's bow and she bends it towards the first grot. Quaking, his arms tremble like leaves in the breeze, but Megan slowly lowers her aim.

Pwyll runs out to her and she buries herself in his neck, sobbing and crying as he cradles her tiny body in his arms. Slowly lifting her from her feet Pwyll carries his love away.

"I did not know…forgive me…I would have brought another!" Pebyn says and his words soften Hyw's heart.

Eventually, Māthōg is secured on the back of his stallion as blood from his body spills onto the ground and down the stallion's side. Pebyn climbs up onto his stead and looks down at Hyw.

"For what it moi-be worth…Oi is sorry…Oi cud-nae stop him…I troi'd, but….He woin-taad ta cum here…he woin-taad toi die…if that moikes any sense…? He woin-taad t' doi at thoi hand!" Hyw is shocked at the message Pebyn bares.

"Every woirrior foices death…he hopes that glory and battle woi'll claim him, but there is no honour here…and foi that oi am soirry!" Pebyn pauses.

"God willing oi will escape Hefydd and his men, but if not…oi am in his hands. Moi he bless thoi life from this time forth." And with his words, Pebyn turns to go, but Hyw is undone and Pebyn has touched his heart.

"Wait up!" Pebyn turns in his saddle. Hyw walks back into his home and sorts through his arrows until he finds the precise one he is looking for. Emerging back into the clearing, scoring around the shaft of the arrow with his knife, close to its sharp and deadly end, he makes his way across to Pebyn's side. Pushing at the head with his thumb against its shaft; it breaks cleanly. Hyw hands Pebyn the arrowhead.

"This is my token; it may bear some sway with Hefydd and his men." Pebyn stares down at the small blade in Hyw's hand, which is neatly bound to the cut-off shaft. Looking back at Hyw with a nervous smile etched on his face.

"Oi thank thee, but woi ha wud ye doo such a thing!" And nudging at his horse's sides, Pebyn disappears into the woods.

Hyw rushes through the door and is met with a beaming smile from Mynddy with Rhyannon and Bryn Ywel both suckling at the abundant nectar of life that flows from their mother's breasts. Quickly looking towards their cot, he sighs, realising all is well.

Sián is dabbing at a cut, hidden somewhere in Mynddy's hairline and Olwyn has a fire raging in the hearth with water boiling in a cauldron. Hyw leans forward, kissing Mynddy on the hair.

"Ye can speak!" He whispers in her ear, but Mynddy just smiles as he cups his hand over Bryn Ywel's head, stroking his son's soft fine hair.

"I came to warn thee Hyw bach…I…!" Dwyr's words wake him to the old man's plight and smiling over at him Hyw's heart is full.

"I know…I…!" Hyw hesitates.

"I saw thy struggle in the night!"

"If not for Dwyr's warning we should never have been here…!" Olwyn looks up at Hyw as she speaks.

"It was all I could do to keep up with the young girl though!" Dwyr continues as Megan sidles into the room.

Epilogue

"There are many endings, but of this life...the life we view...there can only be one, but his time is not yet at hand. And so there remain only questions and new beginnings. Thou hast witnessed many things, but there is yet one last thing I must show unto thee.

Come...come with me now...step into the night. Look upon the rock...the rock of his family's throne...there, see...Hyw has both babies wrapped up safely, one in each arm. See how he holds them up to the stars and the night...listen...he is calling to those he has loved and lost...listen for their names...he calls to his Mam, Isobel; Bryn, his Da and to Ywel. There are tears in his eyes...look. Listen... whose name is he calling...'Bayr', but who stands at his side...it is not Mynddy. Look... see, it is Isobel. His mother stands at his side, one last time. His heart can feel, but his eyes cannot see her. The heavens are open and she must take her voyage beyond the stars...Bryn will finally embrace his love through the veil drawn over this life and take his beloved Isobel home.

Be still now...there is more...there is a stranger here. Come; be quick...if ye wish to witness all. Look...there by the top of the path...see...in the shadows of that bush...it is Megan. Can ye see her, watching and waiting? Listen again...One of the babies is crying. Megan can hear. There see, there are tears set in her eyes and her heart is breaking, but inside her small belly, a little life quickens.

The babies are our future, but their futures are inseparably connected and bound up in the fate of their parents...but their story must also be told. Their time will come, but for now, ye must leave and I alone will wait at their side...until we meet again."

Author's Notes

I describe myself as an 'un-historical fiction writer'. That's not to say I consider my work as not being historically accurate, but I do not write about known characters from history, nor do I describe the known corridors of our times past; rather I write about the people history has forgotten or never even known. The old adage is true; history is written by the victors and although those I write about have their victories and losses, they certainly weren't recorded within the histories of our times.

'The Last Celt', as a story, has been coaxed from the uncertain histories surrounding the Brythonic Tribes of Western Europe, or the Celts as we have a want to call them. Whilst that is a romantic notion, I have used some words inspired by, and drawn from, the Brythonic languages (Welsh mainly), although I have tried to keep this to a minimum. Personally, I find a certain joy in the interpretation and pronunciation of the more obscure words and unusual names found in some of the books I read, so I will keep these notes brief, hoping you find a similar joy in my work.

Hints on the pronunciation of certain letters: 'DD', sounds as the softer sound of 'TH', as in 'this'; 'NG', as in 'hang'; 'RH', is pronounced with a soft exhale of breath as in reel or rent; SI, as 'sh', 'F' as 'v', as in vale and 'W', as the 'oo' in 'moon'.

The following may be pronounced as such or similar:

Ywel…	You-ell
Mynddy…	Min-thee
Sián…	Sharn
Siôn (John)	Shown
Taid (Grandfather.)	Tide
Nain (Grandmother)	Nine
Blaidd (Wolf)	Blaith
Hefyn…	hevin
Cilydd…	Kil-ith
Geddyn…	Gethin
Hefydd…	Hevith
Angharydd…	Ang-ha-rith

Annwn: 'Hades' to the Greeks and Romans; the closest Christian translation would be 'Hell', but from my limited knowledge – gleaned from the modern-day commentaries of the Celt's obscure beliefs – I have come to understand 'Annwn' as a Spirit World, the place from which we have wandered and, following our deaths, that place to which we will return; – if only for a short time – a world of spirits, encompassing both good and evil.

I am not a linguist and my spoken language skills are quite poor. At school, in my last French exam, at thirteen, Mr Shaw gave me two marks; one for writing my name at the top of the paper and another for spelling it correctly. But in my life, I have grown to love language and our differing languages.

Within my writing, I have tried to give a flavour of the various tongues and dialects of the people involved in Hyw's life, but in doing so, I have also tried, as much as possible, to keep the flow of my writing and make their varying languages understandable.

Irish:

Māthōg; (The main antagonist) is the leader of The Scotti; The Blood Red Crows. In history, The Scotti were the Irish. They invaded in their droves the lands northward across the sea and that is why Scotland, is called Scotland. In my efforts to convey their beautiful language, I have concentrated on accent, rather than Gaelic (A beautiful and poetic Language). My main inspiration has come from some Irish in-laws we have in our family and, unbeknown to them, I have tried to mimic the way they talk and the phrases they use.

The Doric.

The Sons of Gododdyn; The Painted Men of The North: In history are described as coming from 'The North'; whether that is the north of England or southern Scotland I cannot establish fully, but here I have made them Scottish. In portraying their beautiful language, rather than using Scottish Gaelic as a base, I have leaned towards The Doric; a Scottish dialect spoken in the North-East of Scotland, which I believe is classed as Scotland's third official language. In portraying The Doric, I have relied heavily on three different sources. Two dear friends; Albert Brown and Iain McNeish, with great reference to doricphrases.com.

Printed in Great Britain
by Amazon